THE ROAD TO WINGS

T0125825

Visit us at www.boldstrokesbooks.com

THE ROAD TO WINGS

by

Julie Tizard

2017

THE ROAD TO WINGS

© 2017 BY JULIE TIZARD. ALL RIGHTS RESERVED.

ISBN 13: 978-1-62639-988-4

THIS TRADE PAPERBACK ORIGINAL IS PUBLISHED BY
BOLD STROKES BOOKS, INC.
P.O. BOX 249
VALLEY FALLS, NY 12185

FIRST EDITION: OCTOBER 2017

THIS IS A WORK OF FICTION. NAMES, CHARACTERS, PLACES, AND
INCIDENTS ARE THE PRODUCT OF THE AUTHOR'S IMAGINATION OR
ARE USED FICTITIOUSLY. ANY RESEMBLANCE TO ACTUAL PERSONS,
LIVING OR DEAD, BUSINESS ESTABLISHMENTS, EVENTS, OR LOCALES
IS ENTIRELY COINCIDENTAL.

THIS BOOK, OR PARTS THEREOF, MAY NOT BE REPRODUCED IN ANY
FORM WITHOUT PERMISSION.

CREDITS
EDITOR: CINDY CRESAP
PRODUCTION DESIGN: STACIA SEAMAN
COVER DESIGN BY JULIE TIZARD

Acknowledgments

Thanks to everyone at Bold Strokes Books for taking a chance on a new author who spends more time in the air than in front of a keyboard. Thank you to Patricia Hennig for making my cover vision into something gorgeous. To VK Powell, for your advice in getting this baby off the ground. To Cathy Osweiler, for being a great beta reader and for forty years of crazy friendship. To Kathleen McGrane, for your love, support, and encouragement. I couldn't have written this without you.

Finally, to the courageous women military pilots it has been my honor to fly with, you are superstars. And to women everywhere who refuse to take "no" for an answer. Keep reaching for the stars.

For Maddix Grace
You are the most amazing young woman I know.
I love you to the stars and back.

In loving memory of
Captain Jody M. Combs
Navigator, United States Air Force
9 Oct. 1958–13 Jan. 1993
Your love and your service will never be forgotten.

When once you have tasted flight,
You will always walk the earth with your eyes turned skyward;
For there you have been and there you will always be.

—Leonardo da Vinci

PROLOGUE

May 1987

Captain Kathryn Hardesty stood on the wide ramp watching the planes in the airport traffic pattern. As flight safety officer, she was responsible for the safety of the flight operations, and this was her first duty shift. She never got tired of the sight of the massive jets flying different approach and landing patterns to the runway. It was an amazing demonstration of precision and power. The radio brick on her hip crackled to life. "Flight Safety, this is the control tower."

Her insides clutched as she keyed the mike button. "Tower, this is Flight Safety, go ahead."

"Spokane Approach Control is declaring an emergency for a KC-135 aircraft, call sign Copper 21."

"What's the nature of the emergency?"

"They are reporting Copper 21 as a missing aircraft."

"When did they last have any radio contact?"

"Last contact was when the aircraft entered the traffic pattern at the auxiliary practice field at 1545 hours. Time now 1615 hours."

"Are there any search and rescue aircraft in the area?"

"They report Elite 85 is inbound to the practice field, ETA ten minutes."

"Has the fire department at the auxiliary field been notified?"

"Affirmative."

"Roger, Tower, I copy all. Is there anything else?"

"Elite 85 also reported a column of smoke southwest of the practice field."

"Copy, Tower. I'm responding now. Flight Safety out."

Oh, God, please don't let it be her.

CHAPTER ONE

March 1992

First Lieutenant Casey Tompkins smiled looking out at the perfect day. The air was cool, the sun shining, the sky a blazing blue, and she was starting the new life she'd always dreamed of. Today was the first day of Air Force pilot training. Driving due east on the long, straight road through the Arizona desert, she recalled everything she had done to get here.

She'd already beaten the odds just to get accepted. Thousands applied every year, and only a few hundred were chosen. Most didn't make it past the grueling flight physical. She had to prove she was almost physically perfect with twenty-twenty vision, perfect hearing, no color blindness, and on and on. She'd scored very well on the battery of written tests after studying every night for months. It was two full days of examinations covering math, physics, electronics, mechanical engineering, aerial photo recognition, and flight instrument interpretation. She'd put in extra work to get outstanding personal recommendations from her commanders, and earned an exemplary service record in her first three years in the Air Force. Every spare dollar went to flying lessons to get her private pilot's license just to make her application more competitive.

She also remembered the women she left behind. One in particular came into her mind—Lynn. She was sweet, kind, loving, and ready to quit her job and sell her home to move to Arizona to be with her. Casey had broken her heart when she told Lynn not to come with her. It had to be done. She had to focus all her time, energy, and attention to make it through pilot training. Now she was on her way. The struggle and sacrifice evaporated into the clear desert sky as anticipation buzzed through her veins.

There was nothing but cotton and alfalfa fields as far as she could see with the rugged Superstition Mountains on the far horizon. Something in the distance caught her eye. It looked like a swarm of gnats or maybe a beehive. Driving closer, she could tell they weren't bees but were, in fact, airplanes. She pulled over for a better look and saw dozens of planes banking, descending, and climbing in a crazy, coordinated dance. She had never seen so many planes so close together in her life.

She recognized the T-37, the primary jet trainer, and the sleek T-38, the supersonic advanced trainer. The T-37 would soon be her jet, and this would be her new world. A T-37 flew right over her head making a hard banked turn with the high-pitched whine of jet noise. The pungent smell of jet exhaust was intoxicating. The ground rumbled and she looked up as a four-ship formation of white T-38 jets roared overhead in a tight line approaching the airport. Transfixed, she watched the lead aircraft snap into a ninety-degree bank turn followed immediately by the second, third, and fourth jets as they executed identical maneuvers. The landing gear came down on the lead jet, then two, three, and four as they flew a graceful descending turn to the runway with perfect symmetry. She was so filled with exhilaration she thought she might spontaneously combust. This was her life's dream coming true before her eyes. In her soul, she knew someday that would be her leading a four-ship formation of supersonic T-38s to a perfect landing. Only one thought came to her mind: *Please, God, don't let me fuck this up.*

She drove to the main gate, got out her green military ID card, and watched the cute security police airman wave the cars through. The young woman snapped to attention and saluted Casey when she recognized the officer decal on the car.

Casey returned the salute. "Could you please tell me where the 82nd Student Squadron is? I'm new here and starting pilot training today."

The airman gave her a big smile as she pointed down the road. "Yes, ma'am, the student squadron is the third big building on the right. You can park in the rear."

"Thank you, Airman."

"Any time, ma'am. Congratulations and welcome to Willie, ma'am." She gave Casey another smart salute and waved her in.

Casey read the big sign just inside the main gate. "Welcome to Willie. Home of the Best Trained Pilots in the World."

She walked up to the student squadron building fifteen minutes early and headed toward the group of men in blue uniforms with fresh, very short haircuts. They were in excellent physical shape and were gesturing and talking like they were already the hotshot pilots they thought they were. Casey sized them up. They were her classmates but also her competition. She could easily match any man here in physical conditioning, intelligence, ambition, and hard work. They were chatting with each other and glanced at her but didn't speak to her. She approached the nearest one and asked him, "Is this UPT class 93-02?"

"That's us. I'm Mike Harris," he said as he extended his hand to her.

"Nice to meet you, Mike. I'm Casey Tompkins." She returned his handshake with a firm grip.

A loud voice boomed, "All right, everyone, fall in and take a seat."

They filed into a large, austere-looking classroom with chalkboards at the front, large airplane models around the room, posters of electrical diagrams, and a giant-sized "whiz wheel," the portable mechanical flight computer, off to the side. In front of each seat was a big stack of books, a regular-sized whiz wheel, a green flashlight, and a large briefcase. Casey scanned the titles of her books—*Weather for Aircrews, T-37 Flight Manual, Aerodynamics, Instrument Flying, Aircraft Weight and Balance, Aerospace Physiology, Instrument Flight Rules, USAF Air Navigation*.

She saw only one other woman in the group. The woman had a big smile on her face as she talked to the guy in the seat next to her. She was pleasant looking but not remarkable. She definitely looked straight, but Casey was glad she wasn't the only woman in the class.

"Room, ten-hut!"

The entire group jumped up and snapped to attention as a middle-aged man in a green flight suit walked to the front of the room. He surveyed the group, let everyone stand ramrod straight for a few minutes, then said, "At ease.

"I'm Lieutenant Colonel Gary Oscar, commander of the 82nd Student Squadron, and I want to welcome you to your first day of pilot training. You've accomplished a lot just to get here, but now the real work begins. You're going to have a very busy day today, and every day, for the next year. Your only job right now is to complete this training program and learn to fly as an Air Force pilot. Here are a few points I want to touch on. Be on time. Lateness will not be tolerated whether it's showing up for class or dropping a bomb on a target; you *will* be on time for everything. Don't get in trouble with the locals. If any of you gets a DUI or gets arrested, even off base, you will be out of this program immediately and probably out of the Air Force as well. And finally, we are here to help you. If you have any problems, of any kind, my door is always open. Come and talk to me and I'll do whatever I can to help you. Once again, welcome to Willie, and now I'd like to introduce your class commander, Captain Steve Morgan."

Another voice shouted out, "Room, ten-hut," as the squadron commander left the room. Casey watched the commander walk past her out of her peripheral vision and knew the last thing he'd said was a complete lie. In her three years in the Air Force, and the four years of ROTC in college before that, she'd learned that you *never* go to the commander with any problems, certainly not any personal problems. That was the quickest way to end your career. The statement "We're here to help you" was a required platitude in every commander's speech. No, Casey would never talk to this man about any problem, would prefer he not even know who she was, and would maintain a very low profile while in pilot training.

"I'm Captain Morgan, your class commander, and we have a jam-packed day today, so you need to pay attention because I won't be repeating myself. On top of your manuals is your schedule for the next month. You'll be doing ground training, academics, and physiological training for the first four weeks before you go to the flight line. You'll be taking three to five written tests every week, and you'll be evaluated on everything you do at every stage of training. Unlike the way some of you got through college, we do not use the 'Pump and Dump' system here. You cannot cram the night before the test, regurgitate the material, and then forget everything you just learned. Everything here is based on the building block approach. You need to thoroughly understand the material, memorize it, retain it, and correctly apply it in the air. You need to hit the ground running if you are going to make it through this program. Put your books in your briefcase and follow me to equipment issue."

Casey was a little nervous as she packed up her books, but her nerves were overcome by the excitement of being here. *How am I ever going to learn all this?* She vowed to never let any of her classmates ever see any of her nervousness.

The group filed out and went down the hall to a big room with a sign reading "Individual Equipment Issue." Arrows on the concrete floor showed the direction of movement through the giant room with piles of gear stacked on long tables. There were three small fitting rooms to try on flight suits. When Casey got her turn in the fitting room and tried on her flight suit for the first time, she almost whooped out loud as she stepped into the green coveralls. There were a dozen zippers on it, and the synthetic fire-retardant Nomex material was stiff and scratchy at first. She pulled up the long zipper from her crotch to her throat and stared at herself in the mirror in amazement. She pulled in the Velcro tabs at the waist so it wasn't quite so baggy and admired herself in the mirror. The flight suit made her shoulders look broad, her waist tapered, her legs long, and nicely showed off her firm butt. She couldn't wipe the huge grin off her face. This flight suit made her look and feel butch, powerful, and hot. This would definitely be her favorite Air Force uniform ever.

They each received a green padded helmet bag, four olive drab flight suits, a Nomex flight jacket, a pair of black leather flight boots, leather flying gloves, and a duffel bag. They were herded into another room labeled "Helmet Fittings," where Casey watched with fascination as each of her classmates had a large metal contraption put on their heads followed by an enlisted technician pouring a liquid resembling pancake batter into the top of the device. The first man cried out like a little kid, "Ow, that's hot!" as the liquid turned into foam and oozed out from the holes all over his head. It solidified instantly and the technician scraped off the excess with a knife, then released the man from the head mold. Another technician removed the rigid foam skull from the mold, labeled each one with the student's name, and stacked them like a skull collection in boxes on the wall. When it was Casey's turn, the liquid felt like a warm hug on her head. *This is for* my *very own helmet, custom made for* my *head.*

The class commander shouted, "Drop your gear off in the classroom and you have thirty minutes for lunch. The dining hall is across the street. Be back here at 1300 hours. Do not be late!" As they hurried across the street to the dining hall, her classmates were talking and joking with each other. None of them spoke to her with the exception of Mike, the guy she met when she first got here.

"That's quite a pile of books they gave us, huh?"

"Yeah, I'm sure I'll be up late reading every night."

"I noticed you're a first lieutenant, not a second lieutenant 'butter bar' like the rest of us. What did you do before pilot training?" Mike asked.

"I worked at a research lab in Ohio. It took me three years of applying to pilot training before I got accepted." She avoided telling him anything more about herself. If her classmates knew she had designed prototype flight simulators, they might think she had an edge over them and see her as a potential threat. She just wanted to fit in, be accepted, and get through this training course.

She hurried back over to the student squadron and flipped open her T-37 flight manual. She scanned the chapter titles: Engines, Electrical System, Landing Gear, Flight Controls, Hydraulics, Fire Protection, Flight Instruments, Weight and Balance, Emergency Procedures. It seemed overwhelming, but she couldn't wait to dive in. She had a hunger to learn everything she could about this airplane.

Captain Morgan came back into the classroom and announced that the class was going on a walking tour—first stop, the flight simulator building. This was the newest and most modern building on the base. As they walked in, Casey saw the cavernous interior and the dim lighting and felt the frigid air conditioning. Captain Morgan showed them the sim sign-in area, the eight simulator bays with full T-37 cockpits on large platforms, and six giant hydraulic actuators underneath each one. It was eerily quiet in the big building except for the squeaks and groans from the moving sims. The simulator platforms moved like big insects as the giant pistons pushed and pulled them from underneath.

"You will do all your emergency procedures training in the sim and you will learn ninety percent of your instrument flying here. You will NEVER intentionally crash the sim. You will treat the sim as if it is the real aircraft at all times. Is that understood?"

The entire class answered, "Yes, sir." Casey was comfortable with flight simulators and hoped she would do well with this part of the training.

"All right, everyone, next stop, the flight line."

As they walked into the big, windowless, gray building, Casey looked out onto the huge concrete ramp at row after row of white T-37 jets. The noise from the engines was almost painful, a high-pitched whine as the jets taxied in and out like an organized ant colony. She couldn't wait to get her hands on one of those jets.

The squadron building was rather dim inside with a wide hallway down the center filled with students and instructors rushing to and from the flight rooms on either side. Captain Morgan took them to their flight rooms. The class would be divided with half the students going into Warlock flight and the other half into Good Grief flight. The logo for Warlock was an eagle descending with a big spear in its talons. Good Grief's logo was Snoopy flying a T-37 instead of his doghouse Sopwith Camel. Casey decided she liked Snoopy better and hoped she was assigned to Good Grief.

The flight room was the heart of pilot training. It was a noisy, busy open room with a dozen conversations going on simultaneously. Casey saw the instructor pilots teaching their students using model airplanes, drawing diagrams, and flying with their hands. The IPs sat across from their students at tables around the perimeter. There was a podium in the corner, airplane murals on the walls, and a giant sheet of Plexiglas on the front wall with the names of the students on the left and rows and columns of numbers across the rest. This was the master schedule board with most of the entries written in black or blue grease pencil. There were a few entries circled in red. Casey didn't know what this meant, but she sensed it was somehow bad.

Captain Morgan led them to the front of the building to the supervisor of flying desk. "This is the SOF desk, where you will sign out your jet and sign in at the end of the mission with your flying time." Casey saw a male student pilot and a woman instructor pilot approach the desk. They both had deep red lines across their cheeks and nose from the oxygen masks, hair wet with sweat, and the student had sweat stains all over his flight suit. Casey couldn't help but stare at the woman instructor. She wasn't tall, maybe five feet four inches with a trim, slight build. Even though her hair was wet, Casey could tell it was sandy brown, straight, collar length, and parted on the right. She had a determined look on her face with high cheekbones, full lips, dark arched brows, and hazel green eyes. She wasn't pretty in the usual sense but had classic features that gave her a striking kind of beauty. Casey couldn't take her eyes off her. The male student was at least a foot taller than the IP and was the size of a football linebacker with a grim, dazed look on his face. He went over to the sign-in log to fill in the flight time. The woman IP pointed to the sheet and said, "No, the flight time was 1.4, not 1.3 hours."

"But, ma'am, I wrote down the takeoff and landing times, and I came up with 1.3 hours."

"Do NOT argue with me, Lieutenant!"

"I'm not, ma'am, I just—"

The IP slammed her checklist on the counter, stepped into his personal space, and poked her finger into his massive chest. Her eyes blazed with fire as she tilted her head up to look him in the face. Her voice was low and threatening, "I am sick and tired of all your excuses, Johnson. You have fucked up every single thing on this ride today, including the sign-in."

"But, ma'am—"

"Forget it, Johnson. You just busted this ride, I'm done with you, and you're out of this program. Wait for me in the flight commander's office."

"Yes, ma'am." He walked off, his head slumped down like a beaten dog.

"Goddamn it," the IP muttered under her breath as she corrected the sign-in log. She glanced up at the crowd of new students staring at her, made eye contact with Casey for a moment, then stormed off down the hall.

"Captain Morgan, who was that?" one of her classmates asked after they were out of earshot.

"That, Lieutenant, was Captain Hard-Ass, uh, I mean Hardesty. She's the chief of flight safety."

Casey was horrified at the tragic scene she'd just witnessed. She couldn't take her eyes off this powerful, compact woman. She was intrigued by her but also felt fear in the pit of her stomach. She heard her classmates mutter, "What a bitch," and, "Hard-Ass is right." *I hope I never have to fly with her.*

CHAPTER TWO

Casey had stayed up until midnight studying her flight manual, got five hours of sleep, but was still exhilarated and alert. Academics today consisted of aircraft systems, jet engines, the AC and DC electrical systems, then fundamental laws of aerodynamics. The instructor went through everything at a breakneck pace, and Casey was glad she'd read all the material and done the review questions the night before. This type of class was completely different from any college course she'd ever taken. This wasn't just learning theory for the sake of learning it; it was all focused on applying the information to flying an airplane. They were scheduled for ejection seat training in the afternoon, but before they broke for lunch, the instructor announced a guest speaker, the chief of flight safety, Captain Kathryn Hardesty.

Captain Hardesty strode to the front of the classroom. She looked completely different from the way she'd looked yesterday when she was destroying that student pilot's dream. Her sandy brown hair looked much neater than it did the day before. Her trim build showed some nice curves visible even under the baggy flight suit. She wore the sleeves of her flight suit pushed up to mid forearm and stood in front of the class with her hands on her hips surveying the whole group. She calmly waited for everyone's undivided attention.

Kathryn surveyed the new group of student pilots. *Great, this is the group of students who saw me rip into Johnson yesterday when I had to bust him on his final check ride.* After four years as an instructor pilot, all the new students looked the same to her—eager and cocky. They swaggered like they were fighter pilots already and thought they were invincible. They wrote the same things on their application letters: "I plan to graduate at the top of my class, fly the F-16 fighter, become a test pilot, then fly the space shuttle." Despite the fact that they were arrogant, brash, and way too full of themselves, Kathryn felt protective toward them. She saw them all as *her* students, and she would do everything in her ability to try to keep them from killing themselves. She was tough on them because she had to be. She didn't care if they called her "Hard-Ass" or said she was intimidating. She'd seen too many students killed because they didn't have what it took to be a pilot. It didn't matter how hard they worked, how much they studied, or how bad they wanted it, some people were just not meant to fly. If they couldn't cut it, it was her job to get rid of them before they killed themselves or someone else. She had no problem washing out the weak ones, like Johnson. It had to be done and she had no guilt about it.

She saw the two women students. One was average looking, the other one was very striking with short, dark, wavy hair, intense blue eyes, and a look of fierce determination on her face. She had handsome features with a strong jawline and a long, elegant neck. *I hope they both make it.*

"I'd like to add my welcome as you start your flight training to become Air Force pilots. Everyone on this base is here for one reason only—to help you learn to fly and graduate from this program. This is the most demanding thing you will ever do in your life. Flying Air Force jets is an amazing thing we do for a living, but it is also a deadly serious business. Thirty percent of you will be washed out of pilot training, and we average five to six aircraft crashes a year in Air Training Command. You will be required to learn to fly at a very accelerated rate. You have to learn how to solo a jet in just twelve rides. If you can't do that, you're out." The gravity of her words hung in the air.

"You'll be going to ejection seat training this afternoon, then physiological training tomorrow to learn the anti-G straining maneuver. *Pay attention.* Properly learning how to do this is a matter of life and death. The number one cause of student pilot fatalities is G-induced loss of consciousness, also known as GLOC. You will be pulling three to four Gs every time you fly, and frequently, we pull five to six Gs doing aerobatics and formation flying. Pulling Gs in a jet is not like riding a roller coaster at an amusement park. You have to be able to withstand sustained G-forces, breathe while you pull Gs, look for other aircraft, and fly the jet all at the same time. Don't let *anything* distract you from the mission of earning your wings. Once again, welcome to Willie. We're glad you're here, and I look forward to flying with you."

As she ended her remarks and left the classroom, Casey heard her classmates quietly whispering to each other. She was surprised that such a petite woman could be so intimidating to a room full of cocky men.

Casey reported to physiological training and learned about the cockpit ejection seat they would be flying in, including the explosive charges inside the seat. She had to reach down, find the hand grips, brace her body into the proper position, and squeeze the triggers as the ejection seat shot her up a metal rail. The instructor yelled critiques at each student. "You're burning up! Find the hand grips!" "Get your head braced or you'll break your neck!"

When it was Casey's turn, she found the ejection hand grips behind her calf muscles at the lower sides of the seat. When the instructor yelled, "Bail out! Bail out! Bail out!" she pulled the grips up, braced her back against the seat, and pulled the triggers as the seat bottom slammed her up the rail. She felt like she'd been shot out of a circus cannon.

"Not bad, Tompkins. Remember to keep your head and spine in alignment so you don't get a broken back. Try it again, this time with your eyes closed like the cockpit is filled with smoke."

Casey did it again with no critique this time. *Remember this, remember this.*

The next day, Casey listened to lectures on the hydraulic system, landing gear, and flight controls. Her first written test was tomorrow on aircraft systems and she would be up late again studying. She wanted to ace the first test so badly she could taste it.

Casey paid rapt attention as the physiological training officer briefed them on the anti-G straining maneuver.

"This is your primary defense against GLOC. When you pull positive G-forces, blood is pulled from your brain into the lower parts of the body. When your brain is deprived of oxygen, you will black out. Sometimes a pilot grays out first, meaning they lose sight in their eyes, but are still conscious, before they black out completely. The only way to prevent this is to raise the blood pressure by tightening the muscles of the stomach, butt, and legs."

Casey watched frightening films of pilots slumping over from GLOC in the training centrifuge and gun camera film of actual crashes due to GLOC. She was stunned how fast it could happen to a pilot. One minute, they were flying and pulling Gs, the next, they blacked out. If this happened in the air, the plane just flew itself into the ground with an unconscious pilot in the seat.

Casey tried not to laugh at her classmates struggling with the anti-G straining maneuver. They made themselves red in the face and looked like they were having difficult bowel movements as they grunted and strained. She had to take short, forceful breaths as she contracted her lower body muscles. Casey was getting the hang of it. She couldn't wait to fly upside down and pull Gs.

The next day was the first time they got to wear their new flight suits. Casey loved the feel of the heavy black leather boots and the long-sleeved green flight suit. She carefully thought about what she would put in all her zippered pockets and wore her blue flight cap low on her forehead. When she reported to the altitude chamber, she was issued her new white helmet. It was very snug on her head and was fitted with a tight oxygen mask on her face. The mask snapped into the helmet, smelled of rubber, and it was claustrophobic as she tried to relax her breathing.

They filed into what looked like a giant steel box with thick windows. They sat in numbered seats and checked their masks and microphones, and counted off their seat numbers. The airman inside the altitude chamber reviewed what they had learned in class the previous day about the symptoms of hypoxia, or oxygen starvation, the difference between hypoxia and GLOC, the effects of unpressurized flight, and what to expect during an explosive decompression. Casey saw looks of stern concentration, and maybe a little fear, on the faces of her classmates. Her buddy Mike sat across from her and gave her a thumbs-up. Casey mentally reviewed the emergency procedure for hypoxia and tried to control her nerves by focusing on deep breaths.

She watched the large altimeter dial inside the chamber go up as they climbed in altitude. A rubber surgical glove dangling from the ceiling by a string slowly inflated like a balloon as they climbed. The instructor's voice in her headset explained the principle of expanding gasses. "That rubber glove is like your stomach. As we climb in altitude, the gas inside your intestines expands as the outside air pressure decreases. There is only one thing you can do to equalize the pressure in your body and avoid injury. Just let 'em rip." Casey felt uncomfortable pressure in her bowels as they climbed. She was grateful she was breathing one hundred percent oxygen through a hose and mask as she let loose with some major flatulence. She saw her classmates shift from side to side and knew they were doing the same thing.

When they reached thirty-five thousand feet, the instructor had them unsnap the mask from one side of the helmet and told them to prepare for the explosive decompression. She heard a loud boom, felt her ears pop, and the chamber immediately filled with a cold, thick fog. Casey reconnected her mask, went to one hundred percent oxygen on the regulator, and tried not to hyperventilate. *Shit, that was scary.*

"Your time of useful consciousness at thirty-five thousand feet is thirty seconds. If you don't get your mask on and go to one hundred percent oxygen within that time, you will pass out. Next, we'll climb back up to twenty-five thousand feet, you will remove your masks, and we will go through the hypoxia demonstration. You will learn to recognize your own personal hypoxia symptoms, which are different for each person, and you will see the insidious nature of hypoxia from an undetected oxygen leak. You will write down your symptoms as you feel them and complete some simple tasks so you can see how hypoxia affects your mental capabilities. Once you recognize your symptoms, put your masks back on and go to one hundred percent oxygen. Acknowledge with your seat numbers."

Casey called out her seat number and tried to control her apprehension as the chamber climbed again. She mentally reviewed the list of possible hypoxia symptoms from class: light-headedness, confusion, tingling, anxiety, euphoria, numbness, cyanosis/blue fingernails, belligerence. When the altimeter read twenty-five thousand feet, the chamber chief directed them to remove their masks. When Casey took her oxygen mask off, she thought it would be like suffocating, but she was surprised to find she could breathe normally. The technician inside with them handed out clipboards with childish-looking quizzes on them.

"Complete as many tasks on the clipboards as you can. Remember to write down your hypoxia symptoms as you feel them."

Casey whipped through the first line of the quiz, 2 + 2 = 4, 3 x 3 = 9, A B C D _. She knew another letter followed D, but she couldn't remember which letter it was. This struck her as very funny. She looked around at the other students in the chamber. Some were hard at work on their quizzes and some were just staring blankly ahead. The whole scene struck her as hilarious, and she tried not to burst out laughing at them. *I think this is euphoria. I should write this down.* She tried to write the word but couldn't remember how to spell it. Then she started to feel tingly. She definitely felt tingly and hot all over. *Oh, I think I like this. I feel VERY aroused right now—this is great. I'm really, really liking this.*

She became aware of an annoying sound. "Number six, put your mask on. Six, put your mask on now." *Wait, I'm number six. He's talking to me.* "Number six, mask on now!" *Why is he shouting? I'm having such a good time right now. Oh, I think I need to put my mask back on.* She put her mask over her face, took a deep breath, and the fuzziness in her brain went away immediately. She looked at her quiz on the clipboard. She'd only filled in the first line. Under symptoms, she had written "uforia." She quickly filled in the rest of her symptoms before she forgot them—euphoria, tingling, very warm, aroused. She secured her mask to her helmet and looked around at her classmates. About half of them had their masks back on, some were still writing, and Mike was staring straight ahead and not moving. She heard the chamber chief yell, "Number five, get your mask on!" Mike didn't move. "Airman Rogers, put the mask on number five."

As the chamber technician moved toward him, Mike started jerking, his eyes rolled back in his head, and he looked like he was having an epileptic seizure. The airman rushed to him, forcefully held the oxygen mask to his jerking head, and slowly, Mike started to regain consciousness. After a few very tense minutes, Mike gave the technician an "okay" signal and clipped his mask back into his helmet.

"As you can see from this demonstration, hypoxia can be very subtle, and if you fail to recognize your symptoms, you will black out. After a certain point, the hypoxia effects will prevent you from saving your own life. The altitude chamber ride is now over. Be alert for any signs of residual symptoms such as joint pain, ear or sinus pain, or the bends."

Casey watched her classmates as they filed out of the chamber. They had very somber expressions on their faces, especially Mike.

CHAPTER THREE

Casey was pleased when she scored one hundred percent on the first written test of aircraft systems. A passing score was eighty-five percent, and everyone in her class passed, although some just barely. The guys were talking about going out to the Officers' Club after class on Friday night. Casey didn't really like hanging out at a bar with a bunch of straight men, but she needed to make an effort to connect with her classmates, so she decided to join them.

After a long, stressful week, Casey was actually looking forward to having a few drinks with the guys. In addition to Mike, a few guys were warming up to her and even chatted with her. The Officers' Club was divided into two sections. The tradition area, a formal place for dinners where most people dressed up, and then the casual bar in the back, which was a completely different story. This was the official place where the pilots came to blow off steam, and it was unlike any bar Casey had ever seen.

It was one big, dark room that reeked of stale beer with a bar the full length of one wall. There were very few tables or chairs with the exception of a strange-looking long rectangular table in the middle of the room. The place was packed with men in green flight suits at five in the afternoon, and they were all very loud, rowdy, and half drunk. Casey maneuvered her way to the bar to order a beer when she heard someone yell, "Carrier landing!"

She turned toward the commotion and saw six men hoist another man over their heads, running with him toward the long table in the middle of the room. The table was painted to look like a runway, and other men were pouring beer over the tabletop. As the guy held up in the air approached, the other men started chanting, "Whoop, whoop, whoop." The six guys holding the man up lowered him to the table and shoved him down the length of it. He yelled as he slid down the table, getting soaked with beer in the process. Casey was stunned at this but tried not to show it as she watched the whole ritual unfold. *This is going to be interesting. They better not try that with me.* The men were laughing and hooting just as Captain Kathryn Hardesty walked in with another woman instructor pilot and sat at a table in the back. *Well, Captain Hard-Ass is here with another woman—very interesting.*

Casey watched Captain Hardesty sit down and she heard another guy in the bar yell, "Dead bug!" The entire room of pilots threw themselves on the floor, landed on their backs, and flung their arms and legs into the air. As they wriggled their limbs, the room looked like it was filled with giant dying cockroaches. The whole bar was on the floor with the exception of her new classmates.

"New class buys!" someone yelled.

The bartender turned to the new students and said, "That'll be twenty bucks from each of you for a round of drinks and for being stupid enough to not know how to play dead bug."

Casey and her classmates put their money on the bar while the other pilots returned to their feet, laughing, yelling, and drinking again. *This is the strangest thing I've ever seen.*

❖

"I don't know why you insist we always come here on Friday nights. You know I can't stand this macho bullshit," Barb said.

"I've told you this many times. I need to see what's really going on with the IPs and students, and this is the best place to see the animals in their natural habitat," Kathryn replied.

"You have a sick sense of humor. Well, it looks like the new class has found the casual bar. More fresh meat—at least for a while." Barb nudged Kathryn's elbow. "She's cute, the tall one with the dark hair at the bar."

Kathryn looked at Casey. She was indeed very cute. She recognized her from briefing their class but took in her appearance more closely this time. She was about five feet nine inches tall with broad shoulders, long legs, and a trim, athletic look. She chugged a beer, laughed with her male classmates, and occasionally flashed a dazzling smile. Just as Kathryn was admiring her, Casey glanced over, and their eyes locked for a brief, hot second. Casey turned away quickly, and Kathryn had a nice view of her firm backside.

Just as Kathryn felt her face heat up, she heard another guy yell, "Carrier landing!" She watched with disdain as the other woman student from the new class was hoisted into the air and thrown across the beer-covered runway table.

"Have you seen enough for one night? Can we please go?" Barb asked.

"Yeah, I've seen plenty. I need to stop at the restroom first."

When Kathryn walked out of the restroom, she almost ran headfirst into Casey.

"Oh, sorry, ma'am, I didn't see you," Casey blurted out.

"It's okay, Lieutenant."

"Is it always this crazy in here on Friday nights, ma'am?"

"Yes, it is." Then Kathryn looked straight into her eyes and put her hand on Casey's forearm. "Lieutenant, I hope you're not driving anywhere tonight."

"No, ma'am. I'm walking to my room on base."

"Glad to hear that. Lieutenant Tompkins, one more thing."

"Yes, ma'am?"

"Please be careful in there tonight. Don't drink too much. Not all those guys are your friends." With that warning, Kathryn let go of her arm, walked past her and out the front door.

"Thanks, ma'am," Casey muttered. *How does she know my name? Why does she care if I get too drunk with these guys?* She rubbed her forearm. It still felt warm from where Captain Hardesty's fingertips touched her skin.

Casey walked back to her room after drinking several beers at the O Club. Her first week of pilot training had been overwhelming, but she loved every minute of it—even the scary stuff like the ejection seat and the altitude chamber.

She also remembered the feelings of arousal from her hypoxia in the altitude chamber. Combined with the stress of her first week, the beers, and the hot, lingering touch of Captain Hardesty on her arm, she was buzzing and needed some womanly attention. She called her college roommate, Trish, to see if there was any action she could get in on.

❖

Casey walked up to Trish's house. She heard the sound of women's voices and started to relax just to be in the presence of women after working around only men for the first week of pilot training. She grabbed a beer, scanned the crowd of women, and found several lovely prospects. Trish introduced Casey to her friends, and Casey gave Trish's partner, Rhonda, a big hug. The evening was filled with drinking and laughing, and Casey enjoyed herself immensely.

One woman in particular, Marilyn, kept eyeing Casey throughout the evening. As the party started to break up around eleven, Marilyn hung around and found every excuse she could to touch Casey or look at her. As Trish and Rhonda were cleaning up from the party, Marilyn sidled up to Casey and whispered in her ear with her hot breath, "Why don't you stay with me tonight, honey? You look like you've had a long, hard week, and I think you and I could have some fun."

A shiver ran down Casey's spine at the warm breath in her ear, and she thought, why not? Marilyn was older than Casey with luscious curves and full, ripe breasts. She had shoulder-length red hair, green eyes, pale, soft skin, and long red fingernails. Marilyn took Casey by the hand and led her out to the dark, quiet patio. Marilyn pulled her down onto a chaise lounge, lay down next to her, turned Casey's face toward her own, and placed a warm, wet kiss on her lips. Marilyn's lips were full and luscious, and Casey could do nothing but respond. She opened her lips and Marilyn slid her wet tongue into Casey's mouth and proceeded to devour her with hungry kisses. She rolled on top of Casey, pressing her thigh into Casey's center and grinding her hips onto Casey's pelvis. Casey felt heat from the apex of Marilyn's thighs through her clothes and knew exactly what she wanted. Marilyn wanted what most women wanted from her. She wanted Casey to take her, to dominate her, to make her moan and cry out, and to bring her to climax again and again. Casey didn't feel any real emotional connection to Marilyn, but she certainly was aroused. She was hot and needed sex. She was more than happy to oblige Marilyn because she wanted a connection with a woman, any woman, and she wanted it now.

They stole off to the guest bedroom, exchanging knowing looks with Trish and Rhonda, and ripped each other's clothes off. Marilyn was voracious and spread her legs wide open, her glistening center beckoning. Casey's mouth watered at the sight and scent of her. She held Marilyn's thighs open as she lowered her mouth, deliberately tasting the delicate folds. Marilyn moaned, and she tilted her hips up, giving Casey the signal she wanted more. Casey entered her, stroking her deeply as Marilyn got louder. Casey was intent on giving her a long, slow ride, but Marilyn started gyrating her hips faster. Casey matched her deep strokes with the rising hips. Marilyn went quiet and clamped down on Casey's pummeling fingers. Casey drove in harder and gave Marilyn exactly what she wanted over and over again.

After Marilyn's breathing returned to normal, she rolled Casey onto her back, settled between her thighs, and gave Casey her own tongue-lashing. Casey loved the feel of the hot tongue on her flesh and climaxed quickly with a short, hard spasm. Casey was more than happy to satisfy Marilyn many times, but she knew Marilyn could not give her what she really needed. After Marylyn dozed off, Casey slipped out of the bedroom, gathered up her clothes, and started to leave. Just as she was about to make her escape, she ran into Trish walking down the hall in her T-shirt and boxers. "Hey, girl, you leaving so soon?"

"Yeah, I have to get up real early tomorrow and study. I have several big tests this week."

"Thanks for coming over. You know you're welcome any time. We both love you and want you to knock 'em dead."

"Thanks, Trish, you guys are the best. Give Rhonda a big hug for me. I'll call you next week."

Casey kissed Trish on the cheek and slipped out of the house. She drove back to the base for a hot shower, then went to bed. She'd achieved her objective and connected with a woman even though it was not exactly spectacular. The need to be in the presence of other women, to feel surrounded by the comfort and safety of their energy—this was what she needed more than the sex. The overwhelming "maleness" of pilot training made her keep her guard up all week. She drifted off to sleep with the lilting sound of women's laughter in her mind.

CHAPTER FOUR

April 1992

The first month seemed to fly by in a blur. The academics made sense to Casey and she continued to ace the written tests. The day Casey was waiting for finally came—their first day on the flight line. She and Mike were assigned to Good Grief flight. They reported to their new flight room at 0500 hours, looking for their names on the big schedule board. Each instructor pilot had three student pilots assigned to them, and Casey was happy that she and Mike, along with Jeff Parsons, a former enlisted Marine, were assigned to the same IP, Lieutenant Dave Carter. They went to the table with their IP's name on an airplane sign hanging from the ceiling and anxiously waited for him.

"Room, ten-hut!"

They all stood at attention as the instructors came in and stayed that way until someone said, "Take seats."

"Welcome to Good Grief flight, the best flight in the Air Force. I'm Captain Stavros, your flight commander, and I hope you are all ready to hit the ground running. I want to introduce our head scheduler, Captain Arnau."

Casey recognized the woman she'd seen with Captain Hardesty at the bar. Captain Arnau was tall and slender with short, sandy brown hair, blue eyes, and a very intense look.

"The first thing you need to know is NEVER touch my schedule board. Every day on the line with your name, you'll see your activity for that day. Flights are written in black, sims in blue, and other assignments in green. If you fail a ride, that mission will be circled in red. We don't want to see any red."

Next, they heard from the flight standardization and evaluation officer, Captain Harrison. "Every day we start with a time hack, a weather briefing, and stand-up. During stand-up you will be presented with an in-flight emergency. I will call on one of you. You will stand at attention, tell me how you will maintain aircraft control, analyze the situation, apply any emergency boldface actions, then bring the aircraft to a safe landing or an ejection, if necessary. If you analyze the situation incorrectly or state the boldface wrong, you just busted stand-up and you will be grounded for the rest of the day. I will then call on someone else until we get the correct information out of you."

"Nothing like being humiliated in front of the whole flight," Mike whispered to Casey.

After the flight room briefings, Casey, Mike, and Jeff listened intently to their new instructor.

"I'm Lieutenant Dave Carter, but when it's just us, don't call me 'sir,' call me Dave. I want you guys to be the best studs in this flight because how you fly reflects on me. I want you to work together to learn this stuff."

He reminded Casey of a mellow California surfer dude. He briefed them on their first simulator ride to introduce checklists flows, starting the engines, takeoffs, and straight-in landings. Jeff had the first sim, so Casey and Mike studied furiously while they were gone.

Casey was nervous and excited as she walked over to the sim building with Lieutenant Carter. The cockpit forward canopy was replaced with large television monitors that projected a visual scene for the pilots to see as they were flying the sim. The IP could change the view out the windscreen to look like day or night, fog, snow, or even zero visibility. They walked past giant terrain model boards with three-dimensional miniature landscapes and a camera gliding over the surface. The camera was controlled by the pilot flying in the sim to give a visual picture out the cockpit windows.

Casey climbed into the simulator and put on her helmet. Lieutenant Carter showed her how to strap in, run the preflight checklists, and how to start the engines. She smiled as she heard the sound of the jet engines whine as she started them. Even though she was in a simulator and the sounds were recorded, it felt real. They practiced several takeoffs, turns, and a few straight-in landings. Casey was surprised at how sensitive the control stick was, much more responsive than the Cessna 150 she'd flown when she got her private pilot's license. She barely touched the stick and she was all over the sky. By the time the sim was over, she was sweating and exhausted.

They continued with basic sims for the first week as they got ready for their first flights in the real airplane, the "dollar ride." The tradition was that the student would "pay" the IP one dollar for giving them their first flight like an homage to the early barnstorming pilots. Casey had butterflies in her stomach the whole day but was disappointed to see that she was in the last group of students to fly their dollar ride. Jeff was scheduled to fly first with Lieutenant Carter, and Mike was flying with Captain Hardesty.

"Oh crap, I'm flying with Captain Hard-Ass on my dollar ride," Mike said.

"Hopefully, she won't be too mean to you since it's your first flight." Casey tried to reassure him.

There was a buzz in the air as the IPs came in to brief the missions. The dollar ride only happened once in a pilot's career, and it was the beginning of something special. Casey listened and took notes as Lieutenant Carter briefed Jeff on their first flight. She would be as prepared as she could be when it was her turn to fly. She sensed Captain Hardesty's presence behind her before she heard her voice.

"Lieutenant Harris, are you ready to go fly?"

"Yes, ma'am, I am," Mike answered as he jumped up out of his seat.

"Let's brief up in the flight commander's office since all the tables are being used."

Casey felt a pang of jealousy as everyone got ready to fly while she had to wait.

After an hour and a half, the first period students and IPs started to return. Casey saw Mike walk in with a giant grin on his face, a deep red mask mark across his face, and wet hair plastered to his head.

"So, how'd it go, Mike?"

"It was great, and I saw so much. It's a thousand percent better than the sim."

"How was Captain Hardesty?" Casey whispered.

"She's good. She showed me tons of stuff."

"She didn't scream at you?"

"No, she made me feel really comfortable in the jet. She even showed me some acrobatics."

Just then, Lieutenant Carter stormed into the flight room cursing and swearing. He was covered in vomit from his chest to his knees, and the disgusting smell started to fill the flight room.

"Jesus, Dave, couldn't you change into another flight suit before coming back in here? You reek," Captain Arnau said.

"I don't have a spare flight suit with me, goddamn it. I need to go home and change."

"Great. Now I have to take you off the schedule and find someone else to fly with your other student."

Casey realized that Jeff, having thrown up on their IP, might prevent her from flying today.

Captain Hardesty then walked in to debrief Mike on his flight.

"Captain Hardesty, my *favorite* guest help IP, I need you. I need you, bad," Captain Arnau said.

"What's up, Barb?"

"Carter's student barfed all over him and he didn't bring a spare flight suit. I need an IP to fly with his other student, Tompkins. Please, I don't have anyone else."

"He showed up for dollar ride day without a spare flight suit? What a dumb shit. I need to call my office and reschedule my meeting with the T-38 maintenance chief first. Anything for you, Barb. I'd rather fly again than go to a meeting anyway."

"Thanks, Kath, I owe you."

"Lieutenant Tompkins, front and center, you're flying with Captain Hardesty now," Captain Arnau said.

Casey was both relieved and apprehensive as she walked over to Captain Hardesty.

"Ready, Lieutenant?"

"Yes, ma'am."

"Then let's go fly."

CHAPTER FIVE

As Kathryn briefed the flight, Casey looked back at her with such intensity that it almost derailed her train of thought. After a momentary hesitation, she ran through the briefing items in her checklist like she had over a thousand times before. "I will demonstrate the first takeoff, point out the ground references, then have you fly. When I want you to fly I will say, 'You have the jet,' and you will shake the stick and answer, 'I have the jet.' If I say, 'My jet,' let go of the stick immediately. If we have any emergency, I will take the aircraft. If I say, 'Bail out! Bail out! Bail out!' eject immediately or you'll be flying solo because I will be gone. Do you understand, Casey?"

"Yes, ma'am, I do," Casey answered nervously.

Their first stop was Life Support. There were rows of wooden locker spaces, each with a metal bar holding a parachute and an open cubbyhole above it with a helmet inside. The room smelled like a men's locker room with a hint of rubbing alcohol and rubber mixed in.

The life support technician showed Casey the proper way to clean the helmet visor and her oxygen mask.

Casey put on her helmet and checked her communication cord and oxygen mask in the tester. She hoisted the forty-pound parachute onto her back and buckled the chest and leg straps of the harness. Captain Hardesty scrutinized her up and down, shaking her head with a frown on her face.

"Lieutenant, your parachute harness is too loose. If you have to use this, your body will be hanging in midair attached by only these three straps. Make them tighter."

Casey tugged on the ends of the heavy nylon straps.

"No, like this." She grabbed the end of Casey's chest strap and yanked hard, crushing her breasts in the process. Captain Hardesty went to reach for her leg straps, Casey grabbed them herself and pulled down hard until it hurt her thighs. Her face flushed having Captain Hardesty so close to her body. "I can't stand up straight with them this tight, ma'am."

"You're not supposed to be able to stand up with them on correctly. They'll feel okay when you're sitting in the jet. You can unbuckle them when we walk to the plane."

"Yes, ma'am."

They walked across the ramp together with rows of white jets in front of them. Casey was tingling with excitement. She glanced at Captain Hardesty walking with her. She walked with authority and purpose—the epitome of confidence. She gave friendly waves to several of the aircraft crew chiefs as she walked.

When they got to the jet, she showed Casey how to review the aircraft logbook and where to stow her gear. It was very loud on the ramp as planes taxied around them, so she had to shout so Casey could hear her. "Follow me as I do the walk-around inspection. I'll show you what to look for." Casey nodded and followed dutifully.

Casey watched intently as Captain Hardesty's gloved hand slid across the leading edge of the wing. She moved the ailerons up and down scrutinizing every inch of the plane—looking, checking, and testing. She pointed out hinges and locking nuts on the control surfaces and where to check for oil drips. Casey watched her trail her fingertips across the other wing like she was caressing a lover. Her touch on the plane was firm, precise, in control. If this was a horse instead of a machine, the animal would have been calmed by the sure touch of her mistress.

Captain Hardesty had Casey climb into the jet on the left side and watched her strap in. Casey tried to remember everything she'd practiced in the sim—parachute harness, lap belt, shoulder harness, parachute key, oxygen hose, comm cord, gloves, and helmet visor.

"Pull the lap belt as tight as you can, Casey. Remember, *you* are the one flying, not the airplane flying you, and you want to strap this jet to your body."

Captain Hardesty climbed into the compact jet on the right side, her shoulder brushing against Casey's as she strapped in, in one-tenth the time. Casey heard her voice through the flight intercom and felt calmed by the sound of it.

"Can you hear me, Casey?"

"Yes, ma'am, I can."

"I've got you loud and clear also."

Casey started her preflight checks very conscious of her every move being watched.

"I'm going to start the engines and show you the hand signals we use with the crew chief to check the speed brake, pitot heat, and flaps. I'll do the initial taxi out, then I'll have you taxi the plane."

"Yes, ma'am."

The sound of the jet engines coming to life with their high-pitched whine filled Casey with electricity. The crew chief motioned them forward with his hands, gave them a thumbs-up indicating everything on the jet looked good, then he snapped to attention and saluted as they taxied out. Captain Hardesty returned the gesture of respect with her own salute.

"The most important thing when you are taxiing is to look outside. You will steer the jet with your feet using the rudder pedals and step on top of the pedals for braking. The horizon should look like it's halfway up the windscreen. Remember this picture. You will see this again for the level flight attitude. When I take off, I will pull the nose up so it looks like one-quarter ground and three-quarters sky. That will be the takeoff pitch attitude. When I'm flying, I want you to put your right hand on the stick and your left hand on the throttles and follow along with me as I move the controls."

Casey finished the taxi out checks, lowered the big canopy, and waited anxiously at the end of the runway for their turn to take off.

"Tango 61, cleared for takeoff, runway three-zero left."

"Tango 61, cleared for takeoff," Captain Hardesty responded over the radio. Her radio voice was lower in pitch than her speaking voice. She sounded confident and a little bit sultry. Casey wanted to sound like her on the radio.

"Step on the brakes hard to keep the jet from moving as we run the engines up to full power and check the engine instruments." Casey felt Captain Hardesty push both throttles forward under her left hand. The plane shook and the engines whined loudly, like the plane couldn't wait to get into the air. "Four green lights, no reds, no ambers, two good engines, release brakes."

The plane jumped forward as they accelerated down the runway. "Look down at the end of the runway and use your feet to steer and stay on the centerline. At sixty-five knots, we rotate and pull the stick back so the nose comes up to that one-quarter ground, three-quarters sky picture. At ninety knots, we lift off."

Casey smiled under her oxygen mask as the plane gracefully lifted up into the air.

"Positive climb, landing gear up, accelerate to one hundred and ten knots, flaps up," Captain Hardesty said. "Casey, you have the aircraft." She shook the stick with a short side-to-side movement indicating the exchange of control.

"Roger, ma'am, I have the aircraft." Casey shook the stick in reply. *I'm flying, I'm actually flying!*

"All right, Casey, start a left turn to depart the traffic pattern, keep climbing, and trim the airplane for one hundred sixty knots."

"Trim for one hundred sixty, ma'am?"

"Didn't you learn that in the sim?"

"No, ma'am, I'm sorry, I didn't."

"My aircraft, Casey. This is one of the most important things you'll ever learn about flying. Trim is your friend. This small button on the top of the stick is the trim button. Use your thumb and flick this button forward or backward to trim off the pressure of the stick in your hand. If I feel the stick push forward against my fingers, I flick the trim button back. If the stick is pushing against the palm of my hand, I push the trim button forward. We trim the airplane for the airspeed we want to maintain. If it is trimmed properly, you can take your hand off the stick and the plane will stay right there. Your goal is to fly with just your fingertips. No death grips on the stick. Understand? Your airplane, Casey."

"Roger, I have the aircraft." Casey tried the trim button and discovered that it was so much easier to control her airspeed and altitude. It felt like she had received a revelation from God.

"Casey, I have the jet."

"Roger, ma'am, you have the jet." Casey wondered what she had done wrong.

"I'm going to show you a few things so you can feel the airplane. Flying is not just about memorizing procedures. You need to be able to look outside and to *feel* what the jet is doing. We're at two hundred knots in level flight, and I want you to listen to the sound of the plane and the air."

Casey was confused but tried to hear the sounds the airplane was making. It was kind of a low roar mixed with the engine whine.

"Now I will pull the power to idle and slow the plane to one hundred and twenty knots. I want you to hear how the sounds change."

Casey heard the roar sound decrease and the pitch of the engines change.

"Now I'll push the power up to full military thrust, one hundred percent RPM, and accelerate to two hundred and fifty knots."

It was clear as a bell as the air noise increased to a loud roar and the pitch of the engine whine went up the scale.

"You don't have to look at the airspeed indicator to know that you are flying fast or slow, just listen to the jet."

"Yes, ma'am. That makes perfect sense." Casey understood she was listening to a master of her craft, that every word this woman spoke to her was pure gold.

"Let's try some maneuvering turns. Unlike civilian flying, we don't make gentle turns. We yank and bank and make sharp, aggressive turns. Show me a sixty-degree bank level turn."

Casey pushed the stick to the side, looked at the attitude indicator for the sixty-degree mark, then pulled back on the stick. The plane started climbing and Captain Hardesty took the jet again.

"You're looking inside at the instruments, not outside. Do it like this." Captain Hardesty snapped the plane into a sixty-degree bank. "Look at where the horizon intersects the windscreen. This is the sixty-degree bank picture. Then pull on the stick to keep the horizon in the same place on the windscreen and your turn will be level. Try it again."

Casey repeated the turn and was amazed that the bank was exactly at sixty degrees and the altimeter showed level.

"Better. You pick things up quickly, Casey. How are you feeling? Are you queasy at all?"

"No, ma'am. I feel great."

"If you feel airsick, tell me. Now I'm going to pull some Gs so you can practice your anti-G straining."

She rolled the jet to ninety degrees of bank into a tight spiral as she pulled back on the stick. "This is three Gs." Casey felt her oxygen mask pull down on her face as she sank into her seat. "Start your straining. Here is four Gs." Casey tightened her leg, butt, and stomach muscles. Her arms felt heavy and she had a hard time holding her head up. "Keep breathing, Casey, short, forceful breaths. Here's five Gs." Casey had to keep all her muscles tight as she huffed out air and quickly sucked in hard.

"It's...like...an...elephant...is...sitting...on...me," Casey grunted.

"That's right. Keep your muscles tight and use quick short breaths," Captain Hardesty answered.

Casey was tingling all over and saw sparkles of light on the edge of her vision.

"I'm rolling out now and easing off the Gs. How do you feel, Casey?"

The heavy weight lifted off her body as they returned to wings level. "I think I feel okay. That's hard, ma'am."

"You'll get the hang of it. Remember to start your muscle contractions as soon as you start to feel the G-forces. If you're at high speed and you pull back hard on the stick, you'll get into high Gs very quickly. Would you like to try an aileron roll?"

"Could we? Oh, yes, ma'am!"

"Follow along on the controls with me. Entry airspeed is two hundred and twenty knots. We pull the nose up so the air vents look like they are on the horizon. That's ten degrees up, then snap the stick all the way over to the side and hold it there but don't pull back." The airplane quickly rolled upside down then back upright. "As we approach wings level to the horizon again, snap the stick back the opposite direction to stop the roll. Now you try one."

Casey tried to do exactly what Captain Hardesty did but rolled out with twenty degrees of bank instead of wings level. "Crap."

Captain Hardesty laughed. "Not bad for your first try. Let's head back for some touch-and-go landings."

On descent into the auxiliary airfield, Captain Hardesty pointed out ground references for the entry points to the traffic pattern. Casey could see the ground points clearly through the big canopy and took a moment to look at the beauty of the desert they were flying over—the buttes, the dry riverbeds, the mountains—it was spectacular.

"I'll demonstrate the first landing, then I'll have you fly a few landings. The most important thing in landing is keeping the aim point, the threshold of the runway, one-third of the way up from the bottom of the windscreen. Keep the aim point at the same place in the windscreen, and that's how you control your glide path. Then set the power to seventy percent and check your airspeed. That's all you have to do. Watch your aim point and airspeed, then flare the jet and touchdown."

She makes it sounds so simple.

Casey felt Captain Hardesty's hands through the stick and throttles, like they were connected.

"As we slow down and get the landing gear and flaps down, be sure and trim off the stick pressures." Captain Hardesty's thumb flicked the little button on the top of the stick.

"When landing is assured, power idle, bring your head up, look at the horizon, then pull back smoothly, and hold that landing attitude picture." The plane touched down softly on the centerline of the runway.

"Lower the nose, power to military, use the rudder pedals to stay on the centerline, then lift off at ninety knots." As she got airborne, she brought the gear and flaps up, then snapped the plane into a sharp turn, rolled out exactly perpendicular to the runway, and said, "Your jet, Casey."

Casey flew the next pattern, but it didn't quite look the same as Captain Hardesty's. Just as she pulled the power to idle to land, she felt Captain Hardesty on the controls and the throttles move forward rapidly. The plane slammed onto the runway and bounced into the air as she heard, "My jet."

"You started your flare too early and ran out of airspeed. Next time don't pull the power to idle that soon. Fly it down closer to the runway, then flare. Try it again, Casey."

Her second attempt was better. It was firm but not bone jarring, still nothing like Captain Hardesty's landing. This was tough.

"Let's fly back to Willie and make this one a full stop landing."

Her last landing was sort of decent with only small inputs from Captain Hardesty.

They taxied in and she completed the after landing checks. As they climbed out of the jet and filled out the logbook, Captain Hardesty put her hand on Casey's shoulder. "Not bad for a dollar ride, Casey."

The warmth of Captain Hardesty's hand on her shoulder, even through her flying gloves, gave Casey a little tingle. She was on cloud nine.

CHAPTER SIX

Casey was so excited after her flight with Captain Hardesty she didn't even care that every maneuver she'd flown was graded U— Unsatisfactory. She took notes on everything Captain Hardesty said and wrote down everything she'd seen. She was scheduled to fly with her regular IP, Lieutenant Carter, the next day and couldn't wait to get back in the air.

Her second flight with Lieutenant Carter was very different from her first flight. Her initial takeoff was good, but when she started her turn to depart the traffic pattern, Lieutenant Carter jerked the stick out of her hand and yelled, "No! Turn the jet like this." He yanked the nose around the turn and rolled out with a snap. Casey felt her stomach lurch when he pushed forward and got some negative Gs.

The rest of the flight only got worse. He yelled at her constantly and took the stick out of her hands throughout the whole ride. She was dizzy and nauseous when she climbed out of the jet after her second flight. "You're going to need a lot of work to get through this program, Lieutenant."

Casey felt like she'd been punched in the gut. How had things gone from good to bad so fast? She tried to listen to his debrief after the flight, but everything he said to her made her feel like an idiot.

"You need to chair fly these maneuvers a lot, and I expect you to know all the ground references and the traffic pattern procedures down cold before the next ride."

Casey had a big systems test the next day. She would be up all night studying and memorizing this stuff.

After Lieutenant Carter left the table, Casey turned to Mike. "Did he scream at you on your flight?"

"Yes, he's an asshole. I didn't learn a thing, he was so busy yelling at me."

❖

The next several rides didn't go a whole lot better than her first ride with Lieutenant Carter. Casey knew the procedures down cold, but he still screamed at her. On the rare occasions when she did something right, he would bang his fist on the glare shield and scream, "Well, goddamn it, you finally got it right this time. Now, don't fuck that up again!"

She was a bag of nerves and was starting to doubt whether she could ever solo. She'd worked so hard to get into pilot training that the thought of washing out made her sick to her stomach. Her life would be ruined and she could never live with herself if she failed this.

Her first emergency procedures simulator ride was coming up, and she was determined to be fully prepared for it, no matter how much he screamed at her. She went over and over the required memory steps and the checklists for engine fire, takeoff abort, single engine approach, ejection, electrical failure, and all the other emergencies. She steeled herself for the verbal abuse she knew was coming from Lieutenant Carter but tried to focus on only the emergency procedures.

She was a coiled spring inside as she started the takeoff roll in the simulator, waiting to see what he would throw at her. He gave her an engine fire just before liftoff. She was startled by the flashing red light fire light but quickly executed the takeoff abort as she called out, "Throttles—idle, wheel brakes—apply." She kept the airplane on the runway centerline and brought it to a stop quickly.

"What do you do now, Tompkins?" Lieutenant Carter yelled.

"Um, I call the tower, declare an emergency, then I do an emergency ground egress."

"Then do it, Tompkins! Or do you just want to sit here on the runway and burn to death!"

Casey was so flustered she got tangled in the lap belt and shoulder harness as she tried to jump out of the simulator cockpit. She finally untangled herself.

"Well, you're dead now. Get back in and do it again and don't fuck it up this time."

The emergency procedures simulator ride seemed to go on forever with no decrease in screaming. When they got back to the flight room

Lieutenant Carter wrote U on all the maneuvers, threw the grade sheet at her, and gave her a grade of Fair on the ride.

"You're lucky I don't bust you on this sim ride, Tompkins. You know what you did wrong. You need to pull your head out of your ass or you're not going to get through this program. You're dismissed," he said with disgust.

Casey walked out of the flight room completely dejected.

❖

Captain Hardesty walked through the squadron building in the late afternoon. Most of the IPs and students were either gone for the day or out flying as she went to each flight room looking through student grade books. She could scan a grade book in a few seconds and spot training problems immediately. She knew the trends to look for to see a problem before it occurred. The door to Good Grief flight was locked, so she used her master key to let herself in.

"Jesus, Kath, you scared the crap out of me," Captain Arnau said after she jumped at the noise.

"Why are you still here, Barb? You're on early week and you came in at 0300 hours. It's 1600 hours, and you're over your twelve-hour max duty day limit."

"I know, I know. I'm here because my schedule for tomorrow isn't finished. That's why the door is locked. And why are you here, by the way?"

"I'm just checking grade books looking for training problem trends. Your class and Warlock's are getting near first solos, so the problem children are starting to show up."

"Tell me about it, Kath. That's why I have to fix my schedule board before tomorrow because we have so many students on busted rides."

"Warlock has already washed out three students so far, including their only woman student."

"Who?"

"Lieutenant Carol Stevens. She couldn't get over her airsickness."

"Well, you can't do much about that if they keep getting airsick."

"Uh-huh," Kathryn mumbled as she flipped through the grade books.

She stopped when she got to Tompkins, Lieutenant C. She studied Casey's grade sheet and scowled.

"What's the matter, Kath?"

"I think Carter's setting up Casey Tompkins to wash her out pre-solo."

"He gave her a Fair on her EP sim today, but I thought she was doing okay."

From her previous job as the Good Grief flight commander, Kathryn knew exactly what you had to do to build a case against a student you wanted to get rid of. Carter was sly about it. He didn't bust Tompkins directly on any of her rides. That would have required the flight commander to fly with her. Instead, he wanted to control all her flights and was documenting a failure to progress in the individual maneuvers, then giving her a grade of Fair. Seeing this, anger burned in her stomach like a bad meal.

Even though women had been in pilot training for sixteen years, and had performed exceptionally well as Air Force pilots, some male pilots still resented women in pilot training. They felt they had the right to try to get rid of women student pilots just because they didn't like them. Clearly, Carter was one of these guys.

She remembered with excruciating clarity all the crap she'd put up with to earn her wings. She'd endured blatant and subtle harassment every day of pilot training. Not all the male IPs were bad, but some of them had intentionally tried to make her airsick or tried to black her out with G-forces. She'd been excluded from their camaraderie and regarded as a threat by her own classmates. They expected her to put up with the bullshit of their "boy's club," not complain about it, but she was never allowed into their clubhouse. She'd earned her wings in spite of them. She'd done it by developing a tough skin like a rhino and flying better than any of her male classmates.

As an instructor pilot, she'd vowed that every student would be treated equally. She was protective of all students, but she especially watched over the women students to make sure they were getting a fair chance. She knew in her gut Carter was planning on busting Casey on her next two rides and washing her out of pilot training before she even had a chance to solo. Bastard.

"Barb, I need to fly with Tompkins. What's her next ride?"

"She has her last emergency procedures sim ride tomorrow."

"Put me in that sim ride with her."

"Dave Carter will throw a fit if I remove him from flying with one of his students."

"I'll take care of him. Don't worry about it. Just put me on the schedule with her. I need to find out if she really can't fly or if it's some other issue."

"If you say so. You've got the EP sim with Tompkins at 1100 hours. Hey, I'm playing softball with the base team tonight. Why don't you come and play with us?"

"I don't think so, Barb. I still have a lot of work to do at my office."

"Come on, Kath, it'll be fun. When was the last time you had some fun?"

"I can't play this time, but I'll stop by and watch your game if I get a chance."

"Okay, you can join us afterward."

"Don't work too late, Barb. I'd hate to have to write you up for a safety violation," she said as she left the flight room and locked the door behind her.

She walked down the hall to the operations officer's office. "Hey, Colonel Miller, got a minute?"

"Captain Hardesty, how's my favorite safety officer? What can I do for you, Kathryn?"

"Just trying to keep you out of trouble, as usual, sir. Can you do me a favor? I want you to put Dave Carter on the upgrade training program for runway supervisory unit observer."

"He's a Good Grief IP, right? He's been an IP for at least a year, so, yeah, I'll move him up to RSU observer. Why are you so interested in him?"

"No particular reason, sir. He's just due. Oh, and can you put him on the board to start training tomorrow morning?"

"Sure, Kath, anything for you. Does this mean I no longer owe you a beer for my hard landing last week?"

"Yes, sir, we're even—for now." She laughed as she left his office.

❖

Kathryn looked at her watch as she finished up her last report. It was 1800 hours. She could still see the end of the softball game if she went over to the field right now. She smiled as she walked from her office in the Wing Headquarters over to the ball field in the cool evening air. The softball field was the unofficial gathering place for all lesbians in the Air Force, and she usually avoided it, but Barb had asked her specifically to come tonight.

She was one of only a handful of fans sitting in the bleachers watching the game. She recognized most of the women on the team—aircraft mechanics, hospital techs, security police, Barb, two IPs from the T-38 squadron, and, surprisingly, Lieutenant Casey Tompkins at third base.

Casey had a look of fierce concentration on her face as she leaned forward, her weight shifting from foot to foot, ready for the next ball. The batter hit a hard drive right down the third base line. Casey launched herself to her right and snagged the ball with her mitt. She spun in midair and fired off a rifle shot as she threw the ball perfectly to first base, completing a flawless double play. *Well, she can certainly handle a ball and has great reflexes.*

Casey had a dazzling smile on her face as they jogged into the dugout for their turn at bat. As she approached the bench, Casey looked up into the stands and locked eyes with Kathryn for a moment, then quickly looked away. Kathryn admired her long, firm legs, well-defined arms, and the lithe way she moved on the field. Casey was the next batter and they were behind by two runs. *Let's see how she handles the pressure.* Casey stood tall and relaxed in the batter's box. She let the first two balls go by, then smashed a home run with a graceful, powerful swing. The ball sailed over the fence with ease as she trotted around the bases. *She's smart, coordinated, thinks on her feet, is cool under pressure, and has excellent situation awareness on the field. I can work with that.*

The whole team cheered Casey as she came across home plate. Her three-run homer won the game for them and they were ready to celebrate.

"Kath, glad you came out to see us win! We're going over to Cosmo's for some pizza and beer. Why don't you join us?" Barb said.

"No thanks, Barb, I can't."

Barb walked over to her. "Why not, Kath? Everyone on the team is cool. You have nothing to worry about. Besides, I have a friend meeting us there who I want you to meet."

"It's not that, Barb. Tonight's the five-year anniversary. I wouldn't be good company for anyone."

"Jeez, Kath, I didn't realize what day it was. I'm going to call you later. Take care of yourself, okay?"

"You guys played a great game. You all have fun. Nice home run, Casey."

Casey looked surprised Kathryn had spoken to her. "Thanks, ma'am."

"Aren't you coming with us, Casey? Come on, you're our star hitter tonight. Barb's buying."

"Sorry, I can't. I have to study tonight. Maybe next week. See you guys later," Casey said after them as she hurriedly packed up her gear and made a quick exit off the field.

Kathryn watched Casey leave. *What's the problem with your flying, Casey?*

The five-year anniversary. It was just another date on the calendar as far as everyone else knew, but for Kathryn it was a reminder of the worst day of her life. It was the day the love of her life burned to death in a fiery plane crash. It was the day everything good and bright left the world, never to return. It was a day she had to endure getting through— once again. A day filled with guilt and regret.

Her grief had been a deep, dark pit of despair that went on endlessly. She couldn't tell anyone at work about her loss and she had to suffer in silence. The only escape from the crushing sadness was when she flew a plane. When she was in the air her total focus was on flying the jet and she got a brief reprieve from pain. Then she landed, and the heavy cloak of depression settled on her again.

She reflected back on the previous anniversaries of this day. One year she'd gotten so drunk she'd made herself sick for two days. Another year, she'd had sex with a complete stranger to try to forget, which had been useless. She'd even gone to a Catholic cathedral, lit a candle, and begged God for mercy and relief from her hopelessness. She now knew the only way to survive it was to let the sadness come. She'd learned the hard way that resisting grief was futile. She just needed to be by herself, let the memories come, and not fight the tears as they ran down her face. Since she had come to accept her fate, the misery was not quite so overwhelming this year as it had been in the past. Maybe there would be an end to the sadness some day in the future—not today, but maybe someday.

Chapter Seven

Casey showed up at the flight room the next morning dreading her next EP sim with Carter. Looking at the big schedule board, she saw that he was scheduled for RSU Training all morning. When she realized she didn't have to fly with him today, she let out a sigh of relief. Instead of postponing the sim until tomorrow, she was still doing the EP sim but with Captain Hardesty instead. She wasn't sure what she was more scared of, Carter or Captain Hard-Ass.

Captain Hardesty walked in the flight room, checklist in hand, and sat at Lieutenant Carter's table. "Ready for your sim today, Casey?"

"Yes, ma'am."

"Good, because we have a lot to cover. Our sim starts in one hour and I will brief EP stuff right up until we walk out the door. First, tell me what's the emergency boldface for takeoff abort?"

"Throttles—idle, wheel brakes—apply."

"Now ejection."

"Hand grips—raise, triggers—squeeze."

"Correct. What is the single engine best glide speed?"

"One hundred and twenty knots."

"Good. You know your stuff. These EP sims are probably the most valuable training you will ever get in pilot training. You get to face disaster and practice recovering from it without killing yourself. Emergencies in an aircraft are not a matter of 'if it will happen,' it is only a question of *when* it will happen. The most important thing you have to do in any emergency is *fly the jet*. What are the three rules in handling any emergency?"

"Maintain aircraft control. Analyze the situation and take proper action. Land as soon as conditions permit."

"Correct, and those rules are in order of importance. Flying the jet always comes first. We're going to go through your checklist and discuss the different scenarios and decisions for each emergency procedure. That way when it does happen to you, you will have already considered the options, come up with the best solution for that situation, and then you can focus on flying the airplane to a safe landing or ejecting, if required. You'll want to take notes, Casey."

"Yes, ma'am."

Other students gathered around them as Captain Hardesty briefed the emergencies. They wrote down every word like she was the Oracle of Delphi. They knew this information was vital to saving their lives some day.

They walked to the simulator building together and Casey was focused, but calm. She climbed into the sim, strapped in, and heard Captain Hardesty's calm voice in her headset.

"All set, Casey?"

"Yes, ma'am." She was ready for this simulator mission this time.

Captain Hardesty gave her engine start malfunctions, a ground fire, and engine failure on takeoff. Casey handled them correctly and with confidence. If she made a mistake, Captain Hardesty stopped the sim, explained what she did wrong and how to correct it, then let her try it again. The emergencies got more challenging as the ride went on. Captain Hardesty had Casey close her eyes then said, "Recover." When she opened her eyes, Casey was upside down, in simulated clouds, with an engine fire light flashing.

"Oh shit!" She tried to right the aircraft and pull the fire handle at the same time, resulting in burying the nose into a steep dive.

"My aircraft, Casey. Remember—fly the jet, fly the jet, fly the jet. In this situation, you do a nose low recovery first, then deal with the fire. You won't fall out of the sky or blow up if the engine is on fire, but you will die if you hit the ground. Let's try it again."

Casey took a deep breath, repeated the maneuver, and performed correctly on the second attempt.

When the sim was over, they walked back to the squadron building together. It was a beautiful, balmy spring day in the desert with a sunny blue sky and birds chirping. Casey's hair was wet with sweat and she had a headache from the intense simulator ride. She couldn't help but notice the golden highlights in Captain Hardesty's sandy brown hair. It looked soft as the slight breeze blew through it.

"What's going on with Lieutenant Carter, Casey?"

"I'm not sure I know what you mean, ma'am." *Is this a trick question?*

"You know exactly what I'm talking about."

"Um, he just gets frustrated with me because I don't seem to be able to pick up things as fast as he thinks I should. He's a good instructor. I'm sure it's just my fault."

"That was very diplomatic, Casey. Now, how about the truth. This goes no further than you and me. I promise."

Casey knew in her heart she could trust Captain Hardesty. "He yells at me all the time. He makes me feel like I can't do anything right." A huge weight came off her shoulders as she spoke the truth for the first time.

"That's what I thought it was."

Kathryn stopped and turned to face Casey, looking directly into her eyes.

"Dave Carter is an IP who is a known screamer. This is an ugly tradition that's a carryover from pilot training of the past. It's kind of like child abuse. Some IPs were yelled at when they were students, and they think they have to do the same thing to their students. My Tweet IP was a screamer, so I know what it's like to fly with a guy like that. It's difficult to learn anything, it destroys your confidence, and it's poor instruction. Casey, you have done nothing to deserve this. I've trained a lot of student pilots in my career, and you have what it takes to fly. You have to learn how to fly under intense pressure as an Air Force pilot, and you will encounter your share of assholes in the process, but don't let *anyone* take this from you. You deserve to be here."

"Thanks, ma'am," Casey answered softly.

When they got back to the flight room, Captain Hardesty filled out her grade sheet for the sim ride. "Do you have any questions on any of the EPs you saw today that we didn't already debrief?"

"No, ma'am."

"Remember what I said today, Casey. Good job." She stood, handed the grade book back to Casey, and walked out of the flight room.

Casey opened her black grade book and looked at her grade sheet. Every maneuver was graded Good or Excellent. Overall mission grade, Excellent. She fought back tears as relief flowed through her.

❖

Casey walked into the flight room the next morning with a new confidence and resolve. She could handle anything Carter threw at her today. She was hoping to see Captain Hardesty again to thank her, but her name wasn't on the schedule board. She found her own name on the board—a second period flight with Carter. She had three flights left before she was supposed to solo and knew he had to see dramatic improvement in her flying before he would let her solo. She was fully prepared to show him that today.

They went out to the jet, and he started in on her almost immediately, yelling at her for the way she put the canopy handle down. *I'm a duck. I will let his shit roll off my back.* She repeated this mantra for the whole flight as he continued to scream at her. Even as they taxied in, he pounded the glare shield with his fist and yelled, "Well, goddamn it, you finally made a decent landing!"

His debrief was short and he gave her an overall grade of Fair on the ride, and he still didn't give her very good grades on the individual maneuvers. She had to earn grades of "good" or better on all the maneuvers before she could solo the jet. Her grades were not even close.

After everyone left the flight room to go fly, she was alone in the room with Captain Arnau, who was working on the schedule board for the next day's flights. An idea came to her.

"Excuse me, Captain Arnau, can I ask you a question?"

"Sure, Lieutenant."

"Is there any way you can schedule me to fly with Captain Hardesty for the rest of my flights?"

Captain Arnau stopped what she was doing and turned to look at Casey. "She's a guest help IP, Casey. She flies with all the flights in the squadron, not just ours."

"I know, ma'am, but I was really hoping she could solo me out."

"Why?"

"Um, she's just really experienced and she communicates really clearly."

"We don't normally have guest help IPs solo out students unless there is a problem with your regular IP. Are you having a problem with Lieutenant Carter?"

"Well, ma'am, I'd rather not go into that. I'm just more comfortable flying with Captain Hardesty. Please, Captain Arnau, I'd really appreciate it if you could help me out."

"Casey, I'd like to, but I can't unless the flight commander authorizes me to. Maybe you need to go talk to him."

"Yes, ma'am. I'll think about that. Thanks anyway."

"Sorry, Casey."

She had a very big decision to make now. Most student pilots didn't ever want to talk to the flight commander. You only spoke to him if you were about to be washed out or had committed some big infraction. Student pilots didn't ever complain about their IPs. It simply was not done. You were supposed to suck it up, endure whatever abuse was dumped on you, and just get through it. If she asked the flight commander to change her IP to Captain Hardesty, this could be seen as weakness on her part—like she couldn't hack it. This was a huge risk she was contemplating, and she had to decide fast. She could either get what she wanted, to solo with Captain Hardesty, or it could blow up in her face and Carter would be even more enraged with her. She had to be tough and show Carter she could fly in spite of his abuse. Her future as a pilot, and her life's dream, depended on it.

❖

"Captain Hardesty, could you come into my office for a minute?" asked Captain George Stavros, the Good Grief flight commander.

"Sure, George, what's up?"

"Guess who just asked the scheduler to not fly with their assigned IP? The first such request from anyone in this class, by the way."

"I give, George, who?"

"Lieutenant Casey Tompkins. And guess who she wants to fly with, to solo her out?"

"Me?"

"Yes, you. She hasn't spoken to me or made this an official IP change request yet. Care to tell me what's going on with her?"

"I'm honestly surprised she asked to fly with me, but I'm not surprised she asked Barb to not fly her with Carter."

"And why is that, Kathryn? What do you know that I, as the flight commander, obviously do not know about my own troops?"

"First, Dave Carter is a screamer. She just doesn't respond to instruction like that. Plus, he didn't teach her how to trim, he's been giving her low maneuver grades, and he's trying to document a failure to progress. He's setting her up to wash her out, George."

"Dave is going to throw a hissy fit if I have her solo with you, you know that, don't you."

"Yeah, so what if he does? What's more important here, George? Catering to a screaming IP's delicate ego or teaching a student how to fly?"

"I was your assistant flight commander for two years, you taught me everything I know about running this flight, and you know I have nothing but the highest respect for you, but you are putting me in a very difficult position here."

"George, there is a student pilot who needs help. She wants an IP who will teach her to fly and not scream at her, but she's reluctant to ask you because she doesn't want to look like a wimp. If anyone put you in a bad spot here, it was Dave Carter, not Casey Tompkins. Why don't you let me solo her out. If she can't cut it, I will bust her and build an airtight case for you to wash her out. As always, the decision is up to you. Do what you think is best."

"I'll let you know what I decide."

"Sure thing, George."

Well, well, well. Lieutenant Casey Tompkins, you've got some guts, girl.

CHAPTER EIGHT

Casey had no idea what to expect as she walked into the flight room the next morning at 0315 hours. She might have gotten her wish to fly with Captain Hard-Ass and gone right from the frying pan into the fire. She looked at the schedule board. She was flying with Captain Hardesty in exactly one hour and fifteen minutes. She sat at her table with Mike and Jeff. Mike was flying with Carter first period, and Jeff was flying with him second period.

"Why are you flying with Captain Hardesty again, Casey?" Mike asked.

"I guess they didn't have any one else to fly with me."

"Well, she can't be any worse than Carter. He's been passing me on my rides, but I don't know why. I feel like I can't do anything right because he screams and swears at me so much."

"He does?" For some reason, she assumed he only screamed at her, not the other guys.

"Does he scream at you too, Jeff?" Mike asked.

"Yeah, all the time, but I'm used to it. I used to be in the Marine Corps. We're used to people screaming at us. You guys are just whisky deltas."

"What's a whisky delta, Casey?" Mike whispered.

"It means 'weak dick,'" she answered.

"Jeff's as bad as Carter sometimes."

The room was called to attention as the IPs walked in for the morning briefing. Carter sat at his table and didn't even look at Casey. He started briefing Mike and Jeff on their flights, then she sensed Captain Hardesty standing behind her.

"Let's brief up in the flight commander's office, Lieutenant Tompkins."

Carter glared at both Casey and Captain Hardesty as she got up from the table.

"Casey, I'll be real honest with you, you're way behind where you should be for this stage of training."

"Yes, ma'am, I know, and I really appreciate you flying with me today."

"You may regret saying that. I didn't get the call sign 'Hard-Ass' for nothing. I'm not cutting you any slack just because you're a woman. I'm going to do my best to get you up to speed, but ultimately, this is on you. What's the main problem with your landings?"

"I'm not sure. They just don't seem to be very consistent."

"What pitch picture are you using in the final turn?"

"Pitch picture? I'm setting the power at seventy percent and flying at one hundred and ten knots."

"Do you know what pitch attitude you should be seeing in the final turn?"

"I'm not sure I do, ma'am."

"That's what I was afraid of. You're not looking outside when you fly. You're only looking inside at the instruments. Okay, this is going to be a pattern only ride today. I'm going to demonstrate the first pattern and landing for you and tell you exactly what you should be seeing out the windscreen. Do you remember from your dollar ride what I told you about hearing and feeling the plane when you fly?"

"Yes, ma'am."

"We're going to work on that today. You don't have to look at the RPM gauges to know the power setting. You just have to set the throttles in the correct position and listen for the sound of the engines. If you set the right pitch attitude in the final turn by looking out the window, you'll be exactly on the correct glide path at the right airspeed. We are going to beat up the pattern until you get it right."

This made so much sense to Casey.

When they walked together across the ramp to the airplane, Casey was more at ease already than in her previous flights. This ride would be tough, but she was optimistic for the first time.

"Casey, I'm going to fly the initial takeoff and the first pattern and landing. I want you to put your hands on the stick and throttles and follow along on the controls with me. The most important thing I want you to do today is look out the windscreen. Look at the picture of where the horizon is during the climb, as we slow down, the final turn, final approach, and the flare during the landing. Got it?"

"Yes, ma'am." Casey's hands were connected to Captain Hardesty's hands as she felt her move the stick and throttles. Energy flowed between them into her hands from Captain Hardesty as she flew the jet.

"Tango 76, request closed pattern," Captain Hardesty transmitted over the radio.

"Closed approved," replied the runway supervisory unit.

She rolled the airplane sharply into a turn, pulled three Gs as she climbed up to traffic pattern altitude, and leveled off at precisely the correct altitude.

"I'm checking my spacing. The runway should look like it's under the Air Force star on the wing." Casey understood what she was looking for. The spacing from the runway was perfect.

"When we are abeam the runway numbers, power idle, slow to one hundred twenty knots, and trim, trim, trim." She pulled the power to idle and flicked the trim button on the top of the stick with her gloved thumb several times as the airspeed decreased to final turn speed.

"Look back over your left shoulder. The runway touchdown point should be on a forty-five-degree line behind us. This is the perch point." She extended the speed brake, put the landing gear down, and lowered the flaps.

"Tango 76, gear down, touch-and-go."

"Tango 76, cleared touch-and-go," the RSU replied.

"I set the pitch attitude at one-third sky, two-thirds ground, thirty degrees of bank. Remember this picture. Bring the power back one knob width, this is seventy percent RPM, and trim off the stick pressure. Don't look at the end of the runway yet. Imagine there is a football goalpost off the end of the runway and we are going to fly right through it like we're a football. As we approach the 'goalpost,' start to look for the threshold of the runway. That's what you're aiming at. Check your runway aim point is one-third the way up the windscreen, then glance at your airspeed. It should be pretty close to one hundred knots. Cross-check aim point, then airspeed, and make small corrections. When the beginning of the runway starts to go under the nose, landing is assured, bring your head up and pick up the horizon. Power idle and start your flare for landing. Bring the nose up just slightly, hold that picture as the speed comes off, then touchdown."

Her words were perfectly timed with her actions as Casey watched Captain Hardesty fly a flawless pattern and landing.

"Your turn, Casey. You have the aircraft."

"Roger, I have the aircraft."

She requested a closed traffic pattern and tried her best to make it look just like Captain Hardesty's. Casey performed the landing sequence just like she'd seen and was amazed when she rolled out on final exactly on speed and on glide path. She focused on her aim point and her airspeed and saw out of the corner of her eye that Captain Hardesty had her hands near, but not on, the controls. She pulled the power to idle, held the landing attitude, and touched down smoothly for the first time. She wanted to whoop out loud.

"My airplane, Casey."

"Roger, your aircraft, ma'am." Casey wondered what she did wrong.

"That wasn't too bad. You lost a little altitude before you started your final turn because you're not quite trimming enough. Every time your power or speed changes, you have to re-trim the aircraft. Good touchdown. Let's try it again."

The ride continued with Casey flying, Captain Hardesty giving her critiques and corrections to fix her landings, and no yelling. After a few tries, Casey was flying simulated single engine landings, no flap touch-and-go landings, left and right overhead patterns, traffic pattern breakouts and re-entries, and she even greased on one landing. *I'm getting this. I think I'm actually getting this.*

"It's my turn to fly, Casey."

Captain Hardesty yanked the jet into a ninety-degree banked turn, pulled hard on the stick with five Gs of force, ripped the throttles to idle, slammed the landing gear handle down, and rolled the plane into a very tight descending turn to the runway.

There's no way she's going to make this landing.

She rolled out on a very short final approach with the power still at idle, perfectly on glide path at exactly the correct airspeed, then gently touched the airplane down with a slight squeak from the tires.

Wow. So that's how it's done.

❖

When they went back into the flight room for the debrief, Lieutenant Carter was sitting at his table already debriefing Mike. Carter was scowling and muttering under his breath as Mike was nodding with a very dejected look on his face. Casey could only cringe at what Carter might be saying to him.

"Captain Arnau, do you mind if we debrief at your table?"

"Sure, Captain Hardesty, it's all yours." Even though they were friends, Casey noticed they always addressed each other with their military ranks in front of the students.

"Casey, I saw improvement in your flying today. You still have a long way to go, but if you keep this up, I think you'll be able to solo."

A weight lifted off Casey's shoulders. She felt encouraged for the first time.

"You were getting too bogged down in the details and not looking out the window at the big picture. You know the correct sight pictures and you know the procedures. You need to chair fly the landings as much as you can. When you are doing this, close your eyes and visualize in your mind the images you saw today as you were flying. Move your hands just like you're flying, especially using the trim button, and this will come together for you. I also want you to go out to the RSU and observe the traffic pattern. Listen for all the radio calls and look at where the planes are in the pattern. This will help with your situation awareness. For the next ride, I need to see more improvement, show me that you can consistently land the airplane safely, and that you can handle any situation in the pattern. Overall grade, Good."

Captain Hardesty handed her grade sheet to Casey as she stood to leave. Casey stared at the individual grades for a long time: normal overhead pattern—good, single engine overhead—good, no flap landing—fair, normal landing—good. *I earned these grades. I think I can really do this.*

The next morning, Casey was energized and excited about flying. She'd practiced the maneuvers in her room several times, chair flying exactly as Captain Hardesty told her to. She'd taken the photo of the instrument panel from her flight manual and had it enlarged so it was life-sized and propped it up on her coffee table. She used her tennis racket handle as the aircraft stick, and she put her racquetball racket between the couch cushions to use as the throttle. She was able to picture flying perfect landing patterns seeing the correct pitch attitudes and moving her hands at exactly the right time. She was ready to show Captain Hardesty that she could fly this jet.

The pre-brief was short and sweet.

"Same as yesterday, Casey, except we're going out to the practice area for stalls, slow flight and spins, then into the auxiliary field for landings and back here for more landings. I'm not saying much today. I expect you to make all the decisions, correct your own errors, and fly like you are solo."

Casey walked out to the airplane with a new confidence. She moved her hands swiftly over the gauges and switches as she completed her preflight checks. She made a good takeoff and departure to the practice area. She went through the practice maneuvers without hesitation. Captain Hardesty sat next to her without saying a word and her hands in her lap. The traffic pattern was busy as she descended into the aux field. She listened on the radio for the call signs of the other planes to figure out where they were located in the traffic pattern.

She flew up to the initial point at two hundred knots, one thousand feet above the ground, cleared the airspace to her right, snapped the airplane into a sixty-degree banked turn, and pulled hard on the stick. The three Gs of force on her body felt familiar and comfortable now as she rolled out on altitude with proper spacing from the runway. Her movements were almost automatic—gear, flaps, speed brake, trim, radio calls—as she looked out the big windscreen. She knew exactly what pitch picture to set and talked to herself out loud as she really *felt* the airplane for the first time. "A little high, lower the nose. A little fast, power back." She rolled out on final on centerline, on glide path, on speed. Her focus was on the end of the runway. "Aim point, airspeed, aim point, airspeed." She held the stick lightly with just her fingertips, trimming off even slight pressure. "Landing assured, power idle." She brought the nose up for the flare. "Hold that picture, hold that picture," she told herself as the jet settled to the runway for a smooth touchdown.

The rest of her landings went equally well until the airplane in front of her flew a "bomber pattern." They were too wide and delayed their final turn too long until it was obvious she didn't have the proper distance behind them to land.

"Tango 61, going around," she called as she added full power, brought the landing gear up, and retracted the flaps. She couldn't fly over the other plane, so she banked to offset her jet from the runway to keep them in sight. She departed the pattern and flew back to Willie for some more landings until the fuel gauges showed it was time to land. Captain Hardesty hadn't said a word to her the entire flight. Her silence was disconcerting, and Casey hoped she hadn't messed up too bad.

Casey completed her shutdown checklist, filled out the aircraft logbook, and walked back into the parachute room in silence with

Captain Hardesty next to her. Casey was dying inside. She *had* to know how she did.

"Well, Casey, you showed me today you can fly the jet by yourself. Good job."

Casey wanted to scream out loud. Instead, she maintained her composure as she listened to the rest of the debrief, looking intently at Captain Hardesty.

"Your landings were consistently good, and you were analyzing and correcting your own errors. You showed good judgment when you decided to go around at the aux field. The guy ahead of us screwed you over by flying a bomber pattern, and you handled that situation exactly as you should have. I expect you to do that tomorrow when you solo, and every other flight from now on. For your solo flight tomorrow, we'll fly together for the first pattern and landing. Assuming that all goes as well as it did today, we'll taxi back in, I'll jump out of the jet, and then you're on your own. Do you have any questions about your ride today?"

"No, ma'am."

"You did well today, Casey. Don't fuck up tomorrow."

When she got up to leave the flight room, Kathryn put her hand on Casey's shoulder and gave it a firm squeeze.

There was a little electric tingle that ran down from Casey's shoulder to her spine.

CHAPTER NINE

May 1992

Casey hardly slept anticipating her solo flight. When she walked into the flight room, she noticed two names were erased from the big schedule board. It was scary how quickly you could be washed out of pilot training if you screwed up. Bust three rides in a row, and you were gone in less than a week.

She banished that thought from her mind. Her whole life would be ruined if she got washed out. Failure was not an option. She had to put doubt and fear in a little box in the back of her mind, lock it, and not think about it.

The tradition was to buy a bottle of your IP's favorite alcohol as a gift to them for soloing you out, but she had no idea what kind of booze Captain Hardesty liked.

"Captain Arnau, can I ask you a question?"

"Sure, Casey. What's up?"

"Do you know what kind of alcohol Captain Hardesty likes?"

"She doesn't drink, Casey. But I have heard she's fond of See's chocolate, especially dark chocolate."

"Thanks, ma'am."

Casey was antsy as she watched the flight room door waiting for Captain Hardesty. She didn't have to wait long. Captain Hardesty strode into the flight room like she owned it. She had a smile on her face as she made a straight line for Casey.

"Ready to go fly, Lieutenant?"

"Yes, ma'am, I sure am."

Casey knew she had to show Captain Hardesty she could handle everything today. She checked the logbook to make sure there were no maintenance issues with the jet, climbed in, and strapped the airplane to her body. She was sure and confident as she completed her preflight checks. She taxied out to the runway, took off, and entered the traffic pattern for her first landing. The pattern was busy with about a dozen other jets in the air with her. She saw all of them, adjusted her spacing for them, and flew two flawless approaches and landings.

"Casey, make this one a full stop. You're ready."

"Yes, ma'am." *Oh my God, she's actually going to let me solo.*

She landed, turned off the runway, taxied back to the ramp, and shut down both engines.

"After I get out, the crew chief will come over and secure the right seat, then he will signal you to start the engines again. Fly three touch-and-go landings, then a full stop. If you need to go around or break out of the pattern, then do it. Don't try to land out of a bad approach, just go around and try it again. If you have any emergencies, handle it. You're the pilot in command now."

Captain Hardesty climbed out of the jet and, instead of leaving, she stood over to the side, just past the wing tip. Casey waited for the visual signal from the crew chief, then started up both engines. She checked her engine instruments and called for taxi clearance.

"Ground, Hook 27 Solo, ready for taxi."

"Hook 27 Solo, taxi to runway three-zero left."

When she cleared the area before taxi, she saw Captain Hardesty snap to attention and bring her hand up to salute her. She felt a lump in her throat as she returned the salute, pushed the throttles up, and taxied to the runway.

After she climbed out of the plane, Kathryn stood just past the left wingtip watching Casey. No matter how many students she'd taught to fly, and there were many of them, this moment always gave her mixed emotions. She knew Casey was ready, but she also knew anything could happen up there, especially in a very busy traffic pattern. Her judgment as an instructor pilot was on the line, as well as the student's life, whenever she let a student solo a jet for the first time. She'd never been wrong in this decision, and she knew Casey wouldn't disappoint her. She was happy with her own ability as an instructor pilot to correct Casey's flying problems, but she was bursting with pride for Casey. She had seen her confidence as a pilot grow before her eyes. The desire to fly was so strong in Casey she'd risked asking the head scheduler for an IP change, an unheard of request from a student, to get to her goal. Now, as she watched Casey from outside the plane go through her preflight checks, this was the moment they had worked for together. This was why she loved being an instructor pilot.

Kathryn smiled looking at Casey get ready to taxi out. She resembled a large insect in the plane with her white helmet on, dark, shiny visor over her eyes, green mask covering her face, and an oxygen hose dangling from the mask like a big proboscis. Not all instructors waited by the jet for their students to fly, but Kathryn knew this was important. She always thought of her own solo and the gesture of respect her IP had shown her. When Casey looked at her before she started her taxi, Kathryn came to attention and gave Casey her best salute. Casey paused a moment, then returned the gesture. She felt like a mother eagle nudging her own fledgling out of the nest. *Enjoy this, Casey. It only happens once in your life.*

❖

The plane seemed oddly empty without Captain Hardesty sitting next to her. Everything went just as Casey had practiced it. She talked to herself out loud as she maneuvered around the pattern looking for other airplanes and executing her approaches and landings. Her first landing was a little firm, but not too bad. Her second and third landings were grease jobs.

"Hook 27 Solo, gear down, full stop." She saw a plane still on the runway in front of her. *Come on, bucko, get off the runway.*

"Hook 27, go around, traffic on the runway."

"Roger, Hook 27 Solo, going around."

"Crap, I hope they don't bust me for that."

"Just fly the jet, Casey," she heard Captain Hardesty's voice say in her head.

After the go-around, she flew her last pattern and landing, made a good touchdown, and taxied back in. *God, I hope Captain Hardesty didn't see me go around.*

After filling out the aircraft logbook, Casey saw a large group of her classmates in a crowd by the parachute shop. They surrounded her, took off her parachute, took her helmet from her, and hoisted her into the air. They all were shouting, "Whoop, whoop, whoop," as they carried her over their heads to the solo water tank.

She remembered the sunny Saturday afternoon two weeks ago when her whole class came out to paint the solo tank with their class patch and motto, "Fire on High." It was a fun tradition that every class decorated the solo tank, but at the time, she didn't picture herself being thrown into it. Now her moment had come. She'd soloed a jet for the first time, and her class was honoring her by hurling her into the ice-cold water tank. Her joy was overflowing.

Just before they threw her into the solo tank, Casey sought out the one person she wanted to see. She locked eyes with Captain Hardesty and was happy to see her laughing at her expense with the traditional dunking festivities. Their eyes stayed on each other as Casey flew through the air and hit the water with a big splash.

❖

Kathryn applauded with the other IPs and students as Casey climbed out of the solo tank dripping wet. The flight commander, Captain Stavros, came up and shook her hand as did everyone else, with the notable exception of Lieutenant Carter. Kathryn stood back a little observing Casey. Even though soaking wet, she looked tall, happy, and confident as she shared her accomplishment with her classmates. *She looks different now. Beautiful and radiant.*

The first solo flight was a milestone for anyone, but for an Air Force pilot, soloing a jet and getting thrown in the solo tank was a baptism. You were no longer thought of as just a dumb student, you were now a pilot—an inexperienced, beginner pilot, but a real pilot nonetheless. Kathryn relished watching Casey enjoy her success. She appreciated seeing all women student pilots succeed, but Casey was special. She loved the bright smile on her face, and even in a soaking-wet, baggy green flight suit, Casey was a striking-looking woman. Kathryn was proud of her but also surprised at the sensation of a small tingle in the depths of her belly. *Casey really is gorgeous.*

At that instant, Casey saw Kathryn and made a beeline for her. Kathryn couldn't help but return her big smile. *Uh-oh, Casey—no hugs, no hugs—not in front of the guys.* Before giving Casey the chance to commit the fatal error of showing affection for an IP, she stepped forward and offered her handshake. Casey paused, indicating she understood the unspoken rule, and grasped Kathryn's hand in a firm grip.

"Good job, Casey," Kathryn said as she returned the firm grip.

This was the highest praise an IP could give a student pilot. Anything more would be unseemly.

"Thanks, ma'am, I really appreciate your help. I couldn't have done it without you."

"Sure you could have. I just helped you see your own mistakes. You soloed all on your own. Don't ever forget that."

"I won't, ma'am."

CHAPTER TEN

Mike and Jeff soloed the next day, and when the flight room was somewhat quiet, Casey asked Captain Arnau if she could be excused for half an hour to run an important errand. Captain Arnau granted her a thirty-minute leave and she rushed over to the Wing Headquarters building. She found the flight safety office on the second floor and asked the secretary if Captain Hardesty was available.

"Second door on the right, Lieutenant."

"Thank you, ma'am," Casey answered.

The door read, "Captain Kathryn Hardesty, Chief, Flight Safety." Just as Casey raised her hand to knock on the half open door, she heard music coming from inside. She stopped and listened for a minute. It sounded like classical music, maybe opera. It was something grand and soaring. Casey glanced into the office and saw Captain Hardesty's back as she was looking out the big windows watching the planes in the traffic pattern. Casey couldn't take her eyes off her. Just before she was about to announce her presence, feeling a little guilty for staring, Captain Hardesty turned to face her.

"Casey. Sorry, I didn't hear you knock. Guess the music is a little loud," she said as she turned the volume down.

"I don't mean to disturb you, ma'am, I just wanted to give you this." Casey handed her a white box.

"Thanks, Casey, but I don't drink."

"It's not alcohol, ma'am. I just wanted to say thanks for your help. Have a good day." Casey set the box on the desk.

Kathryn unwrapped the box, her eyes got big when she saw the two-pound box of See's dark chocolate candy. "Well done, Casey," she said as she ripped into the famous treats.

❖

Casey's next big hurdle was passing her first check ride. She would have to pass six check rides to graduate from pilot training. Proficiency checks were a big part of every pilot's life, and she already knew how this game worked. You had to fly like you were solo, even though the check pilot was sitting next to you, and he judged you on everything you did. If you screwed up, the check pilot might let you repeat the maneuver to try and make it better. If it was an unforgiveable error, such as forgetting to put the landing gear down, he just flew the plane back to the base and you busted the check ride. If you passed all the flight maneuvers, the check pilot then grilled you on aircraft systems, emergency procedures, and flight regulations. If you answered his questions wrong, you could still bust the ride. If you busted a check ride, you got one or two practice rides, then a recheck. If you failed the recheck, you were kicked out of pilot training. In short, the whole process was a nerve-rattling minefield.

Casey had to fly with Carter, and he still screamed at her, but she didn't let it get to her. He showed her the loop, aileron roll, and split S, and she loved every second of flying acrobatics.

Casey hoped to fly with Captain Hardesty again, but she wasn't on Good Grief's schedule board. The day before her check ride, Captain Hardesty showed up in the flight room even though she wasn't on the flying schedule.

"Lieutenant Tompkins, let's do a pre-check ride ground eval."

"Yes, ma'am," Casey answered. Other student pilots gathered around them to listen in. She ran through aircraft systems questions like it was a game of *Jeopardy*. She asked flight regulation questions and grouped them together so they made a lot more sense. She summarized the emergency procedures into the most important points to remember.

"Don't allow yourself to get nervous. You *will* make mistakes in the air. The check pilot wants to see you recognize your errors and correct them yourself. Remember, the ground eval is like a hostile interrogation. Only answer the questions he asks. Do *not* bullshit the check pilot. If you do, he will know it, and rip you a new asshole. Just fess up if you have no idea how to answer a question. Good luck, everyone."

"Thanks, ma'am," the students said as she got up to leave.

"Lieutenant Tompkins, a word please."

"Yes, ma'am?"

"You've got Captain Pescado tomorrow. His favorite systems are hydraulics and fire warnings. Make sure you are up on that."

"Yes, ma'am."

"You'll do fine, Casey. Just don't get flustered if you make a mistake. Think of this as an opportunity to excel, to show him what you can do."

How was it that she always knew just the right things to say to make Casey feel better?

The next day Casey was ready and also nervous to show Captain Pescado that she could fly this jet. He was completely silent as she went through all her maneuvers. She was satisfied with her stalls and landings. After her single engine landing at Willie, Captain Pescado finally said, "I have the jet."

Oh no, did I mess something up?

Captain Pescado requested an overhead pattern and flew the plane without saying anything.

He's not going to even let me try it again? I'm screwed.

He did a touch-and-go, requested another pattern, then called for a full stop landing. Casey was dying inside. She felt hot tears well up in her eyes, but knew she could not let him see that. He didn't say a word as they put their parachutes away.

Finally, he said, "Meet me in my office at the end of the hall, Lieutenant."

"Yes, sir." *Here it comes, the end of pilot training, the end of my dream.*

After washing her face, with her head held high, like she was facing the executioner, she walked into his office.

"Well, Lieutenant Tompkins, you passed the flying part. Let's see how you do on the ground eval."

She wanted to scream in relief. He asked her every possible question about hydraulic malfunctions, fire warning systems, and a smattering of everything else from her flight books. She knew the answers to every question, replied without hesitation, and knew she had this.

"Good job, Lieutenant, you passed." He stood and shook her hand.

"Thank you, sir."

It was a Friday afternoon, she was done with this ordeal, and she really wanted to see Captain Hardesty and tell her all about it. Instead, she went to the Officer's Club for several well-earned drinks.

❖

All weekend, Casey found her thoughts turning to Kathryn Hardesty. She wanted to talk to her, to fly with her, to sit next to her in the jet, and to feel the connection to her when they both had their hands on the stick together. She had to watch her conversation so that she wasn't constantly talking about her. She was looking forward to the next phase of training—advanced acrobatics—and she wanted to ask Captain Hardesty about flying acro. More than anything, she wanted Kathryn Hardesty to be proud of her. She knew it was a waste of time to think about her all the time, but she didn't care.

She and Mike were scheduled to fly with Carter during the first and second periods while Jeff was flying with another IP. Carter briefed all three of them on the advanced aerobatic maneuvers. "These acro maneuvers were invented by the first fighter pilots as combat tactics used in air-to-air dog fighting. They involve high-speed and high-G maneuvering, and you guys need to know all the entry speeds and power settings cold."

This was what distinguished Air Force pilots from all other pilots, and Casey could hardly wait to try it.

In the practice area, Lieutenant Carter demonstrated the first maneuver, an Immelman.

"This is a half loop followed by a half roll," Carter explained. "Lower the nose, accelerate to two hundred and fifty knots, tighten your leg muscles, and then pull the stick straight back to your belly button."

The five Gs of force pulled Casey's oxygen mask down her face and pushed her into the seat. She clenched hard on her lower body muscles to withstand the G-forces.

"Check both wingtips are even as you pull through the horizon. When you are upside down at the top of the loop, pause, then roll upright to wings level. You should be at one hundred and twenty knots now. You try one."

Casey's attempt sort of looked like her instructor's demo but she was too slow at the top, and when she tried to roll upright, the aircraft started to rotate into a spin.

"My jet," Carter said as he took the airplane and recovered from the spin.

"We are now flying the jet at the edge of the performance envelope.

You'll be pulling high Gs and flying near the stall speed during all these maneuvers. Don't screw that up again."

"Yes, sir."

He quickly went through the other acrobatic maneuvers—Cuban eight, split S, barrel roll, chandelle, lazy eight, loop, and cloverleaf. When they left the practice area for the auxiliary field, Casey was exhausted from pulling Gs, and her mind was spinning trying to remember everything she'd just seen.

Back on the ground, his debrief was short. "You will practice all the advanced acro you saw today on your next solo ride. Don't let the jet get into a spin again. Chair fly this stuff. Overall grade, Good."

Casey looked at her grade sheet where all the new acro maneuvers were graded U. She feverishly started writing notes in her book trying to remember what the different maneuvers looked like and the entry parameters.

The next day, both she and Mike were scheduled for their first area solo rides. Carter briefed them both at the same time.

"Check your orientation and don't fly out of the practice area. I want you to work on all the acro maneuvers. Then go to the aux field for two to three landings, then back to Willie. When you see five hundred pounds of fuel remaining, call for a full stop landing. Any questions?"

"No, sir," they answered in unison.

They went to the supervisor of flying desk for their solo brief.

"Lieutenant Tompkins, your tail number is 0086 and your call sign today is Hook 21 Solo. Lieutenant Harris, you're in tail number 8081 and your call sign is Hook 22 Solo. Call me on the radio if you have any problems. Bingo fuel for landing is five hundred pounds. Any questions? Have a good mission today."

Casey tingled with excitement as she checked her gear and walked across the noisy ramp to her jet. *It's my jet today.*

She was thorough with her preflight checks and her takeoff was picture perfect. She started to relax as she flew the departure to the practice area. She meticulously completed her required in flight checks—oxygen check passing ten thousand feet, fuel balance check, instrument checks—all perfect. When she entered her practice area, she did a few clearing turns looking for other aircraft. She was right in the middle of her area at exactly the right airspeed and altitude.

"I think I'll warm up with an aileron roll first," Casey said out loud.

She pulled the nose up slightly, then sharply moved the stick to the full right stop. The airplane quickly rolled upside down, and she snapped the stick back to the left to stop the roll.

"Not too bad. I'm wings level right at two hundred and twenty knots. How about a loop next."

She lowered the nose to accelerate to two hundred and fifty knots, tightened her legs for the Gs, then pulled the stick back toward her crotch. She checked her wingtips even with the horizon as the jet was pointed straight up at the sky, then threw her head backward to find the horizon.

"Wings level inverted, check airspeed—ninety knots. Crap. I'm slow. I'm supposed to be at one twenty. Keep pulling."

She felt a slight burble in the stick warning her that she was close to the stall speed.

"Don't pull too hard, just keep the nose tracking through the top of the loop."

As the nose came through the horizon and she was pointed directly at the ground, she heard the sound of the airspeed increasing rapidly. She tightened her lower body as hard as she could as she completed the pull to wings level.

"I'm supposed to be at two hundred and fifty knots at the end of the maneuver and I'm at two seventy. What the hell did I do wrong?"

Casey did a few gentle turns as she checked her position and climbed back up to the correct altitude for her next maneuver. She tried the chandelle but got slow again at the top of the maneuver. Then she tried the lazy eight, and it sort of looked like it was supposed to, but not really.

"I think I'm ready to try another over the top one now. What was the entry speed for the Cuban eight again? Oh yeah, two hundred and fifty knots and one hundred percent power."

She lowered the nose to accelerate and pulled straight back like she was beginning a loop.

"Three-quarters of a loop, pause, then half a roll. Find a section line on the ground to follow, then reverse back the other direction."

As she talked herself through the Cuban eight, the G-forces increased and decreased as her speed changed throughout the maneuver. She rolled out thirty degrees off her section line with her airspeed accelerating through two hundred and seventy knots.

"Goddamn it, what am I doing wrong? These don't look anything like the way Carter did them. I'm going to try one last maneuver, then go to the aux field. The cloverleaf looked pretty easy, and I think the starting airspeed is slower."

She glanced down at the cheat sheet on her knee board to check the entry airspeed.

"Power ninety percent, entry speed two hundred and twenty knots, pull up smoothly like the beginning of a loop. When it feels like my feet are on the horizon, eyes right, roll, and pull to a point on the horizon abeam my right shoulder. I should be at one hundred and twenty knots inverted going through the horizon. Then three more leaves just like it. This should be easier than the other over-the-top ones."

She pulled back on the stick at two hundred and twenty knots, at sixty degrees nose high, she looked to her right and saw a small white puffy cloud. This was her target as she slowly rolled the aircraft upside down toward the cloud and kept pulling back on the stick. Everything looked good until she checked her speed inverted coming through the horizon. She wasn't quite wings level and was too fast at one hundred forty knots instead of one hundred twenty knots.

"Pull the nose up a little more on the next leaf," she said to herself.

On her second leaf, she started at two hundred fifty knots instead of two twenty, and she continued the maneuver to try to fix it on the next leaf. She pulled up through the horizon, looked right again, and saw a mountain peak to use as a target.

"Up and over, nice and smooth."

She glanced down at her airspeed indicator as she was inverted coming through the horizon. It read one hundred seventy knots instead of one twenty knots this time.

"Goddamn it. I'm too fast again. Fix it on the last leaf." She was getting frustrated with herself.

She looked for the section line on the ground to try to straighten out the backside of the cloverleaf. She heard the air noise around her increase to a deafening roar as she realized she was going way too fast. Her altimeter was unwinding at a furious rate, and her altitude was rapidly approaching the bottom of the practice area. She saw her airspeed going through three hundred knots toward the red line.

"Shit! Pull up!"

She yanked back hard on the stick to slow her screaming descent. Instantly, her vision went gray and she couldn't see anything.

"Fuck! I'm graying out!"

She was pointed straight at the ground, and if she pulled any harder, she would black herself out. If she didn't pull up hard enough, she would slam into the ground. She was blind but still conscious for the moment. She had to decide right now. Either eject, or fly the jet blind and keep pulling back on the stick, hoping she didn't hit the ground.

"Pull, Casey, pull!"

CHAPTER ELEVEN

Kathryn was supposed to be finishing her quarterly wing safety reports, but instead she was standing at the big window in her office watching the planes fly around the traffic pattern. She never got tired of looking at all the aircraft in the crazy, organized chaos of the busiest airport in the world.

The radio brick on her hip crackled to life. "Flight Safety, this is the Control Tower."

Her insides clutched and she keyed the mike button. "Tower, this is Flight Safety, go ahead."

"Albuquerque Center is declaring an emergency for a T-37 aircraft, call sign Hook 21 Solo."

"What's the nature of the emergency?"

"They are reporting Hook 21 Solo as a missing aircraft."

"When did they last have any radio contact?"

"Their last contact with Hook 21 Solo was when the aircraft entered the low-altitude practice area at 1545 hours. Time now 1605 hours."

"Are there any search and rescue aircraft in the area?"

"They report Sage 85 is inbound to the practice area. ETA ten minutes."

"Has the fire department at the auxiliary field been notified?"

"Affirmative."

"Roger, Tower, I copy all. Is there anything else?"

"Sage 85 just reported a column of smoke southwest of the practice area."

"Copy, Tower. I'm responding now. Flight Safety out."

Oh, God, please give me a student pilot with a successful ejection on this one.

With that unspoken prayer, she ran as fast as she could to the blue Air Force pickup truck.

Kathryn raced across the desert to the coordinates of the smoke column as memories of another terrible aircraft accident five years earlier flooded her mind like a dam breaking. She had just finished flight safety school after eight weeks of training in aircraft accident investigation at the University of Southern California. The intensive training and getting a new job on the wing staff was good for her career, but she'd been very lonely for Marie.

Kathryn never believed in "love at first sight" until she laid eyes on Marie in pilot training. They were in different flights, but they noticed each other immediately. Marie was cute, smart, and funny, and everyone liked her. They started out studying together, but things quickly progressed to a physical relationship. They'd been very happy together, especially in bed, then they ran into a major hurdle.

Kathryn was doing well with flying, but Marie struggled right from the beginning. She tried to help Marie learn the huge volume of material, but Marie got flustered when she was in the sim or the airplane. She would make minor errors, get mad at herself, then fall apart and not be able to fly the jet. She couldn't pass the first check ride because of her nerves, and she washed out of pilot training. Marie had done well academically, so she was offered a slot in navigator training. They parted tearfully when Marie got sent to a different training base but vowed to stay together despite where the Air Force sent them.

Kathryn excelled in pilot training, and at the time she was graduating in 1983, women were very restricted with the airplanes they were allowed to fly. She was fighter qualified because of her skills but women weren't allowed to fly fighters, attack aircraft, bombers, or even reconnaissance jets. They could only fly air refueling tankers, big airlift transports, or training jets, because the men didn't want those jobs. She was asked to stay on at the pilot training base as a T-38 instructor pilot, which was a great honor, but she requested to fly the old KC-135 tanker so she could be stationed with Marie. Her class commander was baffled but gave her the assignment she wanted.

Kathryn breezed through KC-135 school and was in lesbian bliss when she finally got to Fairchild Air Force Base in Spokane, Washington. Her life with Marie was perfect. She upgraded from copilot to aircraft commander as soon as she could, Marie was her navigator, and they flew around the world together.

Kathryn loved Marie with her whole heart, she thought Marie was her soul mate, and they planned their future together. When she was offered the job as a wing flight safety officer, she jumped at the chance to advance her career. She was optimistic when she got home from training and was looking forward to flying with Marie again. Little did she know the first accident she would be tasked to investigate would be the death of the love of her life.

"This isn't the same accident. Stay focused on the present. The student might have gotten out." She tried convincing herself as she drove faster through the desert.

She mentally assessed her emergency response kit—camera, maps, flags to mark debris, evidence bags. She had everything. She just had to steel herself to the possible scene that awaited her. The memories of that first accident scene came rushing back to her, and she couldn't stop them.

It started the same way with the radio brick calling her to an accident scene. A KC-135 tanker had gone down at night in the traffic pattern at the Fairchild practice field. They were practicing instrument approaches with touch-and-go landings. It was a cold, clear night in Spokane, but the fire from the wreckage could be seen for miles. Kathryn had been focused, and scared, responding to her first real accident. The tanker had a midair collision with a light aircraft that flew right through the traffic pattern. They didn't have a chance. The flaming debris was scattered over a relatively small area, but it was clear there were no survivors. Kathryn remembered that fateful radio call like it was yesterday.

"Flight Safety, this is Operations."

"Go ahead, Ops."

"We have the crew manifest for the mishap aircraft."

Kathryn's blood ran cold before she even heard the names. Somehow she sensed Marie's name would be on the list.

"Stop it, Kath. This isn't Marie. This is a student pilot who may still be alive," she told herself.

As she rounded the corner in her safety truck, she saw the column of black smoke and the flashing lights of the fire trucks. She drove up to the accident scene slowly, staying out of the way of the emergency response vehicles. She got out of her truck and went up to the on-scene commander.

"Any survivors, Chief?"

"Sorry, Captain Hardesty, no news yet. We've almost got the fire out. I'll clear you to go to the site in a few minutes."

She walked around the perimeter of the accident site and started taking photos. The crash site was fairly contained, without a lot of wreckage strewn about, indicating the aircraft didn't break up in flight but hit the ground intact. She looked up into the sky—perfect blue skies, no clouds, no thunderstorms.

"Flight Safety and Medical, this is the on-scene commander. The fire is out and the accident site is now safe. You are cleared to enter."

"Flight Safety copies. Proceeding to the site now."

As she slowly walked among the smoldering pieces of metal that used to be a beautiful airplane, she consciously put her emotions in check. There was an important job to do, and she was the officer to do it. She needed to know if the student got out. She went first to the smoking cockpit section.

Most of the airframe was gone, having burned up in the post-crash fire, and there was a scorched outline of the plane on the desert floor. It was a black shadow of a T-37 with only a few big pieces left—both engines, the tail section, and the cockpit section with a melted canopy. *Oh, no.*

Bile started coming up her throat, but she forced it down. She continued to take evidence pictures as she approached the black mass in the center of the wreckage. Then she saw what she'd prayed she wouldn't see—the charred remains of the student pilot in the left seat. It was all she could do not to hurl the contents of her stomach when she inhaled the unmistakable smell of burning flesh. *Keep it together, Kath. Keep it together.*

She took pictures—the lap belt, the ejection seat handgrips, the parachute, the flight instruments—it was all there. The student had made no attempt to eject. Her job would be to figure out why. The flight surgeon came up and tapped her shoulder.

"Sorry you have to see this, Doc. This is your first aircraft fatality, isn't it?"

The young doctor nodded, but he couldn't speak. He looked like he was about to faint.

"Master Sergeant Gutierrez knows the drill. They'll remove the remains, then have the body sent to Wilford Hall Medical Center for autopsy and toxicology testing. You just have to sign the death certificate when it's ready."

The aircraft maintenance team showed up to haul out the pieces and analyze the aircraft systems for any mechanical malfunctions.

"How's it look, Captain Hardesty?" asked the team leader, Chief Master Sergeant Rand.

"Nothing obvious at this point, Chief. It looks like the plane was in one piece when it hit the ground, but we'll look at everything. I want your best techs on the engines, flight controls, and avionics."

"You got it, ma'am. We'll figure out if anything was wrong with this jet."

"Have you impounded the aircraft maintenance and service records?"

"Already done, ma'am."

Kathryn finished marking the crash site on her maps and completed her accident photos. The medical and maintenance specialists had everything else under control, and the security police had the site secure, so Kathryn returned to the base to start the next phase of her investigation—the part she dreaded most—determining the identity of the dead student.

As she drove back across the desert to the base, she was struck at how beautiful the sunset was. The sky was streaked with soft shades of pale lavender blending into subtle hues of salmon and silver on the clouds. She loved the sunsets in the desert sky, but this one just made her sad. *That student pilot will never see this again.*

The crackle of her radio brick snapped her out of her thoughts.

"Flight Safety, this is Squadron Ops."

She recognized the voice of the squadron commander. "Go ahead, sir."

"Come up on secure channel seven."

"Safety is on secure seven, sir."

"We heard about the fatality. We've identified the student, and the class commander has impounded the grade book and training records. They're in my office when you get back here."

She reached for her pencil in her left sleeve pocket. "I'm ready to copy, sir."

"The student pilot is First Lieutenant Casey Tompkins, Good Grief flight, call sign Hook 21."

Kathryn dropped her pencil, stunned by the news.

"Safety, did you copy?"

"Yes, sir, I copy," she answered softly. "Sir, I believe she lives on base in the bachelor officer quarters. I'll head over there now to examine her personal effects."

"After you're done at her quarters, report to my office. We need to get the preliminary press release together. This one's going to get a lot of attention."

"Yes, sir."

"Squadron Ops out."

Kathryn had to stop driving. She struggled to breathe as tears blurred her vision. *Oh, my God, Casey.*

CHAPTER TWELVE

Kathryn stood in front of the door to Casey's quarters waiting for the BOQ manager to let her in. She was dreading this task even more than seeing the accident site. The horrid memories of going through Marie's personal effects after her plane crash made her physically ill. Just then, the BOQ manager showed up to let her in.

Kathryn felt guilty being in here, like she was violating Casey's private space. She recognized the subtle scent of Casey's shampoo in the air. The room was tidy and well organized, just like Casey was. Apprehension rose in her as she looked around at Casey's personal things—a framed photo on the desk, some books on the nightstand, dirty laundry in the basket by the closet, a cork bulletin board with her weekly schedule on it. Kathryn picked up the picture on the desk, looking closely at Casey and her family. She had a beautiful smile on her face and was almost as tall as her father, with her arm draped across her mother's shoulders. She seemed to look right into Kathryn's soul.

Casey's flight suits hung in the closet. Kathryn slowly ran her hand down the sleeve as sadness descended over her. The grief from Marie's death, and now Casey's, merged together and overwhelmed her. She had to sit down on Casey's bed. Holding her face in her hands, hot tears flooded over her, and she cried out, "Oh, my God, Casey, what happened to you?"

Fighting the grief, she shook her head hard and wiped away the tears. "Get over yourself, Kath. You've got a job to do here." She stood and looked around the room, noticing a rainbow-colored button on the bulletin board. It read, "Dip me in honey and throw me to the lesbians!" *Oh, crap. I can't let anyone else see this.*

Kathryn was quite sure Casey was gay, but she certainly hadn't talked to her about it because she was a student. If the investigating board found out Casey was a lesbian, it would make it into the official accident report, maybe even as a related cause of the accident. She had to protect Casey's reputation from the homophobes in the Air Force even if it meant jeopardizing her own career as the accident investigator. She owed Casey that much.

Images of hiding her relationship with Marie after her crash came flooding back. She remembered the sadness of removing their love letters and pictures. Protecting Marie's reputation with the Air Force was the last act of love she ever did for her.

Kathryn grabbed a trash bag from under the sink and rapidly scanned the room for anything gay. She snagged the rainbow button off the bulletin board, then looked at the titles of the books on the nightstand—lesbian romance novels. Into the bag they went. She opened the drawers and removed a photo album and a small bundle of letters tied with a red ribbon. Just as she was putting these in the trash bag, she sensed someone else in the room. She quickly turned.

Casey.

Kathryn was sure she was hallucinating.

"Captain Hardesty? What are you doing here? Am I in some kind of trouble?"

Kathryn slowly stood up, frozen with disbelief. This apparition of Casey was speaking to her.

"Captain Hardesty?"

Kathryn slowly walked over to Casey and gripped her shoulders to see if she was real. She stared directly into Casey's eyes for a long moment. Then she reached up, put her arms around Casey's neck, and pulled her into a tight hug.

Casey was stunned. First, she'd almost killed herself on her solo ride, and now Kathryn Hardesty was holding her in a full body hug. What the hell was going on today? How in the world did Captain Hardesty know what happened on her solo ride when she grayed herself out doing a very bad cloverleaf? Did Albuquerque Center see her on radar and report her to the supervisor of flying?

Casey's mind raced as she stood there letting Captain Hardesty hold her. After she lost her vision when she was pointed straight at the ground, she had pulled blindly to what she guessed might be the horizon. After a few tortuously long seconds, her vision slowly came back when her blood returned to her brain and eyes. She'd been amazed to find that the airplane was sort of level with the horizon in a twenty-degree bank turn. After realizing that she'd almost blacked herself out, she'd scared herself so badly she just flew around the border of her practice area until she'd burned enough fuel to head back to the base. Just as she was about to return, she heard Albuquerque Center broadcast that all aircraft were to return to Williams Air Force Base immediately. It took her a while to get back because the other aircraft were trying to return at the same time. When she did get back to the base, they told her to make a full stop landing. The parachute room was strangely empty when she hung up her chute. When she went back to her flight room, the doors were locked with a sign on it directing the students to return to their quarters. She was confused but glad to leave the squadron building after her near-death experience on her flight. She still didn't understand why Captain Hardesty was hugging her, but she was enjoying the feel of her warm, firm body pressed against her.

Captain Hardesty let go of Casey and stared at her again.

"Casey, I thought you'd been killed in a plane crash. I'm very glad I was wrong."

"What? You thought I'd been in a plane crash? My flight today was pretty bad, but I certainly didn't crash. I don't understand what's going on."

The radio brick crackled to life. "Flight Safety, this is Squadron Operations."

"Safety here, go ahead, sir."

"We misidentified the student in the accident. Maintenance just gave me the correct tail number from the accident site. It's 8081, not 0086. The mishap student used the wrong call sign. His call sign was Hook 22, not Hook 21. It's not Lieutenant Tompkins; it's Lieutenant Mike Harris."

"Safety copies, sir. I'll head over to his quarters now. Can you have the BOQ manager meet me again to let me in?"

"Roger. Ops out."

"Oh, my God. Was Mike in a plane crash, Captain Hardesty?"

"Yes, Casey, he was. I'm very sorry, but he's gone," she said softly.

"I was just talking to him two hours ago. We went out to fly our solo missions at the same time. This can't be true."

"I'm afraid it is true. And I'm really sorry for the confusion, but we thought you were the student pilot in the accident. I'm so glad you're okay, but I have to get over to Mike's quarters. Do you know where he lives?"

"He lives next door to me, ma'am. I have a key to his room."

"You do?"

"Yeah, we studied together and hung out all the time. He did my laundry for me and I made flash cards for him. He was my best friend in the flight, my only friend really. We decided to exchange keys in case either one of us forgot to set their alarm and slept in on early week. He has a key to my room too. Or he had one. Oh my God, I still can't believe this." Casey had to sit down as she choked up thinking of her friend.

"Please take me over to Mike's room and let me in."

"Yes, ma'am."

They went next door and Casey opened the door to Mike's room. The furniture was identical to all the other rooms in the bachelor officer quarters except that the linoleum floors were gleaming and the room looked like it was ready for a Saturday morning white glove inspection. The twin bed had perfect hospital corners, and the blanket was tucked in so tight you could bounce a quarter on it. Every Air Force officer knew how to do this from their initial weeks at basic training, but no one continued this practice after graduation. The room was so neat it looked staged, not like a real person lived here.

❖

Kathryn looked around the room, but nothing was out of place. She looked more closely at the standard cork bulletin board. Mike had a calendar with his flights and sims marked on it. Next to each flight or simulator day, Mike had written a note in tiny, precise handwriting. Kathryn started reading the notes by the flight entries.

Screwed up the takeoff today.

Carter yelled at me again. Can't make level turns.

Messed up in the EP sim. I'm such a fuckup.

I don't feel ready for my check ride. I think I'm going to bust.

Kathryn was shocked at what she read. Every note was a severe reproach on himself. Mike was severely self-critical. This might be an explanation as to what happened in the air today. She wouldn't allow herself to jump to any conclusions. She would complete a comprehensive investigation then report her findings, but she had a gut feeling where the evidence would lead her and it wasn't good.

Casey also saw the notes on Mike's calendar as she looked over Kathryn's shoulder.

Kathryn turned to her. "Casey, you are not to say anything about this to anyone. This is part of an accident investigation now, and I need your word you will not discuss what you've seen here with anyone."

"Yes, ma'am, I understand."

"Did Mike ever talk to you about his flying? How he felt he was doing or about these notes?"

"No, he didn't, but I suspected he was struggling. He complained about Lieutenant Carter screaming at him in the plane, but he never did anything about it. I told him to ask for an IP change, but he wouldn't do it because he didn't want to look like a weak dick."

"When I realized what Dave Carter was doing to you, I should have flown with him. I flew his dollar ride with him and he seemed so happy. I had no idea he was having a hard time."

"Mike tried to hide that. He had to call his father every week to give him a progress report and I could hear him yelling on the phone from my quarters."

"It sounds like Mike was used to putting up with bullies. Please don't say anything about this, Casey. I need to continue going through Mike's personal effects, so you can return to your quarters now. I'm sorry for the confusion earlier, but I'm really glad you're all right."

Kathryn reached up, put her arms around Casey's neck, and pulled her into another firm hug. This time, Casey hugged her back and they held each other for a long moment.

❖

Casey left Mike's room struggling with shock and sadness at his death. He had been the first guy in her class to treat her like an equal. He was smart, funny, but also insecure. She had no idea how insecure he really was until she saw his notes, and she wished she'd made more of an effort to help him. They talked all the time about what an ass Carter was and how they couldn't wait to get to the T-38 so they could have a different IP.

She'd come very close to death herself today, but for whatever reason, her number wasn't up yet. Captain Hardesty could just as easily be investigating her crash today instead of Mike's. She'd been so shocked to see Kathryn in her quarters when she walked in. She thought she was in big trouble until Kathryn pulled her into that embrace. She'd been frozen when Kathryn put her arms around her in that long, warm hug. She didn't know why Kathryn was hugging her, but she didn't want it to end. She had a strange mixture of feelings about Kathryn Hardesty.

She looked down and saw the trash bag Captain Hardesty had been holding. Casey opened the bag and was surprised to find her lesbian books, her love letters from Lynn, and her rainbow button. Captain Hardesty thought she had been investigating Casey's death and was trying to "straighten up" her room so the Air Force wouldn't find out she was a lesbian. *She was trying to protect me.*

CHAPTER THIRTEEN

The mood in the classroom was quiet and somber. Mike's seat was empty and no one even looked at it. Their class commander, Captain Morgan, walked up to the front of the classroom.

"Today is a hard day for all of us. Lieutenant Mike Harris was a friend to everyone in this class. There will be a time for grief, but today is not that day. We have a job to do, and we cannot let this accident distract us from that job. Unfortunately, death of a friend is a part of being an Air Force pilot. This is a dangerous job, and every pilot on this base has lost a friend in an aircraft accident at some point in their career. We have to learn to deal with it. There will be an accident investigation, and we'll get the results of that investigation when it is complete. Do not waste time speculating on what may or may not have happened. The best way to honor Mike is to learn from this accident and go on to be better pilots for it. There will be an informal memorial in the O Club casual bar this Friday at 1600 hours. Everyone needs to be there."

Casey struggled to fight back tears. Mike's absence left a gaping hole in her heart. She'd never known anyone her own age who had died, but she needed to put her sadness aside and deal with it later. Air Force pilot training stopped for no one.

When the class got to the flight room, the master schedule board had a big X through the flights and sims scheduled for that day. Instead it said, "Safety Down Day." Several of the IPs, including Lieutenant Carter, were absent. The flight commander, Captain Stavros, walked to the podium as the room was called to attention.

"Take seats, everyone. We won't be flying today as several IPs are being interviewed by the safety investigation board. Instead, we're going to have a ground day focused on flight safety and accident prevention. We are coming into a very intense phase of training, with more solo flights, and there is no IP sitting next to you to save your ass if you screw something up. You've all soloed the jet, and the responsibility is on you to save yourself. The best way to get through this is to continue to work hard, learn your stuff, and be heads up when you fly."

Casey looked up at the schedule board. There was a blank line under her name where Mike's name had been. He had been erased from the flight just as if he'd washed out of the program. She tried to concentrate on studying her instrument flying manual but was having a hard time keeping her mind focused. Her thoughts kept drifting back to that sustained hug from Captain Hardesty in her room. She was surprised when she felt little tingles move into her stomach remembering the feel of Kathryn in her arms.

Lieutenant Carter came back to their flight room the next day and grumbled about wasting his time with the safety board. Casey sensed he seemed nervous. Maybe they thought there was something wrong with his screaming instructional technique. Maybe they thought he was to blame for Mike's crash. They would find out soon enough after the investigation was complete. She kept looking for Captain Hardesty's name on the schedule board, but she didn't see her all week. She assumed she was tied up with the investigation.

The whole class was glad when Friday finally came and they could go to the O Club to blow off steam and remember Mike. Casey had several beers as they told stories about Mike. Her favorite story was the one where Mike borrowed Jeff's flying gloves, then barfed into them on his second flight because he forgot his airsick bag. They raised their glasses in a final toast to Mike led by their flight commander, Captain Stavros.

"To Mike Harris, who has flown his final flight west into the sunset. To us, and those like us, damn few left. Hoo-ah!"

No one cried for Mike in public. It wasn't "manly," and there was no crying in the Air Force. Casey looked across the room and noticed Captain Hardesty standing in the corner watching the activities. She looked subdued until she locked eyes with Casey. She gave her a head nod and a slight smile. Casey felt warmth spread in the pit of her stomach and she smiled back.

She noticed Captain Hardesty quietly leave the bar shortly after the last toast to Mike. Casey stayed for another half hour but was feeling antsy as the drinking increased and the volume of the men got louder. She was overwhelmed by the reek of testosterone and beer in the air and needed to get away from the maleness that had surrounded her all week. What she needed right now could only be found at a lesbian bar. She drove into Phoenix to the Incognito Lounge. She didn't feel particularly good about what she was looking for, but she wasn't feeling guilty either. Casey wanted a quick hookup—that's all. She needed the intimate company of a woman to free her mind from thoughts of Mike, plane crashes, and pilot training.

The bar was packed with a cloud of thick, blue cigarette smoke and the pounding disco beat of the Village People. She scanned the crowd looking for a potential lover for the night. No women really caught her eye until she saw a cute, sporty-looking woman walk in by herself. Casey observed her as she walked up to the bar to order a Coors. She was shorter than Casey, with shoulder-length straight brown hair and a nice smile. Casey struck up a conversation with her, then asked her to dance. The woman seemed interested in Casey as she pressed her hips into her on the dance floor.

"Would you like to come over to my place where we could have a drink in private?" she asked Casey.

Here it was, Casey's objective, right in front of her, but a strange nagging in the back of her mind kept her from closing the deal. "Thanks, but I can't tonight. I have to get up real early tomorrow. Maybe some other time."

The woman walked off with a shrug.

Casey drove back to the base frustrated with herself. She looked at the clock—eleven thirty. She hoped Rhonda and Trish would still be up.

"Hi, Rhonda, I was wondering if I could invite myself over. It's been a rough week."

"Sure, come on over. Why don't you spend the night? We're having a pool party tomorrow."

A weight lifted from her as she drove to her friends' home. They didn't ask her any questions, they just got her a beer and some snacks. After a while, Casey told them about Mike's death, her own near crash on her solo ride, and finding Kathryn Hardesty in her room thinking she'd been killed. They listened without comment, but both gave her a big hug.

When she went to their guest room, she wondered again why she couldn't complete her hookup plans with the cute girl at the bar. Then it struck her—that girl resembled Kathryn Hardesty. She turned over and tried to dismiss the disturbing thought. Instead, she let herself sink into the sheets, feeling surrounded by the sanctuary of her friends.

❖

Kathryn closed the thick folder of the accident investigation report. She was almost finished with the formal written part and was just waiting for a few more evidence analysis reports to come in. They were just formalities since she had her causes and conclusions already written. The cause of this accident was difficult for her to accept. A young student was dead, and he shouldn't be. She'd put in long hours for weeks working on this investigation, and the heavy stress was getting to her. She knew what she needed and went to where she could get it.

Kathryn spotted Barb hard at work on the big schedule board as she entered the flight room.

"Captain Arnau, I have a favor to ask."

"Captain Hardesty, where have you been? Done with your investigation, I hope."

"Almost, Barb, but I really need to fly. I'm going stir-crazy from this paperwork. Do you have any jets available today? Pleeease?"

"Sorry, Kath, I don't. Let me call the squadron scheduler and see if I can rustle up a plane for you. I don't have any other IPs available to fly with you. Can you do a student sortie?"

"I'll fly with anyone. I just need to get up in the air."

After a quick call, Barb motioned Kathryn over. "I got a Warlock jet for you that was on a mechanical delay but is fixed now, and you can fly with Tompkins. She's up for an advanced contact ride."

"You're a gem, Barb, thanks." Kathryn had a little twinge of apprehension because this would be the first time she would see Casey after she'd hugged her in her quarters. She had to put her awkwardness aside and treat Casey like any other student. She needed to fly, and Casey needed her to be a good IP.

"Lieutenant Tompkins, are you ready to fly?"

Casey jumped when she heard her name called. "Yes, ma'am, I am."

"Let's brief this up and go fly."

❖

Captain Hardesty had Casey complete the preflight inspection, take off, and climb out to the practice area.

"Casey, I need to update my spin currency, so I'll fly the first spin recovery, then I'll have you do one."

"Yes, ma'am."

"My airplane. I'm climbing to twenty-five thousand feet. Confirm your loose items are stowed."

"Your jet, loose items stowed."

Kathryn talked as she set up the spin maneuver, like she couldn't fly if she wasn't instructing.

"Nose up twenty degrees, throttles idle, hold this pitch attitude as the speed drops off. At the first stall indication, smoothly feed in full right rudder and hold it."

Casey felt the aircraft shudder as it ran out of airspeed and started to stall. She looked out the big canopy as the plane rolled to the right, almost upside down, then started rotating into a spin. The ground looked like a record on a turntable as the rotation increased and the nose was pointed almost straight down.

Captain Hardesty called out the emergency recovery steps as she executed them. "Throttles—idle. Rudder and ailerons—neutral. Stick—abruptly full aft and hold. Spinning right, turn needle right—left rudder."

She kicked the left rudder hard to the full stop, held it for one turn, then slammed the stick full forward to break the stall. The jet accelerated like a spinning ice skater, then suddenly popped out of the spin with the nose pointed straight at the ground. "Recover from dive. Tighten up, Casey." She smoothly pulled back on the stick to return to level flight with G-forces pulling them hard into their seats. "Okay, Casey, your turn."

Casey climbed the airplane back up to twenty-five thousand feet and tried not to be intimidated by the perfect spin recovery Captain Hardesty had just demonstrated. Her spin wasn't bad, just not perfect.

"Let's descend into the low area and practice some acro. Tighten up, Casey."

Captain Hardesty rolled the jet upside down, pulled the throttles to idle, pulled back on the stick with five Gs, and did a split S maneuver, losing ten thousand feet of altitude in a matter of seconds. Then she rolled upside down again, doing another split S, and had the jet in the exact center of the low practice area.

Slick. I'll have to remember that.

"Casey, why don't you show me your Cuban eight? Your jet."

Casey set up the maneuver to fly it as precisely as she could. She was tilted off-center after the first half of the maneuver and didn't do a very good job of fixing it on the second half.

"My jet, Casey. What are you looking at when you do the reverse turn?"

"Um, I think I'm checking my heading."

"That's what I thought. These are fighter pilot maneuvers, and you have to look outside the jet, as if a bad guy is on your tail trying to kill you as you are flying them. You only glance inside at the instruments to check your airspeed and heading. I want you to *feel* the jet, Casey, not just mechanically go through the steps. Let's try something. Pretend there is a giant tube of red lipstick at the tip of the pitot probe on the nose. I'm going to do a barrel roll around that puffy cloud in the distance, and I want you to visualize drawing a big red circle around it. Follow along with me on the controls."

Captain Hardesty lowered the nose to get the entry airspeed with the cloud right in front of her. She smoothly rolled and pulled the airplane around, up, and over the cloud in a complete circle. Casey could truly *see* the pitot tube on the aircraft nose draw a perfect circle in the sky around the cloud. She had been struggling with her acrobatics, but this was so simple. She finally understood.

Casey tried a barrel roll around the same cloud, and instead of ending up in a dive like she usually did, her maneuver was almost perfect. It was a revelation. They went through the rest of the acro maneuvers with Captain Hardesty providing only minor critiques.

"I think you've got the picture. My turn," Captain Hardesty said as she took the controls and descended toward the bottom of the practice area where there was a layer of scattered cumulus clouds. The white puffy clouds looked like giant pieces of popcorn.

As she was descending, Captain Hardesty started quizzing Casey on some of the flight rules. "What are the VFR cloud clearance and visibility minimums in the practice areas?"

"Three miles in flight visibility and clear of clouds."

"Correct. But what does that mean?"

"I don't understand the question, ma'am."

"It means we can get as *close* to the clouds as we want, as long as we don't fly through them. Like this." She abruptly rolled the plane upside down, yanked back on the stick, flew around and under a puffball cloud while just skimming below the base of the cloud. The cloud was so close it looked like Casey could reach her hand out and touch it. She maneuvered the jet like it was her own private playground as she wheeled, dove, and rolled around the puffy clouds. She started doing figure eight rolls with just the wing tip of the plane touching the clouds. Captain Hardesty wasn't instructing now—she was just *flying*.

Casey didn't say a word as she watched this demonstration of precision and skill. She knew these clouds were just condensed water vapor, but they were so beautiful in shades of dazzling white and pale gray within a blazing blue sky. Captain Hardesty was chasing the clouds like she was one of them. Casey put her hand on the stick to feel Captain Hardesty's movements. She sensed a lightheartedness she'd never felt from her before. She wasn't instructing or grading Casey; she was just flying with joy. It was beautiful and just plain fun.

"Okay, Casey, your turn."

"My jet, ma'am. Um, what should I do?"

"Anything you like. Just don't over-G or overspeed the jet and don't fly into the clouds."

Casey tentatively maneuvered banking left and right around the clouds.

"Get closer, Casey. Do an aileron roll right over the top of that big cloud. It's okay to yank and bank the jet."

Casey aimed the jet toward the top of the cloud. It looked like she was going to hit it, but she pulled up a little just as she rolled upside down right over the top of it.

"Good one, Casey. Now fly right between those two cloud columns."

She flew toward the two clouds and rolled to ninety degrees of bank as she approached the small space between them. The nose went down and she went right into the clouds with white momentarily filling the windscreen, then she popped back out into blue skies.

Captain Hardesty laughed. "With ninety degrees of bank you lose all your lift. You have to step on the top rudder to keep the nose up. Think of it as if you are a knife edge." They continued this game for several thrilling minutes before Captain Hardesty said they had to head back to the base. Casey had never felt such freedom in her entire life as when they were chasing those puffy clouds. She'd just shared something magical in the air with Kathryn Hardesty.

❖

Kathryn had Casey fly the plane back to the base. She was able to relax a little watching Casey confidently fly the arrival procedure and make the radio calls. Casey was growing into a pilot almost right before her eyes, and she let herself feel pleased. Flying a plane was the only thing that made sense in her life right now—pull back on the stick and you climb; push forward and you descend. It was logical and predictable and, unlike a human being, you could count on an airplane to not betray you or break your heart with a senseless death.

As they flew back to Willie, the sun, low on the horizon, reflected on the Gila River beneath them, making the water shine like a ribbon of liquid gold. The light slowly changed as the day gave away to the inevitable night. The bright blue sky transformed into pale turquoise, and the land changed to subdued, soft colors with a line of deep lavender separating the sky from the earth. This was Kathryn's favorite time of day to be in the air as the daylight retreated into the beauty of the night sky. She had successfully exorcised the terrible images of a charred aircraft and a dead student pilot. She was, once again, at one with the twilight, the airplane, and the sky.

CHAPTER FOURTEEN

June 1992

Kathryn reviewed her briefing notes as the squadron auditorium filled with instructors and students. She would be presenting her findings from the investigation of the crash of Lieutenant Mike Harris. The flight yesterday with Casey had cleared her mind so she could focus on this important but difficult duty today. She scanned the audience. All the IPs, students, and both the T-37 and T-38 squadron commanders were present. She also saw Lieutenant Dave Carter scowl at her as he sat next to Captain Bailey Grant. They were often seen together at the O Club bar, usually leering at the local women. Now here they were whispering and laughing as a briefing about a dead student was about to start. The group jumped to attention as the wing commander walked in and took his seat in the front row center.

A hush fell across the room as she started with slides of the accident site and pictures of the burned plane. "This accident was not the result of anything mechanically wrong with the aircraft, the engines, the oxygen system, or the physical condition of the student pilot. The weather was not a factor, neither was air traffic control. The cause of this accident was G-induced loss of consciousness by the student pilot." She paused to let her words sink in.

"This was the first solo flight after the introduction of advanced acrobatics. The GLOC was most likely caused by a poorly flown acrobatic maneuver where the student was unable to recover from a high-speed dive and consequently blacked himself out. The student had seen the advanced acrobatic maneuvers one time, with a grade of Unsatisfactory on all maneuvers, prior to this mishap. He had been

briefed by his IP to practice all the acrobatic maneuvers on this flight."
A mumbling rippled through the audience.

Kathryn stopped and asked the student pilots to leave the room as she had additional information for the IPs only. She noticed Casey and Mike's IP, Lieutenant Carter, looking around nervously.

"There are some other facts concerning this student pilot, Lieutenant Mike Harris. During the investigation, we discovered that Lieutenant Harris was extremely self-critical about his flying. He had notes in his room documenting and berating himself on every flight where he made mistakes. Now, we critique every student on every maneuver on every ride, but this student took this critique very personally. There were also letters from his father demanding that Mike excel in this program. We will never know what kind of internal, self-imposed pressure this student put on himself, but we can still try to learn from this mishap. We need to pay more attention to our student pilots and how they're dealing with the stress of this program. We need to be mindful of the demands we impose on them, and the type of instruction we give them, especially when we send them out on solo missions." She looked directly at Lieutenant Carter. He couldn't look at her.

❖

Life went on in pilot training as they entered the instrument flying phase of training. There were a million things to remember when flying on instruments. Casey had to figure out where she was in the sky by looking only at the navigation instruments, think about where she wanted to go and how to get there. There were all kinds of new procedures to memorize for flying course intercepts, holding, precision and non-precision approaches, and all the instrument flying rules. Some of the guys who had been hotshots at the beginning were, all of a sudden, busting instrument sim rides and getting washed out.

Lieutenant Carter had been taken off the flying schedule for ten days after Mike Harris's accident report came out. None of the IPs would talk about it, but the student rumor mill said he had to go through remedial instructor training with wing standardization and evaluation. Casey and Jeff got a break from his screaming and flew with other flight IPs. Casey liked flying with most of them, but she was mentally exhausted after an hour and a half in the simulator looking only at round dials.

Casey was excited, and a little bit scared, to see she was flying her next instrument sim with Captain Hardesty. She knew she had to study hard to learn all the procedures and chair fly the approaches because Captain Hard-Ass wouldn't cut her any slack.

Casey felt claustrophobic in the instrument sim with no horizon picture out the windscreen and just the reddish glow of the instruments illuminating the small space. Captain Hardesty had her fly simple climbs and descents, but then made it more difficult by having her also turn to headings. Casey was missing the rollouts and level-offs. She was chasing the altitude and airspeed and failed to notice when her heading drifted off course. *This is so difficult. I don't think I'll ever get it.*

"Let go of the stick, Casey."

Crap. I forgot to trim the plane.

When Casey let go of the stick, the nose abruptly pitched down and she lost three hundred feet of altitude.

"Who is your friend, Casey?"

"Trim is my friend, ma'am," she answered sheepishly.

"That's right. Having the airplane trimmed is absolutely essential to instrument flying. Your cross-check is all over the place and you're chasing the instruments. The main thing you need to look at is the attitude indicator. This is your horizon. Take your pencil out of your sleeve pocket and hold it in your hand like you are going to write something. Now hold the stick with the pencil in your hand. You can't have a death grip on the stick as long as you have the pencil in your hand. This will force you to trim the jet."

"Okay, I'll try that." Casey was pleasantly surprised. She had to keep a very light grip on the stick and fly with just her fingertips because of the pencil. She trimmed the plane to keep it level and she was able to detect tiny pressures on her fingertips when the plane was out of trim. She wasn't flailing nearly as much.

Captain Hardesty showed her several tricks to make the approaches more stable and improve her instrument cross-check. After the sim, Casey was still mentally exhausted but was relieved the instrument flying was starting to make sense.

"You have to be able to fly the jet in the present moment and think about the future—where am I, and where do I want to go? This is one of the most difficult things you will ever do in an airplane, Casey. Overall, your instrument flying is coming along and you know your procedures. You are well ahead of your classmates. Sim grade, Excellent."

"Thanks, ma'am." Casey felt herself flush with heat at the compliment.

❖

Casey studied navigation in academics and learned how to read aeronautical charts, plot courses, make flight plans, calculate en route leg times and fuel burns. She couldn't wait to go on her cross-country flights and fly to another base. She flight planned a low-level navigation leg to Davis-Monthan Air Force Base near Tucson, then they would fly back to Willie at night. She used dead reckoning navigation for the low-level flight, checking the terrain to determine her turn points. She would be flying on instruments for the return flight at night.

Carter was back flying with Jeff, and she was flying with Captain Hardesty. They listened to the weather brief, which included gusty winds for the landing at Davis-Monthan and the possibility of thunderstorms developing.

Captain Hardesty sat down with Casey with her own sectional chart, whiz wheel, and instrument approach book for Arizona. "Casey, brief me on what we're doing today."

"I plotted the low-level route using turn points of a pair of buttes, Coolidge Dam, a railroad crossing the freeway, Picacho Peak, then direct to Davis-Monthan."

"You'll be flying at two hundred and fifty knots, only one thousand feet above the ground, so the most important thing you have to do is clear, clear, clear. Look outside the jet for other aircraft, terrain, and obstacles like antennas or power lines."

They reviewed the return leg from D-M back to Willie and talked about the different instrument approaches she would fly. At base operations they filed their flight plan, got a weather briefing, and Captain Hardesty showed her how to set up the cockpit for a navigation flight.

It felt like they were flying really fast because they were so close to the ground as they skimmed over the mountain ridges. She spotted her first turn point, the twin buttes, checked her timing, and started her turn to the next point. When she wasn't hyperventilating, she was starting to think this was actually kind of fun. The sky looked sort of fuzzy in front of her.

"What is that, ma'am?"

"That's virga, rain that evaporates before it hits the ground. We may not be able to complete this low-level if the visibility gets any worse."

Just then it sounded like they were hit with machine gun bullets as big raindrops struck the canopy. Captain Hardesty took the stick, made a hard turn to the right, slammed the throttles forward to full power, and pulled the jet into a climb. "My jet, Casey."

The plane started to rock and roll as turbulence hit them, pushing Casey hard against her shoulder straps. A wall of dark, ominous clouds was in front of them as the ground faded away. *Oh my God. I have no idea what to do.*

"Albuquerque Center, this is Sage 75," Captain Hardesty transmitted.

There was only static.

"Albuquerque Center, Sage 75. Do you copy?"

Again, no answer.

"We're on our own since we're too low to receive any radio signals. Casey, find our current position on your map, draw a line heading west, and look for the nearest navigation facility."

Casey's hand shook as she drew a rough line on her chart. "I think Stanfield VOR is the nearest nav fix. I'll tune that up."

The needle on the navigation instrument slowly spun as it searched for a signal.

"We're too low to get a nav lock. We need to climb higher." They were surrounded by dark gray clouds as the turbulence got worse. An amber warning light came on—the engine ice light.

"Uh, Captain Hardesty?"

"I see it. Unfortunately, this plane has no weather radar, no deicing or anti-ice capability. That light just tells us that ice is forming in the engines and we need to get out of this as soon as possible."

The clouds surrounding them were disorienting. Casey was enveloped in grayness. The turbulence threw her against her seat harness and made it difficult to read the instruments. She couldn't tell if she was upside down or straight and level. She fought hard to keep her fear in check.

The needle on the navigation instrument stopped and pointed to one-two-zero degrees.

"Casey, tell me where we are."

"We are northwest of the Stanfield VOR."

"Good. Now where do we want to go?"

I can't believe she's still quizzing me as we're about to die.

"Back to Willie?"

"Correct. Figure out which direction we need to go."

"I think we should turn to a zero-three-zero heading, ma'am."

"That's exactly right. I'm descending to six thousand feet to get out of this icing since we're over a flat part of the desert. Let's see if we can get Phoenix Approach on the radio now that we're away from the high terrain.

"Phoenix Approach, this is Sage 75 passing ten thousand for six thousand, northwest of Stanfield," Captain Hardesty transmitted.

"Sage 75, Phoenix Approach, radar contact. I show your destination as Davis-Monthan, but they are closed due to thunderstorms. What are your intentions?"

"We'd like vectors to Williams for the instrument approach. What's the current weather at Willie?"

"They are reporting a two-hundred-foot ceiling, visibility one-half mile with blowing dust, wind two-four-zero degrees at fifty knots, runway three-zero in use."

"Fuck. Maybe we can make it to Luke," Captain Hardesty muttered to herself.

"Phoenix Approach, what's the current weather at Luke Air Force Base?"

"Sage 75, Luke is closed for wind shear on the field."

"Okay, Phoenix, request vectors to Williams."

"Sage 75, turn right heading zero-four-five, descend and maintain five thousand feet."

"Ma'am, can we land in that weather at Willie?" Casey asked nervously.

"You tell me, Casey. Can we?"

This woman is maddening! "Well, we have the minimums for the approach, but I'm not sure if the winds are out of limits."

"What is the crosswind limit for the T-37?"

Casey hesitated. She knew the answer to the question but was having a hard time focusing with fear choking her and the turbulence banging her head around.

"Twenty-six knots?"

"Are you sure?"

Casey was getting more and more irritated with her. "Yes, the crosswind limit is twenty-six knots."

"Good. Now go to your checklist and figure out the crosswind for runway three-zero."

Casey's gloved hand shook as she looked up the table in her checklist. "I come up with a twenty-five-knot direct crosswind."

"So, can we land in that?"

"Yes, ma'am, we can."

"Good. Yes, we can land with those winds at the moment. But if the wind velocity gets worse or the direction changes, we may have to divert to Phoenix Sky Harbor airport."

"Can we land at the commercial airport?"

"Not generally, but we'll be an emergency aircraft if we have to divert so we can land there. I'm going to have to fly this approach, Casey, and I need you to back me up on the altitudes. We're going to be flying as a crew on this—not IP and student. Do you understand?"

"Yes, ma'am." This was serious now. Very serious.

They broke out of the clouds momentarily. Casey saw massive columns of towering black clouds on either side of them as if they were flying through a deep canyon. Lightning flashed all around them and inside the clouds. The lightning strikes were happening so fast it looked like paparazzi flashbulbs going off. They were still flying through heavy rain, but with the bright landing lights on, the big drops looked like they were shooting past them at an incredibly fast speed. It resembled the starship *Voyager* going to warp speed through a star field. The raw power of the weather surrounding them made her feel very insignificant flying through this in a small trainer. It was terrifying and beautiful all at the same time.

"Attention all aircraft. This is Phoenix Approach. Phoenix Sky Harbor is now closed due to wind shear on the field."

"Shit," Captain Hardesty muttered. "Casey, listen to me very carefully. We have one shot to get this plane on the ground. We don't have enough fuel to try another approach, and the other airports in the area are closed. If the winds get worse, or I can't see the runway, I'm going to immediately zoom the jet up to two thousand feet and we're going to eject. I will say, 'Bail out, bail out, bail out,' then we go."

"Yes, ma'am, I understand."

"Sage 75, Phoenix Approach. Turn right heading zero-nine-zero, descend to three thousand feet. You're cleared for the ILS three-zero center approach, contact tower."

"Sage 75, cleared for the approach."

"Gear down, Casey."

She put the wheel-shaped handle down and checked for three green gear-down lights.

"Speed one ten, flaps to fifty."

Casey moved the flap lever to the one-half mark and tried to watch the instruments as Captain Hardesty flew the approach. The attitude indicator looked like a dancing meatball, and the turbulence was so severe the instruments appeared to bounce around like they weren't even attached to the front panel. They were in complete, blind grayness, and Casey wanted to put her hand on the stick as Captain Hardesty flew the jet, just to feel connected to her. She moved the stick so fast it looked like she was furiously stirring a pot as she struggled to fly the jet.

She had to shout so Casey could hear her over the deafening sound of the pounding rain. "On glide path, on speed, flaps full, Casey."

"Flaps full. At the final approach fix."

They were only fifteen hundred feet above the ground and descending rapidly surrounded by dark, violent weather. Casey's heart pounded as she checked the distance to the runway: five miles to go. Her eyes burned as sweat ran down her forehead from her helmet. She had to do her job even if it was the last thing she would ever do on this earth. "Three miles, one thousand feet."

"Willie Tower, Sage 75, gear down, full stop."

"Sage 75, cleared to land, wind two-four-zero degrees, thirty-five gusting to sixty knots. Wind shear advisories in effect."

"Sage 75, cleared to land."

There was no talking between them as they continued the descent toward the ground. Casey glanced at the little instrument they were betting their lives on, the ILS indicator. It was the size of a silver dollar and showed centered crosshairs indicating they were on the glide path and lined up with the runway. Casey looked at the bouncing altitude dial thinking about her next call as they approached three hundred feet above the ground.

"Approaching decision height," Casey called.

She stole a peek out the front of the windscreen hoping to see the runway but saw nothing. *Oh, my God. Altitude, Casey, call out the altitude!*

"Decision height! I can't see the runway!" Casey shouted.

"I have a light at two o'clock low," Captain Hardesty said.

Casey saw one dim, pale fuzzy white light, then another, then three—they were the lead-in lights. She couldn't see the runway and Captain Hardesty was still descending. They were one hundred feet above the ground.

"Runway in sight—landing!"

Casey saw the green runway threshold lights and the white stripes of the landing zone. The nose of the plane was twenty degrees angled off from the runway. It looked like they would go off the edge of the pavement. Captain Hardesty stepped on the rudder pedal to swing the nose around as she banked the plane into the wind. Bam! They hit the runway hard and Captain Hardesty slammed the stick full forward to keep the nose on the runway. Her feet danced on the rudder pedals trying to stay on the center line with the wind buffeting them ferociously.

The centerline lights were barely visible through the torrential rain. "Tower, Sage 75 is clear of the runway, taxiing to parking."

"Tower copies. Did you experience any wind shear on final?"

"Yes, we had a twenty-knot loss of airspeed at two hundred feet."

"Glad you made it back, Sage 75."

"So are we, Tower."

CHAPTER FIFTEEN

Captain Hardesty pulled into a parking space without guidance from a crew chief since the mechanics were not allowed to be on the ramp with lightning on the field. She shut down the engines and they sat in the jet with the canopy closed waiting for the storm to pass. The air inside the jet was close and humid as the loud rain continued to pelt them. The rain brought the outside air temperature down to ninety degrees, which was cool for Arizona in June, but it was still hot. Casey thought she should say something but wasn't sure where to start. She wanted to laugh and cry at the same time because they had just cheated death. *Why isn't she quizzing me or debriefing me? Did I screw something up?*

"Um, Captain Hardesty, I just wanted to say, that was amazing flying you did to get us on the ground."

"Not now, Casey."

"Ma'am?"

"It was not amazing flying. It was complete stupidity. We are both lucky to be alive. Don't EVER do what I just did."

"I don't understand, ma'am. We got back to Willie and the plane's okay."

"I'll discuss this with you when we get inside." Her tone meant business, and Casey didn't utter another word.

❖

Fuck, fuck, fuck, fuck! I still can't believe we are not both dead in a smoking hole right now. Shit. How did I let this happen? Calm down, Kath. Don't take your screw-up out on Casey.

Kathryn made herself breathe deeply to exhale her anger and bring her heart rate back to normal. Once her shaking stopped and the adrenaline subsided, she tried to reconstruct how they got into such a dangerous situation in the first place. Casey had been doing well on the low-level mission. She was finding her turn points, keeping the airplane trimmed, and making good course corrections. She was expecting Casey to notice the deteriorating weather and was waiting for her to decide what to do about it. It was a classic case of overconfidence in a student pilot's ability. It was a rookie IP mistake, and Kathryn was kicking herself for it.

Why had she overestimated Casey's flying judgment in the first place? She knew the answer before she even asked herself the question. She just didn't want to acknowledge the truth.

It was because Casey was special.

Crap. She couldn't allow herself to think of Casey as special. None of them were. They were all the same—student pilots who tried to kill her three times a day on every mission. Still, Kathryn had taught enough students to fly in her career to be able to recognize the truly exceptional ones when they came along, and they were very rare. She made a point of flying with as many students in the different flights, in all the phases of training, as she could, and Casey was far above most of them. She was smart, hardworking, prepared, and paid attention to every critique. Casey didn't have the usual arrogance of the male students, but she had the hunger—the hunger to fly as well as she possibly could. Kathryn had allowed herself to think of Casey as more than just another student pilot. Kathryn *wanted* Casey to be more, but where was this coming from? Kathryn had no idea, but it bothered her just the same.

Casey could be washed out of this program at any time if she busted three rides in a row. She could kill herself, like Mike Harris did, on a solo flight. She might fail at formation flying or never be able to keep up with the supersonic T-38 jet. There was no reason to think of Casey as special, and yet, she was.

Kathryn would get a grip on her feelings and explain during the debrief, in a calm manner, what had gone wrong on this flight. Hopefully, this would be a valuable learning experience for both of them that they would never have to repeat.

Their shoulders touched as they sat in the compact jet waiting for the rain to subside. The air around them was warm as their breath mingled. Kathryn took off her helmet and oxygen mask and Casey followed suit. Kathryn was calm and in control once again. They sat in awkward silence as the rain pounded the canopy. Kathryn knew her tone with Casey had been sharp and uncalled for. She prided herself at never yelling at a student because she had hated it so much when she was a student pilot. Guilt and shame made her squirm in her seat. She glanced sideways to look at Casey's face. She was quiet and stoic, but looked like a hurt puppy. Her chest tightened with compassion for having hurt Casey.

She turned in her seat to look directly into Casey's eyes. "I didn't mean to yell at you, Casey. You didn't do anything wrong. I was just angry over the situation we got into."

"It's okay, ma'am," she answered with relief in her voice.

"I think this rain is starting to let up. Put everything into your helmet bag so it doesn't get wet and let's head back to the flight room."

When Casey opened the canopy, they both got pretty wet, but at least the torrential rain had stopped and now it was just a steady rain. The pungent smell of mesquite was heavy in the freshly washed desert air. It was a rare treat from the normally dusty, dry air. Kathryn inhaled deeply of the intoxicating, spicy scent. Even being somewhat soggy in her wet flight suit, she was glad they both were back on terra firma.

They were greeted with the smell of pizza as they entered the flight room. Kathryn was surprised to see Barb Arnau already there talking to her student. No other IPs or students were in the room.

"Did you land ahead of me, Barb?"

"Hell no. We didn't even get off the ground. We were about thirty minutes behind you guys. We had a mechanical. By the time we got it fixed, the gust front from that massive storm rolled a giant *haboob* dust storm right across the runways. We barely got inside. Did you just land in that?"

"Yes, by the skin of my teeth."

"I'm amazed you got in. Everybody else diverted. I've got two jets at D-M, three at Fort Huachuca, and that idiot Carter landed at the emergency field in Gila Bend. So Parker and I ordered a large pizza from Cosmo's. Help yourselves."

"Thanks, Barb."

They both grabbed a large slice and sat down to debrief the ride. Somehow the near-death experience in the airplane made them both ravenously hungry.

"You started out really well on your low-level leg. You found your turn points and you were making good course corrections. Did you see the clouds start to build up south of us?"

"No, ma'am, I didn't. I guess I was so focused on being that close to the ground and looking for my turn points that I didn't notice the weather around us changing. I'm really sorry."

Kathryn reached across the table, took Casey's hand in hers, and looked her straight in the eyes. "Casey, this was not your fault. It was mine. I should have pointed out the weather to you a lot earlier so you could have figured out how to exit the low-level route and divert to a safe airport. You're the student pilot. You're not expected to know what to do with thunderstorms like that. I'm the IP and I let you down. I waited too long to let you notice the weather was deteriorating, and I let us get into a very dangerous situation, not you. I'm very sorry, Casey. I endangered your life and I should have known better."

Casey couldn't believe what she was hearing—an instructor pilot apologizing to a student. She was stunned and relieved. "You didn't endanger my life, ma'am. I knew I was safe with you. It was just really scary."

Kathryn squeezed Casey's hand slightly, then withdrew her own. "Yes, Casey, I was scared too."

Casey knew the moment of connection with Kathryn was over and took out her notepad to start writing.

"I wasn't trying to harass you by asking you questions when we were in the air fighting those storms. In actual instrument conditions, you have to be able to figure out where you are, where you want to be going, where the terrain is relative to your position, and then come up with a plan. You have to be able to apply the instrument flight rules and airplane operating limits in real time while you're flying—all at the same time. That's why we have to know those numbers and procedures down cold. You don't have time to look stuff up in the book when you need to get on the ground right now. You have to know what to do from memory and make the right decision."

"Yes, ma'am, I can certainly see that." Casey wasn't writing down notes; she was only able to look into Kathryn's eyes.

"You did a good job as copilot on the approach. You kept your wits about you and you did your job calling out the altitudes. That was a no-shit emergency situation. You can never allow yourself to panic or give up. You have to keep fighting and flying to the very end, until you're safely on the ground."

"Yes, ma'am."

"I also need to tell you I violated some very serious flight rules when I was flying that approach. The last wind reading we got from the tower was sixty degrees off the runway at sixty knots. That's a direct crosswind of thirty knots, four knots greater than the operating limit of the plane. We were lucky the landing gear didn't collapse from the side loads. I also descended below the decision height without the runway in sight. I went fifty feet below the decision height altitude to try to see the runway lights. I'm going to have to write myself up in a safety report. I'm telling you this, Casey, because I don't want you to ever do what I just did. It was wrong and dangerous."

"But you got us on the ground, ma'am."

"I know, but it was still wrong. Every aviation rule we have is literally written in blood. Every single regulation is because someone died in a plane crash. Don't ever forget that. Go home, have a few drinks, and just be glad that our number wasn't up tonight. You're dismissed, Casey." Kathryn stood up without looking at Casey, walked out of the flight room, and went directly into the flight commander's office, closing the door behind her.

Casey sat by herself for a long moment looking down at her blank notebook page. Her classmate Parker came over and sat in the seat next to her.

"Casey, I heard your debrief. What the hell happened out there tonight?"

"I guess I used up the second of my nine lives. I'm just really glad I had Captain Hardesty with me tonight. Her flying was amazing. Thanks for the pizza. See you tomorrow."

Casey got into her car, but her mind and body were a complete jumble of emotions. She was elated she wasn't dead, excited by the flying demonstration she'd seen, humbled by what she didn't know yet about real flying, and she was warm all over from the electricity of Kathryn's touch. Sitting in the jet with the rain pounding, their shoulders touching, their breath intermingled, she couldn't tell if the fear she'd felt was just from the bad weather or from the stirring in her belly being next to Kathryn.

CHAPTER SIXTEEN

July 1992

Casey worked on flight planning for her upcoming cross-country trip. This was one of the biggest highlights of T-37 training. Casey and Jeff worked together to plan a five-leg weekend trip. Since everyone else was also planning their trips, a lot of the military bases were full, with no room for more out-of-town jets. They came up with a plan for two legs on Friday to Cannon Air Force Base in Clovis, New Mexico, then Dyess Air Force Base in Abilene, Texas. Day two would be a low-level mission to Randolph Air Force Base in San Antonio, then on to Biggs Army Air Field in El Paso, Texas. The last day was one leg home to Willie on Sunday. Lieutenant Carter approved their flight plans and told Casey to ask the head scheduler who she would be flying with. She hoped it would be Captain Hardesty.

"Captain Arnau, can you tell me who I will be flying with on my cross-country?"

"I don't know yet, Casey. I'm still waiting to hear back from my guest help IPs. Let me guess, you want to fly with Captain Hardesty again?"

"Yes, ma'am, I would." *Is it that obvious?*

"I'll see what I can do."

❖

Kathryn looked forward to flying a cross-country mission after being inundated with safety paperwork for the last several days. She was relived the squadron commander had not given her an official letter of reprimand after her safety report on herself. He'd made her stand at attention in front of his big desk while he slowly read the report. Then he looked her square in the face and said, "Kath, you got lucky this time. Don't ever do that again or I'll have to make it official. Do you hear me, Captain?"

"Loud and clear, sir."

"Now get out of my office, and—you didn't hear this from me— nice flying getting that jet on the ground in that shitty weather."

Warlock flight had all their cross-countries covered, so she went over to see Barb to volunteer to fly with Good Grief flight. She tried hard to fly with the different flights and not show favoritism to anyone, but she secretly wanted to fly with Casey. She needed to show her good training in instrument flying, not just a near-death experience.

"Captain Arnau, my favorite scheduler, I am at your service to fly a cross-country this weekend."

"Captain Hardesty, I'm very glad to see you. I need IPs to fly with Montgomery, Keller, and Tompkins—take your pick."

"How about Tompkins?"

"You got it, Kath. I think she has her flight plans already done."

Kathryn walked over to Casey and Jeff's table. "Lieutenant Tompkins, tell me where you've planned for us to go this weekend."

"Yes, ma'am. Jeff and I have flight plans for Cannon and Dyess on Friday, Randolph and Biggs on Saturday, then return to Willie on Sunday."

"Clovis, New Mexico, Abilene, San Antonio, and El Paso, Texas? I don't think so. I hate fucking Texas. Throw out those flight plans. It was a good practice exercise. I want you to work with Keller and flight plan for March Air Force Base in Riverside, California, then a low-level to Miramar Naval Air Station in San Diego on day one. We'll fly to Mather Air Force Base in Sacramento and end up in Las Vegas at Nellis Air Force Base on Saturday, then one leg back to Willie on Sunday. Be sure to stay out of the airspace around LAX on the leg from March to San Diego." Kathryn had her own personal plans for her layover in Las Vegas. She was considering the idea of dating again after a very long dry spell, and the possibility of a date percolated in her mind. This could turn out to be a very good cross-country trip.

"But, ma'am, those bases said they were full and they couldn't handle any more planes from Willie."

"Don't worry about landing permissions, Casey. I'll take care of that. You and Keller just put together the flight plans."

"Yes, ma'am, I'll get right on it."

"I'll meet you in base operations Friday at 0900 hours. Don't bring too much stuff with you. The baggage storage on the Tweet is pretty small."

"Yes, ma'am, I'll be ready. See you Friday."

Casey walked over to Keller's table. "Hey, John, guess what? We're going to California and Vegas for our cross-country flights! We're supposed to flight plan together."

"How'd you pull that off? I heard those places were full up."

"Don't ask me, dude. Captain Hardesty is taking care of it."

"Sweet. I don't even know where to start with these flight plans. Do you know how to do this?"

"Yeah, I do. We'll do it together. It's not that tricky."

"Captain Hardesty, did I hear you mention you were going to Nellis this weekend?" Captain Arnau asked.

"Why, yes, Barb, you did. Do you have a problem with that?"

"Certainly not. I was just wondering if you were planning on seeing *her*, that's all," Barb whispered.

After checking no students or IPs were listening to them, she said, "I don't know yet. Maybe. It depends on if she wants to see me."

"Oh, I'm sure she's going to want to see you again, Kath. Look, I'm really glad you're considering seeing someone again. Lord knows it's been a long time, but you know what I think of her. Just be careful, that's all I'm saying."

"Thanks, I will."

Kathryn walked back over to her office, and she felt a little stir in her belly at the thought of actually having a date this weekend. It had been such a long time since she'd been involved with anyone. Marie's death had hung over her like a heavy blanket for the past five years. Only recently had she started to see glimpses of light at the end of the dark tunnel of grief.

She realized the exact moment her heart started to thaw—watching Casey play softball. She smiled at the recollection of seeing Casey's toned legs as she ran around the bases. That's when the scales fell from her eyes.

Then there was that dream. The dream she'd had twice now. She walked into her office, closed the door, and sat in her chair. She closed her eyes and let her mind drift back to it.

Kathryn felt warmth on her left shoulder. She was flying a Tweet at night in bad weather. She was getting bounced around pretty good and was having a hard time controlling the plane. She felt tense and looked over to see who was sitting next to her. It was Casey. The lights of the instrument panel cast a red glow on her face, making her look sensual and warm. She wasn't wearing a helmet or mask. She looked back at Kathryn and smiled. Her smile was so beautiful, like she had every confidence in Kathryn. She reached over and put her strong hand on Kathryn's hand. There was no fear between them, of the bad weather, or of each other. They were in sync, as one.

Then she woke up. Yesterday, when she woke from the dream, she was warm all over and felt aroused for the first time in a very long time.

It was ridiculous to even think about Casey. Anything between them was out of the question. Casey was her student, and she was junior in rank. There had been one or two relationships between IPs and student pilots, usually male IPs and their female students, and it always ended in disaster with severe, career-ending punishment. No, there would never be anything between her and Casey, but the dreams had opened her eyes to the possibility of trying again with another woman. She would call her old flame in Vegas and see what might happen. The idea gave her a welcome tingle.

❖

Casey did most of the flight planning and let Keller mark the aeronautical charts. She was as prepared as she could be when she got to base operations early, and she was beyond excited for the upcoming trip. Captain Hardesty strolled in precisely at 0900 like she owned the place.

"All right, Casey, brief me on what we're doing today."

Casey explained the routing, the en route weather, the emergency airfields, and the arrival into March. Captain Hardesty showed Casey some whiz wheel shortcuts to calculate ground speed and fuel burn.

"Casey, Southern California is some of the busiest airspace in the entire country, and you will be flying under the hood doing different types of instrument approaches. I'll work the radios and you just fly good instruments. We will fly like a crew."

"Got it, ma'am."

They went out to the jet and Captain Hardesty showed her the secret storage cubby holes in the Tweet. They took off, and as soon as they passed four hundred feet, Captain Hardesty took the stick and told Casey to put on the instrument hood. She used a folded chart stuffed under the top visor of her helmet to block her field of vision so she could only see the instruments. The departure went well, and Casey leveled off at twenty-five thousand feet. She was concentrating hard on holding her altitude but missed a few radio calls. This was a lot harder in the real airplane than it was in the simulator.

Captain Hardesty showed her how to do a ground speed check and triangulate her position. Casey was flying fairly well on instruments until they got into the airspace for Los Angeles Center. The radio calls were so fast it was like drinking from a fire hose, and Casey could barely understand what the air traffic controllers were saying, much less when they were talking to her. She had never heard such fast and furious radio chatter and was getting completely overwhelmed.

"Sage 21, Los Angeles Center, turn right heading two-seven-zero, descend and maintain five thousand, contact SoCal approach on two-three-five point two."

"Um, Sage 21, say again?"

Captain Hardesty jumped on the radio with the reply to LA Center. "Casey, you just fly the plane and I'll handle the radios."

Casey was a little less overwhelmed but still had to concentrate as hard as she could to keep up with the jet. They didn't give her the arrival she had planned on, but instead a completely different routing. Casey was mentally behind the jet and she had no idea where she was or where she was going.

"Descend to four thousand feet, Casey, power idle, slow down, get the landing gear down. You're on a dogleg to the runway final and five miles from the final approach fix. Trim, trim, trim, Casey."

All she could do was try to hold her heading and keep the wings level. *Fly the jet, just fly the jet.*

"If I don't take off the hood at decision height you must go around and fly the missed approach procedure. Think of what that is as we descend."

Crap. What's the decision height altitude? How do I fly the missed approach? Her brain went blank. *Oh yeah, do a go-around, then fly runway heading to three thousand feet, turn right to heading zero-three-zero.* Her mind was swimming as she was descending toward the ground.

"Approaching decision height. Decision height. Can you see the runway, Casey?"

"No, ma'am, I can't."

"Then go around. You are only two hundred feet above the ground. Execute the missed approach now!"

Casey's brain finally engaged and she was able to fly the missed approach.

"My airplane, Casey." Captain Hardesty took the stick. "Relax, take a breath, take the hood off, and look around."

She removed the chart from her helmet visor and looked out at thick, brown smog. She saw the giant runway at March through the haze over her shoulder. They were turning to a downwind leg. Now she understood where she was, and her situation orientation came back.

"Feeling less overwhelmed, Casey?"

"Yes, a little bit, ma'am."

"You are doing okay. This is hard. Just try to fly good instruments, keep trimming the jet, and try to visualize where you are in relation to the runway. I'm going to have you put the hood on again and we'll try the ILS approach to a touch-and-go landing."

The next approach went better. Casey felt like she was able to keep up with the jet mentally a little better. At the decision height, Captain Hardesty pulled the hood from Casey's helmet, and she saw the big runway right in front of her. She flared high and dropped in the landing from thirty feet for a rather firm touchdown. She lowered the nose, added full power, and lifted off for another approach.

"Sage 21, request closed pattern."

"Sage 21, closed approved. Use caution for a B-52 on a three-mile final. How will this approach terminate?"

Captain Hardesty jumped on the radio. "Tower, this will be a full stop.

"My airplane, Casey."

"Roger, your jet, ma'am."

Captain Hardesty yanked the airplane hard into a tight, climbing turn. They were abeam the touchdown zone as she ripped the throttles to idle, threw the landing gear handle down, and put the plane into a steep, descending final turn.

"March Tower, Sage 21, gear down, full stop."

"Sage 21, cleared to land."

This was the tightest overhead pattern Casey had ever seen. They were screaming toward the ground as Casey looked out and saw a giant green and black B-52 bomber headed right for them on final approach. *Oh my God, that thing is huge. It's going to overrun us. How is she going to pull this one out of her ass?*

Captain Hardesty rolled the jet out on a very short final approach, perfectly on glide path, and on speed. She greased on the landing, then got on the brakes hard, slowing the jet to taxi speed in a few seconds, and made the first runway turn-off. She stopped the plane when they were clear of the runway, and they both looked back over their shoulders just as the massive bomber touched down right next to them. Casey saw black smoke come out of the eight engines as the behemoth accelerated, then gracefully lifted off for another practice approach.

Casey was exhausted, sweating, and brain-dead as she climbed out of the jet. When they went inside, Captain Hardesty said, "Would you like a Coke, Casey?"

"Yes, ma'am, I think I would."

They walked over to the bank of vending machines on the wall. "This is the official food of cross-country flying, Casey." Captain Hardesty got two Cokes, bags of Cheetos, and two Snickers bars. They sat in companionable silence eating their junk food.

"Let's debrief a little. Your overall instrument flying was pretty good and you did an okay job on the approaches." Casey was surprised. She thought she'd done a terrible job flying. "You need to work on your situation orientation. That's the hardest thing about instrument flying, but that will come." Casey smiled inside at Captain Hardesty's confidence in her. "The low-level leg to Miramar should be easier now. We have to be very heads-up going in there because we'll be mixing it up with a bunch of Navy F-14s and F-18s going really fast. Sorry I had to take a last landing in here, but I knew we had to get in front of that B-52. We were starting to get low on gas."

"How did you know you could get in front of them?"

"Oh, just a few thousand landings in the Tweet. By the way, that's how you fly a tight overhead pattern if you ever have to. Just make sure you're stabilized on final. Ready for the next leg?"

"Yes, ma'am, I guess so." She was a little less brain-dead after the sugar and caffeine.

The low-level leg to Miramar was a lot less stressful than the previous one. She found all her turn points and even enjoyed the view. The Navy controller gave her a precision radar approach that turned out to be a piece of cake. Casey was glad to see two other Tweets parked in front of base operations. Her classmates Keller and Montgomery were waiting for her inside operations with room keys to the visiting officer quarters.

"Just drop off your flight gear in your rooms and come over to the O Club. Don't change out of your flight suits. Captain Stavros and Captain McClain are already there, and they have a head start on us."

"Thanks, guys, see you in a few," Captain Hardesty said. "Good job on the low-level, Casey, and the approach. See, that radar approach isn't so tough."

"No, ma'am, it was easier than I thought it would be."

"Well, they have to keep things real simple for these Navy pilots."

Laughing, they both went into their respective rooms.

Casey noticed how stark the quarters were compared to Air Force quarters. Air Force rooms were not plush, by any means, but this was positively Spartan and tiny. "I guess it's better than being on a boat." As she washed her hands and face, she heard the sound of the shower next door, in Captain Hardesty's room. An image of her all soaped up with her sandy brown hair wet against her face came into Casey's mind. *What does she look like under that flight suit? Does she like to play in the shower?* Casey enjoyed the fantasy a few moments until she heard the water shut off. "Oh my God. Where did that come from?" She splashed more cold water on her face, then hurried out the door to the Officers' Club.

Casey found the IPs and her classmates standing at the bar sharing a pitcher of beer.

"Tompkins! Come and join us. You look like you need several beers. Bartender, we need another glass."

Casey relished the cold, sharp taste of the beer as she took a big swig. She definitely felt like relaxing after two challenging flights today, and she needed to get her mind off the shower fantasy of Kathryn Hardesty. This bar was as noisy as the bar at Willie but filled with Navy and Marine Corps pilots. There were several young women here, but she was the only woman in a flight suit. She felt very conspicuous. She heard a scream over her shoulder and turned to see a bunch of Marine pilots laughing as they "played a harmless game" with some of the local girls. They would sneak up behind a girl, bend down, then bite her on her butt cheek. The girls didn't seem to be enjoying it nearly as much as the Marines did. Casey sensed Kathryn standing right behind her. She turned, looked at Kathryn's damp hair, and tried not to choke on her beer as she reached for a glass for her.

"Fucking jarheads."

"Don't say that too loud, Hard-Ass, or they'll eighty-six us right out of here. Have some beer and chill," Captain Stavros said.

"I'll have ginger ale instead."

"Uh-oh, she's going right for the hard stuff. Watch out."

"Shut up, you assholes, and give me my ginger ale."

Casey enjoyed their good-natured ribbing. Other than Captain Arnau, she'd never seen Kathryn joke around with any other IPs. It was nice to see her cut up with the guys. She rarely ever smiled at work. Away from Willie, relaxed in this Navy bar, she laughed with abandon and showed her killer dimples when she smiled.

Casey caught movement reflected in the mirror behind the bar. Two Marines were trying to sneak up behind Captain Hardesty. Before she even thought about it, Casey quickly turned with her knee bent and caught the first one hard in the chest. He fell back with an "oof" and hit his head on the floor. Everyone at the bar turned to see what the commotion was, and they were surprised to see a big, tough Marine splayed out on the floor with a woman Air Force pilot standing over him. Then they started laughing at him. "Smooth move, Ex-Lax!" "Wochowski just got shot down by the Air Force!"

"Do you need some assistance, Lieutenant?" Captain Hardesty said, looking down at the man on the floor.

"Uh, no, ma'am," he muttered.

"Then I suggest you leave now before my student really kicks your ass."

The Marine pilots shuffled off in disgrace as the rest of the pilots in the bar howled at them.

"Maybe we should go get some food before Tompkins takes out any more jarheads," Captain Stavros suggested.

They left the bar laughing and joking and spent the rest of the evening having a pleasant meal together. For the first time in the five months since starting pilot training, Casey felt herself start to relax around her classmates and IPs. *This is kind of nice.*

When they returned to the visiting officer quarters, Captain Hardesty hung back from the group with Casey.

"You did well on your flights today, Casey, and thank you for defending my honor from those drunken Marine pilots."

"Any time, ma'am."

"Try to get some sleep. You've got a very busy day tomorrow. Good night."

"Yes, ma'am, see you tomorrow." Casey watched Captain Hardesty retreat into her quarters, wondering what she slept in.

CHAPTER SEVENTEEN

The morning cross-country flight to Mather Air Force Base was busy with holding, course intercepts, and more instrument approaches. Casey was getting the hang of quick flight planning and was doing better at mentally keeping up with the plane. She was pleased with her flying and was looking forward to going out on the town in Las Vegas with her classmates and IPs. She was especially looking forward to spending time again with Kathryn in a more casual setting. After landing at Nellis, they walked into base operations and Casey saw a young blond woman officer wearing fatigues who was obviously waiting for them.

"Welcome to Nellis. I'm Captain Jill Eller, and I'm the deputy airfield officer. You can leave your flight gear in my office, and I have room keys for you at the Circus Circus hotel since the quarters on base are full."

She handed out their room keys, and she gave Captain Hardesty a big smile when she reached her. Casey disliked her instantly.

"There's a bus outside waiting to take you to the hotel. The bus will be back to pick you up at 0900 hours tomorrow morning. Have fun tonight in Las Vegas, and don't get arrested."

The guys were very excited as they filed out to the bus, and Casey noticed Captain Hardesty wasn't with them.

"Hey, Hard-Ass, you coming? We've got some slot machines waiting for us!" Captain Stavros said.

"I'll catch up with you guys later at the hotel. Captain Eller and I are going to get caught up over dinner. Have fun."

As the bus started to leave, Casey saw Captain Eller wrap her arms around Captain Hardesty's neck in a very big hug.

❖

The guys were in high spirits. They were conspicuous in their fight suits, and the smoke and noise from the bustling casino practically assaulted them.

"All right, troops, change into your street clothes and meet back up in the main bar in fifteen minutes," Captain Stavros said.

Casey entered her room and threw her bag across the room. "Crap. Who is that blond bitch and what's she doing with Captain Hardesty?" Casey wanted to go out with Kathryn and the guys and have a good time, but now she was the only woman in the group—once again. "The hell with her and that blonde. I'm going to have a good time anyway." She quickly changed into her jeans and polo shirt and went down to the hotel bar.

Keller and Montgomery were flirting with two buxom blondes who looked like hookers, and Captain Stavros was ordering drinks. They decided to eat at the hotel buffet, then they were going to a "great show bar" that Captain Stavros knew about.

"Captain Stavros, shouldn't we wait for Captain Hardesty? She said she would meet up with us at the hotel," Casey asked.

"She called me a few minutes ago. She's having dinner with Captain Eller and her husband. I guess they were stationed together at Fairchild. She said she'd meet us in the morning." Casey tried to hide her disappointment, but she was very glad to hear that the blonde was married.

After stuffing themselves at the buffet, they went by cab to Captain Stavros's favorite place, which turned out to be a strip bar. Casey really didn't care to go in, but she couldn't back out without looking like a wimp. She was trying to fit in with the guys, so she decided to keep her mouth shut, put her feminist self temporarily in the closet, and go along with them. The strip bar was reasonably nice inside. This was supposed to be an upscale gentlemen's club. She would need several drinks to get through this experience.

They sat at a table, thankfully, not too close to the stage. Casey chugged her first two drinks to relax and decided to view the whole evening as an anthropology experiment.

She observed the men who came in and the women who worked here. Most of the men looked like college guys or businessmen, not slobbering old perverts. The women serving drinks were young, cute, and trim, and they all had big breasts. They were smiling at the men and collecting big tips. Once the show started, Casey was surprised at how beautiful the performers were. These women appeared to be having a great time putting on a show for the cheering men. One woman came onstage, and Casey couldn't take her eyes off her. She was a talented dancer who'd obviously received professional training. She didn't have huge breasts but had the body of a swimmer or a gymnast. Maybe it was the numerous drinks she'd had, but Casey was sure the dancer was looking at her as she moved on the stage. Her eyes sparked with intelligence and seduction. She was playing with these men, using them instead of letting them use her. Her smile was dazzling and her eyes were green—almost the color of Kathryn's. Casey felt a tingling in her stomach at the sight of the dancer and realized she'd had way too much to drink. She was aroused, self-conscious, and tipsy. She needed to leave. As she rose to go, Captain Stavros touched her arm. "Where are you going, Casey?"

"I'm really tired, sir. I'm going back to the hotel."

"Do you want me to come with you?"

"No, thanks, I'll be fine. You guys stay and have a good time. See you tomorrow."

Outside, the night air was warm, and she was glad to get out of that smoky, noisy strip club. *Why do those gorgeous women do this? Is it just the money or is it something else?*

Pondering the whole experience, Casey was glad Kathryn wasn't here. Watching naked women dance and sitting next to her would have been way too much to handle. Maybe she was still up and Casey could talk to her about this. That's exactly what she wanted to do—discuss this with Captain Hardesty and try to figure out how to fit in with these men, her fellow pilots. She needed to see her.

Back at the hotel, Casey found her way to her room. She'd seen Kathryn's room key and knew her room was right next to Casey's. She felt an urgency to talk to her, to see her, and she checked the time. It was eleven fifteen. *That's not too late. I'll just go listen outside her door, and if she's still up, I'll knock on her door.*

She staggered a little as she quietly walked over to Kathryn's door and checked the hall to make sure no one was watching. She leaned her ear against the door and was surprised to hear two different voices and the sound of laughter. *What the hell? Is someone with her?* In Casey's drunken state she was both confused and irritated. *Is she still with the blonde from base ops? I thought she was married?* Casey was just about to raise her fist to knock on the door when the sound seemed to change. She heard murmuring and something else. This was driving her crazy. She had to know what was going on in there. Her thinking was fuzzy, but she came up with a plan that seemed reasonable.

She went back to her room and stepped out on the small balcony. Maybe she could hear more clearly what they were talking about. She couldn't hear any better because Kathryn's sliding glass door was closed, but she could see dim light inside and some kind of motion in the room through the gauzy drapes. *I could just climb over my balcony railing to her balcony and steal a little peek into her room.* It seemed perfectly logical.

After looking down the twelve floors to the glittering lights of the Vegas strip below, Casey pretended she was a stealthy cat and carefully climbed up on top of her balcony railing. She quietly stretched her foot the four feet over to Kathryn's railing. Delicately balancing on the railing, she slowly lowered herself to Kathryn's balcony, being careful to stay in the shadows. She bent down low and crept over to an opening in the drapes. Her heart was pounding with fear, but she had to see— she had to know.

She peeked through a small slit in the drapes into the dimly lit room and squinted to make out the dark images. She threw her hand over her mouth to cover her gasp and almost fell over backward at the sight. Kathryn's compact form was unmistakable, and the movement was as clear as a slap in the face. The blonde was on all fours kneeling on the bed, and Kathryn was behind her. Casey wanted to run, but she was frozen by the sight in front of her. She was mesmerized as she watched Kathryn's arm move like a powerful piston as she pounded the blonde from behind. The blonde had her head thrown back in ecstasy with her legs wide apart as her moaning got louder and louder. Kathryn reached forward with her left hand to grip the blonde's shoulder as she increased her pace and slammed her own hips into the woman's behind. *Oh my God, I have to get out of here now.*

CHAPTER EIGHTEEN

Casey swore as she threw on her flight suit. She was late for the bus, her head was pounding from all the alcohol she'd drunk the night before, and she was dreading seeing Captain Hardesty this morning. She expected to be chewed out for being late, but when she got to the bus, the flight commander was missing and so was Montgomery. Captain Hardesty was sitting by herself in the bus, and Casey preferred to stay outside waiting for the rest of the crew. Captain Stavros and Montgomery showed up a few minutes later looking rather green, and they were both wearing sunglasses. The bus ride out to the base was unusually quiet. Casey sat way in the back, away from Captain Hardesty, next to a snoring Montgomery.

This was the epitome of awkward. Casey would have to sit next to Captain Hardesty in a compact airplane all day, concentrate on flying complicated instrument maneuvers, and try not to think about what she'd seen and heard last night. After spying on Kathryn having sex with the Blond Bitch, Casey's desperate need to flee caused her to slip and almost fall off the twelfth-story balcony as she leapt to her own balcony. *Maybe that would have been better.*

Last night was a terrible mistake filled with regret. She wished she could purge the images from her mind. After she'd made it back to her own room, Casey couldn't stand the thought of hearing them through the hotel wall, so she'd gone down to the bar and had two more stiff drinks. Some guy kept hitting on her and wouldn't take no for an answer. She finally escaped his clutches by pretending to be sick in the ladies' room and went back to her room via the service elevator. When she walked down the hall to her room, she couldn't prevent herself from stopping at Kathryn's door to listen for more sounds of sex. Silence this time. Maybe the Blond Bitch had gone home to her husband or maybe Hard-Ass had fucked her to death. *Screw both of them.*

Casey had begged for sleep as her emotions fought a pitched battle. She knew Kathryn was gay, but she hadn't imagined that she might have a girlfriend. She never would have pictured Kathryn with a married, bleached blonde with big, fake tits who wasn't even cute. The whole scene made her angry and disappointed, but worst of all, jealous. How could she possibly be jealous? Kathryn was her instructor, not her lover. She couldn't allow herself to think about this anymore, as they were almost back to the base. She would have to focus on flight planning her mission back to Willie, fly the jet as best she could, and process the whole incident after she got home.

Inside base operations, Casey efficiently plotted her course on the chart, wrote out her flight plan, and did the fuel and time calculations with her whiz wheel. Captain Hardesty looked it over and made no corrections.

"What departure are you expecting out of here?"

"The sign says to expect to fly runway heading, then get a vector to the Boulder VOR, ma'am."

"Brief me on the weather." Captain Hardesty's questions were clipped and short, like she was irritated with Casey.

"The weather briefer said to expect moderate turbulence until we climb above fifteen thousand feet, then clear skies the rest of the way to Willie."

"Let's get out of here." She snatched up her helmet bag and stomped out the door.

"Great. This is going to be a fun ride today," Casey muttered.

They got airborne before the other crews and hit the turbulence on climb out just as predicted. The heat of the desert and the turbulence was not helping Casey's headache or her stomach. She was fighting the jet just to keep her airspeed under control, and she wanted to cheat with the instrument hood and peek outside at the horizon.

"Watch your speed," Captain Hardesty barked.

"I'm trying, ma'am, but this turbulence is really rough."

"Stop making excuses and just do it."

The rest of the ride only got worse after that. Casey couldn't get her brain out of first gear, and she was mentally behind the jet. She started to turn the wrong way in holding because her situation orientation had completely abandoned her, and she missed intercepting the localizer on her first approach.

"My jet, Casey. Take the hood off and look around. I don't know what's wrong with you, but you are flying like crap today. Get your bearings, then put the hood back on and let's see if you can get this jet on the ground."

"Yes, ma'am." *Fuck. Get it together, Casey.*

The next approach was slightly better but still not good. It was as if all her flying progress had left her and she could barely hold her heading, altitude, and airspeed. After they finally got on the ground, Casey was dreading the debriefing. They walked back to the flight room in silence. Casey got a great big drink of cold water to try to make her head feel better before she went to face the verdict.

"I should bust you on that ride, Casey. That was the worst I've seen you fly. What is going on with you?"

"I'm sorry, ma'am, I don't know. I didn't get much sleep last night, and I don't really feel that well. I know that's no excuse. I won't let it happen again, ma'am."

"You're damn right you won't let it happen again or I'll bust you so fast it'll make your head spin. Did you stay out all night drinking with the guys?"

"I had a few drinks with them, ma'am."

"Well, I'm going to pass you on this ride, but just barely. You're better than that, Casey. Now go home and get some sleep. You're dismissed."

"Yes, ma'am." Casey left the flight room glad to get out of there.

Kathryn heard Barb Arnau walk into the flight room with her student. She overheard Barb say to him, "We debriefed everything in the air already, and you know what you need to work on. If you don't have any questions, you're dismissed."

"Thanks, ma'am. See you Monday."

The flight room was momentarily quiet since none of the other crews had returned from their cross-country trips yet.

"How was your cross-country, Kath? Do anything exciting?"

"It was fine."

"Well, we had a lovely trip to Dyess. Did you know they actually have a gay bar in Abilene, Texas? I snuck away from the group and had a good time despite it being a tiny place."

"Good for you." Kathryn never looked up from her grade book.

"What's up? Is anything wrong?" Barb sat next to her.

"I screwed up big time, Barb."

"What happened?"

"It was after we got to Nellis."

"Do *not* tell me you hooked up with that whore, Jill Eller."

"I'm afraid I did. It was a complete disaster."

"Where was her macho fighter pilot hubby, Sam? Screwing every woman in Las Vegas, I assume."

"Jill said his unit was deployed to Korea for two weeks. She didn't tell me he was out of town until after we had already gotten there."

"Kath, are you actually surprised she just 'forgot' to mention that her husband was nowhere around? Even you aren't that blind when it comes to conniving women."

"I guess if truth be told, I was kind of feeling the need to be with someone, even if it was Jill."

"And what led to this urgent need to hook up with Miss Skank?"

"I'm not sure. I've just been feeling really lonely lately. So I let her seduce me and, once again, it was extremely disappointing."

"Goddamn it, Kath, if you just wanted a woman to sleep with, I could recommend several nice actual lesbians here on base. Instead, you hook up with a selfish slut who pretends to be bisexual because she doesn't have the guts to admit she's really gay but can't live without heterosexual acceptability. Did you really think it would be different this time?"

"I don't know what I was thinking. I just needed to connect with someone."

"So, how was it with Jill?"

"One-sided, as usual. She begged me to do her, but she didn't reciprocate."

"So what else is new? I have a suggestion for you, Kath. After this class graduates in four weeks, the base softball team is playing in a tournament in Flagstaff. Why don't you play with us? We can get out of town for a bit, there will be lots of women there, and maybe you'll meet some real lesbians for a change. What do you say? It'll be fun."

"I'll think about it. It does sound fun, though." Kathryn smiled for the first time all day.

❖

Casey rang the bell at Trish and Rhonda's house. She'd come straight over after her disappointing last flight. She was thankful they didn't mind if she just dropped in.

"Casey! Come on in, girl. We've missed you. Everyone just left. We were having a pool party earlier." Trish wrapped her in a big hug and held her tightly. Casey's eyes welled up.

"Rhonda made her famous ribs and we've got lots of leftovers."

"Thanks, Trish." Casey's stomach growled at the smell of the delicious ribs.

"Where the hell have you been? We had some hot women here today. Too bad you missed it." Rhonda set a big pile of ribs in front of her.

"I was gone all weekend flying my first cross-country trip. These are yummy, Rhonda."

"So how was it? You don't look too good, Casey. Are you okay?"

There was no use trying to hide it from them. They could always read her like a book.

"My flights were great up until today."

"What happened?"

"I was flying with Captain Hardesty, and it was really challenging flying in Southern California, but I was doing okay. I was learning a lot."

"Is she the instructor you talked about before? The one you call Hard-Ass?"

"Yes, that's her."

"So what went wrong?"

"Well, I did something really stupid and almost busted my ride today. I went out with the guys in Las Vegas, had way too much to drink, and I kind of spied on Captain Hardesty when she was having sex with a woman."

"You did what? Okay, I want all the dirt now. Trish, you have to come and hear this. Spill it, Casey."

"I just wanted to talk to her. The guys took me to a stripper bar, and I felt the need to talk to her about dealing with the guys, plus I just wanted to see her. When I was about to knock on her door, I heard voices inside and I had this burning need to know who she was with."

"So then what happened?"

"I got this crazy idea to climb over to her balcony and spy on her. I saw her having sex with another Air Force woman, who was married to a man, supposedly. I almost fell off the balcony and we were twelve stories high."

"Jesus, Casey, what got into you? You are not normally insane."

"I know. It was really stupid. Then I had to sit next to her today on the flight home, with a nasty hangover, and I couldn't fly for shit. She was mad at me and almost busted me on the ride. I really screwed up this time. I'm not sure how to fix this."

"Casey, why did you feel so compelled to see her? I mean, you almost fell off a balcony?"

"I don't know what I was thinking, but I just *had* to see her. The thought of her with that other woman made me crazy."

"In all the years we've been friends, I've never heard you talk about any woman like you talk about her. Are you falling for her?"

Casey looked at Trish and Rhonda but couldn't speak. *Could this possibly be true? Oh. My. God. I think I may be falling for her. What the hell am I going to do now?*

CHAPTER NINETEEN

When Casey got home, she couldn't stop thinking about Kathryn and what she'd seen in Las Vegas. The images made her alternately angry, then jealous, then aroused. Her mind and emotions were trapped in an inverted spin, and she couldn't fly herself out of it.

After struggling to sleep with no success, she went to the bathroom mirror and looked at her reflection. "It doesn't matter what I may or may not feel for her. We can never have a relationship. I'm her student and I have to get through this program. It's the most important thing in my life, and I will not jeopardize it just because I may have the hots for Kathryn Hardesty." She looked into her own eyes. "You have to get through your instrument check this week, then formation flying, then on to the T-38. If you make it through this and earn your wings, maybe then you can think about her, about Kathryn."

At the utterance of Kathryn's name, Casey could no longer look at herself. She tried to hold back her emotions. "Come on, Casey, just suck it up and leave Kathryn Hardesty alone. Hell, she probably doesn't even notice me. I'm just another dumb student to her." After splashing cold water on her face, she was finally able to get to sleep. If she was lucky, she'd get four hours of sleep before her 0400 hours show time.

Casey was scheduled for her last instrument sim with Lieutenant Carter. She had to show him she could handle anything in instrument conditions. She was focused as she climbed into the simulator. Nothing would rattle her today, not even Carter's screaming. She smoothly flew all the different approaches, and even single engine approaches and go-arounds. She was mentally ahead of the jet as she calmly handled in-flight emergencies using only the instruments.

"I think you're ready for your instrument check ride, Tompkins. Overall grade, Good," Carter said.

Casey was surprised he hadn't screamed at her once. Her confidence in her ability to fly on instruments was solid—just one more check ride to get through in the T-37 phase.

❖

Kathryn walked into the flight room and went to the big schedule board. There were several students' names on the board with missions circled in red indicating busted rides. A lot of students got washed out of pilot training because they could never learn to fly on instruments. This was the most difficult part of the whole year of training.

"Captain Hardesty, I hope you're here to fly with some of my students having major problems. They're dropping like flies," Captain Arnau said.

"Actually, I was hoping to fly with Tompkins on her last instrument flight before her check ride. We have a few things to work out. After that, I'll be happy to fly with any of the guys you need me to."

"I kind of expected that, Kath. You're already in my schedule plan for this afternoon with her."

"Thanks, Barb."

"After you're done with Tompkins, I really need your magic instructor mojo with Parker and Keller."

"Sure thing, Barb."

Flying with other students would be good for her. She loved teaching flying, and the moment when the lightbulb finally came on for a student was the satisfaction she lived for. She could clearly see the student's problem, then show them how to fix it. Most of the students were afraid of her until they actually flew with her. Then they found out her secret, that she really cared about them. She was tough and demanding but fair with them. This last instrument training ride with Casey was important. She needed to make sure Casey could handle any situation under instrument conditions to ensure she passed her check ride, and to make up for their last disastrous cross-country flight. She would put Casey through her paces today and throw everything at her. She just hoped Casey was ready for it.

❖

Casey walked into the flight, saw Captain Hardesty, and suppressed a little gasp. Somehow, she had the idea that Captain Hardesty didn't want to fly with her anymore. Maybe she was flying with another student today. After she saw her name on the schedule board with her, she had to tell herself that this was just another ride. She had to stay mentally ahead of the jet, fly good instruments, and not let anything rattle her. She had to prove to her that she was ready to pass her check ride regardless of what had happened in Las Vegas.

"Lieutenant Tompkins, are you ready to fly?" Captain Hardesty asked.

"Yes, ma'am."

"I'm going to play check pilot today and try not to say anything to you. You will fly as if you are solo and in actual instrument conditions. I will not help you with anything, and you will make all the decisions in the air. If Phoenix Approach Control can't give you the approach you request, have a backup plan in mind. Always be prepared to execute a missed approach. If the check pilot takes off your hood and lets you see the runway, consider that a present. Any questions?"

"No, ma'am." Casey was grateful there was no discussion of their last ride together. Today would be all business.

When they got into the air, Captain Hardesty threw the book at her. She had her fly the most complicated instrument departure with tricky altitude and airspeed restrictions, holding, and simulated emergencies. Casey was in the zone as she flew through each situation and held her altitude, heading, and airspeed like a rock. Captain Hardesty had her request the most difficult instrument arrival procedure. The traffic pattern was very busy, and the controller had to break off her first approach because of a much faster T-38 jet behind her. Casey handled it with calm control as she flew the missed approach maneuver.

Their fuel was getting low, so Captain Hardesty requested an ILS precision approach for the last maneuver. She pulled one throttle back to idle to simulate an engine failure. Casey had to fly the approach single engine and she had to use a higher power setting on the remaining engine. She had the crosshairs of the ILS indicator centered. At the decision height of two hundred feet above the ground, Captain Hardesty reached over and removed the hood from Casey's helmet visor for the first time of the entire flight. Casey was about five seconds from the runway and greased on the landing with just a little squeak from the tires.

When they got back to the flight room, Captain Hardesty grilled Casey on the instrument flying rules and emergency procedures. Casey knew her stuff cold, and Captain Hardesty couldn't stump her on anything. She was definitely ready to pass her check ride.

"You did well today, Casey. Just do everything like you did today and you'll have no problems."

"Thanks, ma'am." Casey was beaming inside. This was the highest praise she'd ever received in pilot training.

Casey would be flying with Major Inman, the chief of check section and a crusty old-school fighter pilot who was known for intimidating every pilot in the squadron.

"Casey, Major Inman is tough but fair," Captain Hardesty said. "Be exactly ten minutes early and be sure and stand at attention and salute him when you report for your check ride. He will not say one word the entire flight. When you've completed your required maneuvers, ask him if he would like to fly, then hang on for dear life. He'll fly a five-G overhead landing pattern. He likes to plant the jet on the runway, then slam on the brakes like he's landing on a dirt strip in the jungle. During the ground eval, don't ever change your answer and don't be surprised if he asks you some very obscure instrument questions."

When Captain Hardesty left the flight room, Casey was glad the ride had gone well today. It was almost like everything was back to normal between them—almost. She still had the disturbing images from Las Vegas burned into her memory, but she would not allow herself to think about that. Nothing would distract her from her mission tomorrow.

❖

Kathryn arranged to make an unannounced safety visit to the runway supervisory unit on runway three-zero center around the time Casey would be returning from the practice area. She sat quietly in the back observing the two T-38 instructor pilots who were the RSU controllers. They were efficiently doing their jobs monitoring the aircraft taking off and landing, and chatting with her during the lulls in the action. She sat up when she heard Casey's voice over the radio requesting a VOR approach. Casey's voice sounded strong and confident. A four-ship formation of T-38 jets was just getting ready for a wing takeoff. If the T-38s requested takeoff clearance right now, the spacing would work out; otherwise Casey would have to go around. *Come on, you idiots, get your shit together and go.*

"The T-38 lead is a solo student. This isn't going to work out. He's not ready," the T-38 controller said to the other controller.

"Tango 37, approach clearance canceled. Fly runway heading, climb and maintain three thousand feet," he called over the radio.

"Tango 37, roger, runway heading, three thousand," Casey replied. *Oh, crap. Don't forget to clean up the jet, Casey.*

Kathryn held her breath as Casey's airplane approached the RSU overhead, and she exhaled when she saw the gear, flaps, and speed brake retract like they were supposed to. *Good job, Casey, now request another approach.*

"Tango 37, turn right heading zero-three-zero at the departure end of the runway and contact departure control," the RSU controller transmitted.

"Tango 37, heading zero-three-zero at the end. Good day," Casey replied.

Kathryn anxiously waited for the sound of Casey's voice over the radio as she came around for another approach. This time there was no other traffic to interfere with her approach. Kathryn saw the white flashing landing light of Casey's jet in the distance. The airplane nose was yawed fifteen degrees to the right of the final approach path—a single engine approach. *Come on, Casey, do it just like you flew it yesterday.*

As the plane approached the threshold of the runway, Kathryn saw the nose of the jet smoothly align with the runway centerline followed by a flawless touchdown right on the runway numbers.

"Sweet," the RSU controller remarked.

"Major Inman is the check pilot in that jet. He's going to ask for a closed pattern to the left runway. You might want to coordinate that for him," Kathryn whispered to the RSU controller.

"Thanks, Captain Hardesty. I don't need another butt-chewing from him."

When Major Inman's gruff bass voice came over the radio, they were ready for him.

"Tango 37, closed approved to runway three-zero left. Contact Mojack control. Good day, sir."

Kathryn stayed a few more minutes to watch Major Inman's overhead pattern and landing.

"Watch what this guy does," the RSU controller told his fellow T-38 IP.

Major Inman was barely abeam the runway numbers when he dumped the nose and dove the jet toward the ground. It looked like a crash was imminent when he rolled out wings level as he crossed the runway threshold, then pranged the jet on the runway right in front of the RSU. The nose of the jet pitched down as he braked hard and made the first runway turn-off.

"That guy is crazy," the RSU controller remarked.

"That's how he thinks a fighter pilot should fly. Fortunately, the Tweet is a tough jet. Good job, guys, see you later." Kathryn was pleased as she left the RSU. Casey had passed her instrument check ride with the toughest check pilot on the base.

CHAPTER TWENTY

After celebrating her check ride victory with Rhonda and Trish, Casey was ready to start the final phase of T-37 pilot training—formation flying. This was something unique to military pilots, and she was excited about learning flying formation with another jet. Casey hit the books hard to be ready for her first formation ride. She learned the hand signals used to communicate with each other without the radio. The videos of the new maneuvers made her heart race. She couldn't wait to see this in a real plane with the other jet flying only three feet away from her.

It was a challenge keeping her thoughts on flying and not on Captain Hardesty. Casey had been disappointed when she wasn't in the flight room after her triumphant return with a grade of Excellent on her instrument check ride. She was still happy with the accolades she'd received from her fellow classmates and the flight commander, but she really wanted Kathryn to see how well she'd done.

There was a subtle shift in the way her classmates treated her after her check ride performance. She was one of only three students in the flight to earn an Excellent on her instrument check ride, and she sensed a new grudging respect from them, like maybe she was an okay pilot after all, even if she was a girl. They even invited her to join them at the O Club on Friday afternoon.

She walked into the flight room anxious to see her name on the schedule board for her first formation flight. Jeff was flying with Lieutenant Carter, and she was in the other jet but with a blank space for the IP name. She hoped Kathryn would fly with her. At that very moment, she strolled into the flight room like she owned it, as usual.

"Captain Hardesty, glad to see you! Ready to fly a beginning formation flight today?" Captain Arnau said.

"Captain Arnau, my favorite scheduler, I live to serve," Captain Hardesty answered her.

She walked behind Captain Arnau's desk into the sacred space of the head scheduler. Casey overheard her whisper to Captain Arnau, "Barb, I'm not flying against Carter. That idiot almost killed me and my student the last time I flew a formation flight with him. I'll do anything else you need, but I'm not flying against him."

"Got it, Kath. Give me a minute to fix this."

"Lieutenant Carter, you and Parsons are now flying against Captain Stavros and Lieutenant Peters. Lieutenant Tompkins, you are with Captain Hardesty against Montgomery and me. Be ready to brief up in fifteen minutes," Captain Arnau called out across the flight room.

"Our call sign will be Tango 27 Flight. Radio check-in will be at 0930 hours on ground frequency followed by engine start. We will taxi out together. I will be the lead for the first half of the flight, then we will position change and Captain Hardesty will be the flight lead for the second half. Final briefing item, Lieutenants Tompkins and Montgomery, what are the only two things the wingman is allowed to say over the radio?" Captain Arnau asked.

"Um, I'm not sure, ma'am," Montgomery answered.

"The wingman is only allowed say, 'Two's in' or 'Lead, you're on fire.' And it's not 'two,' it's 'toop'—sharp and crisp. Now let's get out there and slip some surlies."

Casey had butterflies in her stomach. She completed the preflight inspection of the jet and they were listening on the radio for the flight check-in.

"Tango 27 Flight, check," Captain Arnau called over the radio.

"Toop," Captain Hardesty answered sharply.

"Start 'em up."

"Casey, I'm going to be doing a lot of the flying today to demonstrate formation position. Whenever I'm flying, have your hands on the stick and throttles with me to feel how I'm moving the controls. I'll be making constant, small corrections and I'll tell you where to look to maintain position. The first thing you'll see is a wing takeoff."

At the end of the runway, Casey saw Captain Arnau look over at them, then she reached up and tapped the edge of the canopy. They brought their canopies down together and Captain Hardesty replied with a sharp nod.

"Tango 27 Flight, ready for takeoff," Captain Arnau called on the radio.

"Tango 27 Flight, cleared for takeoff," the RSU answered.

Captain Hardesty lined up on the runway with their wing tip barely a few feet behind the other jet's wing. Captain Arnau tapped the side of her white helmet and gave a big head nod down to command brake release and power up for takeoff.

"Only look at lead, Casey. Glance at the engine gauges to check they are good, then look back at lead. I'm looking to see their nose wheel strut extend, then we rotate with them."

Casey saw the lead jet's nose wheel gently lift off the ground and she felt Kathryn pull back slightly on the stick. Both jets gracefully rose into the air like they were a single being. It was an amazing sight.

"Watch for their gear to come up, then we raise our landing gear. Their flaps come up, our flaps come up." Captain Hardesty reached for the gear and flap handles without even looking at them.

"Safely airborne, we slide into fingertip formation position. Your eyes need to be constantly moving to stay in position."

Casey tried hard to listen to Captain Hardesty as she talked, but she fell silent at the sight of this other T-37 jet flying in the air only three feet away from them. They were so close it looked like they would smash into them at any second. She felt Kathryn's hands through the stick and throttles. She was moving the throttles up and back in tiny increments and she was making small, rapid movements of the stick. Even though she was constantly moving the controls, they stayed in about the same place relative to the lead aircraft. Casey was mesmerized and scared at the same time. *How am I ever going to do this? This is way too close.*

They climbed up through a layer of puffy clouds. Everything went white, but Captain Hardesty stayed next to lead's wingtip like she was glued there. The clouds whizzed past them at incredible speed. "Are you ready to try it, Casey?"

"I think so."

"Your jet, Casey."

Casey was sure she would hit the other jet and she jerked back on the stick, sending them wildly above and behind the lead jet.

"My jet, Casey," Captain Hardesty said calmly. She smoothly glided back into position like it was the simplest thing in the world. "You have to relax. Keep your eyes moving on the whole jet and make small corrections. Try it again."

This time Casey made a conscious effort to relax and breathe. *Small corrections, keep my eyes moving.* She stayed in position about two seconds before falling hopelessly behind lead.

"My jet, Casey." Again, she smoothly flew right back into position as before. "Try it again. Your jet."

They continued this pattern of Casey flailing out of position, then Captain Hardesty flying them back in for some time. Captain Arnau made the symbol of a check sign with her hand against her white helmet.

"That symbol means we check our fuel and oxygen before we enter the practice area. We slide a little wider away from lead so we can safely check our systems without having to worry about hitting them. When lead rocks their wings, we come back into position."

Casey was completely disoriented. She had no idea they were even close to the practice area. She'd been concentrating so hard on trying not to crash into lead she had totally lost her situation orientation. *Crap, this is scary and so much harder than I thought it would be.*

"Casey, I'm going to demonstrate some formation maneuvering with Captain Arnau. Look at where we are in relation their jet. No matter what kind of maneuvering lead does, we stay in the exact same position on their wing. Follow along on the controls with me."

"Yes, ma'am."

Casey saw a vision of flying she'd never even dreamed of. She relaxed knowing Captain Hardesty would keep her safe. Captain Arnau put one finger up with a little spinning motion, banked her jet hard, and they pulled away fast from her plane. "Tighten up, Casey." Captain Hardesty snapped the plane into a ninety-degree bank turn and yanked back on the stick, pulling six Gs of force. The lead plane was barely visible ahead of them and looked like it was the size of a fly.

"There's the wing rock, so now we are cleared to rejoin on them. They will go into a thirty-degree bank turn, then we fly to the inside of their turn with full power and aim right at them."

Casey heard a tinge of glee in Captain Hardesty's voice as she described what she was doing. They were closing on lead very rapidly. It looked like they were going to smash right into them, then she pulled the power to idle, popped out the speed brake, and banked the jet hard. She stopped the collision course just ten feet from lead, then smoothly slid into perfect position. Captain Arnau maneuvered the formation, and when she went to ninety degrees of bank, it looked like lead would slide right into them, but Captain Hardesty kept her position. *How does she do that?*

"Tango 27 Flight, go trail," Captain Arnau called out over the radio.

"Toop," Captain Hardesty replied as she pulled the power back and slid back behind lead. When she was about one hundred feet behind the lead jet, she called, "Toop's in."

The lead jet rolled upside down and Captain Hardesty followed them like she was their shadow. Captain Arnau yanked, rolled, and dove her jet in abrupt acrobatic maneuvers, trying to shake them off her tail. This was better than the wildest roller coaster Casey had ever been on.

After having their lips G-ed off, Captain Arnau gave the change lead signal, and now Casey and Captain Hardesty were the formation lead.

"Look around, Casey, and get your orientation in the practice area, then think about what maneuvers we will put them through."

Casey had no idea where they were at the moment but looked down at the ground and saw the two big dry river beds that formed an X in the middle of the practice area.

"The most important thing we have to do as lead is fly a smooth jet and think ahead. You cannot abruptly turn a formation flight, and we have to protect our wingman at all times since they only look at us and they trust us. We have to work them through the maneuvers plus watch the fuel and our position in the practice area. Flying as a good lead is actually much more difficult than being the wingman. I'm going to lead them through formation maneuvering so she can demonstrate wingman position to her student, then I'll have you fly lead." She touched her fist to the front of her helmet visor to show she was flying and Captain Arnau replied with the same gesture.

It was the most beautiful sight Casey had ever seen in her life. Blazing blue skies with puffy white clouds beneath them as they rolled and climbed with the other T-37 so close she could almost reach out her hand and touch them. She heard music in her head. It was magnificent.

"You ready to be lead, Casey? Just hold the wings level for now so Montgomery can try to stay in position. Your jet."

"My jet," Casey answered. She knew immediately when Montgomery took the controls as he flailed next to them looking like he was about to crash into them, then he got completely spit out of position. Captain Arnau flew them back in, then Montgomery flailed out again. This went on for several attempts with no noticeable improvement by Montgomery. *Was I that bad?*

"What do we do now, Casey? We're coming up on the border of the practice area. Make a decision."

"Um, I'm not sure what to do, ma'am."

"My jet, Casey. This is why you have to think three maneuvers ahead. The only way to quickly change directions with a formation is with a pitchout—like this." Captain Hardesty put up one finger, made a little spinning motion, then yanked the jet into a hard ninety-degree banked turn to fly away from the wingman. She pulled hard until they were headed back into the middle of the practice area, then rolled wings level and the wingman was gone. "I'm going to rejoin the formation, then give Captain Arnau some close trail acro maneuvers and return to Willie for a wing landing." Captain Hardesty did a giant wing rock then put the airplane into a thirty-degree bank turn. "You should see the wingman at the eight o'clock low position."

Casey looked back over her left shoulder and saw the wingman as a small speck in the sky. The number two jet was getting bigger fast as they closed rapidly on what looked like a collision course. *Crap, it looks like they're going to ram right into us.* Fear started to clutch in her chest as the other jet came screaming toward them. Just as she thought death was imminent, she saw the big speed brake extend, they banked, then rolled out about thirty feet away and gracefully slid into position. "Wow, that was close."

"Not really, Captain Arnau just likes to show off. Now we're going to have some real fun with them, Casey."

"Tango 27 Flight, go trail."

"Toop."

"Tighten up, Casey!" Captain Hardesty rolled upside down and pulled five Gs hard into a split S maneuver headed straight toward the ground. "The objective is to shake them off our tail any way we can with abrupt maneuvers," Captain Hardesty grunted between quick breaths. "They are in our high six o'clock position behind us. If this were a combat situation, we would maneuver to get behind them and shoot their brains out." Captain Hardesty yanked and banked so hard it was all Casey could do to not black out from the Gs. It was also the most fun Casey had ever had in her life with her clothes on. "Your turn, Casey. Your jet."

Casey took the controls and did three aileron rolls followed by a Cuban eight right into an Immelman.

"Come on, shake them off your tail—they are trying to kill you! Pull hard!"

Casey checked the throttles at full power, put both hands on the stick, tightened up her legs and abs, and flew as aggressively as she could. She didn't think about the entry parameters for each maneuver, only about getting away from a bad guy. She and the jet were one, and she was controlling it with her mind and her body.

"Good job, Casey. My jet. Time to go home now," Captain Hardesty said.

Casey was reluctant to give the plane back. Her heart was racing, her muscles tingling, and her breathing fast, as she watched the other jet slide smoothly back into position next to them. Captain Arnau gave them a big thumbs-up.

They flew back to Willie, where they would land together. The approach was smooth and flawless with an amazing view of the other jet right next to them. Casey held her breath as both jets gracefully touched down together on the runway. It was the most amazing flight Casey had ever experienced in her life, and she couldn't wait for more.

They did a formation debrief and Captain Arnau complimented Casey on her formation lead and claimed she won the close trail maneuvering. There was good-natured ribbing between Captain Hardesty and Captain Arnau in addition to critique. It was obvious they had great respect for each other's flying skills.

"What did you think of your first formation flight?"

"It was amazing, ma'am."

"You didn't do too bad for your first ride. You were beginning to get the hang of the wingman position a little toward the end. You need to push yourself to get in position and stay in position. Don't be satisfied with flying wide because it feels safer."

"Yes, ma'am." Casey took notes on every word she said.

"Visualize what you saw today, practice staying in position, and know your hand signals cold. Formation flying is the one area where you will see how your flying skills and mental ability stack up against your classmates. More than anything, formation flying is about leadership, mutual support, and trust. Good job today." She filled out the grade sheet and gave Casey a grade of Good.

Casey stood at attention when she left, but she felt like she was floating. She'd been scared out of her wits flying that close to another plane at two hundred and fifty knots. Captain Hardesty made it look so easy and she obviously loved it. Casey got a small amount of praise from both Captain Hardesty and Captain Arnau and she got to see the most incredible sights from the air. She went right over to the learning center to review more videos on formation. She was determined to know everything she could about flying formation and she wanted to get really good at this. This was the way her male classmates would respect her. She would simply fly circles around them.

CHAPTER TWENTY-ONE

As formation flying continued, Casey felt a small amount of lightness in herself. She was progressing well, especially her ability to lead, and she was getting better at staying in position on the wing. The last hurdle was to fly solo in formation. She could not wait.

She hadn't flown with Captain Hardesty recently and the flight IPs were flying with lots of different students. Casey was comfortable flying with any IP now, even Carter. He was doing less screaming lately. When she flew against her classmates, she realized she could stay in position better than most of them, and she had no trouble staying mentally ahead of the formation when she was the lead. Some of her classmates struggled with formation and were close to getting washed out. If you couldn't fly formation, you couldn't be an Air Force pilot.

Casey was excited to see she would be flying with Captain Hardesty today. If everything went well, her next ride after this one would be her formation solo and her last ride in the T-37 before she graduated to the supersonic T-38 jet. She and Captain Hardesty would fly against her classmate Jason Montgomery, who was flying his solo formation ride.

Captain Hardesty came striding into the flight room like she always did and announced, "Tompkins, Montgomery, let's brief this up."

Casey stood at attention at her table as Montgomery rushed over looking harried and disorganized. "Lieutenant Montgomery, Lieutenant Tompkins and I will start out as lead, then position change, and you will lead us back to the overhead pattern for landings."

Casey was keenly aware that Captain Hardesty expected her to be the formation commander and make all the decisions as lead. This ride would be her last check before she was allowed to fly formation as a solo pilot. The check-in, engine start, taxi out, and wing takeoff went well. Casey started a smooth turn to the practice area and noticed Montgomery bouncing around a fair amount on her wing. *Maybe he just needs to settle down a bit.*

She did a slow, smooth rollout from the turn to try to help him out. Casey gave him a cross under, and it took him longer than normal to move from the right wing to the left wing. When she entered the practice area, she gave him a pitchout so he could get a rejoin. After she gave him the wing rock rejoin signal, she looked for him in the usual eight o'clock low position behind her but couldn't see him. "Can you see him, ma'am?"

"Yeah, I see him. He's way too low and forward of the rejoin line," Captain Hardesty answered.

Casey saw Captain Hardesty's hand move to the stick for the first time on the ride. She finally saw Montgomery way low and far forward of where he should have been. "Crap," she muttered to herself. *What the hell is he doing?*

"Overshoot! Overshoot!" Captain Hardesty yelled over the radio.

Casey saw Montgomery cross under her jet and swing wide to the opposite side of her.

"Just continue the turn, Casey. Give him a chance to get back in position."

After what seemed like a long time, Montgomery finally got back into position on her wing. Casey only had time for a few more maneuvers before she reached changeover fuel. She gave him the change lead signal and slid back into fingertip position off Montgomery's wing. He continued straight ahead for several miles without giving her any maneuvers. Casey glanced ahead and saw they were rapidly approaching the boundary of their practice area. *Come on, do something, Montgomery.*

Finally, he gave her the signal for a pitchout. *Good. Well, at least I'll get some rejoin practice.* The lead aircraft abruptly turned into her. She gasped as her windscreen was instantly filled with a white plane coming right at her. The stick jerked down out of her hand and she was held down by her shoulder straps as negative Gs lifted her up out of her seat. They immediately went down as the lead jet crossed over the top of their canopy, missing them by inches.

"Jesus Christ, you fucking idiot, Montgomery! My jet, Casey," Captain Hardesty yelled.

"What just happened, ma'am?" Casey's heart was pounding out of her chest.

"That dumb shit forgot what side we were on, didn't look where he was going, and he pitched right into us. I had a feeling he might do that. That's why I had my hand on the stick. You didn't do anything wrong, Casey. Now's he giving us the rejoin signal. He is completely clueless. Your jet, Casey. Just complete the rejoin and watch out for him."

Her heart was still pounding from their near midair collision. She took a few deep breaths and flew the rejoin. As the flight continued, she was very wary of lead and she didn't trust him. It was a new and very uncomfortable feeling. At one point, he had her go to close trail position and she followed him through acrobatic maneuvering. With a little space behind him she could see the practice area around them and looked at her altimeter. He was leading them out the bottom of the practice area below the minimum altitude. Not knowing what else to do, she said, "Lead, check altitude." He finally noticed his altitude and abruptly pulled up after going out the bottom of the area by two thousand feet.

"Tango 47 Flight, Albuquerque Center, check altitude. I show you two thousand feet low."

Captain Hardesty jumped on the radio. "Roger, Albuquerque, we're correcting now. I'll be filing a report when we land."

Montgomery climbed back up to the correct altitude and departed the practice area to lead the flight back to Willie. As the formation flew up to the overhead pattern, Casey felt relief when he broke away from them to make his landing. She no longer had to follow him. She heard him call "Gear down" over the radio.

Captain Hardesty got on the radio. "Mojack, have Tango 47 Lead make a full stop landing."

The RSU replied, "Roger. Tango 47 Lead, make this landing a full stop."

Montgomery answered, "Roger, Mojack. Tango 47 Lead, gear down, full stop."

Casey could hear the confusion in his voice. *This is going to be ugly when we get on the ground.*

The flight room was noisy, as usual, with lots of students and IPs talking. When they walked in for the mission debrief, quiet descended on the room. Casey felt anger seethe from Captain Hardesty and she hadn't said one word yet.

"So, Lieutenant Montgomery, how do you think the flight went?" Captain Hardesty asked.

"Well, there were a few little things I could have done better, I suppose, but overall, I think it went pretty good," he answered.

"Really? Lieutenant Tompkins, how to you think the ride went?"

"Well, um, I think, um, I'm not really sure, ma'am," Casey answered weakly.

"Lieutenant Tompkins, a vital part of formation flying is the debrief. This is where we give each other constructive critique in order to correct mistakes and improve each other's performance. Don't you agree, Lieutenant Montgomery?"

"Yes, ma'am, I do," he answered brightly.

"Lieutenant Tompkins, tell Lieutenant Montgomery exactly what he did wrong on the ride."

Casey knew this was not a request and there was no way she was going to get out of blasting Montgomery.

"Montgomery, you almost killed us. As wingman, you were way forward of the rejoin line and ended up having to do an overshoot. As lead, you broke right into me when you did your first pitchout. Then you led us out the bottom of the practice area during trail," Casey told him bluntly.

Montgomery looked stunned. "That's not how I recall the flight. You were a very rough lead at the beginning, making it hard for me to stay in position. I may have been a smidge aggressive on my rejoin, but I made the correct decision to overshoot, and that worked out well. I tried to be smoother for you when I was lead, and I certainly did not break into you. I didn't see you except when you took a long time to rejoin." He was quibbling. Casey felt anger radiate off Captain Hardesty. He concluded with, "I think Albuquerque Center's radar was off when they said I went out of the area. I looked at my altimeter and it may have been close, but I was definitely still in the practice area."

"Lieutenant Montgomery, not only can you not fly formation, either as wingman or lead, but you are clueless, and you are a liar. You just busted this ride."

She got up from the table, walked across the flight room to the big schedule board, reached for the red grease pencil hanging on the string, and drew a big red circle around Montgomery's name, breaking the pencil in the process. Casey overheard her as she bent down to speak to Captain Arnau. "Don't *ever* schedule me to fly with that fucking dumb shit again." She turned on her heel and left the flight room. The entire room was silent.

❖

Casey thought about everything that had happened on the disastrous formation ride as she entered her maneuver grades onto the grade sheet. Captain Stavros came over to her. "Lieutenant Tompkins, please come into my office."

"Yes, sir."

"Casey, I'm pleased to tell you that you've been promoted to captain."

"Really, sir? I'd almost forgotten I was even up for promotion."

"You should be very proud, Casey. There's a commander's call this Thursday afternoon, and the squadron commander will pin your new bars on you. Congratulations."

"Thank you, Captain Stavros." She saluted smartly, did an about-face, and left his office.

Casey called Trish and Rhonda as soon as she got home to share her good news.

"Congrats, girl! This calls for a party. Come over on Saturday and we'll have some brats, beer, and cake." Trish sounded more excited than Casey.

Relaxing in the pool with her friends was just what Casey needed. She'd been working and studying so hard she could hardly remember what day of the week it was. She only had her solo formation ride left in the T-37, then she had a few days off before going on to the T-38 squadron. Her body was tired and her mind was fried. She was excited about flying the "White Rocket," the supersonic T-38, but she would miss flying with Captain Hardesty.

Kathryn Hardesty. Just saying her name out loud made Casey's pulse race. She had such mixed emotions swirling around inside her. She wanted to fly like Captain Hardesty, and she knew without a doubt that she was the best IP in the squadron, but she also knew they could never even be friends. Then there was that scene. That view from the Las Vegas hotel balcony when she spied on her with that other woman. It was futile to try to suppress the image. It came to her unbidden when her head finally hit her pillow after another twelve-hour day of training. The scene replayed itself in slow motion with Casey fighting jealousy and arousal at the same time. She usually had to get out her vibrator for a quick release just to get some much-needed sleep. Why was she so obsessed with her? Maybe Trish and Rhonda could help her get her head on right again.

Their home was a sanctuary to her. Tension left her body when she walked up their sidewalk. The sound of splashing pool water and the lilt of women's laughter made her smile. Maybe she would meet some amazing woman today who could take her mind off Kathryn Hardesty. At the very least, she could truly relax and be herself.

When she walked in the door, the whole party erupted with "CAPTAIN Tompkins!"

She couldn't hold back her grin. The women came up to hug her. This was what she really needed—warmth and acceptance from friends who loved her. "Casey's on my team," Trish called out.

"I need a beer first," Casey answered.

Not only was Rhonda a brilliant engineer, she was also a fabulous cook. She'd made a cake and decorated it with Air Force wings and silver captain's bars. Casey started to choke up at what her friends had done for her. Rhonda came up behind her and hugged her. "It'll bring a tear to a glass eye, Cap."

"Thanks, Rhonda, this is great. You guys are the best."

"You need to fill us in on your latest flying adventures. I love hearing all the crazy shit you're doing."

She was relaxing poolside and Marilyn strolled over to her. She'd arrived too late on purpose to play volleyball and she was wearing a tight-fitting T-shirt to show off her ample breasts. Marilyn went around the group hugging everyone but saved a long, lingering hug for Casey. She was polite but pulled away from Marilyn's grip as soon as she could make an excuse to get another beer. Marilyn was an attractive woman, but Casey felt nothing for her, even though six months ago they'd briefly hooked up.

She noticed Marilyn's red nails and thought of Kathryn Hardesty's hands. Kathryn's hands were smaller than Casey's, and she kept her nails short with no polish on them. She remembered her hands in leather flying gloves moving over the wings of a Tweet. Her hands that could make a T-37 do precisely what she willed it to do. Her powerful hands that could poke a grown man in the chest when he screwed up, and precise hands that danced over the stick and throttles even in severe turbulence. Those were the hands that Casey wanted to touch, her hands, not Marilyn's. *Oh crap, I think I've had enough beer.*

Trish and Rhonda sidled over to Casey and propped their feet up on a lounge chair.

"Get enough to eat, Captain?" Rhonda asked.

"Yes, I'm stuffed. Everything was delicious, as always."

"Good. So what's up with you and Marilyn?"

"Nothing's up with me and Marilyn."

"I thought you were kind of interested in her."

"No. We had that one night a few months ago, but I'm only interested in getting through pilot training, nothing more."

"Okay, then what's up with that woman instructor?" Rhonda could be relentless when she wanted information.

"Nothing's up with her. She's my IP, that's all." Casey was starting to squirm under the interrogation.

"It didn't sound like nothing after that trip to Las Vegas with her. You were acting like a crazy woman. Are you interested in her or not?"

There it was—the big question. Right out on the table in front of her. Would she continue to deny the truth to her dearest friends or would she finally speak the words she'd been holding inside?

"Yes. I'm interested in her, but it doesn't matter. Nothing can ever happen between us." A weight was lifted from her as she made her confession.

"What are you going to do about her, Casey?" Trish asked gently.

"I really don't know."

"What about when she's no longer your instructor when you go to that really fast plane? Why can't you see her then?" Rhonda asked.

"I don't know, Rhonda. It just seems impossible right now."

"Well, you've got a few days off after your last flight, don't you? Why don't you think about it and try to figure out a way to at least see if she feels anything for you. What's the worst that could happen?"

"I could get kicked out of the Air Force for being gay, lose my career, and never fly again," Casey answered sadly.

"Really? After all they've invested in training you?"

"It doesn't matter. If you are gay and they find out, your career and your life are over."

"Well, since you know she's gay too, I don't think she would rat you out. You'll figure it out, Casey. You're a smarty-pants and a real catch." They both hugged her as they returned to the party. Her friends had given her a lot to think about.

CHAPTER TWENTY-TWO

The squadron auditorium was packed for the commander's call. Captain Hardesty had given a safety briefing on the hazards of hot-weather flying in Arizona. The executive officer called the room to attention as the squadron commander marched to the front of the room.

"Lieutenants Simmons, Mendez, and Tompkins, front and center."

Casey and the other two joined him at the front of the room and stood at attention.

"Ladies and gentlemen, take seats," Lieutenant Colonel Miller said.

"This is one of the best parts of my job as squadron commander. It is a great honor for me to recognize the outstanding achievements of these young officers as they are promoted to the rank of captain. Lieutenant Tompkins, step forward. You are out of uniform."

Casey took one step forward and stood ramrod straight as the commander removed the first lieutenant bars from her shoulders and replaced them with the shiny double silver bars of a Captain. "Well done, Captain Tompkins," he said as he shook her hand.

"Thank you, sir." She saluted him and stepped back.

After the ceremony, most of her classmates came up to congratulate her. She noticed Captain Hardesty out of the corner of her eye hoping she would also congratulate her. As the crowd started to thin out, Captain Hardesty came up behind Casey.

"Congrats, Casey."

"Thank you, ma'am."

"You don't have to call me 'ma'am' anymore. How about just 'Captain Hardesty' until you graduate from the Tweet program."

"Okay, Captain Hardesty."

"Are you ready for your solo formation ride tomorrow?"

"I sure am. I'm really looking forward to it."

"Well, don't celebrate too hard at the O Club tonight."

"I won't, and thanks again."

Warmth slowly rolled over Casey as Kathryn left the room. This was a moment of pride and accomplishment and she was happy she could share it with her.

❖

The big day was finally here—Casey's formation solo. A tingle ran up her spine. Captain Hardesty and Captain Arnau would be flying in the other jet. She was ready and this would be very challenging with two IPs in the other plane.

Casey was the flight lead and checked her airplane clock—three minutes to check-in. She took a moment to look around the ramp at the taxiing T-37s. They were loud and hot but she felt comfortable and safe flying them. She was going to relish her last flight in the mighty Tweet.

"Tango 41 Flight, check in," she called over the radio.

"Toop," Captain Hardesty answered.

She taxied to the runway and looked over her shoulder at her wingman. She saw the two helmets of her instructors and they both gave her a thumbs-up. Her heart was racing with excitement. "Tango 41 Flight, ready for takeoff."

"Tango 41 Flight, cleared for takeoff."

She gave the hand signal for power up, tapped the side of her helmet, and gave them the head nod for brake release. She roared down the runway and smoothly pulled back on the stick. She rose into the sky and looked over at Two to make sure they were safely airborne. Captain Hardesty slid into formation position like they were a single aircraft. *I'm going to have to challenge her. This is going to be fun.*

She gave Two the signal for a cross under and Captain Hardesty flew to her opposite wingtip in the blink of an eye. When she entered the practice area, she gave them a pitchout and rejoin. Two was closing on her fast, but she didn't fear getting hit by them.

Casey went right into fingertip maneuvering and smoothly rolled into ninety degrees of bank, made the nose slice down, and let the jet accelerate. She rolled wings level and pulled up with three Gs of force. Captain Hardesty never wavered from her wing tip position.

"Tango 41 Flight, go trail." Casey looked for Two behind her. When she saw them in her mirrors, she rolled upside down, tightened her leg and stomach muscles, then yanked back hard on the stick. She glanced at her G-meter—five Gs. *Let's see how you can hang with this!* She yanked and banked as hard as she could like the devil himself was chasing her. She almost lost them on a turn reversal, but then they popped back into position. She was having the time of her life and could have played cat and mouse with them all day.

She gave them the wing rock signal and they returned to position off her wing. Casey's face was sore from smiling so much and her legs trembled from holding her muscles tight. This was better than the best sex she'd ever had. She gave them the change lead signal. They both nodded and Casey slid into position off their wing.

Captain Hardesty was in the left seat and she put her fist against her helmet visor. "Captain Hardesty is flying lead. This should be good. Show me what you got, Hard-Ass!" Casey said.

Captain Hardesty put Casey through her full paces—pitchouts, rejoins, echelon turns, hardcore wing work then she called, "Tango 41 Flight, go trail!" As soon as Casey replied "Toop," they tore away from her in a flash. She'd seen anyone maneuver a plane that aggressively in her life. She kept her throttles at full power as she rolled and pulled as hard as she could to stay with them. She was breathing so hard from the abrupt G-forces she thought she might pass out and was just about to call, "Knock it off," when Captain Hardesty smoothly rolled wings level and gave her the rejoin signal. *Thank God that's over. She almost killed me.*

Casey saw Captain Arnau, who was flying from the right seat, put her fist to her visor, indicating she was the pilot flying now. "Tango 41 Flight, go trail!" *Oh God, round two.*

Casey was ready this time when she answered, "Toop." They rolled upside down and went right into a five-G split S maneuver and Casey went right after them. There were little puffy white clouds near the bottom of the practice area and Captain Arnau headed right for them. She dodged and wheeled the plane through the clouds, getting very close to them but never touching them. Casey hung right with them as puffies shot past her. This high-speed, high-G game of chase went on for several minutes before Captain Arnau gave Casey the rejoin signal. Casey was exhausted and sorry it was over. *This flight has been more amazing than I could have ever imagined.*

As they approached the base, Casey remembered Captain Hardesty's instruction and heard her voice in her head, "Always look good coming back into the pattern. Everyone is watching you. Get in tight and stay in position." *Yes, ma'am, Two's in.*

When the formation neared the break point, Captain Hardesty glanced back at Casey and gave her a salute just before they broke away from her. She saw the full underside of lead's plane as they rolled sharply to ninety degrees of bank. Casey was a solo jet again with a small sense of sadness that this thrilling ride was over. She was also proud of herself. She'd held her own against two of the best pilots in the squadron. She felt like a real pilot today. She'd been Kathryn Hardesty's student for five months, but on this magical formation flight, she'd flown like she was her equal. Their two jets together was like they were one person.

This would be her last landing, on her last flight, in the fabulous T-37. She was determined to make it a good one. For the final time, she keyed the mike button. "Tango 41 Solo, gear down, full stop."

CHAPTER TWENTY-THREE

August 1992

The flight commander, Captain Stavros, walked to the front of the flight room to the podium. "I have an announcement. You students who have completed all your rides by Thursday, you will get four days off from training before you report to the T-38 squadron next Tuesday. Also, IPs who have finished up with your studs, you get four days off too." A collective cheer erupted from the whole flight room at this news.

Wow, four whole days off. Casey had been running at full speed for the last six months with no breaks. She was a little dumbfounded as to what she would do over her precious days off. Maybe she could hang out with Trish and Rhonda.

"Casey, do you have a minute?" Captain Arnau asked.

"Sure, what's up?"

"The base softball team is playing in a tournament in Flagstaff over the weekend and we are short some players. Can you play with the team this weekend?"

Casey thought about it for a millisecond. "Yes. I'd love to play. Count me in."

"Great. Here's my address. We will meet at my house at 0700 hours Friday morning, then caravan up to Flagstaff. Our first game is at 1000 hours. This should be a lot of fun, Casey."

With Casey's plans for her days off solidified, she let out a small sigh of relief. Escaping to the cool air of Flagstaff after all the stress and pressure she'd been under in pilot training might be just what she needed. Not to mention being in the company of a few hundred dykes playing softball sounded like heaven right now.

❖

At 0650 hours, Casey saw a collection of pickup trucks, jeeps, and SUVs parked in front of a tidy one-story house. "This must be the place." Casey had packed light with a small bag of clothes for four days, her softball bag with her favorite glove, and her lucky bat. She'd played with most of the women, but there were a few new faces in the crowd. She saw a very attractive tall, long-legged blonde wearing a Williams AFB hospital scrub shirt. She also recognized the cute dark haired security police airman who'd welcomed her to Willie on her first day of pilot training, which seemed like a million years ago now. She saw a flash of red out the corner of her eye. "Well, well, well, look who's here," Casey said. The whole group turned to look at Kathryn Hardesty in her fire engine red Mustang convertible. She was wearing very short softball shorts, a William AFB Softball cap with her sandy brown hair tucked behind her ears, and a pair of Ray-Ban aviator sunglasses. She looked as hot as her car.

"Kath! You made it. I'm so glad they unchained you from that desk for a few days." Barb rushed up to Kathryn and embraced her in a full body hug. Most of the other women on the team greeted her as well.

"Fall in, everyone. We've got some asses to kick in Flagstaff. I can take five in my truck," Barb said. "Casey, Kath, Donna, and Kim, why don't you guys ride with me, and everyone else can fit in the Mormon Assault Vehicle that Robyn drives."

"Mormon Assault Vehicle?" Casey asked.

"The giant blue SUV that seats nine. The big Mormon families around here drive them. You can fit all your sister wives and kids in them." Laughing, they piled in and took off for Flagstaff and a temporary respite from living on the surface of the sun, which was Willie in the summer.

Casey sat next to Kathryn with their legs touching for the whole two-hour drive. She could hardly focus on anything being said because of the sensation of silky smooth skin against her thigh. Not only was Kathryn's thigh lusciously soft but her skin was also unusually warm. Casey didn't want their contact to end and was reluctant to get out of the truck when they'd arrived.

The ball fields in Flagstaff were gorgeous. The fields were bright green with grass, the skies crystal blue with puffy white clouds, and they were surrounded by a spectacular backdrop of forest-covered mountains. It was hard to believe they were in the same state. Casey inhaled deeply the scent of warm pine sap and freshly mown grass. This was going to be a great weekend.

Casey hung back a little as the team walked over to their dugout. She found herself stealing glances at a certain person's backside and wanted a moment of undisturbed gawking. The ride in Barb's big truck had been very pleasant but also a little unnerving. She needed to get a grip on herself if she was going to play well today. More than anything, she wanted to impress Kathryn with her softball skills, but one last glance at her lovely rear end before she had to get serious wouldn't hurt. Just then, Kathryn stopped, turned around, and looked Casey square in the face, like she could read Casey's lascivious mind. Casey froze in her tracks and looked back into those sparkling green eyes.

"Come on, slowpoke, you're batting first." Kathryn flashed Casey a dazzling smile when she spoke to her. *I'm going to have a hard time concentrating today.*

The Williams team won the coin toss and Casey was the first batter. She walked to the batter's box and heard her team cheering her on, but one voice stood out among the rest—Kathryn's. She relaxed her body, took a deep breath, and let two balls and two strikes go past her without even swinging. She saw the outfielders move in closer to the infield just like she wanted them to. The next pitch was hers, and she focused her eyes on the ball like a laser beam. She took a step, swung with full force, heard the loud "ping" of her metal bat, and watched her ball sail down the third base line. *Sweet.* Her hit went past the outfielder, and it kept rolling even farther. She took off running the bases. She easily made it to third base and had set up the next batter to bring her home for their first run. Yes, this was going to be a great weekend.

After Casey's great start, everyone else got hits and they easily won their first two games. Casey enjoyed watching Kathryn play ball most of all. She couldn't hit the ball as far as Casey could, but she was a very quick runner and a smart player. She particularly enjoyed watching Kathryn's leg muscles as she ran the bases. She looked even better in her softball shorts than she did in her flight suit.

After their triumphant first day, they went to their motel on Route 66 to get cleaned up and go out on the town. Flagstaff wasn't a big city, but they had some fun, funky places to hang out. Casey was sharing a motel room with Barb, Kathryn, and Donna, the cute security police airman. Casey wasn't sure what the sleeping arrangements were, but she was nervous about the possibility of sharing a bed with Kathryn.

She wasn't sure she could restrain herself if she was lying next to her all night. Fortunately, Barb and Kathryn took the first bed, leaving Casey with Donna in the other bed—problem solved, for now. "Everyone form up at 1900 hours. We're going to the Museum Club. It's ladies' night!" Barb said.

They drove to a giant log cabin building that looked like it was at least a hundred years old. Casey couldn't help but notice the unusual front entrance. Above the door was a very large, smooth, Y-shaped tree branch that looked remarkably like a woman's lower torso with her legs spread wide open straddling the big entrance door. It was both amazing and tasteless all at the same time. "I call it 'The Crotch,'" Kathryn said to Casey.

It was a lively, cavernous place with knotty pine paneling and at least fifty large animal heads along the walls. Country music blared and they sat at one of the long wooden tables. There were quite a few women already dancing on the big dance floor with a few straight couples mixed in. A few men in cowboy hats looked at them as they took their seats, but they seemed harmless. This was clearly a place where everyone was welcome, and they settled in for a good time as pitchers of beer started flowing.

Casey attempted to look nonchalant and tried not to stare at Kathryn, but she couldn't help sneaking peeks at her. Kathryn seemed comfortable with everyone and appeared to have a good time, but she didn't join in on the dancing. This was such a totally different environment from the flight room where she normally interacted with Kathryn that Casey felt a little awkward around her. A bar filled with women and music was her natural habitat, and now she didn't know how to act. Thankfully, Donna asked her to dance. Once she was on the dance floor doing the Texas two-step, she felt like her old self again.

After they returned to the table for more beer, Casey heard some very familiar music.

Barb jumped up. "'Cotton-Eyed Joe'! Come on, everybody out on the dance floor. That means you too, Kath."

They scrambled to the big dance floor, linked arms, and started dancing high kicks to the old song. Casey felt Kathryn's arm firmly gripping her waist as they danced, and she could hardly breathe. She wrapped her arm around Kathryn's waist and held on tight as they twirled around the floor. Casey was breathless and tingling. The song was over way too soon, and Casey was reluctant to let go of Kathryn's firm waist. She lingered a little too long holding on to Casey's waist. *Is she really holding on to me, or is this just my wishful thinking?* They sat next to each other back at the table with their thighs gently touching. *I'm not sure what's happening right now, but I like it.*

The next line dance song came on and the group again took the floor together. Kathryn took Casey's hand and led her to the dance floor. This song was another rousing line dance number, but when it was over, the music changed to Patsy Cline singing "Crazy." Kathryn looked at Casey, smiled, and said, "Shall we?"

"Yes," Casey answered eagerly. They moved together during the slow dance music with Kathryn's arm around Casey's waist, Casey's arm holding Kathryn's shoulder, and their hands clasped together. Kathryn's hand was warm and soft and her firm breasts gently brushed against Casey's stomach. Normally, Casey would lead, but it felt perfectly natural with Kathryn leading. Casey thought about nothing else but the sensation of Kathryn in her arms. They glided around the dance floor like they slow danced together every day. It felt natural and very sensuous. Just as she was enjoying the sweet scent of Kathryn's hair, the song was over way too soon and they separated. Casey looked into Kathryn's eyes and felt a desire to lean down and kiss her full, luscious lips. Kathryn held her gaze, took Casey's hand, and slowly led them back to the long table before Casey could do anything she might regret later.

Soon Barb announced they had to get back to the motel for their early game tomorrow. Casey was sad to see the evening end, especially dancing with Kathryn. When they got back to their motel room, she couldn't help sneaking peeks at Kathryn as they got ready for bed. Kathryn came out of the bathroom wearing gym shorts and a thin cotton tank top that did nothing to hide the shape of her firm breasts and pert nipples. She held her breath watching those lovely breasts gently bounce as Kathryn walked across the room. *Oh, my God.*

Casey hurriedly got ready for bed and climbed in next to Donna. Her desire was radiating off her like a big, red warning beacon, and she was sure it was glaringly obvious to everyone. Her arousal throbbed and her heart pounded as she tried to calm herself and get to sleep. *Why was she dancing with me like that? Why did she keep touching me? What about the Blond Bitch in Vegas?* Casey didn't care about any other women, or about Kathryn's motives. She only cared about the sound of Kathryn's breathing in the bed next to hers and remembering the feel of her body as they danced together. This was making it very difficult for Casey to sleep. It was exquisite torture.

CHAPTER TWENTY-FOUR

After a restless night of tossing and turning, Casey woke up still buzzing from the events of the night before. She quickly dressed and went out looking for coffee and to have a moment to herself. She needed to put Kathryn in the back of her mind today regardless of how her body was reacting to her. When she returned with drinks for all of them, they were dressed and ready to go. She'd remembered that Kathryn only drank baby coffee—two creams and four sugars. Kathryn was quiet as they drove over to the ball fields. Maybe she'd had a restless night too.

Their first game went well, but the competition was getting tougher as the day went on. They barely won their second game and they were behind by two runs in the last inning of their third game. Kathryn hit a single just over the shortstop's head and ran to first base to get the bases loaded. Casey was up to bat, they had two outs, and she needed to hit at least a triple to drive in three runs to win the game. She walked slowly to the batter's box, taking several deep breaths on the way. As she approached, the noise from the field was notably quiet except for one voice—Kathryn's. "Come on, Casey, bring us home. You can do it. Nail that ball!"

The other team was no longer fooled by Casey's slacker batter trick. They'd seen her hit and were deep in the outfield waiting for her. Casey watched the pitcher's hand as she released the ball. It flew in a graceful arc, and Casey could tell it would be high and inside, right where she wanted it. She held her breath waiting for it to arrive at the exact spot in the air, then she uncoiled with all the force in her body and smashed the ball down the third base line. She dropped the bat and took off running for first base. The other three runners also tore off toward home. As Casey ran to second base, she looked up in time to see Kathryn rounding third toward home and the left fielder was just now getting to her ball. If the girl didn't have a spectacular throwing arm she might just make it home herself. As she approached third, she heard Kathryn yelling, "Run, Casey, run! You can make it!"

She didn't even look where the ball was, she just trusted Kathryn's voice as she poured on all the speed she had. The catcher was blocking the plate as she ran for home. Casey could slide and risk tearing up her skin or she could plow into her and knock her out of the way. She decided to take this big mamoo out, lowered her shoulder, and aimed right for her. Just then, the ball sailed past her head into the catcher's glove in front of her. The catcher slipped on the dirt reaching for her, then Casey hurdled right over the top of the catcher and landed on home plate. Her whole team rushed up to her, shouting and throwing their arms around her.

"A game-winning grand slam. Not bad, Casey. I knew you could do it," Kathryn said. Casey was beaming.

They decided to try a different place for dinner and drinks after their winning day. Casey wanted to go back to the Museum Club for more slow dancing with Kathryn, but maybe this place would have dancing too. The place they ended up had decent food but only a tiny dance floor and a woman was playing guitar as the entertainment. Kathryn intentionally sat next to her and she kept touching Casey's hand or her arm. She noticed every tiny gesture and felt herself becoming increasingly warm at this closeness. Her face was hot and flushed, and she felt like everyone could see right through her. *I need to get out of here for a minute or I'm going to burst.* "I'll be right back," she told Kathryn.

Stepping outside the bar into the cool night air, Casey tried to collect herself. She walked around the block trying to decide what to do. She knew what she wanted to do. She wanted to kiss Kathryn. Every time she looked at Kathryn's full mouth, she felt butterflies in her stomach. She was dying to feel those luscious lips with her own. She wanted to kiss them for a very long time. She stopped walking. She sensed Kathryn standing behind her. Casey turned to look at her. "Are you okay, Casey? I was starting to worry about you."

"You were?"

"Yes, I was. Is anything the matter? Please tell me." Kathryn took Casey's hands in hers and looked deep into her eyes.

Casey's pulse pounded in her ears. Her eyes locked on to Kathryn's. She loosened her hands from Kathryn's and moved them to gently hold her face. She leaned in to kiss those irresistible lips. Kathryn looked a little surprised but didn't move to stop her. Their lips touched lightly at first, then again, then more fervently. *Her lips feel like warm velvet. I have to have more.*

Casey pulled Kathryn's body close to hers and pressed her mouth more firmly to Kathryn's. She heard a little moan emerge from Kathryn's throat as she deepened their kiss. Kathryn's arms slid around Casey's back, and she pressed her breasts into Casey's belly. Casey's heart was soaring as she devoured Kathryn's lips. She wanted to kiss her for forever. Kathryn started to pull away. Her lips looked a little swollen and she was breathing hard. "Casey, we have to stop."

"Why? I want you so much right now." Casey was confused. Kathryn had kissed her back with the same fervor and now she'd abruptly ended it.

"This can't happen because you're a student and I'm an IP. I'm sorry. I shouldn't have led you on. I have to go." With that finality, Kathryn turned and left Casey standing there dumbfounded.

❖

Kathryn got into the other SUV for the ride back to the motel. She couldn't face Casey right now. *Oh, my God. What have I done?* She was a complete jumble of emotions. It was so amazing to kiss Casey like that. She tasted Casey on her lips and craved more. But this was disaster looming, and she couldn't even explain it to her.

She remembered the incident when she was a flight commander and one of her IPs, a married man with a baby at home, got into a relationship with a female student pilot. She'd just gotten him promoted to be a squadron check pilot, and the woman student had moved on to the T-38 squadron when the scandal broke. He was fired from check section, shipped off to another training base, and given official disciplinary action in his permanent records.

They couldn't kick the woman student pilot out of training because she had passed all her check rides, but they made her life a living hell and gave her the worst assignment in the class when she graduated. Her flying career was effectively over before it had even started.

Kathryn caught the wrath of the wing commander when he had her standing in a brace position before his desk screaming at her because she hadn't known anything about it at the time. Thankfully, he was gone now or she'd never have been promoted to chief of flight safety. No, she could never endanger Casey or her future flying career with a forbidden romantic liaison. She cared about her too much to risk it. Not to mention the fact that they'd both be dishonorably discharged, never fly again, and have both their lives ruined by the Air Force for being gay.

When they got back to the motel, Kathryn avoided contact with Casey and immediately went to bed. Her mind was spinning as she remembered the taste of Casey on her lips and the feel of Casey's strong body pressed into hers. Why had she let Casey kiss her? She'd never felt any kind of attraction to any woman student pilot before. What was it about Casey that she couldn't resist? It was those eyes. Those piercing blue eyes from the first time she'd seen them. Eyes filled with intelligence, intensity, and a hunger to learn to fly that Kathryn had never seen before.

There was something else about her, and now Kathryn knew what it was. Casey always carried herself with confidence and poise in the flight room, but she was also friendly and outgoing with the women on the softball team. The quality that Kathryn had discovered tonight was Casey's passion—her passion for life, for flying, and for love. It was as if Kathryn had touched a live electrical wire when her lips touched Casey's and now she wanted more, but it could never happen. Kathryn drifted off into fitful sleep mourning a loss that could never be.

❖

The next morning they were all sore and sluggish from the previous two days of nonstop softball and partying. They barely won their first game, then lost in the semifinals of the tournament. Casey's hitting was off and Kathryn missed an easy out. They were subdued on the drive back to Phoenix. Casey rode in the Mormon Assault Vehicle while Kathryn and Barb rode in her SUV. Kathryn wanted to talk to Barb about what had happened with Casey, but she couldn't bring it up with other people in the car. Maybe she could talk to Barb when they got home. Barb was her closest friend and they had been through a lot together, including Marie's death. Kathryn worried that Barb would give her hell for letting it go as far as it had with Casey. What a giant mess.

CHAPTER TWENTY-FIVE

September 1992

Casey couldn't permit herself to think about the events of the weekend in Flagstaff with Kathryn. She was starting the T-38 phase of pilot training in two days, and she had to focus her attention and energy on preparing for that.

Flying the supersonic T-38, the "White Rocket," had been her life's dream for as long as she could remember. Studying her flight manual, Casey continued to be impressed at what this jet could do. It was twice the size of a T-37 and twice as fast. It had afterburners on the engines and cruised at over four hundred knots. It was newer than the T-37 and had more advanced instruments. Casey couldn't wait to get her hands on this plane. She could not lose sight of the goal of her life for an attraction to a woman, any woman, even if that woman was Kathryn.

Despite her efforts to not think about her, Casey kept hearing Kathryn's voice in her head. As she was making her flash cards to learn the T-38 emergency procedures and operations limits, she heard Kathryn saying, "All knowledge can be divided into three areas: either need to know, nice to know, or nits." Kathryn had taught her how to study, to prioritize, and to learn a new airplane.

She wanted to talk to Trish and Rhonda about everything that had happened with Kathryn in Flagstaff, but she couldn't bear recounting the story of Kathryn's rejection. It was too sad and pathetic.

❖

Casey arrived early to the T-38 squadron building. There were eight flights instead of the six in the T-37 squadron, and the building looked similar but slightly different from the Tweet squadron. The main hallway was darker and it smelled a little like a men's locker room. The pilots returning from their flights wore G-suits, also known as "go fast pants." They were olive drab, worn over the legs of the flight suit like cowboy chaps, and the guys loved to swagger in them. Casey wondered what they felt like when you were wearing them in the plane.

She glanced into the flight room of Tipper Flight. Their flight patch was a Playboy bunny drinking out of a champagne glass, and there was a giant mural of a naked woman's silhouette along an entire wall. Casey found it tasteless and offensive and was grateful she wasn't in that flight. The overall impression of the T-38 squadron was one of macho men, wannabe fighter pilots strutting about like roosters with excess testosterone. It didn't matter. Casey would do whatever it took to pass this phase of training, and she would not be intimidated by anyone.

Casey was assigned to Gombey Flight and looked for her name on the big schedule board to see who her IP would be. She said a silent prayer that she would get a good instructor this time. Her IPs last name was Pruitt and she looked for his table in the room but didn't find it. "Tompkins?" the head scheduler asked her.

"Yes, sir," Casey answered.

"Your instructor is a guest help IP, Major Pruitt, and you can sit at my table."

"Thanks," she replied. Her tablemate was Tom Jenkins, a guy she didn't know very well, but he was a captain like her and a former navigator.

"Hi, Casey, good to see you again," Tom said as he extended his hand.

"Hi, Tom, good to see you."

The first day was all briefing items and life support checks where Casey got fitted for her G-suit. It was a very tight lower body suit with air bladders against her stomach, thighs and calves. The air bladders inflated automatically when you pulled Gs to improve your G tolerance.

The life support technician told her, "This will not prevent you from blacking out. It only gives you another two Gs of resistance. The most important thing about this G-suit is that when you feel it squeeze your legs, that will tell you when you are pulling Gs, and to get on your anti-G straining maneuver and then you won't black out." *What a revelation.*

Casey saw her name on the schedule board with her new instructor pilot, Major Pruitt, for her first sim ride. Casey had learned all her prefight checklist flows and felt prepared but also nervous.

"Hi, y'all! Where's my next victim?" The whole flight turned to see who was making the loud entrance. A short, stocky, bald-headed man with a neck as thick as his head strolled into the flight room. He had a giant grin on his face and was wearing a worn, faded flight suit. His name tag read "Pruitt."

"Oh, no," Casey muttered. She stood up to greet him.

"You must be Casey. Glad to meet you. Sit down, sit down," he said with a Southern drawl as thick as molasses. He reached out to shake her hand.

"Nice to meet you, sir." His hand was rough and sturdy like he'd just walked off the plantation.

"Oh, Jesus, don't be calling me 'sir.' Just call me Bulldog. Get out your notepad and write down everything I say."

He gave her exact pitch attitudes, airspeeds, and power settings for the initial maneuvers. It reminded her of the way Kathryn instructed, very succinct and precise.

"All right, missy, let's get out there and slip some simulated surlies."

"Okay, Bulldog." *How the hell did I end up with this redneck old fucker as my IP?* At least he would be sitting behind her in the rear seat instead of next to her when he yelled at her.

The wall of cool air-conditioning in the sim building was a welcome escape from the Arizona summer heat. The first thing Casey noticed when she climbed into the front seat of the T-38 sim was how compact this plane felt. It was like a hot little sports car. The instruments were newer and the attitude indicator was huge compared to the meatball-sized one in the T-37.

Bulldog stood next to her on the sim platform. "Show me your preflight setup."

Casey smoothly went through the tests and checks of the instruments.

"Well, somebody's been practicing. Now do an engine start."

Casey knew the engine start procedures and she announced the start parameters as the engines came to life.

"Very nice, missy." He had a teasing, good ol' boy tone in his voice.

"This little bugger up on top of the glare shield is the most important difference between a Tweet and a T-38. It's the AOA indicator, and why do we care about this?"

"That's the angle of attack display. It shows when you are flying near the stall speed."

"Correct. But I like to call this the life-or-death-o-meter. You need to keep this bad boy in the green donut or you will stall the jet. I'll hop in the backseat and we're going to have some fun."

Casey was excited but a little apprehensive as she closed the canopy and realized she was by herself in the front seat.

"Casey, can you hear me?" Bulldog said over the flight intercom.

"Yes, sir, I've got you loud and clear." He had a smooth baritone voice, and hearing his disembodied words felt like God was talking to her.

"You're loud and clear also. I'm going to show you the first takeoff, then have you try one. You have to hold the brakes hard to keep from moving during the engine run-up because this little sweetheart wants to get in the air. Push the throttles up to mil power, check the engine gauges, then push the throttles over the hump into max afterburner power, check for two good nozzle swings, this confirms the burners are lit, release brakes, and hang on."

The sim leapt forward with a lurch as Casey watched the speed rapidly increase. "Speed one hundred thirty-five, rotate to five degrees nose up, and we lift off at one sixty. Safely airborne, gear up, flaps up immediately, and accelerate to three hundred knots." Everything happened so fast Casey was mentally still on the runway as they climbed through ten thousand feet at four hundred knots. *Crap, I'm so behind this jet!*

"Casey, you take her and fly around a little. Hold your speed at four hundred knots and your altitude at fifteen thousand feet."

"My jet." Casey was all over the sky with wild speed and altitude fluctuations. The stick was super sensitive and she couldn't get the airplane under control.

"Whoa, Nelly, my jet," Bulldog said. "This baby is very touchy. Don't try to move the stick, just *think* about putting a tiny bit of pressure on it. Try it again."

Casey tried again by holding the stick lightly with her fingertips and got slightly better. She remembered the exercise Kathryn had her do of holding a pencil in her hand to prevent a death grip on the stick. She tried some turns.

"Just drag that big pitot tube right across the horizon to make a level turn. It's easier than in the Tweet because you're sitting on the centerline of the jet. Try a ninety-degree bank turn."

Casey did more turns like he instructed, and she nailed her altitude. *Sweet!*

Back in the flight room, Casey wrote down everything she'd seen, and her first sim in the White Rocket hadn't been great, but it wasn't awful either.

"Overall grade, Good. You know your stuff, missy. Keep it up. Me and the boss are having a barbecue at the house this Saturday at 1600 hours. You *will* be there. This is a mandatory social event. Here's the directions." He handed her a scribbled note.

❖

Casey abhorred these Air Force social activities. She always felt so awkward. The men would be outside talking with their hands about flying and the wives would be in the kitchen talking about babies and spit-up. She didn't feel particularly welcome in either group. She usually had to fortify herself with several belts of liquid courage before she could even walk through the door. She drove over to Bulldog's house on base and saw Kathryn's bright red Mustang convertible. *Great, now it will be even more uncomfortable.*

When she walked in, she was assaulted with the blaring sound of country music and she recognized both the T-37 and T-38 squadron commanders, many of the flight commanders, lots of IPs, and the wing commander. This was a who's who of all the pilots at Willie.

"Casey, I want you to meet the Boss." Bulldog grabbed her arm and led her into the kitchen.

"Hon, this is my new stud, Casey."

"Hi, Casey, welcome. I'm Merrilee, you know, like in 'roll along.' We're so glad you could join us." She was the epitome of Southern charm with long, dark hair teased so high it almost touched the top of the doorway. Her Southern drawl felt like warm honey.

"Casey, this here's our boy, Chester Junior. Chester, darling, meet Daddy's new student," Merrilee said.

"Hello," he said in a tiny voice. He was about nine with the moon face of a child with Down syndrome.

Casey felt her presence behind her before she saw her.

"Oh, Kathryn, there you are. Will you set these salads on the table, hon?" Merrilee asked.

"Sure thing, Merrilee. These look delicious," Kathryn answered. She exchanged a hot glance with Casey as she carried the food. Casey helped with the food and brushed her elbow against Kathryn's arm as they set them on the table.

"Hi, how are you?" Casey asked.

"I'm good. How about you?"

"I'm okay, a little overwhelmed with the T-38, but overall, good."

"I'm glad to hear that. Everyone is overwhelmed with the T-38 at first, but Bulldog is a great IP."

"Really? I'm not sure what to make of him. Rednecks from the South are not usually the kind of people I like to hang around with."

"Don't let the Southern accent fool you, Casey. He's one of the best pilots you'll ever fly with. Check out his office down the hall."

Casey glanced around to make sure no one noticed her as she slipped down the hall to the office. She peeked in and saw walls covered with plaques, diplomas, certificates, and awards: Top Graduate-Fighter Weapons School, Distinguished Graduate F-16 Qualification Course, magna cum laude from MIT, T-38 Instructor Pilot of the Year, USAF Test Pilot School. *This guy is no slouch.*

Casey noticed Kathryn sitting with the T-37 squadron commander, two flight commanders, and Bulldog. It seemed like Kathryn was avoiding her on purpose. She also saw her former IP, Lieutenant Carter, sitting with another guy. She didn't know who he was, but she felt an instant dislike for him. He had greasy hair, pockmarked skin, and a sneer on his face. The two of them were laughing and pointing at Kathryn. She wanted to punch him in the face. She went over to sit with some other T-38 student pilots.

"So you're Bulldog's new stud?" one of the guys asked her.

"Yes, I'm Casey. Just started this week. Are you his students?" she asked.

"I'm Jeff, I'm in Shatsi. This is Carlo, he's in Beer Can, and this is Ed, he's in Boysan. We're all at different phases in training. Carlo graduates in two weeks. He's got an F-15 to Kadena, Japan."

"Congrats, Carlo. You must be glad that you're almost done with training."

"I'm having fun right now. All my check rides are done and Bulldog has been showing me some fighter maneuvers. You won't believe what they can do in this jet at Fighter Lead-In Training. I can't wait," Carlo answered.

Casey felt a twinge of jealousy because women were not allowed to fly a fighter aircraft. She wanted to make a comment about women being discriminated against but decided to keep her thoughts to herself. "So how do you like Bulldog as an IP?"

"He's the best," they answered in unison. *That's quite an endorsement.*

Casey rose to thank her hosts and was hoping to get a chance to talk to Kathryn. "Merrilee, thank you so much for dinner. It was all delicious. I need to get home and study, so I will say good night."

"Casey, you are so welcome. I'm happy to have met you. You just come on over anytime you want to. You are always welcome here." Merrilee was sincere, and her warmth gave Casey a lump in her throat.

❖

As the party started to break up, Kathryn pulled Bulldog aside. "How's she doing so far?"

"Well, Kath, it's still early, but so far, she's okay. She knows her stuff, but we'll just have to see if she can accelerate her brain to keep up with the T-38. I'll keep you in the loop. If she starts to have problems, you'll be the second to know. She'll be the first to know when I kick her ass!"

"Thanks, Bulldog, I appreciate it."

"Anything for you, darlin'. Why are you so interested in this one? I know you like to help out all the gals, but what's up with Casey?"

"I don't know, really. There's just something special about her. I think she's a natural pilot, and you know as well as I do how very rare those are."

"That I do know, Kath. I'll do my best with her, as always. I better go help the Boss clean up. Thanks for coming. It's always great to see you."

"Thanks, Bulldog, it was fabulous, as always. Good night." Kathryn genuinely enjoyed spending time with their family. They always made her feel at home.

She walked to her car feeling conflicted about Casey. She wanted to see her, and she was as gorgeous as ever, but her attraction to Casey was so dangerous for both of them. All it took was just the suspicion of being gay to destroy your life in the Air Force. At least she'd arranged for Casey to have the best chance to succeed by getting her the best IP in the squadron. She was startled by a figure stepping out of the dark toward her. Casey.

"Kathryn, I need to talk to you."

"Casey, you scared the crap out of me. We can't talk here. We'll be seen by someone. Drive over to the bleachers at the softball field. I'll meet you over there."

"All right, I'll be there in five minutes."

Kathryn was dreading this conversation with Casey. She knew what Casey was going to say, and there was no way to avoid hurting her. None of the possible outcomes was good.

Casey was sitting in the dark on the first row of the bleachers.

"Are you avoiding me, Kathryn? Why?"

"No, it's just that we are under constant scrutiny, and you and I can't be seen together. I'm sorry, Casey."

Casey reached over and took Kathryn's hand in hers. It was as warm and soft as she remembered. "I need to talk to you about what happened in Flagstaff."

"Casey, there's nothing to talk about. I already told you there can't be anything between us because you are a student and I'm an IP."

"I need to know if you feel anything for me. I understand how the Air Force works. I've been around for four years and I've had friends kicked out for being gay. I've seen the witch hunts and I know how to be discreet. But I felt a real connection with you when we were in Flagstaff, and I need to know if you feel anything for me, or was it just my wishful thinking. Please tell me the truth."

Kathryn paused for a long moment. She had a choice to make. She could tell Casey that she felt nothing for her and that would be the end of it. They would go their separate ways. But that would be a lie, and for some reason she couldn't bring herself to lie to Casey—not now, not ever.

"I felt a connection too, Casey. It's just that we can't do anything about it."

Casey squeezed her hand a little tighter. "I understand that. You need to know that I'm willing to wait. I'll wait until I've graduated from pilot training, then we can decide what to do. But can I see you on the weekends, away from this place?"

"No." Kathryn's heart hurt to say that.

She stood up to leave when Casey gently pulled her down to place a soft kiss on her lips. Kathryn tasted the salt of a tear on Casey's lips.

CHAPTER TWENTY-SIX

T-38 training seemed to go as fast as this jet did. Casey progressed rapidly through her simulator rides and was scheduled for her first flight. She was getting used to Bulldog's instructional style and could generally understand his Southern accent. She put on her tight G-suit for the first time and was giddy with excitement.

She walked across the ramp with Bulldog toward their jet and she didn't even try to hide her big grin. This was where she had wanted to be her whole life. The T-38 was much bigger than a Tweet and higher off the ground. She had to climb a ladder to get into the cockpit.

Bulldog climbed into the backseat and checked in with her over the flight intercom. "Pull those lap belt and shoulder harness straps as tight as you can because we're going to pull some serious Gs today, missy. Make sure you connect up your G-suit hose."

"Yes, sir, got it," Casey answered.

She quickly went through her preflight checks and gave the engine start hand signal to the crew chief. These engines sounded different from the high-pitched whine of the Tweet. They weren't as loud, but she felt a low, powerful rumble flow through her entire body as the engines came to life.

"Okay, Casey, my jet. I'm going to demo the first takeoff and I want you to pay attention to the airspeed indicator and the pitch attitude when I rotate. Let's lower our canopies."

She closed the clear canopy and checked that it was locked. The visibility from this jet was tremendous as she looked all around. She could see everywhere without an instructor pilot sitting next to her blocking her view.

Bulldog lined up on the runway. Casey put her hands lightly on the stick and throttles like she had done with Kathryn so she could feel how he was moving the controls.

"I'm holding the brakes real hard so she don't creep forward during the engine run-up. Throttles to military power, check engines good, then push them up over the hump into full afterburner, check two good nozzle swings, release brakes, and hold on."

Casey's head snapped back hard against the head support as the jet jumped forward down the runway. The airspeed was increasing so quickly it was almost a blur.

"Speed one thirty-five, rotate, safely airborne, gear up, flaps up, accelerate to three hundred knots," Bulldog said. It was all happening so fast, her head was spinning. The nickname "White Rocket" was an understatement. "Okay, Casey, your jet." She felt him shake the stick to indicate she was flying now.

The control stick was way more sensitive than the Tweet. She was flailing across the sky.

"Small pressures on the stick, missy. Try to just *think* about moving it."

Casey realized she'd been hyperventilating during the whole takeoff. She consciously slowed her breathing and moved her hand so that just her fingertips were holding the stick. Her huge pitch oscillations started to dampen out and she was feeling marginally in control of this racing beast. She was concentrating so hard on not over-controlling the jet that she was missing every radio call and had no idea where she was.

Bulldog made the radio calls for her and took the jet as they entered the practice area. The T-38 practice areas were much larger than the T-37 ones, and Casey had studied her map to learn the ground references. Once she was in the area, it felt like it was the size of a postage stamp because of how fast they were going.

"Stalls in this jet feel a lot different than they did in the Tweet. The light stall feels like mice are jumping up and down on the wings. You will get comfortable with this because this is where we get max performance and you're going to feel this in the final turn on the landings. The medium stall feels like there are jackrabbits jumping on the wings, and the full stall feels like elephants are pounding on the wings." Casey was quite alarmed at how violent the full stall was. It seemed like the wings could break off. Bulldog had her fly around the practice area to get the feel of the jet, then they headed back to the base for landing practice.

"My jet, Ace. I'm going to demo the first landing." He flew three hundred knots approaching the runway, yanked the plane into a ninety-degree banked turn, pulled four Gs, and ripped the throttles to idle. As the airspeed came down to two hundred and forty knots, he put the landing gear down, then the flaps, then it looked like he was pointing the nose of the jet straight at the ground. The windscreen was three-quarters dirt and one-quarter sky, speed one hundred seventy knots, and a two thousand feet per minute descent rate. Casey felt a slight shudder in the aircraft all through the final turn. "This is the mice jumping on the wings, max performance sensation. You have to pull that nose around the final turn. We're on the edge of a stall, but I keep that AOA right in the green donut." It looked like he would land short of the runway, but then he brought the nose up to the landing attitude and touched down right on the numbers.

"Okay, Casey, your turn."

"Yes, sir, my jet." She felt clueless but tried her best to copy exactly what he had done. Her traffic pattern spacing looked sort of close to the runway, and everything was happening so fast she had to pull the power to idle. She got the gear down, the flaps down, and started her turn to final. She could feel his hand on the stick as she flew the final turn. "Don't get slow, Casey. Get the power in. More power. Burners, NOW! My jet!"

Bulldog slammed the throttles into full afterburner, but the jet was still descending toward the ground. The angle of attack indicator showed a red stall chevron. *Crap, this is bad!* The airplane shuddered into the elephants jumping on the wings heavy stall. They were sinking fast toward the ground and Bulldog was swearing furiously. *Oh my God, are we going to crash?* Just as they were about to hit the runway hard, she felt the afterburners kick in. The plane went into a series of violent wing rocks as they bounced down the runway with one main wheel, then the opposite wheel banging hard onto the pavement. It seemed like an eternity before the jet finally started to accelerate and climb away from the ground.

"Shit, that was a close one, missy! You remember when I told you this jet was a snake in the final turn?"

"Yes, I do."

"Well, we just about got bit by it big-time. That's what's known as being behind the power curve. You can't get slow in the final turn with the power at idle. That wasn't your fault, Casey, it was mine. I should have intervened sooner. I'm glad you got to see that even though I lost a little more hair because of it," he said, laughing.

We almost pancaked into the ground and this old redneck thinks it's funny? I'd almost rather have Carter screaming at me. Casey missed flying with Kathryn big-time.

She was still shaken from her first near crash landing and would not make that mistake ever again. He gave her the jet and she flew another pattern as precisely as she could, adding the AOA green donut to her cross-check. Her landing was very firm, but it was a lot better than her first attempt.

After they put their parachutes, G-suits, and helmets away, Casey took a little break in the refuge of the women's restroom. She had to admit the flight had scared her. Could she ever hope to keep up with this jet? Could she cut it, or would she get washed out like so many others?

She returned to the Gombey flight room and was surprised to see Bulldog laughing as he told everyone the story of their near-death experience.

"I almost crapped my pants waiting for those goddamn burners to light! Then we were doing the T-38 saber dance almost the full length of the fuckin' runway! I'm getting too old for this shit. These studs are going to turn my hair gray. Oh wait, I don't got no hair!" The entire flight howled with laughter. "Casey, there you are. Come on and sit down, missy. Let's debrief this ride."

She sat down and dutifully got out her notepad before he busted her on this disastrous ride.

"Well, you saw a lot of stuff today. You understand the difference in the stall characteristics? You'll get used to max performing the jet right on the edge of a stall. That's what a fighter pilot has to do all the time. You saw a final turn stall today. It's a real eye-opener, ain't it? Now you know why we never let that AOA get into the red. Your last landing wasn't too horrible. Just remember, this jet has a very small margin of error, so don't take your eyes off her for a second in the final turn. Got any more questions for me?"

"No, sir."

"All right then. Overall grade, Good." He stood and left the flight room.

Casey was stunned. She fully expected him to fail her on this ride. She looked at her grade sheet and saw that every maneuver was graded U except for preflight procedures and systems knowledge. *I guess this means I officially cheated death once again and am here for one more day. I need a drink, or several of them.*

❖

Kathryn had arranged a safety visit to the runway supervisory unit when she knew Casey would be returning to the traffic pattern from her first flight with Bulldog. She felt a surge of pride when she heard Casey's strong voice over the RSU radio. This quickly turned into concern, then downright fear when she saw Casey get slow in the final turn. Bulldog yelled on the radio, "Going around!" with a higher than usual pitch in his voice as the T-38 was sinking toward the ground. She saw the focused blue flames behind the engines as the afterburners lit, then looked on with horror as the plane went through a severe wing rock banging the main landing gear from side to side as it careened down the length of the runway. The IP controller reached for the red phone to call crash fire rescue just as Bulldog got the jet under control and they lifted off. She had been holding her breath throughout the ordeal. The controller put the red phone down. "Goddamned new class!"

She sat in the flight safety truck trying to compose herself. The whole thing had happened in an instant and she'd felt so completely helpless. She fought lingering nausea from the sickening fear of almost seeing a plane crash. She was having a flashback to the sight of the black column of smoke from Marie's deadly crash so many years ago. Her eyes burned with tears as the smell of burning fuel and flesh and the sound of roaring fire assaulted her memory once again. *It's not her. She's not Marie. Casey's okay now.* She kept repeating this mantra until the pain subsided.

I don't know if I can handle this.

Despite her rejection of Casey, she hadn't been able to stop thinking about her. She'd done everything in her power to try to help Casey. She'd called in all her favors with Bulldog to persuade him to take her on as a new student. She'd made sure Casey got the best T-38 IP on the whole base. She'd stolen glances at Casey's grade book when she made her squadron inspection rounds, and she watched the Gombey schedule board to make sure Casey didn't get overlooked. Now that Casey was flying the plane, Kathryn just happened to be in the RSU watching her fly in the traffic pattern. Hell, she was stalking her, plain and simple.

She'd sufficiently calmed herself down so she could drive the truck back to her office. She had to have faith that Bulldog would keep Casey safe and that she would start to figure out how to keep up with and fly the T-38. Casey was smart and hardworking. She showed more ability and promise than any student Kathryn had ever taught. She had to admit to herself—she missed flying with Casey.

She also missed touching Casey, and she really missed kissing her. She had no resistance at all when she went to bed at night. Her mind and her body ached for Casey, and she'd even started fantasizing about a future life with her. These thoughts usually only ended up making her feel sad and alone. Casey would never give her a second chance after the way she'd rejected her. She could only hope that someday Casey would understand why she'd done what she had to do to protect them both.

For now, she had to be satisfied with watching her from afar. She was confident that Casey could learn to fly the T-38, but no one was ever sure a student could get through this program until they walked across the stage on the last day and got their wings. Kathryn would just have to get a few more gray hairs watching her get there.

CHAPTER TWENTY-SEVEN

Casey was still shaken from her near crash on her first T-38 ride. She wanted to call Kathryn and talk to her about it, but she knew Kathryn didn't want to hear from her. Even though Kathryn had hurt her, Casey couldn't be angry with her. She understood the danger to both of their careers if anyone found out they were gay, but that didn't stop her from wanting to see Kathryn and to talk to her.

When she walked into her quarters, she heard the phone ringing.

"Casey, it's Tiny. I've got something important to tell you!"

Tiny was a dental tech and the left fielder on the base softball team. She had a part-time job as a barback at the O Club. Casey was surprised to hear from her at this hour.

"What's up, Tiny?"

"It's about Captain Hardesty. There are these two pilots talking about her at the bar, and it doesn't sound good." Tiny whispered into the phone like she didn't want to be overheard.

"Tiny, please tell me exactly what they said." Casey was getting worried.

"Well, they've both been drinking a lot, and the big one said to the other pilot that he couldn't wait to bust that little dyke on her check ride tomorrow. He mentioned her by name and he was bragging that there was no way she'd pass her ride with him as the check pilot. Then the other one said he couldn't wait to see her go down in flames after she'd made him look bad. They both laughed like it was real funny and the big one said one other thing too. He said he was finally going to get his revenge on her. I'm scared for her, Casey."

"Oh my God, Tiny, I have to warn her. Can you do me one more favor? Can you tell me what they look like and what their name tags say, and I need to know what the patch on their right sleeve looks like."

"Okay, I'll be right back." Casey heard Tiny's voice in the background.

"The big one's name is Grant, and he's got bad teeth, greasy hair, and pockmarked skin. The other one's name is Carter, and he's skinny with dark hair. The big one, Grant, has a black patch with silver writing on it. The other one has the boxing bunny on his patch. I hope that helps, Casey."

"You're a gem, Tiny. I owe you big-time. Thanks."

Crap. That was the guy she saw with Carter at Bulldog's party, the one that was sneering at Kathryn. She knew Carter didn't like Kathryn because she had soloed the T-37 with her instead of him. She'd also heard a rumor that Kathryn's safety report about Mike's death was the reason Carter had to go through IP retraining, but she never suspected he would try to ruin her career. That guy, Grant, was an evaluator pilot, the ones who give the IPs their check rides.

Casey reached for the phone to call Kathryn and warn her, but she stopped herself in mid-dial. *What if this phone is bugged?* No, she couldn't risk that. She thought of calling Captain Arnau since she knew they were close friends, but she had the same problem with the phone. No, her only course of action was to drive over to Kathryn's house to warn her in person and just hope that no one from the base saw her. She grabbed her keys and ran to her car. She drove very carefully leaving the base, then she sped up once she got onto Williams Field Road. She'd memorized Kathryn's home address some time ago and knew right where she was going since she'd driven past her house several times. Okay, so stalking wasn't always a bad idea.

Kathryn's street was quiet since it was 2100 hours, and she saw a light on inside the house. Casey checked her mirrors to make sure no one could see her as she walked up to the front door with butterflies in her stomach. She rang the doorbell. She was worried about Kathryn's reaction when she saw her at her front door.

Kathryn opened the front door, saw Casey, momentarily looked stunned, then grabbed her sleeve and yanked her into the house.

"Casey, what are you doing here? I thought we were very clear on everything."

"I'm not here to talk about us. I'm here to warn you. Are you supposed to have a check ride tomorrow?"

"Yes. I'm scheduled for my annual instrument check at 0900 hours. How do you know that?"

"Is your check pilot a guy named Grant?" Casey asked.

"No, I'm supposed to have Glenn Samuels as my check pilot. What's going on, Casey?"

"Kathryn, you're being set up. Tiny works as a barback at the O Club and she overheard two pilots, Carter and Grant from stan/eval, talking about busting you on your check ride tomorrow. They're going to make sure you don't pass. That's why I had to come over and warn you. I hope you're not mad at me."

"Shit, those fucking assholes. Come in and sit down. I need to make a phone call to scheduling."

Casey watched Kathryn as she called the base. She looked around Kathryn's home and took it all in. Everything was neat and tidy, as she would have expected, but the furnishings were also tasteful and warm. It was a very nice home that looked comfortable and calm. Casey felt a little awkward being in Kathryn's home uninvited.

"Sergeant Anderson, this is Captain Hardesty. Can you tell me if there was a change to the schedule for my instrument check ride tomorrow? There was? What time did that happen and who called in this change? Okay, I got it. Do me a favor and put a hold on that aircraft. There's a possibility that the sortie may not go tomorrow. Thanks, Sergeant. Good night." Kathryn hung up the phone.

"That piece-of-crap motherfucker. He had scheduling switch check pilots from Samuels to him at 1800 hours, after everyone else had gone home, so I wouldn't find out. If I could shoot him in the head with my forty-five, I would."

"What's going on, Kathryn? Why is this guy trying to bust you on your check ride?"

"It's a long story, Casey. Bailey Grant has a grudge against me because I made him look bad when we were both T-37 flight commanders. My flight consistently performed better than his. I'm not surprised he's colluding with Carter to try to take me out. He's one of those macho men who doesn't think women should be flying Air Force jets. He's also a sleazy chauvinist pig who makes comments about women's bodies and who cheats on his little Christian wife. He's a dirtbag who's advanced his career by brownnosing the bosses instead of working hard to be a good pilot. He's a fucking creep and he picked the wrong dyke to fuck with."

"What are you going to do?" Casey asked.

"I'm not sure yet, but I'm certainly not going to fly with him tomorrow."

"Please be careful. I'd hate to see this guy damage your career."

"I'll be okay. Thank you for warning me, and please thank Tiny for me too. You should probably get back home. You're on early week and you should get some rest."

Kathryn came over to her and gave her a hug. Casey wanted the hug to linger, but she knew she couldn't. She broke contact and reached for the door.

"I'll see you around, Kathryn. Good night."

"'Night, Casey, and thanks again for looking out for me."

"Any time."

❖

Casey was in her seat in the Gombey flight room at 0325 hours waiting for the morning briefing. She hadn't slept much the night before worrying about Kathryn. She was grateful she wasn't scheduled to fly that day and was looking forward to being the flight room phone person so she could get caught up on studying for her advanced aerodynamics test. She had to wait for the flight room to clear out as everyone went out to fly so she could call her friend in the T-37 squadron.

"Ninety-sixth flight operations, Sergeant Henderson speaking, may I help you, sir?"

"Hi, Nikki, it's Casey Tompkins, are you free to talk?"

"Stand by, sir, I need to switch to the other phone." After a short pause, Nikki came back on the line. "Casey, what's up?"

"I need to know what happened with Captain Hardesty's instrument check ride this morning. Can you fill me in?"

"Oh, girl, you missed quite a show! How do you know about this, anyway?"

"Tiny overheard something in the O Club bar last night. So what happened?"

"Let me close the door first. Well, Captain Grant from stan/eval showed up at the airplane sign-out desk at 0800 hours looking for Captain Hardesty. He had this big shit-eating grin on his ugly face and he made me call the safety office to check on where Captain Hardesty was. Just then, she strolls up to the desk with the chief of stan/eval, Major Lee. Captain Grant looked surprised at the sight of his boss, then pretends to act all friendly to Captain Hardesty. He said to her, 'Ready for your instrument check, Kathryn?' And she stands right up to him and says, 'No, I won't be flying with you today, or any day.' Just as he's about to say something to her, his boss, Major Lee, pulls him into the squadron commander's office for a little chat."

"Wow, then what happened?"

"Then Captain Hardesty starts to fill out the paperwork to sign out her jet for her check ride. I'm confused, so I ask her, 'Who will you be flying with today, ma'am?' and she says, 'Major Lee.' Just then, I see Captain Grant come storming out of the squadron commander's office with a big scowl on his face. He stomps out of the building and Major Lee comes back to the desk to get the tail number of their jet, then he and Captain Hardesty go out and fly."

"That's unbelievable. Well, I guess she showed him."

"That's not the best part, Casey. Guess what?" Nikki asked.

"What, what, tell me!"

"After their flight, Major Lee came back to the desk and wrote on the big 'Attaboy' board, you know the one right by the main door with all the promotions and awards on it, and he wrote, 'Outstanding Instrument Check Ride—Captain Hardesty.' Girl, it was sweet!"

"Damn, that's great news. Thanks so much, Nikki, that makes my day."

"Anytime, Casey. We miss you over here in the Tweet squadron. Talk to you later."

Casey was thrilled and relieved that Kathryn had turned the tables on that asshole, and got an "Outstanding" out of the whole deal, to boot. *I guess he learned his lesson on that one. Hopefully, he won't try to mess with any other women pilots again.*

Casey aced her test the next day, adding to her unbroken record of one hundred percent on all her academic tests. After her death-defying first flight, she'd gone to the learning center and watched films of T-38 patterns and landings over and over while she practiced her chair flying. She would not miss that angle of attack indicator again or get slow in the final turn. She was a little nervous before her next flight with Bulldog, but she felt better prepared this time.

Bulldog was relaxed and unconcerned as he always was during the briefing for her next flight. When she lined up on the runway for her first takeoff, she held the brakes as hard as she could and she ran the engines up to military power. She released the brakes and pushed the throttles up into afterburner. The jet leapt forward and her head snapped back against the headrest. *Shit! This thing is fast!* She lifted off and got the gear and flaps up immediately before she over-sped them. She was barely keeping up with the jet as she accelerated to three hundred knots. It was better than her first ride, but it was still like holding on to the tail of a racing cheetah. She'd been hyperventilating during the entire takeoff again and had to slow her breathing back to normal. At least she was able to make her radio calls on this ride.

She went through all her maneuvers in the postage stamp–sized practice area, including the stall series. The "jackrabbits" and "elephants" jumping up and down on the wings still felt disconcerting. Bulldog only had a few corrections for her, and he never once raised his voice at her. It was such a relief not to be screamed at all the time. They headed back to Willie to practice in the traffic pattern.

"Do you want me to demo another landing for you, Ace?" Bulldog asked.

"No, I'd like to try one myself this time."

"All right, Casey, just don't try and kill me again." He was only half joking.

The pattern was busy and she adjusted her spacing for the traffic. She sharply rolled into a ninety-degree banked turn, pulled hard on the stick, and was at four Gs. She rolled out parallel to the runway, put the gear down, then the flaps, made her radio call, set the power, and went right to her final turn pitch attitude—forty-five degrees of bank, three-quarters ground and one-quarter sky. She pulled on the stick until she felt the max performance "mice-jumping-on-the-wings" sensation, aimed short of the runway threshold, and verbalized her mantra: "Aim point, air speed, AOA." Bulldog wasn't saying anything. As she rolled out on final approach, she brought the nose up slightly, crossed the runway threshold, smoothly pulled the throttles to idle, and flared the jet. The plane impacted the runway firmly but not too hard.

"My jet, Casey. Catch your breath. That landing was much improved. I think you're starting to get the picture."

Casey flew three more touch-and-go landings, getting a little better with each one. By the time she did her full stop landing it felt like the lightbulb was starting to come on a little. When they got back to the flight room, Bulldog didn't have many debrief items for her.

"Well, Champ, I saw a lot of improvement today. You've obviously been practicing. Keep chair flying, and next ride we're going to work on the single engine and no flap patterns and landings. Overall grade, Excellent."

Casey was surprised he'd given her a grade of Excellent for the ride. She was learning that she could face her fear, keep her wits about her, and keep flying the jet in spite of it. She had the desire to pick up the phone and call Kathryn to tell her about her flight. She had taken it for granted that Kathryn would always be there to talk about flying. Now that she wasn't, there was a hollowness inside. It was hard to admit it, but she missed Kathryn—a lot.

Casey found herself glancing around the base when she was driving, looking for the blue flight safety pickup truck, and wondering what Kathryn was doing. She probably had another new student pilot, and Casey had a twinge of envy for this unknown student. One or two of the girls from the softball team had asked her out on dates but she couldn't bring herself to say yes. Even though she knew nothing could ever happen with Kathryn, the thought of going out with another woman made her feel like she was being unfaithful. It was silly and foolish to waste her time hoping Kathryn would change her mind, but Casey couldn't help the way she felt. More than anything, she wanted Kathryn to be proud of her. Maybe someday she would be.

CHAPTER TWENTY-EIGHT

October 1992

The next two weeks of pilot training seemed to race by as Casey was getting ready to solo the T-38 jet. She'd kept Kathryn out of her thoughts by keeping busy with studying, simulator rides, chair flying, and occasionally visiting with her friends Trish and Rhonda.

The solo flight in the T-38 was very different from in the Tweet. The IP didn't hop out of the jet, then let you fly solo. In the T-38, the student pilot just signed out the jet and went flying by herself. The T-38 solo was not limited to flying around the traffic pattern, instead you flew out to the practice area by yourself, then came back to the base for landings. There was no dunk tank to honor your accomplishment and it was not regarded as a very big deal. The student just went out flying solo. For Casey, it was still a very big deal.

Her flights with Bulldog continued to go well. He never raised his voice, but he was demanding. It amazed her how quickly she could learn when she wasn't being screamed at. She still hyperventilated on every takeoff, but she was starting to feel she could keep up with the jet—sort of. She could actually feel her mind accelerating with the jet. It was a strange but exciting sensation.

There was something else she noticed that made her feel good—the blue Air Force pickup truck from flight safety. On her last two flights, as she was in the run-up area next to the runway waiting to take off, she'd seen the blue pickup parked next to the RSU across from her on the other side of the runway. Maybe it wasn't flight safety doing an observation of the RSU operations, but maybe it was. It could have been a communications technician working on something, or maybe it was Kathryn watching her. It gave Casey a little thrill to think that maybe Kathryn was watching her from the RSU. The idea that Kathryn might be stalking her made her very happy. Even though she couldn't see Kathryn or talk to her, she still felt connected to her. During the rare moments when she wasn't thinking about pilot training, her mind always turned to Kathryn. Despite everything Kathryn had said, she still held on to hope that they could find a way to make things work out. It was frustrating, but it also made her happy to think about a possible future together.

Casey was preparing for her next flight, which she hoped would be her last flight before solo, when Bulldog made his usual loud entrance.

"All right, missy, what are we doing today? Dazzle me."

Casey tried not to laugh at him, but he loved being the center of attention.

"We'll go to the practice area, run through stalls, slow flight, acro, then come back to Willie for pattern work."

"Sounds good except I want you to do a pattern delay so you can practice heavyweight single engine and no flap landings, then we'll go out to the practice area. Let's go, Ace."

Casey looked for the blue pickup truck next to the RSU but didn't see it today. *Oh well, maybe next time.* Her heavyweight single engine landing and no flap landings were safe, but not great. After that, she flew out to the practice area and smoothly went through all her planned maneuvers. Bulldog was not saying a word to her today. He was trying to get her used to flying the jet solo with no one's voice in her ear. The traffic pattern was busy when she got back to Willie, but she handled it well and got in her touch-and-go landings.

"Make this one a full stop, Champ," Bulldog said.

Casey configured the jet for landing, felt the max performance shudder as she pulled the nose around the final turn, rolled out on final with the jet on her aim point, and she kept the green donut on the AOA throughout the final turn. She smoothly pulled the power to idle, flared, then heard the slight squeak of the tires as she touched down. She pulled the nose up with full back stick, with the main wheels still on the runway, to aero brake and slow the airplane, then lowered the nose to the runway at one hundred and twenty knots. She stepped on the top of the rudder pedals to slow down with the wheel brakes, then took the high speed taxiway near the end of the runway. She was pleased with her landing as she opened the canopy and taxied back to the ramp.

Back in the flight room, Bulldog grabbed her grade book, sat down, and said, "Well, missy, you ready to go up next time by yourself?"

"Yes, sir, I am."

"I agree, you're ready. I'm signing you off to fly solo. Tomorrow, I want you to go out there and do exactly what you did today minus the stalls. Come back to the traffic pattern with at least fifteen hundred pounds of gas so you can get in three or four good landings. Excellent ride today." He handed the grade sheet back to her. "Oh, and, Casey?"

"Yes, sir?"

"Have some fun out there tomorrow."

Casey smiled as she put her grade book away. Tomorrow she would solo the White Rocket. She couldn't wait.

❖

Kathryn stopped by the T-38 squadron to review a few grade books and to check the Gombey flight schedule board. She was glad to see Casey scheduled for her solo flight tomorrow. She'd seen improvement in Casey's landings from observing her at the RSU. Her frequent safety visits to the RSU were getting noticed. None of the IPs who worked as controllers in the RSU had made the connection between her visits and Casey's flight schedule yet, but she had gotten a few comments as to why she was dropping in on the RSU so much. She decided she would visit the main air traffic control tower instead of the RSU when Casey returned from the practice area on her solo flight.

She enjoyed watching Casey fly, and she loved hearing her voice on the radio. She sounded confident and she was showing some real heads-up thinking when she flew around the traffic pattern. Casey was doing as well as, or frequently better than, any student pilot she'd ever seen. Kathryn was starting to feel confident that Casey would make it through the T-38 and earn her wings. She still had lots to learn—low-level navigation, four-ship formation—but she was definitely showing promise.

Only one thing would make things better right now. If she and Casey didn't have to fear losing their careers and flying because the Air Force found out they were gay. Kathryn wished they could have the freedom to explore the possibility of a real relationship. She loved flying as an Air Force pilot, but having to hide and lie about who she was, was becoming a very heavy burden to bear. She'd always been able to handle the conflict of serving with honesty and integrity while having to lie about her personal life, but now she was questioning how long she could continue this charade. When she was a second lieutenant, having a female "roommate" was not unusual. But she would be up for promotion to major soon and she knew she'd be under even more scrutiny. She had her lesbian friends, and the secret Air Force underground of the softball team, but the price of always being on guard was damaging her spirit.

She might allow herself the luxury of calling Casey tomorrow to congratulate her on her solo flight. That wouldn't be seen as unusual between an IP and a former student. She hoped Casey would be glad to hear from her despite everything that had happened, and not happened, between them.

❖

Casey woke the next morning filled with excitement to fly her T-38 solo mission. She felt prepared and ready. She couldn't wait to fly the jet by herself. She reviewed the weather forecast and it was a perfect fall day in Arizona with light winds and crystal blue skies. She signed out her jet and got her solo briefing from the supervisor of flying.

With her helmet, parachute, and G-suit, she walked across the ramp to her jet with her head held high. The crew chief greeted her and followed her on the aircraft walk-around inspection. The jet looked perfect—tall, shining, and magnificent.

The engines fired up perfectly and she taxied out to the runway. She had a small twinge of disappointment at not seeing the flight safety blue pickup truck next to the RSU.

"AWOL 45 Solo, cleared for takeoff," the RSU said over the radio.

"Roger, AWOL 45 Solo, cleared for takeoff," Casey answered.

She advanced the throttles to mil power, both engines accelerated smoothly as they roared to full power, then she pushed the throttles into full afterburner, released the brakes, and her head again snapped back against the headrest as she shot down the runway. Once they were airborne, she turned the plane to fly to the practice area, calmed her breathing back to normal, and relished the quiet and the view. The only sound was the whine of the high-speed air around the jet and the powerful growl of the engines.

It was a spectacularly beautiful day to fly with puffy white clouds against the blue sky and colorful mountains in the distance. Albuquerque Center assigned her the Globe practice area, which was her favorite, since it was right over San Carlos Mountain. She went through her planned acrobatic maneuvers just as she'd visualized. She set up for her aileron roll and did six in a row—just for the fun of it. The jet rolled so fast she was laughing out loud. She checked her fuel. She wanted to get back to the traffic pattern with plenty of gas in case the pattern was busy.

"Albuquerque Center, AWOL 45 Solo, request clearance to Willie."

"AWOL 45 Solo, cleared right turn direct to Williams, descend and maintain flight level two-five-zero."

She turned the jet toward the arrival fix, and just as she reduced power for her descent, the red master warning light came on. She blinked her eyes and looked at the red light again. It was not an apparition, but instead a real warning light. *Fuck! What the hell is this?*

After a split second of disbelief, her training kicked in. "Maintain aircraft control," she said. The plane seemed to be flying all right at the moment. "Analyze the situation and take proper action." Casey looked down at the lower right side console by her leg, and the amber "Right Generator" light was on. She'd lost her right electrical generator, and the left system had not automatically picked up the electrical load as it was supposed to do.

"Refer to checklist." She opened up the emergency section of the checklist strapped to her thigh and found the procedure for "Loss of right generator with no crossover." She did the first step. "Attempt to reset the right generator by turning the red guarded switch off, then back on." It was no help. She read the next note. "Warning: only attempt one generator reset or there is a risk of electrical fire." She certainly didn't need a fire on top of this situation.

"Okay, what have I lost with no right generator?" Casey verbalized her thoughts just like she'd been taught to do. She could see her system review flash cards in her mind.

"I have no attitude indicator steering bars. Not a big problem. No engine anti-ice, I don't need it today. No pitch trim—crap, the plane is trimmed for three hundred knots and I can't change it, so the stick will be heavy as I slow for the landing. I can handle that. No right tank fuel boost pump, so I can't use the gas in the right tank. I have plenty of gas in the left tank, but I've lost the fuel cross-feed. That will make the right wing heavy and the jet will be hard to keep level. I can still manage that." This situation would be complicated but not impossible. Then she remembered the big system that she'd lost—the flaps. "Oh, fuck. A no flap landing." Things now just went from serious to a no-shit emergency.

Casey keyed her mike button. "Albuquerque Center, AWOL 45 Solo is declaring an emergency."

Now she had to think about the last step: "Land as soon as conditions permit."

"AWOL 45 Solo, state the nature of your emergency and what are your intentions?"

"Center, I've lost half my electrical system, I'd like one turn in holding so I can call the SOF, then I'd like vectors for a straight in approach to Willie."

"Approved as requested, AWOL 45 Solo. Cleared off frequency to call the SOF. Report back when ready."

Before Casey talked to the supervisor of flying, she needed to formulate a plan. She had two choices: she could eject from the plane, or make a no flap, full stop landing. If she ejected, she could get severely injured and she would lose the jet. No flap, full stop landings were prohibited because of the much higher touchdown speed, the excessive braking required to stop the plane, and the high probability of going off the end of the runway. She'd done exactly four practice no flap touch-and-go landings with Bulldog with a grade of Fair. She was in this jet alone, she was the pilot in command, and she had to make this decision. "I think I can land it."

A no flap landing would double her landing distance. She had to add twenty knots to her approach and touchdown speeds due to no flaps. She had to make a straight in approach to the longest runway, three-zero center. She would need every inch of that ten-thousand-foot runway to get this jet stopped. If she didn't stop on the runway, she would hit the arresting cable at the end. That should stop the plane before she went off the end of the runway into the ditch, but it would damage the landing gear. If she missed the arresting cable and the plane went off the end of the runway into the ditch, she would end up in a ball of fire.

❖

Kathryn was in the control tower watching the traffic pattern when she heard Casey's voice on the emergency frequency.

"SOF, this is AWOL 45 Solo emergency," Casey said calmly.

Oh, no. What's wrong?

"Go ahead, AWOL 45 Solo," the SOF answered.

"I've lost my right generator, run my checklist, and I plan to make a straight in, no flap, full stop landing to the center runway, sir." *Crap, that's serious.*

"AWOL 45 Solo, continue holding. I'll get back to you," the SOF said.

Kathryn was fighting with all her might to control her emotions. When she first heard Casey's voice on the emergency frequency, her heart almost stopped. She'd called Bulldog as soon as she heard Casey declare an emergency.

"Tell me the truth, Bulldog, can she land this jet, or should she eject? I'd rather have Casey alive and injured from an ejection than dead from a bad landing she can't handle."

Bulldog thought very carefully before he answered. "I say let her make the call. And yes, I believe she can do a no flap, full stop landing. She might take the arresting gear at the end of the runway, but she'll get the plane on the ground."

"Thanks, Bulldog. That's all I need to know." Kathryn hung up the phone.

She heard the squadron commander's voice on the emergency frequency. "Flight safety, this is squadron ops, come up secure channel seven."

"Safety's on, sir."

"Safety, this is the SOF, are you aware of the situation with this T-38 solo student?"

"Yes, sir, I am. I already talked to her IP, Major Pruitt. I know this student and I have flown with her. Major Pruitt and I are in agreement that she should try and land the jet. She can handle it."

"Roger, Safety, I copy. Have crash fire rescue standing by at the end of runway three-zero center."

"Roger, SOF, they'll be ready. Flight safety out." Kathryn ran down the stairs of the control tower as fast as she could. Casey would be landing her crippled jet in about ten minutes and she had to make sure the fire department was in position to extinguish any fire and to rescue Casey from the damaged jet. It was all Kathryn could do to not scream out loud with fear. She knew Casey was a good student pilot, but this emergency was about as serious as you could get, and it would be a very difficult landing even for an experienced instructor pilot. If any student could get this jet on the ground, Casey could. She was still scared to death for Casey. *This won't be like Marie's crash. This won't be like Marie's crash.* She kept repeating this to herself so she could keep her wits about her and do her job.

❖

"AWOL 45 Solo, this is the SOF. It's your decision to do a no flap landing or to do a controlled bailout."

"I want to land the jet, sir," Casey answered.

"Okay, AWOL 45. Do you need any other help?"

"No, sir, I've already computed my approach and touchdown speeds."

"Very good, AWOL 45. We'll see you on the ground. Good luck. SOF out."

Casey switched her radio back to Albuquerque Center and requested her descent into Willie. As she pulled the power back to idle to descend, she had to fight the airplane to keep the nose up because the trim was frozen. She could see Willie in the distance and tried to remember everything Bulldog had taught her about flying the no flap approach. *"Use a slightly flatter approach angle. The power setting will be less than normal. Don't let her float down the runway. Don't touch the brakes until you're below one hundred and twenty knots or the tires will blow."*

This was going to be a real handful. She forced herself to take several deep breaths to calm her nerves and to focus her mind. She wished Kathryn was in her backseat right now. "And what would she say to me?"

"She'd say, 'Fly the jet, fly the jet, fly the jet. You can do this, Casey.' All right, Captain Hardesty, that's exactly what I'm going to do."

Hearing Kathryn's voice in her head gave her a sense of calm as she descended into Willie. Phoenix Approach Control handed her off to the control tower ten miles from the field. She sensed a small vibration along her right side that she'd never felt before. This was the same side as the failed generator. Casey remembered a diagram from her flight manual. Each engine turned a gearbox that housed the electrical generator, oil pump, hydraulic pump, and the tachometer. If the failed generator was damaged and vibrating, it could also damage her right engine; then she would be in very deep shit. She needed to get this jet on the ground right now.

"Tower, AWOL 45 Solo emergency, I need vectors to final. I'm landing now."

"Roger, understand full stop. Turn right heading two-seven-zero and cleared to land runway three-zero center."

"AWOL 45 Solo emergency, cleared to land, runway three-zero center."

Casey pulled the power back to slow to final approach speed, and the jet was becoming difficult to control. The stick felt very heavy in her hand and the nose kept dropping because the airplane trim was stuck when she was at three hundred knots. She put the landing gear down and lined up with the runway. Her approach speed was one hundred and seventy-five knots and she checked her green donut AOA indicator. She aimed the nose of the jet slightly short of the runway so she could land in the first one thousand feet of pavement. There were flashing red lights from the fire trucks at the end of the runway.

One hundred feet above the ground, Casey pulled the throttles to idle. She tried to pull the stick back to start her flare, but the stick was so heavy she had to pull on it with both hands. She surprised herself when she made a smooth touchdown and landed on brick one of the runway. She pulled the stick back to bring the nose up and aero brake to slow down, but the jet lifted off the runway again. *Shit!* She flew the plane back down to the runway, tried to aero brake again, but the plane kept flying off the ground because of her high speed. *Fuck!* The distance remaining markers on the side of the runway were flying past her as she hurtled down the runway—eight thousand, *zing*, seven thousand, *zing*, six, *zing*, five, *zing*. Her airspeed was still above one hundred and twenty knots. If she stepped on the wheel brakes, the tires would blow. *I'm not going to get this thing stopped!*

Four thousand feet remaining, still too fast for brakes. After what felt like an eternity, the airspeed finally came down below one twenty. She lightly tried the brakes. No skidding so far. Airspeed below one hundred knots, three thousand feet left. She stepped on the brakes as hard as she could. Her legs were shaking. Two thousand feet remaining.

The arresting cable was in front of her on the runway. She saw the high-speed taxiway at the end of the runway turning off to the left. *Could I make the taxiway and not take the barrier? Maybe, just maybe.* She pressed hard on the brakes with all her strength. Her jet looked like it might actually stop. Speed eighty knots. *I'm going to try for the taxiway.* She angled the plane toward the high-speed taxiway. "Oh my God, I'm going to make it," Casey said out loud.

Just as she cleared the runway, there was a giant fire truck right in front of her in the middle of the taxiway. She was headed straight for it. *Oh, shit!* She had nowhere to go, and the fire truck was too slow to get out of her way. She pushed as hard as she could on the brakes and prayed she could stop before she rammed into the fire truck. She finally stopped with the pitot tube of the plane only a few feet from the fire truck. Casey knew the tires would burst into flames any second and she had to get out of this jet right now.

"AWOL 45 emergency has hot brakes." She ripped open her lap belt and shoulder harness, yanked off her comm cord, her oxygen and G-suit hoses, and threw open the canopy. She stood up on the seat, gripped the left side of the cockpit rail, and flung herself over the side of the jet. She let go and dropped the remaining five feet to the ground. As she landed hard on the concrete, she saw thick, white smoke pouring off both main wheels. *They're going to blow!* She ran at full speed toward the giant fire truck. *If I can get behind the fire truck, it will shield me and at least I won't get killed when the tires explode.*

As she rounded the back end of the fire truck in a full sprint, Casey saw the most beautiful sight on the face of the earth—the blue flight safety pickup truck. She had to stop to catch her breath, and she took off her helmet and oxygen mask. Kathryn drove the blue pickup over to Casey in a cloud of dust. She jumped out, took Casey's parachute off of her, set it in the back of the truck, and led Casey to the pickup. She drove off the taxiway so the fire department could extinguish the tire fires on the aircraft.

Once at a safe distance, they both looked over to the plane and saw a dozen firefighters swarm over it wearing silver Kevlar fire suits spraying down the melting wheels with foam. It looked like the plane was going to be all right. Casey breathed a big sigh of relief. Only then did she turn to look at Kathryn.

Kathryn had a look of exhausted relief on her face as well, but she wasn't looking at the jet—she was staring only at Casey.

CHAPTER TWENTY-NINE

"I have to take you back to the squadron to fill out your report," Kathryn said quietly.

"Okay." Now that she was safely on the ground, Casey started to catch her breath. Her heart was still pounding and she buzzed with adrenaline. She wanted to tell Kathryn to stop the truck. She wanted to reach over and hold on to Kathryn for dear life. Instead, she just sat there and tried to breathe.

Kathryn reached across the seat, took Casey's hand in hers, and squeezed tightly. Casey looked back at Kathryn and held on to her hand. Just then, Casey's legs started to shake uncontrollably. Was it muscle fatigue from holding the brake pedals so hard? No. Was it Kathryn holding her hand? She didn't think so. Why was she shaking now that she was safe on the ground? Casey was frightened that she couldn't stop this shaking.

Kathryn let go of Casey's hand and reached over to Casey's shaking thigh. She ran her hand slowly across Casey's trembling knee. "You're okay, Casey. You're safe now and you saved the jet. Try to take deep breaths. The shaking will stop soon." Casey reached over to hold Kathryn's hand again as she tried to take deep breaths and calm herself down. They didn't say a word to each other, but they were connected.

Kathryn pulled up to the squadron building. "I have to go to maintenance to impound the aircraft and the logbooks. I'll call you later. Just go back to your quarters. Don't let them schedule you for anything else today."

"Okay." She was reluctant to let go of Kathryn's hand and leave the safety of sitting next to her. The shaking in her legs had stopped and her breathing was normal again. She got out of the truck, got her parachute and helmet, and went into the squadron building to face the music. She was apprehensive but held her head high.

❖

Kathryn was filled with deep pride watching Casey walk into the squadron building. She would be grilled about every detail and decision she'd made, and there would be a fair amount of second-guessing going on. Everyone in the building would be looking at her and would now know who Casey Tompkins was. The bottom line was that she had handled a very serious emergency with skill and courage, and she'd safely landed the jet.

Kathryn had other things to attend to, such as what the hell happened to that jet to cause this mishap? She met up with the maintenance superintendent, Master Sergeant Gutierrez, in the T-38 engine shop. They already had the melted brakes and tires removed and were installing new wheel assemblies as she walked up to the plane. There was some soot on the underside of the plane, but that would get cleaned off. The right engine access panel was open, and three engine specialists were carefully examining the engine gearbox section. Kathryn took a few photos as they disassembled the components and removed them.

"Oh wow, look at that," one of the techs exclaimed.

"What is it, Sergeant?" Kathryn moved into position to see what they were looking at.

"See all that shiny silver stuff that looks like glitter? Those are metal shavings from inside the gearbox. The generator shaft was vibrating so badly it was disintegrating the whole gearbox. I'd say this jet had been minutes away from having the right engine blow up. And the shrapnel would have taken out the left engine as well."

Kathryn looked at the mess of disintegrated metal and felt her heart clutch. Casey had been only minutes away from a dual engine failure and a loss of all flight controls. If she'd been close to the ground when that happened, she wouldn't have even been able to eject. She would be dead now.

Kathryn couldn't breathe. Her blood ran cold, then rage boiled up inside her. *Who the fuck was responsible for this?* She would have his balls and end his career, if she didn't kill him first.

"Sergeant Gutierrez, I want the complete maintenance inspection history on this jet from the last three years, and get this to me ASAP."

"Yes, ma'am."

Kathryn had to see Casey right now to make sure she was all right. She called her office and told them she would be interviewing the mishap student pilot and to not interrupt her for the rest of the day. She normally didn't speed when driving on base since base cops were everywhere, but right now she didn't care if she got pulled over. Only one thing mattered—seeing Casey.

She ran up the stairs two at a time to Casey's room. Just as she raised her hand to knock on the door, Casey opened it. Kathryn stepped inside and closed the door behind her. She threw her arms around Casey's neck and held on to her as hard as she could. Casey's arms circled Kathryn's back, and she returned the tight hug. They held each other like this, pressing their bodies together for a long time. Kathryn finally pulled back a little and held Casey's face in her hands, looking deep into her eyes.

"I was so afraid I might lose you, Casey," Kathryn said in a choked whisper. She pulled Casey's face down to her own and kissed her lips with a fierce hunger. Casey opened her mouth to take in Kathryn's tongue, devouring Kathryn's mouth as well. Their kisses were hot and desperate. They were in a frenzy of passion that kept them gripped together in a powerful need to connect. Kathryn knew what they both needed. They had to take each other and claim life again. Casey had cheated death, and now Kathryn had to consummate what she could no longer deny.

Kathryn moved her hands down from Casey's face and squeezed her breasts as she kissed her. She took the top of Casey's flight suit zipper and pulled it all the way down. She had to feel her skin. She pulled the flight suit off Casey's shoulders, pulled up her T-shirt, and unhooked her bra. She stared for a long moment at perfect breasts with hard pink nipples beckoning her. She had to taste her skin now. As she felt the tender, warm flesh of Casey's firm breasts, she lowered her mouth to suck them, first the right, then the left. Casey's taut nipples felt amazing in her mouth.

Casey's moans only fueled Kathryn's heat for more. She peeled off Casey's flight suit and boots, then her own, and pushed Casey back onto the bed. She was stunned at how beautiful Casey's firm body looked. Her long legs and glistening center drew in Kathryn like an unstoppable force. She looked up at Casey's face before she went any further. Casey's eyes said yes. That was all Kathryn needed to know. She held Casey's strong thighs open with her hands as she lowered her face to taste Casey's essence. It was like gasoline on fire. Kathryn plunged her tongue into her and sucked on her hard clit. Kathryn was a starving woman and Casey was the food she hungered for. As Kathryn continued to devour her, Casey's hips undulated in the unmistakable rhythm of life. She knew what Casey wanted and she wouldn't tease her or make her wait. She slid her fingers into Casey's wet center as she continued to lick her and was met with hot velvet clamping down on her fingers.

She explored Casey's depths and accelerated her movements. The sounds emerging from Casey confirmed that she was giving her exactly what she wanted. She could tell Casey was close and she held nothing back as she plunged her fingers in deeper and faster. Casey's orgasm broke like a giant wave on them as she shuddered and cried out. Kathryn didn't stop until Casey's trembling hands pulled her head up to kiss her. They melted into one another and became one as their kisses slowed down to tender caresses. Kathryn rested her head on Casey's shoulder, feeling her powerful heartbeat. She would not allow herself to think about the possibility that this heart had almost stopped today.

❖

After catching her breath, Casey rolled on top of Kathryn. Her body was smaller than Casey's, but she was firm and strong. She pressed her thigh into Kathryn's center. She was met with slick heat and a throbbing clit. She moved her leg into Kathryn as she squeezed her breasts and sucked her nipples. Kathryn's breasts were larger than Casey's with prominent, erect peaks. She could suck on these beauties all day. Kathryn's hips moved and her moans brought Casey's attention back to the pulsing clit against her thigh. She started to slide down Kathryn's body to feast on her, but Kathryn stopped her. "No. Stay on top of me. Please."

Casey understood what Kathryn wanted, and the thought of it made a giant shiver run all the way down her body. She pulled Kathryn's legs fully open and settled her legs between them. Her belly and breasts were pressed against Kathryn's, and she slowly pushed her pubic bone into her center. Kathryn rocked her hips in response, wanting more. Casey released one of Kathryn's full breasts and moved her right hand down her body to touch her hard clit. She slid her fingertips across the sensitive bundle to coat her fingers with hot lubrication, then she slowly entered her. Kathryn arched up in response and gasped as Casey filled her. She made long, slow strokes, pushing deeper with each movement. She felt Kathryn relax her inner muscles begging Casey for more. She happily obliged as she pumped harder. She let go of Kathryn's other breast to move her left hand under her back as she gripped her shoulder. Kathryn was hers in this moment, and she wasn't letting go of her for anything. Kathryn wanted to be taken, and Casey was the woman who would give it to her. They continued writhing in their dance of passion until Kathryn's body stiffened and she went silent. Casey continued pounding her until Kathryn cried out. Only when Kathryn put her hand on Casey's arm did she stop pummeling her. They both collapsed in a sweaty heap, finally sated, and fully alive.

Just as Kathryn gently pushed Casey off of her, the phone on the nightstand interrupted them with a jarring ring. Casey was ignoring it as she started moving her hands over Kathryn again.

"Casey, answer the phone."

"I don't care who it is. I only want you."

"It could be important. Please answer the phone."

Casey reluctantly reached for the offending device and answered it. "Hello, Captain Tompkins speaking…Yes, ma'am, I understand." She hung up. "Well, fuck, I have to go over to the wing commander's office. Goddamn it."

"What did they say?"

"It was the wing commander's secretary, and she said I had to report to him ASAP. Crap. I hope he's not going to second-guess everything I did today too. And just when I had you right where I wanted you." She reached for Kathryn's face to kiss her some more.

"Casey, we have to stop. You need to get dressed and get over there now. You do not keep the wing commander waiting."

"Okay, okay, I'm going, but will you please stay here until I get back? I'd really like to continue this."

Kathryn heard the sound of voices outside Casey's door in the hall and suddenly felt very exposed. *What if someone saw me leave her room? We'd both be crucified.*

"I think I need to go, Casey. They'll be looking for me at my office, and I have to get back to my safety investigation." She got off the bed and put on her flight suit and boots.

Casey felt crushed as Kathryn hurried toward the door. "Kathryn? Will I see you again?"

"Sure you will. I just need to go. I'll call you later." She stopped and turned toward Casey. "I'm so happy you're okay." Then she turned, cracked open the door to make sure no one was looking, and slipped out like a thief in the night.

Casey was left standing naked and alone in her room with the scent of Kathryn on her fingers. She had gone from elated to devastated in a millisecond.

CHAPTER THIRTY

Kathryn felt like a coward sneaking out of Casey's room. She thought she'd made a clean escape when she heard behind her, "Hi, Captain Hardesty."

She turned to see a young lieutenant she had flown with last week. "Hi, Lieutenant Rogers. What are you doing today?"

"Emergency procedures sim, ma'am," he said as he rushed off toward the simulator building.

What the hell was I thinking? This is madness. I'm going to get us both court-martialed and kicked out of the Air Force. And what must Casey think of me now? That I treated her like a quick fuck? Shit!

Kathryn continued to beat herself up as she drove back to her office, then she went back to the maintenance hangar. She had a feeling this near crash was the result of some very bad decisions, but she had to find proof before she could say anything. She would get to the bottom of this no matter how many heads rolled.

"Captain Hardesty, I'm glad you're back. I've got some interesting documents to show you," Master Sergeant Gutierrez said. "First, look at this gearbox shaft."

Kathryn examined the heavy metal pieces he handed to her. "It broke as we were removing it from the jet. This thing had maybe a few minutes left before it broke apart in the air." It had the classic seashell look of extensive metal fatigue over ninety percent of the surface with a fracture zone on the last ten percent. *How long had we been flying this jet in this condition? This shaft failure would have caused catastrophic engine and gearbox damage.*

"When was the last time this component was inspected, Sergeant?"

"Almost two years ago, ma'am. Here are the maintenance history records." He handed her a thick folder with tabs for each major aircraft system and orange Post-it Notes in two places.

As she studied the marked sections, she noticed that prior to two years ago, this gearbox shaft had been inspected and documented every year. "Was an inspection missed?"

"Look at the other marked section, ma'am. The inspection schedule protocol was changed from annual to biannual a little over two years ago as a cost saving measure."

"Who was the idiot who did that? Some headquarters bean counter?"

"No, ma'am, it was a local maintenance decision by the deputy chief of maintenance based on a recommendation from some captain in the base budget office. He estimated that we could save one hundred and twenty man-hours per year by extending the inspections to every other year."

"Save one hundred and twenty maintenance man hours? That comes out to maybe six thousand dollars, and this part costs at least three times that much to replace. That was complete stupidity to change that inspection schedule, and why in the world did the budget office recommend an aircraft maintenance change?"

"More like four times the cost savings to replace this part, ma'am, not to mention the expense of the damage to the rest of the engine. Right now, we're looking at over one hundred grand to repair this jet."

"Thanks, Sergeant. Keep me informed if you find anything else." Kathryn would get to the bottom of this disastrous decision and make sure the higher-ups knew exactly who was responsible.

"Captain Hardesty, I went through the computer, and we have thirty-two other T-38s that have gone over a year without the gearbox shaft being inspected. I've told my guys to put everything else on hold and start inspecting those other jets as soon as possible."

"We're going to have to ground all those jets until we're sure they are safe to fly. The T-38 squadron commander and the wing commander are going to shit bricks when they hear I'm grounding half the fleet. Get me the tail numbers of the jets that need inspections, and I'll write up the temporary tech order to ground them. Let me know what you find with those other jets. Thanks, Sergeant." Kathryn rushed out of the maintenance hangar to go tell the wing commander, then inform the flight safety office at the Air Training Command headquarters. This was not going to go over well.

❖

Casey stood outside the wing commander's office looking at the plaques on the wood-paneled walls. Willie had a long and distinguished history, and it was all displayed here in this imposing-looking office.

"Colonel Johnson will see you now," Mrs. Rogers informed Casey.

"Thank you, ma'am."

Casey stood up to her full height as she walked into Colonel Johnson's office. His wood desk was enormous with his official flags behind his giant chair and his personal airplane models and awards decorating the walls. She stopped in front of his desk standing at attention. When he turned to look at her, she saluted. "Captain Tompkins reporting as ordered, sir."

"At ease, Captain. Please take a seat." He seemed cordial, friendly, and not angry. Casey was suspicious and nervous. A junior officer's goal in life was for the wing commander not to even know who she was. It was certainly not in her plans to be sitting in his office having to explain her actions in an aircraft emergency.

"I understand you had some excitement on your solo flight today. I just wanted to talk to you about this." *Is this a trick? Why is he being nice?*

"Can you tell me what happened today?"

"Yes, sir. I lost my right generator with no crossover and had to do a no flap, full stop landing."

"Can you tell me why you demanded immediate landing clearance from the tower?"

"I felt a vibration on the right side of the plane where the gearbox is located, and I thought I needed to get on the ground as soon as possible in case there was any further damage to my jet. Was I incorrect, sir?"

"No, Casey, you weren't. As a matter of fact, your instinct to land immediately was exactly the right thing to do. I've been informed by aircraft maintenance that the gearbox was on the verge of disintegrating and you would have been in a much more dangerous situation if you'd kept flying. Your decision to land the jet was absolutely correct and you landed that jet like an experienced IP. I wanted to meet you and tell you that you did a great job today. You keep up the good work in training, and I'll be keeping my eye on you." Stunned, Casey stood up and shook his hand.

"One last question, Casey. I heard you on the radio during your emergency and you didn't sound nervous or scared at all. Were you?"

"No, sir, I wasn't. I just kept hearing my IP's voice in my head, 'Fly the jet, fly the jet.' So I guess I was just focused on that."

"Is that Major Prewitt you're referring to?"

"No, sir. I was hearing Captain Hardesty's voice."

"I see. Well, good job, again, Casey. I'm proud of you. You're dismissed."

She saluted, did an about-face, and walked out of his office hardly believing what she had just heard—the commander of the entire flying wing was proud of her.

She was practically floating as she left the wing headquarters building when she rounded the corner and ran right into Kathryn.

"Casey! Are you okay? What did Colonel Johnson say to you?"

"He said I did a good job today and that he would be keeping his eye on me. I can't believe it." She wanted to pull Kathryn into a big hug, but other people were standing around. She could only look and smile at Kathryn.

"Casey, that's great. Colonel Johnson is a good guy, and if he called you in to tell you that you did a good job, well, that really means something."

"Can you come back over to my room? Or could we go to your house?"

Kathryn felt guilty as hell. "I'm sorry, Casey. I have to brief the wing commander right now. I'll call you later. I've got to go."

For the second time today, Kathryn made her feel devastated.

❖

Casey showed up at her flight room the next morning to see half the big schedule board crossed out in red grease pencil. The flight commander explained to everyone about the emergency maintenance inspections on the entire T-38 fleet and said they would be flying a lot of sims until the planes were fixed. Thankfully, he didn't elaborate on Casey's emergency from yesterday except to say she'd done a good job. That was the highest praise any student pilot would ever hear.

She had a feeling there would be a lot of questions from guys in the squadron she didn't even know about her emergency. She asked the scheduler if she could be the flight room phone person today so she could study for her instrument flight rules exam. Several of the guys in her flight asked her some questions about her emergency and she didn't mind talking to them. After telling them her story, she sensed some increased respect from the guys.

Kathryn was front and center in her mind today. She had called her late last night and they only talked for a few minutes. When Casey asked her about when they could see each other again, Kathryn sounded evasive and made excuses about being too busy with her safety investigation. Casey didn't push it even though she didn't understand. She was torn between letting her mind create amazing fantasies with Kathryn and studying for her instrument exam. She wanted to let her mind wander to thoughts of Kathryn's luscious body, but how Kathryn felt about her was the big unknown.

❖

Kathryn was buried in paperwork as she worked on the safety investigation of Casey's mishap. Thirty-two T-38s were past due for inspections of the gearbox shafts, and maintenance was working twenty-four hours a day to inspect them as fast as they could. So far, they'd only found three with severe metal fatigue and they had been repaired already. Seven more jets had evidence of damage, but they should be fixed fairly soon.

The more troubling aspect of this investigation was the detective work to find out who instigated this disastrous inspection change. For some reason, she was finding gaps in the records of the maintenance tech order changes, which was very unusual.

Everyone in aircraft maintenance, and especially in Air Training Command, was meticulous about documenting anything having to do with the jets. She'd stayed at her office until two a.m. the night before digging through the paperwork with no luck. When she'd finally gotten home, she'd had a hard time sleeping. Thoughts of Casey kept stirring in her mind. She kept seeing the image of Casey's jet hurtling down the runway then finally stopping with smoke pouring off the wheels. Then the image of Casey's amazing body came into her mind. She'd been so desperate and frantic with her that it could hardly be called lovemaking. It was more like animalistic coupling to affirm for each other that they were still alive. Her feelings about Casey were becoming a huge problem.

Just then, Casey's IP, Bulldog Prewitt, came stomping into her office. "I've got something you need to see, Kath," he said as he pulled a computer disk from his pocket.

"What's this?"

"I keep copies of everything related to tech order changes since I'm a wing test pilot. They hammered this into us at Edwards when I was in Flight Test School. When I heard about Casey's jet and that change to the inspection schedule, I went through my old files and guess what I found?"

"What, Bulldog? You're killing me."

"There're some maintenance records that have been deleted off the main computer system. And they've been deleted just recently, to boot. This floppy disk has a copy of my records from before her mishap. You need to check this with what's in the maintenance computer system now. Very interesting reading."

"Why don't you just tell me what you found out?"

"Because that ain't my job. I'm just cooperating with the records request as part of the safety investigation." He turned and stomped out of her office.

Kathryn inserted the floppy disk into her computer terminal, opened the files, and saw a name she recognized, Captain Bailey Grant. *Why the hell is his name here and why were these erased from the base main computer?*

Kathryn reached for the phone and dialed the base computer information officer.

"Major Hendricks, I need your help in tracing some computer files and documents related to my safety investigation. Can I come over and show these to you now? Great, I'll be there in ten minutes." This could be just the break she needed to solve this puzzle.

The visit with Major Hendricks was enlightening. He was able to identify the computer that erased the suspect documents to a terminal in the wing standardization and evaluation branch. Specifically, the computer terminal on the desk of the chief of stan/eval. The files were erased from the computer at 2200 hours the night of Casey's mishap, and Kathryn found out that the chief was out of town at a conference that day. Someone used his computer terminal to cover their tracks. This was no longer just a mistake or negligence; this was now a deliberate cover-up, and Kathryn knew that Bailey Grant was right in the middle of it.

She was so enraged, she wanted to go home, get her twelve-gauge shotgun, go over to his house, and blow his ugly face off. She had to calm herself while she formulated a plan to catch this bastard red-handed. She would have to wait until tonight to get the evidence she needed to nail his ass.

It was 1800 hours when she heard a knock at her office door. She looked up and saw Casey standing in front of her looking gorgeous and a little apprehensive.

"Can I come in?"

"Sure, Casey, please sit down."

"I know I'm not supposed to be here, but I have to talk to you and I waited until everyone else went home."

Kathryn was dreading what Casey would say next. "Okay, go ahead."

"I have to know where we're going. I'm thinking about you constantly and it's driving me crazy. I'm having trouble concentrating on pilot training. I don't mean to put you on the spot, but I really need to know how you feel about me." There it was—the million dollar question.

Kathryn looked into Casey's beautiful, piercing, blue eyes, took a deep breath, closed her door for some privacy, and pulled up the chair next to Casey. She reached out to hold Casey's warm, strong hand.

"I'm not sure how I feel about you, Casey. I care about you very much, but I'm not sure if I'm capable of a relationship with you, or with anyone else, for that matter. I'm not sure I can give you what you want. I do know this for sure—I want you to succeed in pilot training and earn your wings. That is more important to me than anything."

Casey looked at her silently for a long moment. "I understand that we can't be seen together because I'm a student pilot. But that doesn't mean we can't see each other at someplace off base, like my friend's house, or we could even meet up somewhere out of town. I just want to know if there is something real here, or was I just a quick fuck for you?"

Casey's words were a slap in her face. "You certainly were not just a 'quick fuck' for me. You mean a lot more than that to me." Kathryn could no longer avoid telling Casey the real reason for her reluctance.

"I have to tell you something so you'll understand. I had a partner, Marie, and we met nine years ago when we were both student pilots together. She got washed out, went to navigator school, and got sent to Fairchild Air Force Base in Spokane. I requested to fly the KC-135 tanker so we could be stationed together. I was completely in love with her, then she was killed in a midair collision. I've been grieving her death for five years and I can't get over it. I don't know if I can ever give myself to another person. I'm damaged goods, Casey. I don't think you'd want to be with me if you knew what I was really like."

Casey was stunned at this information and also felt sadness in her heart for Kathryn's pain. "I'm so sorry that happened to you. Kathryn, but I'm not Marie. I can't promise you I'll never die in a plane crash, but I can promise you that I will do everything in my power to stay safe. I may be just a student pilot right now, but I've also been a lesbian my whole life. I know what I want, and I want you. I will graduate and earn my wings in four months and nothing, or no one, will prevent me from doing that. You're not 'damaged goods' to me and I would like to give us a chance. You know where to find me if you change your mind." With that finality, Casey stood up, walked to the door, and left Kathryn's office without another word.

CHAPTER THIRTY-ONE

The big conference room would soon be filled with all the bigwigs on base, and Kathryn checked her presentation slides one last time before they started to file in. She knew her investigation was comprehensive, but she would be leveling some hard facts at the wing commander, and you never knew how he would react. Colonel Johnson was smart, but her report might make his flying wing look bad. Kathryn was nervous, but she stood behind her evidence. She would simply present the information and let the facts speak for themselves.

The base commanding officers came in and took their assigned seats around the big table. Kathryn jumped in with her first slide. It was a picture of Casey's jet right after the fire department had extinguished the fire from the melted tires with smoke still coming off the hot, molten brakes. It was a stark reminder to everyone of just how close they'd come to a disaster. After she let the image linger, she hefted the broken gearbox shaft onto the table for everyone to see. "This is the cause of that substantial aircraft damage and the near loss of life of a student pilot."

She had everyone's undivided attention now. "This is the evidence of severe metal fatigue, which went undetected due to a delayed inspection schedule. The inspection schedule was changed two years ago because of a recommendation from the base budget office to the deputy commander of maintenance."

"Who in the base budget office advised the DCM to change the inspection schedule?" the wing commander asked.

"Captain Bailey Grant, sir."

"Captain Grant? He's a T-37 stan/eval pilot, isn't he?"

"Yes, sir, he is. He works for me," the chief of stan/eval said. "He was assigned to the budget office for a short time before he came to stan/eval."

"The evidence I recovered, with the help of the base computer office, are documents concerning cost savings by reducing the T-38 inspection interval," Kathryn explained.

"Documents you recovered? Explain this, Captain Hardesty."

"Sir, these records were deleted from the base mainframe computer on the night of the mishap—from the computer terminal in the chief of stan/eval's office."

"What? I wasn't even in my office on that day. I was at Randolph for a conference." The chief of stan/eval looked stunned at this information. "Someone must have used my terminal."

"Someone did use your desk computer terminal, sir," Kathryn stated.

"Captain Grant?" he asked.

"No sir, on the night of the mishap, the log-in on your computer terminal was from Lieutenant Dave Carter, T-37 IP, under the direction of Captain Grant. Mr. Jefferson, the building custodian, was an eyewitness to this fact and positively identified Lieutenant Carter."

The situation became obvious to everyone present. Captain Grant had convinced the deputy maintenance commander to change the T-38 inspection schedule for a small cost savings to make himself look good, then he tried to cover it up by using Lieutenant Carter to do the dirty work. He did this when he figured out his inspection change had resulted in the accident. The wing commander got quiet with an ominous look on his face.

"Captain Hardesty, that will be all for now." He stood and abruptly left the room.

"Yes, sir."

Everyone shuffled out of the conference room muttering.

Kathryn had accomplished her mission. She'd figured out what caused Casey's accident and who was responsible. With any luck, the wing commander would destroy Bailey Grant's career and, hopefully, Dave Carter's too.

❖

Casey's flying improved quickly after she successfully handled that big emergency. There was a new confidence and aggressiveness in the way she attacked each mission, and she felt ready for her upcoming check ride.

The next morning, Casey read the base newspaper with great interest. It had a "Welcome to Willie and Farewell" section and mentioned Captain Bailey Grant was leaving immediately for Minot Air Force Base, North Dakota, where he would fly the B-52 bomber. *Ha! Serves you right, asshole.* The B-52 was the least desirable aircraft to fly in the entire Air Force. He would sit alert in an underground bunker for one-third of his life, then fly an ancient plane. It was like being sentenced to a Gulag in Siberia, and she grinned at the thought of him freezing his nuts off. It also said Lieutenant Dave Carter was reassigned to Laughlin Air Force Base in Del Rio, Texas. "Double bonus!"

Her check ride was with Major Case, the chief of check section and an F-4 fighter pilot. The preflight, engine start, and taxi out went smoothly. Just as Casey was about to lower her canopy for takeoff, she saw the blue flight safety pickup truck parked next to the RSU. *Kathryn is watching me.* A gentle warmth settled in her belly.

She was flying well, and everything was just like she'd practiced it with Bulldog. She ran through her stalls and acro in the practice area, then requested her return to Willie.

Her descent into the base was uneventful and she was surprised how easy it was to fly a no flap approach when you had trim available and no fuel imbalance or airframe vibration. After she lifted off from her sweet touch-and-go landing, she asked the check pilot if he would like to fly. "Sure. I've got the jet," he said.

"Your jet, sir," Casey answered. She felt a tiny bit of relief that he hadn't asked her to repeat any maneuvers. He requested a closed pattern, then yanked the jet into a six-G turn.

After a few basic systems questions, Major Case shook her hand and said, "Good ride, Captain. Overall grade, Excellent. I look forward to flying with you again."

"Thank you, sir, me too." She was on cloud nine. Everyone looked at her as she entered the room.

"How'd you do, Tompkins?" the head scheduler asked.

She held up three fingers sideways in the shape of an E.

The room erupted in cheers for her. The flight commander came out of his office to shake her hand. "Good job, Casey."

"Thanks, sir."

"God dammit, girl, I knew you could bring home the bacon!"

Bulldog gripped her hand in a bone-crunching handshake. "Jack Case doesn't give out many Excellents. You must've dazzled him good, Ace. Don't rest on your laurels too much. Next week we're starting formation, and I want you to hit the ground running."

"I will."

She wished she could share her triumph with Kathryn, but she knew she couldn't. It was a little dark cloud on an otherwise great day. She would take Trish and Rhonda out for dinner to celebrate. Maybe Kathryn would call her to congratulate her since she probably already knew about her check ride grade. She had, after all, been watching her from the RSU.

CHAPTER THIRTY-TWO

November 1992

Kathryn walked into her office in a good mood. Bailey Grant and Dave Carter had been exiled and their careers were essentially over, and Casey had aced her first T-38 check ride. There was a phone message marked Urgent on her desk. It said she needed to get over to the wing commander's office ASAP. *Crap. What now?*

Kathryn hurried over to the his office and asked his secretary, Mrs. Rogers, what was up. "I don't know, but he's in a good mood. He'll see you now."

Kathryn stood at attention before his huge desk.

"Captain Hardesty, please take a seat."

"Yes, sir."

"First of all, you did a great job with that safety investigation. You uncovered some serious deficiencies that I wasn't aware of, and I'm happy to tell you they've been resolved. You also got a lot of attention from headquarters, Air Training Command."

"Thank you, sir. I was just trying to do be thorough."

"The main reason I called you here is to tell you that you've been selected to attend Air Command and Staff College in residence. This was a highly competitive field, and you're one of only five officers in the entire command to get selected for senior staff school in residence. You'll report to Maxwell in April."

"Wow. I don't know what to say, sir."

"That's not all. I'm also putting you in for promotion to major one year early. You're my number one captain on the base. You'll pin on major probably by March."

Kathryn was stunned at this news. She knew she was a good instructor pilot and a conscientious safety officer, but she never dreamed the wing commander considered her the top captain on the whole base. "Thank you so much, sir."

"You've earned it, Kathryn. You're one of my superstars. After you've finished your year in Alabama at Maxwell, you'll go to the Pentagon or maybe even to a White House fellowship. This is the first step toward becoming a squadron commander." He stood to shake her hand.

"Thanks again, sir. I'm really thrilled." She snapped to attention, saluted him, then did an about-face to leave his office.

This is incredible. I can't believe it.

❖

Casey watched the formation films a dozen times to get the references down cold. Formation flying was the biggest part of T-38 training, and she wanted to shine. The visual signals and basic maneuvers were the same as the T-37 but the T-38 also had some new formation positions—close trail and extended trail. She couldn't wait to see what these looked like.

Bulldog quizzed her and she knew all the answers. After the briefing, they would start out as the wingman, then position change and lead the formation back to Willie. Bulldog was flying the wing takeoff and was instructing, but Casey could only look at the magnificent sight of the beautiful T-38 right next to her. It was sleek, graceful, and so fast it almost made her head spin. Fingertip position looked so much closer to the other jet than it did in the T-37.

They entered the practice area. Lead went to ninety degrees of bank and three-G maneuvering. Bulldog followed like he was stuck to them, then lead gave the signal for an echelon turn. As lead smoothly rolled into a sixty-degree banked turn, Bulldog rolled with them, and it looked as if her canopy would smash into the underside of lead's plane. Her entire field of view was filled with the underside of the other jet. As lead rolled out, Casey thought their wing tip would hit her on the head. *This is way too fucking close! How am I ever going to get this?*

"Are you ready to try it, Casey?" Bulldog asked. "Remember, don't think about moving the stick, just think tiny pressures on the stick. You have the jet."

"Roger, I have the jet." She tried to hold position but quickly got into an up/down oscillation.

"My jet, Casey." Bulldog flew them back into position. "Try it again."

Casey quickly got spat out of position again and again. Her back, shoulder, arm, and hand got tense as she fought to stay in the right place. Bulldog had to take the jet from her at least a dozen times. *Crap. I thought I could do this.*

"Okay, we're going to position change and be the lead."

Bulldog had her fly the plane. Even though they were in a bigger practice area, she couldn't turn the formation around quickly, so Bulldog had to tell her everything to do. She felt like she was back at square one with this jet. She was so far behind mentally that she could hardly find her way back to Willie. Bulldog flew the formation wing landing. It was beautiful watching them land together but extremely frustrating.

She expected a brutal debrief, but Bulldog said, "You'll get the hang of this, Champ. You'll get to the point where you only have to think about moving the stick and you'll be in position. Watch those films again."

If Casey couldn't master this, it would be the end of her dream.

As the days went on, she did start to show some slight improvement. She was progressing as a lead faster than as a wingman. She was starting to think one or two maneuvers ahead, and it still looked way too close to the other jet, but she wasn't completely hopeless.

Her instrument flying and navigation training were going much better. The speed of the jet made things happen very quickly, especially on instruments, and she had to do quick mental math to keep ahead of the jet.

Four more of her classmates had been washed out. She never felt safe in this program. You could bust a ride or a sim, get two practice rides, and be gone in a week—your dream of flying over for good. Casey wanted to talk to Kathryn about this so badly. She could talk to her friends, but they couldn't understand what she was going through. Maybe she could call her just to ask for some advice to get through T-38 formation training and not mention anything about a relationship.

❖

Kathryn walked through the T-38 squadron on her rounds of random grade book checks. The T-38 squadron did not pay very close attention to the individual needs of the students. Their attitude was, "We're the big boys around here and if you can't cut it, it's your fault and we'll just wash you out."

They were all wannabe fighter pilots and thought they were badasses. The reality was that they washed out students who might have been saved if they'd paid a little more attention to their training.

In Gombey's flight room she went right to Casey's grade book. Her instrument sim grades were good, but she didn't like what she was seeing with Casey's formation grades. They were flying her with a lot of different IPs instead of Bulldog, and it was showing with a lack of progress with her wingman flying. It didn't look intentional, more like benign neglect. If Casey failed to meet the standards in her formation flying, they would wash her out as just another girl who couldn't cut it in pilot training.

Maybe she should call Casey and talk to her about her flying. She was concerned about facing her again, but she couldn't let her get behind in pilot training without doing everything in her power to help her. They would have to meet on neutral territory. She couldn't handle the temptation of being in Casey's quarters again or risk other people on base seeing them together. She wanted to see Casey but was also fearful. She was comfortable talking about flying, but relationship stuff scared the hell out of her.

She thought of Casey so many times during the day. She wanted to tell her something funny a student pilot had done or some juicy gossip. She even wanted to think about a future together. She drove past a new housing development off base and imagined them buying a house together, setting up housekeeping, maybe even getting a dog. It just seemed so impossible right now.

Every time a thought of Casey came into her mind, she kept going back to her relationship with Marie. That was the basis of her fear with Casey—that she would allow herself to fall in love with Casey and then have her heart broken again.

After Marie died, Kathryn could barely function, and she lost the will to live. Her grief was overwhelming, and she had to keep it all to herself because they were gay. The only escape she got from her sadness was when she was in the air flying a plane. She volunteered for the most dangerous missions in the squadron just to run away from the pain. The only time the darkness started to lift was when she got her assignment to come back to Willie as an instructor pilot. She'd found a reason for living again in teaching students to fly and in reconnecting with old friends like Barb Arnau.

Her life was finally back on track again when she got assigned Casey as her student, and now her world was turned upside down. Nothing could happen between them until Casey graduated. Casey would probably get sent away to another base and she would be leaving for Alabama for a year of school in a few months. There was no point in imagining a future that could never be, so why couldn't she get Casey out of her mind?

Because Casey was unforgettable.

She was beautiful, smart, and passionate, and Kathryn couldn't stop thinking about her. If she talked to her about her flying, maybe she could muster the courage to tell Casey the real reason she was afraid to pursue a relationship with her.

❖

Casey was in her quarters studying when the phone rang and startled her.

"I need to talk to you. Are you available tonight? We could go off base and get some dinner somewhere, if you like," Kathryn asked.

Casey was glad to hear from her, but she was also feeling very cautious. "What time?"

"I'll pick you up at 1800 hours on the east end of your building."

"Okay. See you then."

Could it be possible that Kathryn changed her mind about seeing Casey? She suspected that Kathryn Hardesty rarely changed her mind about anything, but she was willing to listen to her. She tried very hard not to get her hopes up, but it was difficult. She put a tiny bit of her favorite perfume on her neck. "No harm in at least attempting to be alluring."

At precisely 1800 hours, Kathryn's red convertible whipped round the corner. Casey noticed the top was up and the dark tinted windows were closed.

"Hi, Casey. Thanks for meeting me."

"Where are we going?" She was hoping maybe they would go to Kathryn's house.

"There's a great old Mexican food restaurant in downtown

Phoenix called Jordan's that I thought we'd go to. It's a bit of a drive, so I hope you don't have to get back too soon."

"Mexican sounds great, and my show time's not until 0900 hours tomorrow, so I'm good."

"I just wanted to get away from the base for a while so we can talk. How's everything been going?"

"Oh, not too bad. I got an Excellent on my contact check ride. I was pretty happy with that. How have you been?" She wanted Kathryn to dive right into whatever it was she wanted to talk to her about.

"I heard. That's great. Your check pilot, Major Case, is a pretty tough nut to crack. You must have really impressed him."

Hearing praise from Kathryn made Casey warm all over. She wanted to reach over the console and hold Kathryn's hand so bad it made her arm hurt to keep it in her lap. She couldn't think of any more small talk, so they sat in awkward silence for the next forty-five minutes on the drive to the restaurant. It was up to Kathryn to bring up the subject she wanted to talk about.

Kathryn turned up Seventh Street, then into the parking lot of a small one-story, rather drab looking restaurant. They certainly shouldn't run into anyone from Willie at this out-of-the-way place. The fabulous smell of Mexican food was the first thing Casey noticed, followed by a sparse crowd sitting in well-used booths.

"Hi, Kath. Haven't seen you in a while. Usual booth?" An older gentleman greeted them.

"Hi, Joe, yes, we'd like a booth in the back room," Kathryn answered.

He led them to a round booth in the corner of the back dining room. They had the whole room to themselves.

As they sat down, Casey couldn't hold it in any longer. "Okay, Kathryn, what's up? You're killing me. What is it that we need to talk about?"

"First of all, I'm sorry it's been so long since I've spoken with you. I wasn't sure what to say to you, so I didn't say anything."

"Okay, go on."

"I need to talk to you about two things. First, your formation flying, and second, about us."

"I'm listening."

"You're not progressing with your formation flying the way you should be."

"How do you know that? Have you been talking to Bulldog?"

"I looked at your grade book. You've flown with six different IPs on your last six rides, and I suspect they're all telling you to do different things. The result is you are not as far along as you should be with your wing formation flying. It's not your fault; it's the scheduler's fault, but you have to fix it."

"Bulldog's son has been sick, so he hasn't been able to fly with me lately. These guys all tell me something different on every ride. It's really frustrating. I only have four rides left before my formation check ride, and I'm afraid I'm going to bust it." It was a relief to finally speak her worry out in the open.

"I called Bulldog. He agreed to fly your next rides with you. You're a good student; that's why they think they can fly you with any IP. You have to take care of your own training."

"Okay, I'll do that. Thanks."

Their food arrived and they completely stuffed themselves. Kathryn got up to leave. Casey touched her arm, "Isn't there something else you wanted to talk about?"

"Yes, but I'd rather talk in the car."

The parking lot was deserted as they got back into the convertible. They were bathed in soft, golden light from the streetlights shining through the windshield. Kathryn turned in her seat, took a deep breath, and took Casey's hand in hers as she looked into her eyes.

"There are not too many things in this world I'm afraid of, but you are one of them. I was so devastated after Marie's death, I lost the will to live, and I'm not sure I'm capable of trusting anyone again."

Casey squeezed Kathryn's hand but said nothing.

"I loved Marie with my whole heart. I'm not sure I'll really get over her death. I still struggle with grief on certain days even five years later. Casey, if I let myself get into a relationship with you and then something happens to you, or the Air Force separates us, I don't think I could survive that hurt again. The bottom line is I'm afraid of getting my heart broken. I'm sorry, but that's where I am right now. I wish I didn't feel that way."

Casey enclosed Kathryn's hand with both of her own and gently brought her fingers to her lips. She tenderly kissed her trembling fingers.

"Kathryn, I am so sorry you had to go through all that. I can't even imagine the pain you've suffered. You are a caring, intelligent, gorgeous, demanding woman, and I believe we have something really special here. I'm not willing to let a chance for real happiness slip through my fingers because of fear. I'm afraid of getting hurt too, but I'm willing to take that risk for you."

Kathryn could feel her heart melt along with the knot of fear in her chest. A thought entered her mind as clearly as if it were spoken out loud—*maybe I really can trust her.* She slowly leaned forward and gently pressed her lips onto Casey's. The kiss was slow and lingering. Casey's mouth tasted like warm honey, and Kathryn wanted more.

Their kissing turned intense, and Kathryn felt Casey's hand move to her breast. The sensation of Casey squeezing her nipple as she slid her tongue into her mouth made Kathryn moan. This only encouraged Casey further as she slipped her hand under Kathryn's shirt. The sound of another car nearby interrupted them and they broke their contact, breathless and hot.

"God, Kathryn, I could devour you right here."

"Me too, but we should get you back to the base."

"Before you start the car, where do we go from here?"

"I'm not sure. There are a lot of things that have to happen for us to even consider the possibilities. The first step is to get you through your T-38 formation check. I know you can do it. I believe in you, Casey."

CHAPTER THIRTY-THREE

December 1992

Once Casey started flying with Bulldog again, everything started to gel with her formation flying. The good thing about flying formation was that she got a clear idea of how good her flying skills were compared to the guys in her class. She could stay in position no matter what the lead aircraft did, and her formation lead was the best in the entire flight. She was finally confident and ready for her formation check ride.

The day of her check ride she was flying against Dan Hopkins, a good ol' boy from Kentucky. He was not particularly bright and had not flown well the last time she flew with him.

She started as lead and ran him through the required maneuvers. She set him up perfectly for a position change and she became the wingman. He continued forward for a long time doing nothing as they rapidly approached the boundary of their practice area. "Come on, do something," she mumbled.

His check pilot in the backseat gave them the pitch out signal as he yanked the jet hard into a turn to get back into the practice area. *Crap, this isn't good.* Dan finally gave her an echelon turn. He rolled out too fast from the turn and almost hit her jet. She had to push the stick forward quickly to avoid getting hit.

Just then she heard her check pilot's deep voice on the radio calling, "Knock it off, knock it off." Then he said, "My jet, Tompkins."

"Yes, sir, you have the jet." *Fuck, fuck, fuck! This asshole is going to get me busted.*

The check pilot smoothly slid away to a safe distance. She was furious at Dan. *Stay calm. Keep flying. There's still a chance you can pass.* It was Kathryn's voice in her head. She took a few deep breaths to stay calm.

Her check pilot said, "Okay, Tompkins, your jet."

"Roger, I have the aircraft."

The check pilot in the lead jet signaled he was flying. He returned to Willie and led the formation to a wing landing. Maybe she hadn't busted the ride because her check pilot was still letting her fly. She would make this wing landing the best one he'd ever seen. Her wing position was rock solid, and she touched down right with lead. If she busted this check ride at least she knew she'd given it her best. She still wanted to kill Dan, the dumbass.

When she walked back into the Gombey flight room, she saw a red circle around Dan's name on the schedule board. She was not surprised he busted his formation check. All eyes turned to look at her.

"Well, how'd you do, Casey?" the flight commander asked.

"I passed with a Good, sir." She was very relieved to have squeaked by with a pass and have this ride behind her.

She would call Kathryn tonight and tell her all about what had happened today.

❖

The wing commander's secretary called Kathryn to tell her that her promotion board would be meeting next week. The board results would be announced in a month. That would be around the same time Casey's class would be getting their flying assignments. That would be a very eventful week, not without its own issues.

She was worried about how Casey would react when she found out that she was supposed to go to Alabama for a year to school, then to the Pentagon to fly a large steel desk for four more years. The odds seemed insurmountable for them to be together. She'd been busy calling in a few favors to arrange a surprise for Casey that she hoped would soften the blow.

❖

Casey was exhausted from the stress of flying, instrument sims, her formation check ride, and now her upcoming cross-country flights. She wished she could just hang out with Kathryn.

She was flying with Captain Taylor from Boysan flight for her cross-country trip. Bulldog had been pretty absent because of his son's upcoming heart surgery. She'd seen Captain Taylor around the squadron but never spoken to her. She was one of only two women T-38 instructor pilots in the entire squadron, and they were on the opposite schedule from her flight. She was an imposing-looking IP. She was six feet tall, had forearms like Martina Navratilova, but Casey had never seen her at any softball games.

"Captain Taylor wants you to come over to Boysan at 1400 hours today to talk about your cross-country flight," the scheduler told Casey.

"Hi, Casey. Have a seat." Captain Taylor sounded friendly. "You've been doing well with your instrument flying, so we're going to concentrate on preparing you for your navigation check ride."

"That would be great."

"Plan a low-level flight to Kirtland Air Force Base in Albuquerque, then we'll do a night flight to Peterson Field in Colorado Springs with lots of approaches. Saturday will be a free day for you because I'm going to the Air Force Academy football game with some friends. On Sunday, we'll fly to Biggs Army Air Field in El Paso, then back to Willie."

"Okay. This sounds like a great trip." Casey was thrilled to have a day off in Colorado Springs.

"Do you know what the nickname for El Paso is?"

"No, I don't."

"It's called El Pinko because so many people have busted nav checks there. The runway is very close to El Paso International and it's very easy to misidentify the runway. I'm going to show you all the hazards of this place so you won't get burned. Meet me in base operations at 0900 hours on Friday. This will be a fun weekend, Casey. Oh, and call me Janie when we're in the jet."

"Got it, see you Friday." Casey couldn't wait to fly with Janie.

❖

Casey met Captain Taylor at 0900 hours and showed her the flight plans. She was pleased with the low-level route. She was used to the high speed of the T-38, but flying at four hundred knots close to the ground was mind-blowing and thrilling. She found all her points on time, Meteor Crater, the Painted Desert, and Monument Valley.

After she completed her low-level route, Casey climbed to altitude and flew to Kirtland Air Force Base. Captain Taylor had her do a circling approach. They took a short break while Captain Taylor debriefed the ride. She gave Casey a grade of Excellent on her low-level.

Casey had to switch to the backseat and fly under the canvas hood attached to the canopy for her instrument flying. Captain Taylor taxied the jet and made the takeoff from the front seat. Casey felt closed in and claustrophobic flying under the T-38 hood. There was no way to cheat and steal a peek at the horizon flying under the bag.

Once she was airborne, Casey concentrated on her instrument flying and her position orientation. The flight to Colorado Springs only took fifteen minutes when she requested the first approach. Captain Taylor next had her fly a non-precision approach, a missed approach, then an ILS approach. She nailed all the approaches, then Captain Taylor took the jet.

"Take a break, Casey. All your approaches are good, and we'll make this last one a precision radar approach. When you call 'Decision height,' I'll take the jet and make the landing."

"Okay, got it." Her flying was precise with the radar controller calling, "On glide path, on course." She kept the jet stabilized until two hundred feet above the ground when she announced, "Decision height." Captain Taylor took the jet and made a great landing.

After landing, Casey pulled back the hood. *You can't see crap from the backseat. How can they see to land this thing from the back?* Captain Taylor pulled up to the parking spot and Casey noticed two other T-38s and one T-37. She assumed they were more Academy grads returning for homecoming. They climbed down the ladders, got their bags, and checked out a car from the base motor pool. All the on base quarters were full, so they got vouchers for an off-base hotel.

Captain Taylor drove them to the hotel, and when they walked into the lobby, Casey saw several other Air Force pilots, including Kathryn.

"Well, look who finally got here. Hi, Janie. Hi, Casey," Kathryn said.

Casey could hardly believe her eyes. She wanted to pick up Kathryn in a bear hug and twirl her around. Kathryn had a gorgeous smile on her face as she beamed at Casey.

"Why didn't you tell me you were flying here?" Casey asked.

"And ruin the surprise? The look on your face when you walked in was priceless."

Captain Taylor was talking to the other T-37 IP who had flown in with Kathryn. She looked familiar, but Casey didn't know her. She figured she must be a new instructor pilot who was getting her aircraft check out from Kathryn. It was obvious that Janie Taylor and this new woman IP were very familiar with each other as sparks flew from the way they looked at each other.

"Here's your room key, Casey. Good job today. This is Stephanie Carson. She's a new Tweet IP. You guys have fun and we'll meet up with you Sunday morning around 1100 hours."

"Shall we go find our room?" Kathryn asked softly.

"Our room? Are you crazy?" Casey was stunned.

"In case you hadn't noticed, this hotel is the unofficial lesbian headquarters for the weekend. Come on, let's go."

Casey followed Kathryn feeling deliciously naughty and excited.

Kathryn put out the "Do not disturb" sign and locked the door. She slowly walked over to Casey but did not turn on the light. The drapes were open and Casey could see the lights shining on the magnificent Air Force Academy chapel. The lights from outside cast a soft blue light throughout the room.

Kathryn reached for Casey's face and slowly drew them together. Her lips were soft and warm as she gently kissed Casey.

Casey returned the soft kisses and put her arms around Kathryn's small waist. There was no hurry or fear of being caught. For the first time, they were alone with no concerns about anyone seeing them. The freedom was intoxicating. They could take their sweet time with each other as they relished each touch and lingered over every caress.

Kathryn slowly pulled down Casey's flight suit zipper and slid her hand inside to drag her fingertips across the pebbled skin. Kathryn's other hand joined in the exploration of Casey's body as both hands moved up her rib cage under Casey's white T-shirt. A moan emerged from Casey's lips at the sensation of Kathryn's warm hands on her chest. She wanted Kathryn to tear her flight suit off, but she knew Kathryn wanted to make her wait. The slow caresses were exquisite torture and Kathryn would not be hurried.

Kathryn reached behind Casey, unhooked her bra as she continued to kiss her and moved her hands to Casey's firm breasts. She massaged them and lightly pinched the hard nipples. Casey was getting damp, and she slid her tongue into Kathryn's hot mouth. Their kisses quickly became more intense as Casey unzipped Kathryn's flight suit and pulled it down off her shoulders. They had to separate in order to get off their flight boots and they both laughed before quickly getting naked on the bed.

Casey was in heaven at the sensation of Kathryn's luscious body on top of her. She couldn't help but writhe when Kathryn pressed her firm thigh into Casey's center. After Kathryn caressed and sucked Casey's breasts, she moved slowly down her body, leaving a trail of hot kisses across her stomach. She settled her body between Casey's legs and dragged her own erect nipples across Casey's hard clit. She was deliberate and agonizingly slow in her lovemaking as she moved her lips to Casey's throbbing center. When Casey's writhing and moaning reached a fever pitch, Kathryn entered her slowly and deeply, bringing her to a powerful orgasm.

Casey pulled Kathryn up to kiss her face. She was breathless and covered in a light sheen of sweat from the giant orgasm, but she wanted to hold on to Kathryn. She loved the feel of Kathryn's breasts against hers and wrapped her arms tightly around her strong back. *I could hold her like this forever.*

"Are you okay?" Kathryn asked gently.

"I'm better than okay. That was the most powerful orgasm I've ever had. My heart is still pounding."

"I know. I can feel your heart beating. I like it." Kathryn placed her hand on top of Casey's heart.

"How did you know to do that to me?"

"Your body told me what you wanted. I just followed where your body led me, like a good wingman. You are magnificent." Kathryn nuzzled her face against Casey's neck. She could feel the strong pulse against her cheek.

Casey gently rolled Kathryn over onto her back. "My turn now."

Casey pressed her taller body against Kathryn's. "Am I hurting you?"

"No. I like the feel of you on top of me."

Casey explored every inch of Kathryn's body. She was unhurried and rolled Kathryn onto her stomach after she'd kissed every part of her front. She massaged and tasted Kathryn's back, slowly moving her hands lower. When she got to Kathryn's cheeks, she gave that area special attention. Casey remembered her last cross-country trip to Las Vegas when she'd spied on Kathryn from her hotel balcony. That image was burned into her brain, and she now wanted to take Kathryn from behind.

Casey pried Kathryn's knees apart and she pulled up her hips.

She felt a slight resistance, but then Kathryn submitted to her. Casey moved her hand lower, finding Kathryn's center soaked with desire. "Oh, Kathryn."

Casey slid two fingers deep inside her as she gripped her hip with her other hand. Kathryn backed into Casey's hand, wanting more. Casey pushed deeper inside her and hooked her leg around Kathryn's thigh so she couldn't move. She moved inside Kathryn harder and faster as she rubbed her own hard clit against Kathryn's ass. She felt Kathryn was close. She accelerated her pace, giving Kathryn exactly what she wanted. Her own orgasm rose from deep within her center as Kathryn cried out her climax. They fell together in a sweaty heap on the bed.

Kathryn turned underneath Casey, wrapping her arms around her neck. Casey held her as small shudders rolled through her. She felt tears on Kathryn's cheek. "Kathryn, did I hurt you? I'm so sorry."

"No, you didn't hurt me." Kathryn choked out the words.

Casey just held her and kissed her face. Some barrier between them was broken now, never to separate them again. They made love all night long, unhurried and unrestrained. As the soft moonlight faded into darkness, they drifted off to sleep wrapped in each other's arms. Kathryn treasured the sensation of Casey's warm body pressed against her back and she held Casey's hand tenderly between her breasts. As she relaxed into the strong arms, a thought came into her mind that she hadn't remembered in a very long time. *I am happy.*

With Casey's warm breath against the back of her neck, Kathryn slid into a deep, safe slumber.

CHAPTER THIRTY-FOUR

They all met up Sunday morning and ate a giant breakfast in the hotel restaurant. Clearly, they all had worked up a good appetite over the weekend.

"How was the game?" Casey asked Janie.

"What game?" Stephanie answered.

After a slight pause, they all burst out laughing. "We got distracted with other things and never made it to the football game," Janie answered sheepishly.

They went to the airport together and did their flight planning.

"How's she doing, Janie?" Kathryn asked discreetly.

"Kath, she's doing great. I gave her one approach after another on Friday night and she handled them all like a pro. She's not going to have any problems on her nav check. I hope she comes back to our squadron as a T-38 IP. She'd be awesome."

They went to their respective jets, but Casey was reluctant to separate from Kathryn after their time together. "What will happen when we get back to Willie? Will I have to pretend to not know you again? I don't know if I can do that." Casey looked worried.

"You know how the game works. We can't be seen together on base. You may not realize this, but lots of people know who you are, and they are all watching both of us. We have to be careful, but I won't ignore you anymore. We'll find a way to work this out. I promise. Stay focused on pilot training. You're doing really well, Casey, and that will give you choices when it comes to your flying assignment."

"Okay, but I'd really like to kiss you right now."

"Soon, Casey, soon. I'll call you tonight after we land. Keep impressing Janie. She's a great IP."

They gave each other a quick hug, grabbed their helmet bags and parachutes, and walked across the ramp to their jets. Four proud women Air Force pilots getting a few stares from the other people around them.

Casey's flight to Biggs Army Air Field was busy. Janie had her roll back the hood so she could see how the runways at Biggs Army Air Field and El Paso International were lined up parallel to each other. It was clear that a pilot could easily get mixed up and land on the wrong runway here.

The last leg back to Willie was also busy, but Casey was mentally ahead of the jet as Janie ran her through everything. The debrief was short with Janie telling her what manuals to review before her nav check. She handed Casey her grade sheet—Excellent.

Casey called Kathryn when she got back to her quarters. They talked for hours until Kathryn reminded Casey that she had an early show time the next day. Casey reluctantly said good night and tried to get to sleep, but her bed felt empty and cold without Kathryn next to her.

The next day, Casey was scheduled for her first four-ship formation ride. She was happy she would be flying with Bulldog again. All eight pilots showed up at the appointed time, and Bulldog led the formation briefing.

Bulldog did an interval takeoff where each plane took off separately with ten-second spacing behind each jet. Bulldog had Casey roll into a thirty-degree bank turn and she could see the other three jets following her. Number Two was lined up for a rejoin with Three right behind them. Two was in position on her right wing, Three slid under her and maneuvered to her left wing when Four joined up on Three's wing.

Casey led them through several maneuvers. It was fascinating looking at the other jets as they gently bobbed in position off both her wing tips. She had to be extra smooth with her flying since there were double the number of planes as usual. She did a position change and maneuvered to the number two slot. The other two wingmen were making tiny corrections to stay in position and she tried to match them. Eventually, she was in the fourth slot and had a great view of the whole formation. They were in an echelon line as they flew up initial to enter the traffic pattern.

"Keep it tight, everyone. We have to look good," called lead.

They all landed right after each other. Casey was exhilarated. She was finally living her dream after almost a year of grueling hard work and a few near-death experiences.

Bulldog led the debrief, and she got some good comments from the other IPs. She couldn't wait to call Kathryn tonight to tell her about her first four-ship flight. She loved talking to her every night even though they couldn't be together. She'd come to appreciate Kathryn's dry sense of humor and loved her full-throated laugh. It was her goal to make her laugh every day.

Kathryn didn't speak to her like she was a student anymore, but more like she was an equal. They didn't just talk about flying, they talked about everything. Her respect for Kathryn grew every day. Casey was beginning to feel confident that she would graduate and earn her wings. Now she allowed herself to think about the future. For the first time, she wanted a future not only as an Air Force pilot, but also a life with Kathryn. This filled her with hope and scared her at the same time.

❖

Casey went over to Bulldog's house for dinner and brought Merrilee's favorite beverage, Dixie beer. Following a delicious dinner of chicken fried steak, they sat outside on the porch.

"How are you doing, Casey? Bulldog says you're tearing up the T-38 program."

"Now, don't go telling her that, Merrilee. Her head will get so big she won't be able to put her helmet on," Bulldog chimed in.

"I really like four-ship formation and I felt pretty good after my cross-country trip. I just have to pass my navigation check ride and not screw anything up."

"Have you thought about what assignment you'd like after you graduate?" Merrilee asked.

"Well, we're pretty limited in the aircraft women pilots are allowed to fly, so I can either fly a heavy, like an air refueling tanker or a transport, or I can be an IP. Right now, I'm leaning toward being an IP in either the T-37 or the T-38. But first I have to be fighter qualified and IP qualified in order to get selected to come back as an instructor pilot, and I'm not sure what the higher-ups think of me in that area."

"Casey, I want to talk to you about your future flying assignment," Bulldog said. "There's a rumor that women might be allowed to fly fighters."

"Wow. I never even considered the possibility of a fighter," Casey answered. This was a huge development, if true. Fighter pilots were the golden children in the Air Force. This change could potentially open doors to major career advancement and command opportunities for her.

"I think you should consider fighters if the ban is ever lifted. Girl, you have the brains, the aggressiveness, and the skills to fly a fighter." She was thrilled he saw that in her flying. "Until that happens, I think you'd make a good IP in either the Tweet or the T-38. You just need to ace this nav check ride first."

"Assuming you get all those qualifications, what do you *want* to fly?" Merrilee asked.

Casey would love to have the chance to fly a fighter, if that was open to her, but she also liked the idea of being an instructor pilot, especially if she could stay at Willie.

An image of Kathryn came into her mind. "I think I'd like to stay here at Willie as an IP, but being one of the first women to fly fighters is also very tempting."

Casey thought about the assignment discussion as she headed back to her quarters. Maybe she and Kathryn needed to talk about her flying assignment, a subject they had so far avoided. Maybe it would be better if she was an IP in the T-38 squadron since Kathryn flew with the T-37 squadron and they would need to continue to be very discreet. Overall, she liked the people in the T-37 squadron better compared to the T-38 IPs, who were all frustrated fighter pilot wannabes, plus she really wanted to fly with Kathryn again even if it was only an occasional IP proficiency ride. This was a big decision, and she wanted to make it with Kathryn's input.

❖

Kathryn ran when she heard the phone ring, knowing it was Casey calling her.

"Hi. I just got back from having dinner with Bulldog and Merrilee. They were asking me about my assignment preferences, and I was hoping to talk to you about this."

"Sure. What're you thinking?"

"Well, I was thinking about an IP slot here at Willie, but Bulldog said they might open fighters to women. What do you think?"

The idea of flying with Casey again caused warmth to flow through Kathryn's chest.

"First of all, I think you'd make a great IP in either jet, and secondly, you have to decide what will be the best assignment for you." Kathryn still hadn't told Casey about her discussion with the wing commander concerning her upcoming promotion and selection for senior officer school in Alabama. This sin of omission was starting to weigh heavily on her.

"You really think they'd want me as an IP? That would be amazing. Would it be better to ask for a T-38 or a T-37? What would be better for us?"

Kathryn delayed in answering the question. She knew what she wanted, but she was afraid they could never work out their careers in the Air Force. "I don't know, Casey. You have to figure that out. I can't tell you what to do."

"Am I overstepping in asking about what would be best for us? I know it's premature, but I've been thinking about you and me together. I'm sorry if I made you feel uncomfortable."

"It's okay, you still have a while to decide. Let's go to the assignment night party at the Officers' Club this Friday. The class ahead of yours will be getting their assignments, and maybe it will make your decision clearer."

"Okay, I'd like that. I'll meet you at the O Club at six."

"Great. I have to get up early and fly with a new student tomorrow. I'll see you Friday." Kathryn felt guilty cutting Casey off.

After she hung up the phone, she was overwhelmed with confusing feelings. She wanted to be with Casey, but she still had doubts she was capable of being in a real relationship. Their time together in Colorado Springs had been a breakthrough for her. She was still afraid of getting her heart broken again, especially if they got separated by the Air Force, but she also knew she was starting to fall for Casey. She wanted the promotion to major and she wanted to be a squadron commander some day. She wasn't thrilled about going to school in Alabama for a year, then four years in a staff job, but that was required to have a chance at command. Almost no relationship could survive a separation like that. She didn't want Casey to make the wrong choice to be with her. For two women pilots to be together in the Air Force—it would take a miracle to make it happen. She just didn't know if she deserved a miracle.

CHAPTER THIRTY-FIVE

The O Club was packed, and all the guys had been drinking heavily. Casey didn't know anyone in this class, and there was one woman student. They were all very cocky and full of themselves with excitement. She saw Kathryn and Barb Arnau enter the back of the big room and maneuvered over to stand with them.

The wing commander, Colonel Johnson, walked up to the raised podium, put his hands up for quiet, and spoke into the microphone.

"Ladies and gentlemen, welcome to Willie assignment night for class 93-01. This is one of my favorite events, and I know it's an exciting night for the pilots in this class who've worked so hard to get here. Some of you may be disappointed with the flying assignment you get tonight. There are no bad airplanes in the U.S. Air Force, and each one has a very important mission. If you don't get your first choice of airplane or base of assignment, I expect you all to behave like officers. Congratulations to each and every one of you. Now let's open some envelopes!"

The air was crackling with anticipation as the first name was called. He was a captain wearing navigator wings and was the top-ranked student in his class. They flashed a picture of him on a big screen behind the podium. As he opened his envelope, they put up a picture of his new jet.

"F-15 to Kadena, Japan!" The room erupted in cheers as he jumped off the stage with a giant smile on his face and a fist pump in the air.

There were five students in the top ten percent of the class who were next. The second guy got an F-16 to Korea and the third person got a KC-10 air refueling tanker to Barksdale AFB, Louisiana. It was a beautiful, huge, new KC-10 painted in Air Force colors. Casey noticed whispers in the crowd because he didn't ask for a fighter, but he got his first choice and was clearly thrilled. The happiness was contagious as everyone cheered and yelled, including the IPs.

After the top students got their jets, the rest of the class went up on stage one by one. The next guy got a B-52 bomber to Malmstrom, Montana, and he looked very relieved that he got any airplane. Casey suspected he was working his ass off just to not to get eliminated from pilot training. She overheard Barb tell Kathryn, "I never thought he'd get this far. I'm amazed he's still in pilot training. He knows he's damn lucky to get a bomber."

Kathryn laughed and added, "The scary part is he'll be flying a plane with nuclear weapons!"

The next guy got an F-4 fighter to Germany, and he was very happy. He was followed by a big guy with an even bigger swagger. He opened his envelope and got a T-37 to Laughlin AFB in Del Rio, Texas. He was clearly crushed. The rest of the assignments continued with a mixture of joy, relief, and some disappointments on the faces of the students. The only woman in the class walked across the stage and got a T-38 to Reese AFB in Lubbock, Texas, and she was overjoyed. At the end of the evening they put up a slide on the screen with all the assignments. Casey was surprised to see that only four of the IPs were going to Willie and the other four were going to pilot training bases in Texas, Oklahoma, and Mississippi.

"Why are there so many IPs going to other bases?" Casey asked Kathryn.

"Because the other pilot training bases can't produce enough of their own IPs to fill their instructor slots. Willie has the highest number of fighter and IP qualified pilots in the Air Force, so we export a lot of pilots to be IPs at the other training bases."

"Wow, I had no idea. What determines who gets sent to other pilot training bases?"

Barb chimed in. "Usually class rank. The higher-ranked pilots stay at Willie. In this class, Carol, the only woman, really wanted to be an IP in the T-38, and that was more important to her than staying at Willie. She wants to go to test pilot school and thinks the T-38 will help her get there even though women aren't allowed to be test pilots."

The wing commander returned to the stage to close the ceremonies.

"Well, this has been a great assignment night. For those of you who didn't get your first choice, work hard in your next assignment, and you'll eventually get where you want to be. I'm going to close with a very significant announcement. I just got the official word from the

Secretary of the Air Force today. Congress has overturned the combat exclusion law barring women from flying combat aircraft. Therefore, starting with the next class, women pilots will now be eligible to fly fighter, bomber, attack, reconnaissance, and tactical airlift aircraft. Have a great evening and don't drink too much."

A collective rumble ran through the crowd at the wing commander's big announcement. Casey overheard one of her classmates say, "Great. Now it will be even harder to get a fighter if they let those bitches fly them." She was surprised to hear his comment. She'd previously thought he was a good guy. Clearly, he was no friend.

"Wow. That's amazing, Kath. I wonder if they'll let any of us cross-train into fighters?"

"I doubt it, Barb, but it would be nice to have the chance to try. I know some of the women pilots from the first classes who have been lobbying Congress for years to get the combat exclusion law overturned. I'm so proud of them."

"Well, Casey, this change means doors are open to you that have so far been closed to all of us. Do you think you want to be the first woman fighter pilot?" Barb asked.

"I never thought that would be possible. I guess I have a lot to think about if I'm ranked high enough to even get one." Casey got very quiet. She had a lot on her mind.

"Well, some of the women from the softball team are going to the Incognito Lounge in Phoenix tonight if you guys are interested in coming." Barb looked anxious to leave.

"Sorry, I can't tonight. Thanks anyway," Kathryn answered.

"Me either. Maybe some other time." Casey was ready to leave, but she wanted to talk to Kathryn alone.

Casey whispered to Kathryn, "Can we go somewhere and talk?"

"Let's go out to the parking lot. Everyone is going to stay here and get hammered tonight."

Out of view in the shadow of a tree, they stood close together.

"What do you think about requesting a fighter? Do you think I should do that?" Casey asked.

"If it was me, I'd try to get more information before deciding. None of us women pilots really know what it's like to fly in a fighter squadron. You'd be breaking new ground. It's a very different culture than flying in a tanker squadron. Maybe you should talk to Bulldog about it. He knows fighter life better than anyone."

"I think I will talk to him. What would that mean for you and me? There are very few bases in the world that have both fighters and tankers, but would you want to fly the KC-135 again? I'm more confused than ever now." Casey looked really distressed.

Kathryn reached out to take Casey's hand. "I will eventually get sent back to the tanker whether I want it or not. It's just a matter of when." She was thinking about her school assignment to Alabama for a year, then the Pentagon. *Maybe I should tell her now.*

"I think it would be amazing to be one of the first women to fly a fighter, but I really want to be where you are too. I guess I have a lot to figure out. Do you want to be stationed where I am? Maybe I'm getting way ahead of myself."

Kathryn could hear doubt in her voice.

"Casey, we both have a lot to figure out right now. You have two weeks before you have to put in your assignment request sheet, so let's hold off on any big decisions for a while." Kathryn could sense her resolve slipping away. She had to talk to Casey about her promotion and school, but she didn't want to add to her confusion right now. The right time would come and she'd tell Casey everything—just not now.

"I'd really like to kiss you good night right now." She squeezed Kathryn's hand.

"Me too, Casey, me too. Good night." She blew her a feeble air-kiss.

Casey took off across the parking lot toward her quarters.

Kathryn saw a small group of Casey's classmates call out to her as they emerged from the O Club. "So, Tompkins, you putting in for an F-16 or an F-15?"

"Maybe both!" she yelled back at them.

"Crap. We thought you'd fill one of our IP slots for us!"

"Well, I guess you'll just have to fly better than me if you want a fighter, won't you!" She was laughing as she ran the rest of way to her quarters building.

CHAPTER THIRTY-SIX

Kathryn's distress at not being open with Casey about her promotion and school assignment was eating her alive. Especially after their weekend together in Colorado Springs. Casey was trying to make a huge decision about her future flying assignment and she didn't have all the facts. She decided she would try and work the system to delay her school assignment to Alabama and try to stay at Willie a few more years so she could have a chance with Casey. She had to talk to the wing commander.

"He will see you now," Mrs. Roberts said.

"Captain Hardesty, what can I do for you?" He looked busy and impatient.

"Sir, I need to talk to you about my school assignment." Kathryn decided to dive right in.

"What about it?"

"I want to know if there is any way I can delay starting school? I have a very important family issue and I need to stay here at Willie."

There was a long pause before he answered. "You realize this is a once-in-a-lifetime opportunity for you, don't you? It won't come around again. You'd be giving up your chance to ever be a squadron commander. Are you sure you're prepared to give that up?"

There it was. The giant question. The career she'd always wanted in the Air Force or a chance with Casey. "Yes, sir, I fully understand what I'm asking. I wouldn't be requesting it if it wasn't essential for my family."

"I have to tell you, I'm very disappointed to hear this from you. There are men on this base who would kill for this opportunity, and you want to give it away. I'll have to get back to you. You're dismissed."

She knew better than to say anything. She did an about-face and left his office immediately, scared but hopeful.

❖

The day finally came for Casey's navigation check ride—her last check ride in pilot training. She'd studied all the different destinations in the check ride profiles and was confident she could fly any of them. She knew her instrument flying rules cold and was prepared for anything the check pilot could ask her.

"Tompkins, your check pilot is Captain Kennedy, and you've got profile number two. Your takeoff time is 1015 hours. Meet him in Base Ops at 0900," the scheduler told her.

"Yes, sir, got it," she answered. *Profile number two—Biggs Army Airfield, El Paso, Texas. Sweet!* She said a silent "thank you" to Captain Janie Taylor for taking her to El Paso on her cross-country trip. She filled out the flight plan, checked the weather forecast, calculated her takeoff data, and checked the notices to airmen. She was ready.

Captain Kennedy showed up and reviewed her flight plan. "Show me how you came up with this landing fuel?"

Casey showed him her performance charts, her ground speed calculations with wind corrections, and her descent planning. "Good. This all looks in order. Let's sit down at the planning table and brief this up."

Casey would be under the instrument hood in the backseat and Captain Kennedy would do the initial takeoff from the front seat. Once airborne, Casey would take the jet and do all the flying and make all the radio calls. She ran into Bulldog in the parachute shop as she was getting ready to go out to the plane.

"Hey, Ace, knock 'em dead today. Take your time when he gives you holding. He loves to try to trip up studs giving them the outbound radial instead of the inbound course. You'll do great."

"Thanks, Bulldog."

It still felt cramped flying from the backseat, especially with the hood covering the whole canopy. The takeoff was normal even though she still hyperventilated every time. The check pilot gave Casey the jet passing four hundred feet.

Just as Bulldog said, he tried to confuse her with non-standard holding instructions, but Casey was ready for him. She quickly drew a picture of the holding pattern and she figured out the correct entry pattern. He had her fly a non-precision approach which she knew would be to a missed approach. Her aircraft control was smooth and positive as she made small corrections and nailed the approach. He had her fly an ILS precision approach next. She was prepared to go around again at decision height, when he suddenly said, "My jet, landing."

After his landing and taxi in, Casey knew she'd flown well and a weight lifted off her shoulders. She climbed down the ladder and Captain Kennedy turned, shook her hand, and said, "Good job, Captain Tompkins. Excellent ride."

She was overjoyed. She'd passed all her check rides and finally knew she would graduate and get her wings. She wanted so badly to call Kathryn and share her good news. The check pilot flew the return leg to Willie and didn't make her use the instrument hood. He quizzed her on instrument procedures, lost communication rules, and instrument emergencies the whole way back to Willie.

His debrief was short and sweet. "You know your stuff and you fly a beautiful airplane. I don't have anything else for you. Overall grade, Excellent. I hope you're thinking about staying here as a T-38 IP or maybe even applying for a fighter."

"I am. Thank you, sir."

When she walked into the Gombey flight room, a cheer rose up from her classmates. She was only the second student to earn an Excellent on her nav check.

Bulldog came over to her and slapped her hard on her back. "Way to go, Ace, I knew you could do it!"

"Captain Tompkins, can I see you in my office for a minute?" the flight commander asked.

"Yes, sir."

"Have a seat, Casey. Good job on your nav check today. I wanted to talk to you about your flying assignment after you graduate. The T-37 squadron let me know they would like you to come back as a T-37 IP, and we hope you will come back here to be a T-38 IP as well. I know you've heard about the recent policy change letting women fly fighters for the first time, and I want to know if you are interested in this. You are certainly both fighter and instructor qualified. Have you thought about what you'd like to do?"

Casey sat in stunned silence as his words sank in. *Both squadrons want me as an IP and he thinks I can fly a fighter? Wow.* She was beaming inside. "To be honest, sir, I haven't really made up my mind yet. I've been so focused on finishing my nav check that I haven't thought too much about my assignment."

"Well, you need to give it some very serious consideration. You have one week left to submit your dream sheet, so let me know what you decide." He stood and reached out to shake her hand.

"Thanks, sir, I'll get back to you as soon as I can." She returned his firm handshake. *I have to talk to Kathryn about this right now.*

❖

They arranged to meet at a famous old steak house in Tempe for dinner. It was far enough away from the base that they felt safe from prying eyes. After they got seated in a quiet booth, Casey decided to dive right into the conversation they needed to have.

"The flight commander told me today after I passed my nav check that both the T-37 and T-38 squadrons want me back as an IP. He also told me that I am fighter qualified and he wanted to know if I was interested in that."

"Wow, Casey, that's so great. I knew you were fighter and IP qualified, but it's great to hear that from your flight commander. I'm so proud of you."

Casey's throat got very tight hearing those words from Kathryn. She'd worked so hard for years to get here, and now to know that Kathryn was proud of her was the icing on the cake.

"I'm not sure what to put on my dream sheet."

"Casey, what do you want more than anything in the world? What is your heart's desire?"

"I want to fly and I want to be with you. I think I could be happy flying any jet so long as I get to come home to you every night." She reached for Kathryn's hand under the table. This felt so right and so complete, right here and now with Kathryn.

Kathryn squeezed her hand in reply. "I want that too, but the plane you fly right out of pilot training is a really important decision. Do you want to teach other people how to fly? Do you want to teach brand-new student pilots in the Tweet, where they *will* try to kill you three times a day, or do you want to upgrade pilots with basic flying skills to the T-38? If you fly a fighter, you have to ask yourself, 'Do I want to try and kill people with an airplane?' because that is what you will be required to do. 'Do I want to be the first woman in a fighter squadron where the men probably don't want me there?' You're the only one who can answer those questions for yourself."

"But what would be the best choice for us? Should we fly in different squadrons here at Willie? I think I would love to fly a fighter, but I would get sent away, maybe overseas even, and I don't want to be separated from you."

Kathryn struggled with telling Casey about her own next assignment. She wanted to tell her the truth, but hopefully, she had fixed things with the wing commander and she wouldn't get sent away to school for a few years. She wanted Casey to stay at Willie with her and become an instructor pilot. She wanted to live with Casey and make a home together, but she also wanted what was best for Casey's career.

"Casey, I can't decide this for you. You have to make the right choice for you. Of course I want to be with you, but you're the one who has to live with it. I can't tell you what life would be like as a fighter pilot because I was never allowed to even try for that, even though I was fighter qualified when I graduated from pilot training."

"Couldn't you apply for it now that fighters are open to women?"

"No. They will never let any of us who flew heavy aircraft, like the tanker, fly fighters. They wouldn't let me cross-train even though I've taught pilots who became fighter pilots. They will only allow new women pilots into fighters. I'm not the best person to talk to about this. Bulldog has tons of experience flying fighters and can tell you what life is really like as a fighter pilot."

"Okay, I'll talk to him. But if I choose to stay at Willie as an IP, what jet do you think I should teach in?"

"Again, you have to decide what's the best fit for you. You'll be a great IP in either airplane. When I came back to Willie as an IP, I had the choice and I wanted to fly the T-37 because I thought I could have the greatest impact on future Air Force pilots as their first IP. Also, I like the people in the Tweet squadron a lot better. They are more down-to-earth, and I thought all the guys in the T-38 squadron were assholes. But that is just my opinion."

"Well, I have a lot to think about. I wish we could fly together again sometime."

"You never know. We just might get a chance to." She squeezed Casey's hand again.

❖

Now that Casey's check rides were complete, she had a few more solo rides and some four-ship formation rides left to fly to complete the program. The students who had finished their check rides talked nonstop about their assignment preferences. As Casey observed her classmates and their IPs, she could see clearly the over abundance of arrogance, cockiness, and testosterone that Kathryn meant when she said they were all assholes. Generally, they all were. Just then, Bulldog came bursting into the flight room just like he always did.

"Champ! How are you doing today?"

"I'm good, Bulldog. Hey, I was wondering if I could talk to you later about my assignment sheet?"

"Why don't you come on over for supper tonight and we'll go over it. I'll tell the Boss to set a place for you."

"Great. I'll see you at six." She was glad she didn't have to talk about assignment choices in front of her classmates. Several of them had been asking her what she was putting on her dream sheet. Before the big announcement that women could now fly fighters, they had assumed she would fill one of the IP slots for their class. They were happy about that since none of them wanted to come back to Air Training Command as an IP. Now that she could be in competition with them for a fighter, they'd become more wary of her.

❖

Casey got to Bulldog's house with a six-pack of Dixie beer.

"Oh, hi, hon! Come on in. Well, aren't you just as sweet as pie to bring me some Dixie beer." Merrilee greeted her with a big hug.

"Hi, Merrilee. Whatever you're fixing, it smells delicious."

"Oh, I'm just whipping up a batch of fried chicken."

After another delicious dinner, they went outside on the patio to crack open a few Dixie beers. Even though it was December, it was still balmy in the Arizona evening.

"So Bulldog tells me you two got to talk about pilot stuff, so I'm going to clean up in here so you can chat." Merrilee got up and went back into the house.

"Bulldog, I need you to tell me the truth about flying a fighter. Do you really think I have what it takes?"

"Of course you do, Ace, or I wouldn't have passed you on your rides. You fly as well as, or better than, any man I've ever trained. The question you've got to ask yourself is, 'How much shit am I willing to put up with to fly a fighter?' because they're going to make your life hell in a fighter squadron, that's for sure."

"But why? Women have been flying Air Force planes for seventeen years now."

"That doesn't matter. You're trying to get into their boys' club and they don't want you, or any women. I was around when the first gals started at the Air Force Academy, and those women got nothing but abuse and harassment for the entire time they were there. Do you know what the class patch was for the pilot training class before women started flying here at Willie in 1976? Their motto was LCWB—Last Class With Balls, and they all wore that patch on their flight suits. There are still some asshole IPs here who try to wash women studs out even today. It doesn't matter how well you fly, those fighter boys will try to wash you out too. Do I think you can stand up to them and fly circles around them? Yes, I do, but you're going to pay a high price for it. You won't be getting any invites to squadron parties or barbecues, and the wives will resent you, big-time. It's going take a while before those fighter jocks get used to the idea that women pilots can fly as well as them. Do you want to be the first one to bash her head through that door?"

"Wow, I had no idea, Bulldog." She was feeling defeated before she even got a chance to try and fly a fighter.

"On the other hand, you could stay here at Willie as an IP for four years, really improve your own flying skills, then apply for fighter training. You'd be a senior captain in the squadron and have more flying hours than most of them guys in the unit. Fighter lead-in training would be a piece of cake after being an IP at Willie. But if you really want to fly a fighter, you can do it, Casey."

"Why did you leave fighters and come back to Willie to be an IP, Bulldog? Most people think that's a crazy thing to do."

"I suppose it is, but most people don't have a boy like ours. When the doc told Merrilee and me that our baby would have Down's, well, it just about broke our hearts. I'd dragged Merrilee and our two older kids all around the world chasing my dream of being a hotshot fighter pilot squadron commander. Merrilee told me, 'It's the Air Force or us,' so I chose my family. The doc told us he wouldn't make it to age eight, and he's already two years past that. I'm just damn lucky I've got a few friends in high places who got me a job at Willie where I can still fly and be home every night. That's very hard to do in the Air Force. I've had a great career and I still love strapping on a jet and flying, but coming home to the giant smile that my li'l punkin' gives me when I walk through the door is worth more than anything. We just try to treasure every day we have with him." Bulldog got very quiet after that.

"Thanks for talking to me, Bulldog. You've given me a lot to think about. I should go, it's getting late."

"See you tomorrow, Ace."

Casey got up to leave and say good-bye to Merrilee while Bulldog stayed outside sitting in the dark.

"Merrilee, thank you for another delicious dinner. It was great."

"Did you and Bulldog get everything straightened out?"

"Oh, I don't know, I've got a lot to think about with my assignment request."

"I want to tell you something, Casey. Bulldog told me you're the second best student pilot he ever flew with, and that you could fly any jet the Air Force has."

"Really?"

"Yes, he did, and you know who was the very best student pilot he ever flew with? Kathryn Hardesty."

"Wow. I didn't know she'd been his student."

"She's a very special woman, as I'm sure you know."

Casey was starting to feel nervous. *Where is she going with this?*

"Casey, the Air Force is a great life, but don't let it be the only thing in your life. Make the right decision for your career and for your *family*, regardless of what the Air Force says. You get what I'm saying here?"

"I think I do, Merrilee." She had no idea what to say next.

"We love both you and Kathryn, and if you choose your family first, you won't regret it." She pulled Casey into a big hug and kissed her cheek. "Good night, darlin'. Don't be a stranger."

"Good night, Merrilee. Thanks for everything."

She could hardly believe what she'd heard as she walked to her car. *They know about Kathryn and me. How can they know about us? They know about us, they want us to be together, and they love us. I am blown away.*

CHAPTER THIRTY-SEVEN

As Kathryn walked into her office, her secretary said, "You need to get over to the wing headquarters building immediately. The deputy wing commander said he wants to see you ASAP."

"Do you know what he wants?"

"No, but it sounds serious."

Kathryn ran over to his office wondering what the big rush was about.

"Colonel Marcus will see you now, Captain Hardesty."

"Thank you," Kathryn answered as she went into the deputy wing commander's office which was almost as big as the wing commander's office.

Colonel Marcus let her stand at attention in front of his big desk for a long minute before he finally looked at her.

"The wing commander wanted me to fill you in on the status of your request to delay your school assignment. Frankly, I was surprised he'd even offered it to you in the first place when I think there are other officers on this base who are much more deserving of this opportunity."

She listened to his words without moving. She'd never liked this self-serving ass and was usually able to avoid dealing with him.

"Captain Hardesty, you have exactly two choices here. One, accept this assignment to go to school and get promoted, or two, decline the assignment and you will immediately be sent to Thule, Greenland, to work in a non-flying job in their command post, which will effectively end any future career advancement you will ever have in the Air Force. So what's it going to be?"

Kathryn tried not to gasp as his words sank in. After everything she'd done as an instructor pilot and accident investigator, after all the sacrifices she'd made for the Air Force, this was his response to her request to delay school? To punish her like she was a traitor? "Sir, may I have a few days to evaluate my options before I give you my decision?"

"If it was up to me, you'd be out of here tomorrow, but Colonel Johnson told me he'd give you twenty-four hours to make up your mind. If you're smart, you'll choose the school assignment, but it's up to you. Report back to me by 0900 hours tomorrow. Now get out of my sight."

"Yes, sir." Kathryn did an about-face, then left his office trying to hold her head up.

She walked the few blocks back to her office. What was she going to do now? Her mind was spinning as she thought about her options, none of which were good. If she went to Alabama for Air Command and Staff College, at least she could fly home to Phoenix one or two weekends a month to see Casey, and the school assignment was only for one year, so maybe they could be together after that. Where could they be stationed together? What airplane would Casey fly? Kathryn knew the Air Force would send her back to fly the KC-135 tanker, but maybe Casey could get a fighter assignment to a joint base. A lot of pieces would have to fall into place to make that happen. A weight of dread descended on her shoulders.

❖

Casey was happy to see her name on the big schedule board for her last solo contact flight today. After the heavy discussion with Bulldog and all the thinking about assignments, she would be grateful just to get up into the sky and slip some surly bonds for a while. She was relaxed and confident as she climbed the ladder into the front seat of her jet. She quickly went through her preflight checks and was glad the backseat was empty of an instructor pilot. It would be just her and the White Rocket today.

As always, when she released the brakes for takeoff and pushed the throttles up into afterburner, her head snapped back against the headrest and she started to hyperventilate. She shot down the runway, lifted off, got the gear and flaps up, and calmed her breathing back to normal. It was a gorgeous day without a cloud in the sky and she was at one with the jet. She could sense every little vibration as her speed accelerated to three hundred knots. She didn't have to look at the engine gauges to know where her power was—she could set the throttles by feel. She could hear her speed without looking at the airspeed indicator.

She was the one flying through the sky, with this T-38 merely strapped to her body.

She wanted to run through all her acrobatic maneuvers. This practice area, which used to feel like it was the size of a postage stamp, was now her playground. She seamlessly went from a loop to a perfect barrel roll to a slice back to an Immelman. Her mind was three maneuvers ahead of the jet as she weaved her tapestry in the sky. She laughed out loud as she flew ten aileron rolls in a row. She heard music in her head and smiled. She had no doubt that she could handle any situation in this jet. After surviving the near-death experience of her electrical malfunction and no flap high-speed landing, she no longer had any fear flying the T-38. For the very first time during the year she'd been in pilot training, she was sure and confident in her ability to fly and felt like she was now a real Air Force pilot. She was higher than her altitude of thirty-nine thousand feet. The only thing that would have made this flight any more perfect would be to have Kathryn fly with her. She wondered if they would ever get to fly together again.

As she requested her clearance to return to Willie, she saw some small, white puffy clouds at the bottom of her practice area. They called her name to come and play. She lowered the nose to pick up speed and yanked and banked as she flew between, over, under, and around them.

After three touch-and-go landings and a picture perfect full stop landing, Casey taxied clear of the runway, opened her canopy to the crisp air, and now understood what she would put on her dream sheet— first choice, T-37 instructor pilot to Willie; second, T-38 to Willie; and third, F-15 to Luke Air Force Base, Arizona. She was very excited about her decision and thought she had a good shot at getting her first choice. She couldn't wait to tell Kathryn her news.

❖

Kathryn had been on the phone all morning trying to figure out what to do before she had to give her decision to the wing commander. She'd been calling in markers all over the Air Force to see if she could find a way out of this situation. She'd spoken to an old friend who now worked in tanker pilot assignments at the personnel center in Texas. Her friend hadn't given her much hope and confirmed that it was within the wing commander's power to send her to Greenland if he wanted to. It seemed her only option was to accept the school assignment and hope that she and Casey could survive a one-year separation. She was worried about that separation. Her friend Barb lost her relationship over a separation from her partner, as had many other women she knew. Maybe she and Casey would be different. They had something very special and she hoped they would be strong enough to make it. She would give her answer to the wing commander tomorrow and accept the school assignment, but she'd still try to find another way to work around this dilemma. She did not take no for an answer easily or she never would have become an Air Force pilot. She decided to hold off telling Casey until she had exhausted all her angles.

She didn't want to ruin the surprise she had for Casey with this bad news. She'd been working on this for a while and was really looking forward to seeing Casey's face when she found out.

Casey's class was having their assignment night party in two days and she still hadn't heard what she was asking for on her dream sheet. Despite trying not to influence Casey's choices, she secretly wished Casey would ask to stay at Willie as an IP. She could be one of the first women to fly fighters, but Casey would also make a great IP. She was so smart and had developed into a very strong pilot. She communicated well, worked hard, and would be very dedicated to her students. Kathryn felt a pang of sadness that she wouldn't be here to watch Casey grow into a great instructor.

Kathryn had been the only woman in her pilot training class, the only woman in her instructor pilot class, the only woman IP in her flight, and she'd wished for a woman mentor to help guide her, but there was no one at the time. Now, at least, there were some other women IPs who could help out Casey even if she couldn't.

The O Club was jammed as Casey's classmates lined up to receive their new flying assignments. Casey was the third person in line, so she wasn't the top stick, but she was in the top ten percent. The wing commander was at the podium and gave his usual admonition that all assignments were good and that the needs of the Air Force came first.

The first guy got an F-16 to Germany and he was elated. The next one got a KC-10 to Louisiana and was thrilled. Casey was next and Kathryn held her breath as they read out her assignment, "T-37 to Willie!" Casey was beaming as she pumped her fist into the air. Her entire class cheered for her, and Kathryn was filled with pride as she looked at Casey's beautiful, radiant face. Kathryn couldn't wait to tell Casey how proud she was of her and to throw her arms around her neck.

"Another one for our team!" Barb said as she slapped Kathryn on the back.

The assignments continued as the rest of the class got their airplanes. Almost everyone was happy, then the wing commander came back to the podium.

"I want to congratulate all of you on your flying assignments, and I want to share some more good news. We have three officers who just got selected for promotion to major: Captain Stavros from the 96th Squadron, Captain Marshall from the 97th Squadron, and Captain Hardesty from Wing Safety. Also, I'm happy to announce that Captain Hardesty got selected for Air Command and Staff College in residence at Maxwell Air Force Base, Alabama. This is a very significant achievement. Please join me in congratulating all these fine officers. Oh, and you three new major-selects, you're buying drinks for everyone!" A huge cheer erupted from everyone except Kathryn. *I can't believe he just did that in front of everyone. Oh my God, I have to talk to Casey.*

Kathryn was surrounded by a throng of people, but she was desperate to find Casey and explain everything to her. She looked everywhere but couldn't find her. She went out to the parking lot to look for her.

"Why didn't you tell me?" Casey sounded hurt.

"Casey, I had no idea the wing commander was going to say that tonight. I was going to tell you about it as soon as I was sure. I'm so sorry. Please believe me." Kathryn reached for Casey but she stepped away from her.

"How can I, Kathryn? All you had to do was pick up the phone and talk to me. I requested my IP assignment to Willie so we could be together. Now what's going to happen? I can't believe you did this to me on the most important night of my life. I don't think you really want to be with me at all. You lied to me. I have to go." She turned to leave.

"Casey, wait, please let's talk about this."

"Now you want to talk about it? It's too late. It's a done deal. I hope you're happy in Alabama." She turned her back on Kathryn and walked away into the darkness.

CHAPTER THIRTY-EIGHT

January 1993

Casey hadn't spoken to Kathryn since the assignment night fiasco. She'd been so happy to get her Tweet to Willie, then so completely crushed by Kathryn's betrayal. The part that hurt the most was the realization that Kathryn had chosen her career advancement in the Air Force over their relationship. She'd really thought they were in love with each other, but maybe her idea of love was different from Kathryn's.

There was still so much she didn't understand. Why didn't Kathryn talk to her about her school assignment? Did she think Casey couldn't handle it? Why didn't Kathryn even try to make it work?

There was a knock at her door. When she went to answer it, Kathryn was standing there looking more beautiful than ever. She started to close the door, but Kathryn blocked it with her foot.

"I don't want to talk to you. Please leave." Casey lowered her voice so she couldn't be heard.

"I know you don't, but I have to talk to you. I'll talk to you standing here in the hall or you can let me in. It's your choice, but I'm not going anywhere." The look of steely determination on her face was one Casey was very familiar with.

"All right, come in, but it won't change anything."

Kathryn sat on the bed and motioned for Casey to sit next to her. Casey stayed standing.

"I need to tell you the full story of what happened. When I'm through, you can ask me any questions, or you can ask me to leave and I will never bother you again. Deal?"

"I'm listening." Casey stood with her arms folded over her chest.

"The wing commander told me he put me in for promotion and

for the school assignment about a month ago. I was honored, but then I realized it would be impossible for you and me to be together if I accepted it. So I asked if I could delay school to give us a chance to be together. He got mad and had his deputy threaten to send me to Greenland immediately for four years if I refused the school assignment. I felt stuck. I had to accept it so I could try and figure out a solution for us. Casey, it was so wrong of me to not tell you about this. I'm so sorry."

"I already know all this. Is there something else relevant you want to tell me?"

"Yes, there is. I figured out a solution for us. I'm leaving the Air Force."

"You're what? You can't do that. You're the best IP on this base. I could never forgive myself if you left what you love doing because of me. I can't let you do that, Kathryn." Casey sat on the bed next to her and took Kathryn's hands.

"Casey, loving you is the most important thing in my life. No job, or promotion, or school, or even flying Air Force jets is worth losing you. I thought I lost the love of my life once before, but I was wrong. You are the woman I love, and I will not let anything come between us. This is the only way we can be free. I'm trusting you with my heart. I'm in love with you and I want to be with you forever." Her last words were choked with emotion as her eyes welled up.

Casey wrapped her arms around Kathryn. "I love you too, Kathryn, more than anything. But I want to fly too."

"I know you do, and you will. You'll be a great Tweet IP. I want that for you and I'll be supporting you all the way. Please tell me you forgive me. I'll never lie to you again, ever."

"You damn well better not. Yes, I forgive you. I couldn't stay mad at you even if I tried. I adore you, Kathryn. What will you do if you're out of the Air Force?"

"I will get an airline job. I have a lot of friends flying for them. I'll be fine as long as I get to come home to you." Kathryn reached for Casey's face and kissed her soft, velvety lips.

"I want you in bed." Kathryn was breathless. Their kisses soon became intense as they removed each other's clothes. They fell back into the bed and Casey pressed her full body against Kathryn's, inhaling deeply of her unique sweetness. Kathryn's skin was liquid warmth in her arms and she wanted contact with every inch of her.

"I've missed you so much," Casey murmured into her neck.

"I've missed you too. You're so beautiful, Casey, I almost can't handle it." Kathryn held Casey's face and kissed her with fierce abandon. She wanted to consume Casey and to be consumed by her in return. She hungered for Casey's tongue in her mouth, her fingers deep in her body, and her soul inside her heart. Nothing else in the world existed at this moment, only their bodies, this bed, and their love.

They moved together in perfect harmony—rising, falling, tasting, giving. Kathryn pulled Casey's face to her own. "I love you. I love you so much. I'm yours, only yours." She held Casey as hard as she could as tears came to her eyes.

"I love you," Casey answered softly. She gently kissed Kathryn's damp cheeks. "I love you, only you, Kathryn." They made love to each other the rest of the night, sealing their love once and for all.

❖

Casey had one last student flight before she graduated. She thought back to her very first day at Willie, when she saw that gorgeous T-38 four-ship fly right over her head and now, here she was about to achieve the dream of her life, and lead that same T-38 formation, with the love of her life, Kathryn, waiting for her. She could barely contain her happiness.

She prepared her formation brief, then the other pilots took their seats for the mission brief. The last crew arrived right at briefing start time. Major Bulldog Pruitt and Captain Kathryn "Hard-Ass" Hardesty would be flying the number two jet. Casey tried to be professional, but she couldn't help smiling at them.

"Flight Safety will be observing our mission today. Y'all know Captain Hardesty," Bulldog announced.

Casey had to avoid eye contact with Kathryn so she could complete her mission briefing without getting derailed. They all went to the parachute shop, and Kathryn and Casey ducked into the restroom. Casey grabbed Kathryn in a big hug. "Why didn't you tell me you'd be flying with me today?"

"Surprise! I arranged with Bulldog to fly in his backseat. I couldn't miss your last student flight. Excellent brief, by the way." She reached up and gave Casey a quick kiss.

Casey was beaming as she climbed into her jet. She quickly completed her preflight inspection and checked the formation in on the radio. "AWOL 47 Flight, check in."

She was pleased to hear a crisp, "Toop." "Three." "Four."

They taxied out together, and Casey checked her flight was ready at the end of the runway. She looked over her left shoulder to see Bulldog's red and black helmet in the front seat and Kathryn's blue and white helmet in the backseat of the number two jet. Kathryn gave her a gloved thumbs-up and touched her fist to her visor, indicating she was flying the jet. They took the runway as two-ship elements with Casey as lead, Kathryn as Two, doing a wing takeoff followed fifteen seconds later by Three and Four.

Casey rolled to thirty degrees of bank for the rejoin and Kathryn was right on her wingtip like she flew this jet every day. Three and Four joined on the opposite wing as they flew to the practice area in a perfect blue sky.

❖

Kathryn couldn't stop smiling flying three feet away from Casey at three hundred knots. She didn't fly the T-38 often, but when she did, she loved it. It was like riding a bike. Once you mastered the White Rocket, you never forgot it. She could see Three and Four on Casey's other wing holding good position. Casey made a quick wing rock to signal all the jets go to her right side, then she gave the "hook 'em horns" signal and rolled into a sixty-degree banked turn as all four jets rolled with her into an echelon turn. She smoothly rolled out and she continued to lead the four-ship through some very challenging maneuvers. She was a smooth, strong leader who thought well ahead of the jets.

"Bulldog, take the jet. I want to get some pictures."

"Roger, my jet," he answered.

Kathryn took several pictures of Casey flying her jet with the Arizona mountains in the background. It was a spectacularly beautiful day and an impressive sight with all four jets flying together.

Casey gave the formation the position change signal and she and Kathryn became Three and Four. Kathryn remembered what Casey was like as a brand-new student pilot. She was so serious and hardworking. Kathryn had been impressed with her from their first flight together. How could she have ever known that Casey would become her favorite student pilot ever, or that she would lose her heart to this beautiful, driven, passionate woman, the love of her life.

Kathryn was bursting with pride. Casey had grown into a skilled, confident pilot with exceptional leadership abilities. Her flying skills exceeded Kathryn's and she would be a great IP. Kathryn was humbled and honored to love, and be loved by, this amazing woman.

After a picture-perfect formation arrival into the overhead pattern and a greased landing, they met in the flight room for the last debrief.

"Excellent ride, as always, Ace. Well, I guess this is the end of the line for us. You've done a great job and I'm proud to have been your IP." Bulldog reached out to shake her hand.

"Thanks for everything, Bulldog. I'm so glad you were my IP." Casey pulled him into a big hug.

"All right, that's enough of that. Now, get out of my hair. Oh, wait, I still don't got no hair!" They all shared a laugh, then went their separate ways.

CHAPTER THIRTY-NINE

The big day was finally here. Graduation day for the newest group of Air Force pilots. Casey enjoyed her last few days off as her classmates finished training. She spent every night at Kathryn's house and she'd gotten her new squadron patches sewn on her flight suits—the Boxing Bunny of the 96th Flying Training Squadron. This was a unit with a long, proud history and she couldn't wait to go back and fly the mighty Tweet.

"There's something I want you to see before we go over to the graduation ceremony."

"Great, what is it, Kathryn?"

"You'll see." They hopped into her red convertible and drove over to base operations.

"Hard-Ass! How are you?" A very cute blonde ran over to Kathryn and threw her arms around her.

"Mary, I'm so happy to see you. This is Casey Tompkins, who is graduating today. Casey, this is Mary Morrison, one of my former students and the aircraft commander of this beauty."

"You guys want to see my plane? Come on. Did you tell Casey your news?"

Casey turned to Kathryn. "No, she didn't. What news is that?"

They walked outside to the ramp. "Check out my new ride." Kathryn pointed to an enormous KC-10 aircraft parked right in front of them. "I'll be flying this in the Air Force Reserve at March Air Force Base."

"What? That's amazing. This plane is so huge."

Mary gave them the deluxe tour of the massive three-engine jet from the flight deck with at least a thousand dials and buttons, through the cavernous interior, to the boom operator's station in the back.

"This plane weighs over half a million pounds, carries fifty thousand gallons of fuel, can fly over twenty-five hours, and can receive gas from another tanker." The size and capabilities were awe-inspiring.

"Thanks for the tour, Mary. See you at March in a few weeks," Kathryn said.

❖

"I can't believe you're going to fly the KC-10 in the Reserves. I'm so happy for you, Kathryn."

"It won't be easy. I'll be in training while you're at instructor school and I'll have to go to March to fly, but I think we can work it out. I'll work on an airline job after I'm through with training." She pulled Casey into a kiss. "Hey, we have a graduation to get to, Captain."

After an entire year of constant study, near-death flying experiences, and the hardest work Casey had ever put into anything in her life, today she would pin on the silver wings of a real Air Force pilot. She could hardly believe she'd actually made it.

They both put on their dress blue uniforms with all the medals. "Kathryn, I want you to pin on my wings."

"Are you sure?"

"Yes. I don't think I would have made it to this day without you."

"I'd be honored to, Casey."

The base theater was filled with family, friends, IPs, and students as the graduating class took their seats at the front. They all stood for "The Star Spangled Banner," then a visiting general gave a speech, then they asked all the IPs to stand. Casey looked for Kathryn, and her class stood in ovation to their instructors. The wing commander made some remarks, then the class commander called up the new pilots to get their wings and diplomas.

As each person was called, they projected a picture of the pilot next to a picture of their new airplane. Casey looked very dashing in her picture standing on the ladder of her T-38 holding her helmet and wearing her G-suit with a picture of a T-37 next to her. When they called her name, she stood up to her full height, held her shoulders back, and marched up to the stage. This was the moment she'd dreamed about for years, the achievement of her lifetime.

The wing commander said, "Congratulations, Casey. I'm so glad you'll be staying with us at Willie."

"Thank you, sir." She saluted, marched off the stage, and looked for the face that meant more than anything to her. Kathryn stood and applauded with a huge grin on her face. Kathryn's look of sheer happiness was the icing on the cake to this amazing day. After everyone got their wings, the entire group stood up and sang a rousing version of "The US Air Force Song."

Casey went outside to see Kathryn, Bulldog, Merrilee, Barb, Trish, and Rhonda waiting for her.

"Captain, you're out of uniform. Let's get those wings on!" Bulldog said.

Casey handed her new wings to Kathryn so she could pin them on.

"No, those are the wings you have to break first," Bulldog explained.

"What do you mean?" Casey asked.

"The Air Force tradition is that you have to break the first wings you are ever given. This is so you will always have good luck in the sky when you fly. Then we pin on your real wings," Barb explained.

"But I don't have any other wings."

"I have your wings, Casey. These are my first wings," Kathryn said.

Casey was speechless. Kathryn was passing on her very own wings to her. She was humbled and overwhelmed.

"You have to break these new ones first and keep the two halves forever." Kathryn handed her the new wings back.

"I sure will," Casey said as she broke the first wings.

Kathryn gently put her hands on Casey's shoulders and turned her to face her. She opened a small box and took out her own first set of wings. She reached up to the area of Casey's dress blue jacket, just above the rows of medals. Casey felt the warmth of Kathryn's hands through her uniform shirt as Kathryn pinned on her wings. The wings felt substantial on her uniform jacket, and she understood the full weight of responsibility she now had.

"Captain Tompkins, I am honored to present you with your wings. You are now officially an Air Force pilot." Kathryn saluted her, Casey returned the salute, and they smiled, and hugged each other for a long time.

"I'm so proud of you, Casey, and I love you so much," Kathryn said into her ear.

"I love you too, Kathryn, to the stars and back."

AUTHOR'S NOTE

Women were first accepted into U.S. Air Force undergraduate pilot training in 1977. They were very restricted in the aircraft they were allowed to fly. Women could only fly air refueling tankers, airlift transports, and training aircraft. Women had to meet the exact same flying standards as male students, including leading four-ship T-38 formations. Women selected as instructor pilots had to be fighter and instructor qualified to fly the T-37 and T-38 aircraft.

Congress overturned the Combat Exclusion Law in 1993. The repeal of this law finally allowed women military pilots to fly fighter, attack, bomber, tactical airlift, and reconnaissance aircraft.

Over 100,000 LGBTQ service members were given dishonorable discharges from all branches of the military until President Obama removed the prohibitions to their service in 2011.

About the Author

Julie Tizard has been a professional pilot for over thirty-five years. She is one of the earliest women pilots to graduate from U.S. Air Force pilot training. She was an Instructor Pilot flying the T-37 jet trainer and an Aircraft Commander flying the KC-10 air refueling tanker. She served in several leadership positions including Flight Commander, Chief of Pilot Upgrade, Chief of Flight Safety, and Squadron Commander. She retired as a Colonel from the Air Force Reserve after twenty-five years of service.

Julie is a captain at a major airline and currently flies the Airbus 320. She has flown the Boeing 737, 757, 767, and the DC-10. She was an instructor pilot and line check airman on the Boeing 737. She also flies her own aircraft, a T-67 Firefly, a military trainer. When not flying, reading about flying, talking about flying, or attending air shows, she can be found renovating houses, playing a baritone horn in the local LGBT band, and traveling like a normal person. She is the first woman military pilot to be writing lesbian fiction. She lives in Arizona, and *The Road to Wings* is her first novel.

Contact her at JulieATizard@gmail.com or at www.JulieTizard.com.

Books Available From Bold Strokes Books

A Date to Die by Anne Laughlin. Someone is killing people close to Detective Kay Adler, who must look to her own troubled past for a suspect. There she finds more than one person seeking revenge against her. (978-163555-023-8)

Captured Soul by Laydin Michaels. Can Kadence Munroe save the woman she loves from a twisted killer, or will she lose her to a collector of souls? (978-162639-915-0)

Dawn's New Day by TJ Thomas. Can Dawn Oliver and Cam Cooper, two women who have loved and lost, open their hearts to love again? (978-163555-072-6)

Definite Possibility by Maggie Cummings. Sam Miller is just out for good times, but Lucy Weston makes her realize happily ever after is a definite possibility. (978-162639-909-9)

Eyes Like Those by Melissa Brayden. Isabel Chase and Taylor Andrews struggle between love and ambition from the writers' room on one of Hollywood's hottest TV shows. (978-163555-012-2)

Heart's Orders by Jaycie Morrison. Helen Tucker and Tee Owens escape hardscrabble lives to careers in the Women's Army Corps, but more than their hearts are at risk as friendship blossoms into love. (978-163555-073-3)

Hiding Out by Kay Bigelow. Treat Dandridge is unaware that her life is in danger from the murderer who is hunting the woman she's falling in love with, Mickey Heiden. (978-162639-983-9)

Omnipotence Enough by Sophia Kell Hagin. Can the tiny tool that abducted war veteran Jamie Gwynmorgan accidentally acquires help her escape an unknown enemy to reclaim her stolen life and the woman she deeply loves? (978-163555-037-5)

Summer's Cove by Aurora Rey. Emerson Lange moved to Provincetown to live in the moment, but when she meets Darcy Belo and her son Liam, her quest for summer romance becomes a family affair. (978-162639-971-6)

The Road to Wings by Julie Tizard. Lieutenant Casey Tompkins, Air Force student pilot, has to fly with the toughest instructor, Captain Kathryn "Hard Ass" Hardesty, fly a supersonic jet, and deal with a growing forbidden attraction. (978-162639-988-4)

Beauty and the Boss by Ali Vali. Ellis Renois is at the top of the fashion world, but she never expects her summer assistant Charlotte Hamner to tear her heart and her business apart like sharp scissors through cheap material. (978-162639-919-8)

Fury's Choice by Brey Willows. When gods walk amongst humans, can two women find a balance between love and faith? (978-162639-869-6)

Lessons in Desire by MJ Williamz. Can a summer love stand a four-month hiatus and still burn hot? (978-163555-019-1)

Lightning Chasers by Cass Sellars. For Sydney and Parker, being a couple was never what they had planned. Now they have to fight corruption, murder, and enemies hiding in plain sight just to hold on to each other. Lightning Series, Book Two. (978-162639-965-5)

Summer Fling by Jean Copeland. Still jaded from a breakup years earlier, Kate struggles to trust falling in love again when a summer fling with sexy young singer Jordan rocks her off her feet. (978-162639-981-5)

Take Me There by Julie Cannon. Adrienne and Sloan know it would be career suicide to mix business with pleasure, however tempting it is. But what's the harm? They're both consenting adults. Who would know? (978-162639-917-4)

Unchained Memories by Dena Blake. Can a woman give herself completely when she's left a piece of herself behind? (978-162639-993-8)

Walking Through Shadows by Sheri Lewis Wohl. All Molly wanted to do was go backpacking...in her own century. (978-162639-968-6)

Freedom to Love by Ronica Black. What happens when the woman who spent her life worrying about caring for her family finally finds the freedom to love without borders? (978-1-63555-001-6)

A Lamentation of Swans by Valerie Bronwen. Ariel Montgomery returns to Sea Oats to try to save her broken marriage but soon finds herself also fighting to save her own life and catch a murderer. (978-1-62639-828-3)

House of Fate by Barbara Ann Wright. Two women must throw off the lives they've known as a guardian and an assassin and save two rival houses before their secrets tear the galaxy apart. (978-1-62639-780-4)

Planning for Love by Erin Dutton. Could true love be the one thing that wedding coordinator Faith McKenna didn't plan for? (978-1-62639-954-9)

Sidebar by Carsen Taite. Judge Camille Avery and her clerk, attorney West Fallon, agree on little except their mutual attraction, but can their relationship and their careers survive a headline-grabbing case? (978-1-62639-752-1)

Sweet Boy and Wild One by T. L. Hayes. When Rachel Cole meets soulful singer Bobby Layton at an open mic, she is immediately in thrall. What she soon discovers will rock her world in ways she never imagined. (978-1-62639-963-1)

To Be Determined by Mardi Alexander and Laurie Eichler. Charlie Dickerson escapes her life in the US to rescue Australian wildlife with Pip Atkins, but can they save each other? (978-1-62639-946-4)

True Colors by Yolanda Wallace. Blogger Robby Rawlins plans to use First Daughter Taylor Crenshaw to get ahead, but she never planned on falling in love with her in the process. (978-1-62639-927-3)

Heart Stop by Radclyffe. Two women, one with a damaged body, the other a damaged spirit, challenge each other to dare to live again. (978-1-62639-899-3)

Undercover Affairs by Julie Blair. Searching for stolen documents crucial to U.S. security, CIA agent Rett Spenser confronts lies, deceit, and unexpected romance as she investigates art gallery owner Shannon Kent. (978-1-62639-905-1)

Taking Sides by Kathleen Knowles. When passion and politics collide, can love survive? (978-1-62639-876-4)

boldstrokesbooks.com

Bold Strokes Books

Quality and Diversity in LGBTQ Literature

victory
EDITIONS

Drama

MATINEE BOOKS

E-BOOKS

SCI-FI

MYSTERY

erotica

BSB SOLILOQUY

EROTICA

BOLD STROKES BOOKS

YOUNG ADULT

LIBERTY

Romance

W·E·B·S·T·O·R·E

PRINT AND EBOOKS

Printed in the USA
CPSIA information can be obtained
at www.ICGtesting.com
JSHW081418281223
54470JS00001B/19

9 781626 399884